"Five will ride the Roaringburn,
But only four will e'er return.
Urgan sits in Gael's Royal House,
Warriormaid and Warriormouse,
Say hasten, and give aid."

Immediately a murmur arose from the assembled Red-wallers.

'Five are to go, which five?'

'The rhyme never said?'

'Aye, but only four will come back, that's what he said!'

Simeon's stick rapped the tabletop sharply. 'Silence, please, friends!' he said. 'You must wait until Joseph has finished speaking.'

The Bellmaker bowed slightly to the blind Herbalist. 'Thank you, Simeon, I have not much more to say now. My dream ended with many images, swirling water, flames, the sounds of battle, and above all the voice of Martin calling aloud.'

By the same author:

Redwall
Mossflower
Mattimeo
Mariel of Redwall
Salamandastron
Martin the Warrior
Seven Strange and Ghostly Tales

BRIAN JACQUES

The Bellmaker

Illustrated by Allan Curless

RED FOX

A Red Fox Book

Published by Random House Children's Books
20 Vauxhall Bridge Road, London SW1V 2SA

A division of Random House UK Ltd
London Melbourne Sydney Auckland
Johannesburg and agencies throughout the world

Copyright © text Brian Jacques 1994
Copyright © illustrations Allan Curless 1994

5 7 9 10 8 6 4

First published in Great Britain by
Hutchinson Children's Books 1994

Red Fox edition 1995

Printed and bound in Great Britain by
Cox & Wyman Ltd, Reading, Berkshire

RANDOM HOUSE UK Limited Reg. No. 954009

Papers used by Random House UK Limited
are natural, recyclable products made from wood
grown in sustainable forests. The manufacturing
processes conform to the environmental regulations
of the country of origin.

ISBN 0 09 943331 1

To the memory of Alan Durband,
gentleman and teacher

Many warriors own the glory
But the saying in Redwall is
'This is the Bellmaker's story
Because the dream was his.'

Storm-bruised clouds, heavy and lowering, dropped teeming rain into the howling March wind, slanting in from the northwest to batter the last of winter's snow that clung to the stones of Redwall Abbey. Inside the gatehouse it was snug and warm, though there was not much room. All the available chairs and floor space had been taken up by little creatures – moles, mice, squirrels and hedgehogs. They watched in silence as an ancient squirrel, silver haired and bent with age from long seasons, banked up the fire with two beech logs. He turned slowly and, shooing two very young mice from his armchair, the aged squirrel sat, a twinkle in his eye as he watched his audience.

'Sit still, be good my Dibbuns, the special breakfast will soon be here. Listen for the knock now, my ears don't work very well these days.'

The little ones, who were collectively known as Dibbuns, cupped paws about their ears, listening intently. All that could be heard was the spattering rain on the windows and the wind mourning its dirge around the outside walls. The knock came upon the door like a spell being broken. A bass-voiced molebabe stood up, shouting, 'Hurr et be, brekkist!'

Several of the young ones had to force the door open against the gale. A fat old hedgehog backed himself inside, pulling a trolley loaded with a cauldron, wooden bowls and spoons. No sooner was he inside than the wind whipped the door shut with a loud slam. Shaking rainwater from his venerable grey spikes, the hedgehog lifted the cauldron lid. A delicious aroma from the steaming vessel caused cries of delight. He wiped the corners of his eyes on a spotted kerchief and winked at his companion in the armchair.

'*Pearl Queen* Pudden, messmate, nothin' like it on a cold wet day. Come on, me little mateys, pass these bowls 'n' spoons around while it's still nice an' hot.'

All that could be heard was the scrape of spoon upon bowl as they sat eating breakfast. The ancient squirrel finished his portion and ruffled the ears of a mouse sitting on the chair arm. 'You enjoying that, Jerril?'

The little mouse licked his spoon. '*Pearl Queen* Pudden's nice. What's in it?'

'Ask my mate. He made it.'

The old hedgehog cleared the Dibbuns from his armchair on the other side of the hearth and sat down chuckling, his huge stomach shaking like a jelly. 'Hohohoh! I'll tell ye what's in *Pearl Queen* Pudden, young Jerril. Anythin' a beast can lay his paws on. Apples, nuts, berries, plums, an' memories, lots o' memories. Ain't that right, messmate?'

The squirrel's eyes shone as he gazed into the fire. 'Aye, that's right. Memories. Long seasons gone an' high old summers that never fade from our minds.'

The bass-voiced molebabe looked up from his second helping. 'Do that mean ee goin to tell us'n's a tale, zurr?' he asked.

'Well there's nothing else t'do in weather like this,' said the ancient squirrel, as he put aside his bowl and spoon. 'Aye, I'll tell you a story, but my mate will have to help me out in parts, because it's a very long tale.'

Jerril was licking his bowl, but he popped his head out to say, 'Did yer make it up, sir?'

The squirrel shook his grizzled head vigorously. 'Make it up? Indeed not. No, young feller, this story is true. 'Tis not just my story, it belongs to many creatures. I gathered their own bits from each one of 'em.'

The hedgehog in the armchair opposite nodded. 'Aye, though it would've never happened but for one, a mouse called Joseph the Bellmaker, for the dream was his.'

Outside, the rain flattened young grass and the wind rattled leafless branches that were trying hard to put out small buds. A delicately thin icicle tinkled from the gate-house roof, like the last tear of winter. Inside, the ruddy firelight gleamed on the young faces, each one watching the ancient squirrel as he leaned forward and began the story.

BOOK ONE

The Dream

1

It is said that in the hungry land of ice and snow from whence he came the beast was known and feared by the names he had taken. Foxwolf! The Urgan Nagru!

He and his mate Silvamord commanded a vast horde of savage grey rats. They ravaged the northlands unopposed – tundra, forest and mountain lay under the claws of Nagru and his vixen. But the Foxwolf knew there was one enemy he could never defeat, one foe more ruthless than any living thing. Winter!

Snow, ice, howling blizzards and famine were the real rulers of the country he had despoiled, a bone-chilling starkness that conquered all. Nagru and Silvamord were forced to yield, realizing that starvation and death stalked the country they had stripped bare. So it was that Nagru took Silvamord and all the horde in three great ships to search for the sun.

Those were the dangerous seasons. Battered across dark, roaring seas they went, narrowly dodging huge floating ice mountains, the ships' sails and riggings frozen stiff with rimy spray. Sometimes they lay becalmed in ghostly latitudes, wreathed in spectral mists with the waters beneath them still and fathomless. Completely lost, the Foxwolf ploughed onwards, driven across trackless wastes where no vessel's bow had ever cut spray, avoiding leviathans of the deep and shoals of unnamed seabeasts. Strange hostile waters closed over their wake as the weary convoy sailed deeper into the unknown.

Then one morning the lookouts saw that the seas were gentler. Small fish swam playfully alongside the wave-scoured hulls and the weather turned fair. Gazing upward, the eyes of Foxwolf beheld fleecy white clouds with sun peeping between them. Looking out to the horizon he saw the thin green-brown line of land. The Foxwolf threw back his head and howled triumphantly.

He had defeated the wide, wintry seas. Silvamord joined him on deck and together they bayed their defiance at the blue spring sky. Roaring and screeching, the grey rat horde thronged decks and rigging to cheer their leaders. It was a curious sight: three big, battered ships, swarming with thin, wild-eyed creatures, tattered sails flapping above creaking decks as they rode the ingoing swell towards shore. And so it was that Urgan Nagru came to the far south!

The land lay like a dream out of time under the spell of early spring. Southsward! A soft, peaceful region of plenty which had never felt the cruel breath of war. Stowing the three ships up a heavily wooded creek, Nagru waded ashore with Silvamord and their ragged, murderous followers. Lean from hunger and privation, eager for loot and conquest, they pressed hurriedly inland. The time of the Foxwolf had come to Southsward!

From his vantage point on a wooded hilltop, Rab Streambattle gazed across the valley to Castle Floret. The otter had watched and planned almost every day as spring passed into summer. Castle Floret stood atop a high flat plateau, its north side abutting the sheer cliff face. The castle's other three sides were surrounded by a crescent-shaped moat. A mighty drawbridge commanded almost a third of the front south side, and at this edge the plateau had a long flight of broad steps carved into the living rock from top to valley floor.

Rab stared sadly at his old home. It resembled a beautiful forgotten cake left standing on the green-clothed tableland. Against a sky of dusty blue, cream-coloured towers shimmered beneath quaint, circular red-tiled roofcaps. Dark green ivy and golden saxifrage flourished amid the crenellations. Campion and climbing roses burgeoned carelessly over windowsills and framed doors. The hot afternoon did not contribute the slightest breeze to ruffle the variegated pennants draped idly round tall flagpoles.

Rab dismissed the dreamlike qualities of his old home, riveting his worried brown eyes on the window alongside the drawbridge top. Had something gone wrong? Did Nagru know of the escape that had been planned? His friends, Gael Squirrelking, Queen Serena and little Truffen, had they received the message from Relph the blackbird? The otter clutched his bow tightly, staring at the window, awaiting the signal as thoughts raced through his troubled mind.

Why, oh why, had Gael not listened to him? Rab recalled the day he had first argued with his friend. The quarrel had become furious and bitter and had ended with Gael ordering his old friend either to curb his tongue or leave the castle. Stone-faced, Rab stalked angrily out of Floret, taking the entire otter castle guard with him. Not because he feared Nagru, but because he could see the evil that Gael was blind to.

Rab hated and loathed the cunning Foxwolf with an intensity that banished all fear. Now his friend the Squirrelking and his family were prisoners in their own home. The wickedness of Nagru was a spectre that would soon blight the whole of Southsward. Gael should have heeded the warnings Rab had issued, but instead he chose to play the king and offer the Foxwolf hospitality.

Suddenly, Rab's eye caught a flutter of iridescent blue-black wings carrying a scrap of red cloth to the window by the drawbridge.

Rab Streambattle notched an arrow to his bowstring. The escape was on!

The sun hung like a hot merciless eye, watching two small creatures huddled in the shade of a shale outcrop on the wasteland floor. The mousemaid Mariel of Redwall shook an empty flask over the outstretched tongue of her friend Dandin. Two single drops fell slowly, then no more.

'Put your tongue away,' she said, sadly. 'The sun will think we're mocking him.'

The young mouse nodded skyward as he withdrew his parched tongue. 'Huh, he's been mocking us for the last week.'

They both sat staring at the empty flask. Mariel gently kicked her slack haversack. 'Two stale oatcakes in there, d'you fancy one?'

Dandin smiled ruefully. 'No thanks, they're the two you said you'd keep as a memento of Redwall Abbey. It's four seasons since we left there – I'd break every tooth in my head trying to chomp on them, besides I'm too dry to eat. Whew, it's too hot even to talk!'

Mariel closed her eyes, settling back into the shade. 'Sleep then, we'll carry on tonight when it gets cooler.'

Dandin lay down clasping his paws behind his head, and called out to the sun, 'Did you hear that? We're going to sleep, turn the heat down a bit, will you!'

Mariel opened one eye. 'Get to sleep, thirstygut,' she said.

Dandin closed his eyes. There was a moment's silence, then he began talking aloud to himself. 'It'll be teatime back at the Abbey now, I bet I know what they'll be having, too. Cold strawberry cordial from deep in the cellars, October Ale, dark and cool in foaming tankards. Prob'ly mint tea as well, icy cold, brewed since dawn, clear and fragrant, just right for sipping on a hot day like . . . Yowch!'

Mariel brandished the haversack over her friend. 'One more word and I'll let you have it again!'

'Can't hear, you old mouseypaws,' Dandin said as he flopped against her, rolling his eyes comically. 'You've knocked me senseless with those two oatcakes in there.'

'Good, perhaps you'll be quiet now.'

'Quiet? I haven't said a single word!'

'Right, then I'll say a single word. Goodnight!'

'Don't you mean good afternoon?'

'I mean goodnight or I'll brain you with this haversack!'

'Oh, righto. Goodnight!'

Mariel woke in darkness. Warned by her warrior instinct, she lay motionless. Somebeast was trying gradually to sneak the haversack out from under her head. It was not Dandin – she could hear his snores drifting gently up to the canopy of the starstrewn night. As the final corner of their supply bag eased slowly away, she sprang into action. Slamming a footpaw hard on the haversack, she prevented the thief making off with it. In the dim light, Mariel could make out a small fat figure scurrying off into the wasteland. Snatching one of the two ancient oatcakes from the bag, the mousemaid hefted it like a discus, yelling as she flung it.

'Redwaaaaallll!'

Thonk!

It struck edge on, right between the robber's ears. He dropped in a heap. Dandin leapt up, still half asleep, his paws waving.

'More October Ale there! Wha . . . Who . . . Mariel!'

As she ran towards the felon, the mousemaid was yelling, 'I knew those oatcakes'd come in useful, got the blaggard!'

Dandin followed, rubbing sleep from his eyes. When

he arrived upon the scene Mariel was kneeling crest-fallen over her quarry. 'Oh dear, what've I done?' she wailed. 'He's only a little un!'

It was a small hedgehog. Dandin stooped to feel the big bump in the centre of its head.

'Middle of the night, running target, great shot I'd say.'

Mariel turned on him, her eyes brimming tears. 'Oh Dandin, how could you say that, I'd never have thrown at such a little feller intentionally. But it all happened so quickly, I couldn't see who it was.'

Dandin picked up the oatcake and chuckled. 'Not to worry, look, the little rogue's coming around fine. Haha, this is a true Redwall missile. See, there's not even a mark on it!'

The small hedgehog sat up slowly, gingerly pawing his head. He blinked at them and said, 'Ooh! Where be I, wot 'appened?'

Before Mariel could answer, Dandin chipped in, 'You tripped and bumped your head, old lad.'

Glaring at Dandin, the little beast bristled. 'Me name don't be ol' lad, I be Bowly Pintips an' I'll thank ee to address I proper!'

Dandin adopted a look of mock fear and bowed respectfully. 'Accept my humble apologies, your Royal Bowlyness!'

Bowly snatched the oatcake and brandished it. 'See this 'ere rock as I tripped over, well you make sport o' me an' I'll biff ye with it! Wot's yore names? Speak up now afore I loses me temper with ye both!'

The hedgehog's impudence caused Mariel's mood of pity to vanish instantly. She grabbed Bowly firmly by his nose, pulling him up on tip paw, and said, 'Listen to me, you cheeky little robber. I'm Mariel of Redwall and this is Dandin. We're both warriors. So keep a civil tongue in your head or we'll give you two more lumps to go on top of the one you've aleady got!'

Tears streamed from Bowly's eyes as his nose was squeezed. 'Yowow! Leggo ob be doze, yore hurtig bee!'

Mariel released him and he grovelled in the sand, rubbing at both bump and snout. The mousemaid nodded as she sat by him.

'That's better. Now, what's a little snippet like you doing out in the wastelands all alone? Where's your mum'n'dad?'

Bowly shrugged glumly. 'Never 'ad none as I c'd remember. Two weasels 'ad me catchered south of 'ere, made me slave for 'em, tied me to a post at nights, but I 'scaped an' runned away.'

Dandin's friendly face grew grim. 'How far south are these two weasels, Bowly?' he asked.

'About arf a night's march from 'ere, I only 'scaped just afore dark, mister Dandy.'

'My name's Dandin, not mister Dandy,' said Dandin, pawing the long dagger at his belt. 'These two weasels, have they got food and drink?'

'O aye, they got vittles aplenty, robs travellers they do.'

Mariel had retrieved the haversack. She knotted the carrying ropes together, exchanging a slow smile with Dandin. 'Let's go and pay these two weasels a visit,' she said.

The sand and shale were still warm from the day's heat, but the night air was cool as the three creatures strode south. Bowly Pintips giggled aloud when Dandin explained their plan to him.

2

Spurge and Agric the weasel slavers sat by their fire as dawn's rosy paws probed the eastern horizon. They were trying to brew a pan of mint tea, and making a total mess of it. At the side of the fire lay a stack of raw apple pancakes. Spurge burned his paw on the pan handle and danced about waving it. 'Rot me ears, 'ow does that liddle spikedog brew this stuff?'

Agric prodded the pancakes with a wicked-looking willow cane. 'Search me,' he said. 'Huh! I ain't sure 'ow t'cook these pancakes the rascal made las' night. Rotten liddle pincushion, we'll track 'im down, he can't go far without water in the wastelands. Wait'll I lay claws on 'im, I'll make that runaway weep fer a season or more!' He swished the cane through the air, grinning crookedly in anticipation of giving Bowly a severe whipping.

'Mornin' sirs, sorry I runned off like'n that las' night!'

Spurge's jaw dropped. There was Bowly, ambling around the big shale rock that marked their camp. Quivering with rage, Agric pointed with the cane to a wooden post driven into the ground with a heavy shackling rope attached to it.

'Yew liddle scum, I'm goin' to bind you t'that post an' lash the prickles offa yore hide. Cummere!'

Spurge knocked the cane aside. 'After brekkfist matey, we want 'im fit t'cook our vittles first. Get to it, yew lazy lump!'

Obediently, Bowly stirred crushed mint leaves into the bubbling water, setting the pancakes on a thin shale slab which he balanced over the fire's edge. As he worked, Mariel strolled into the camp, smiling foolishly. She waved a paw at the two weasels.

'Morning! Lovely day, isn't it? Any breakfast going spare for a hungry traveller?'

Spurge and Agric could not believe their luck. Not only had the runaway surrendered, but they had suddenly got themselves a simpleton mousemaid travelling alone. It surely was turning out to be a nice day.

'Wot y'got in there, mousey?' said Spurge, eyeing the haversack their new arrival was carrying.

Mariel winked and wrinkled her nose. 'Oh, a bit of this'n'that, y'know.'

The weasels went into a huddle, sniggering and whispering. After a while Agric turned to Mariel, saying, 'If yew wants to eat you gotta 'elp, see. There's fresh fruit an' water in that holler under the rock. Yew 'elp that lazy 'edgepig to ready the vittles, then we'll see yew gets somethin' nice, won't we, matey?'

Spurge gave a malicious chuckle. 'Ho yerss, it'll be a real surprise!'

The food stock was good. Mariel busied herself preparing a fruit salad of strawberries, apples, plums and pears. Pouring honey and water into a gourd, she crushed damsons in and began shaking up a cordial. The weasels sat in the shade of the rock as the morning sun got up. They nudged each other, sniggering with ill-concealed mirth.

Mariel winked at Bowly as she called out,

'Morning's risen and breakfast's here,
Eat, my friends, and be of good cheer!'

15

Flipping his long dagger from paw to paw, Dandin strode boldly into the camp, kicking the weasels' foot-paws out of his way, instead of stepping over them.

'Well, well, Mariel the Gullwhacker, am I invited to eat?'

Mariel gave a roar of laughter quite inappropriate for a simple travelling mousemaid. 'Hoho! Dandin, you old Warrior, welcome!'

Mariel and Bowly lay the food down on the floor.

Dandin sat down between the two astonished weasels, calling out to Bowly, 'Come on, little un, grab a plate and spoon, join us.'

Bowly obeyed with a will, helping himself to a hot apple pancake and a cooling beaker of damson cordial. As the weasels reached out for food Dandin dealt them a couple of sharp slaps with the flat of his dagger blade, and clucked disapprovingly at them. 'Tch, tch! Where's your manners? Guests and young uns first. I'll tell you when it's your turn.'

By this time the two weasels were looking distinctly uneasy. A lone mousemaid was one thing, but this Dandin looked like a seasoned warrior.

Mariel, Dandin and Bowly ate heartily, letting the mint tea cool as they sipped damson cordial and treated themselves to hot apple pancakes and fruit salad.

'You'd have to be a robber and travel wide to get stuff like this, eh, young un?' Dandin said cheerfully to Bowly.

Bowly nodded sagely. 'Aye, that y'would, Sir Dandy.'

'Robbers must have to be good cooks, what d'you say, Bowly?' said Mariel, sipping some mint tea appreciatively.

'No marm, some robbers is slavers too, they catchers a liddle slave an' makes 'im do all the work. Robbers is awful creatures, they beats their slaves an' ties 'em up nights to a post wi' a big 'eavy rope, like that'n yonder.'

16

The weasels were very nervous now. Dandin caught their attention as he slit a pancake neatly in half with the keen edge of his dagger. His voice was low and dangerous as he said, 'I don't suppose honest creatures like you would know of two such slavers, would you?'

Agric developed a sudden stammer. 'N . . . n . . . no S . . . sir!' he squawked, his throat bobbing nervously.

Bowly gurgled, spraying mint tea as he tried to suppress an attack of the giggles. The weasels were robbers and bullies, but when faced with the two warriors they were cowards.

Dandin stared hard at the trembling slavers, and picking up the willow cane he swished it under their noses. 'Mariel, what d'you think, are these two telling the truth?'

The mousemaid strode across to the wooden post the weasels had driven into the ground to tether Bowly. She unfastened the short heavy rope from it. Winking at Bowly and Dandin, she began tying a solid, complicated knot in the rope's end. 'Oh I don't know,' she said. 'They look like fairly respectable beasts to me.'

From the weasels' food cache she produced half-a-dozen mixed beech and hazelnuts, still in their shells. Placing them in a line on a flat rock, she turned to Spurge and Agric.

'See this knotted rope, I used to own one like it – called it my Gullwhacker. I could lay a big seabird flat with one blow. Now I can't see any gulls hereabouts, but there'd be other things to whack if I thought certain creatures were lying to us.'

Spinning the knotted rope in a skilful blur, Mariel dealt six lightning blows to the nuts on the rock.

Whack! Smack! Crack! Thud! Bang! Splat!

The weasels squeaked with fright. Trembling, they stared wide-eyed at the line of kernel and shell fragments, which was all that remained of the six nuts. Mariel dangled the Gullwhacker a fraction from their noses. 'See what I mean?'

Bowly grinned from ear to ear as he patted the weasels none-too-gently on their heads. 'Nay, nay, you've made a mistake, I c'n see these are two good vermints. Why, I wager given arf a chance they'd thank us for callin' in to brekkist an' give us water'n'vittles to 'elp us pore travellers on our way, wouldn't you?'

Spurge and Agric took the hint swiftly. Leaping up, they loaded their food and drink store into the haversack. Bowly stood by, tossing the two hard oatcakes up and down.

'These be my throwin' rocks. I been knowed to fetch foebeasts down at fair distances with 'em, cos I be a warrior too, see.'

Dandin removed sufficient supplies for a day from the pack, and laid them in front of the weasels. 'You haven't had breakfast yet, here, take this with our compliments. We're travelling south, which way are you bound?'

Spurge shrugged unhappily. 'North, I think, Sir.'

Mariel swung the Gullwhacker expertly across her shoulders. 'Well, keep an eye out for those two thieving robbers we mentioned, and be careful, it's dangerous country out here.'

Dandin spun his dagger in the air. Catching it by the hilt, he thrust it into his belt. 'Aye, take care, never know who you might bump into!'

And the three friends strode off calling cheerful goodbyes to the crestfallen weasels.

Thoroughly refreshed, they stepped out with a will. A mere half-morning's walk brought them in sight of green hilly scrubland and the promise of gentle, fertile countryside. Bowly trudged alongside Mariel, tossing his two oatcakes in the air.

The mousemaid caught one, and said, 'Now then, you young rip, what are we going to do about you?'

The small hedgehog snatched the oatcake back indignantly. 'I've told ye my name be Bowly Pintip, I ain't no young rip. I be goin' wi' you an' Dandy, I be a warrior from now on!'

Dandin sliced an apple into three with his dagger and gave them each a piece, winking at Mariel over the small hedgehog's head. 'What d'you think, has he got the makings of a warrior?'

Bowly scrunched his face into a ferocious scowl to show that he had. Mariel returned Dandin's wink. 'Being a warrior doesn't always mean a fierce face, warriors are also renowned for their gentleness.'

Bowly immediately changed his expression until he thought he looked gentle enough to charm baby birds from their nests. Stifling their smiles, Mariel and Dandin carried on extolling warrior virtues, while Bowly took note of all they said.

'Oh yes, warriors are handsome beasts.' Bowly wobbled his head, fluttered his eyes and tried hard to look handsome.

'You're right, Dandin, but I've known warriors who can look very stern too.' The handsome Bowly suddenly transformed into one with a grim jaw jutting and what he imagined were cold, gimlet eyes. Mariel spluttered and coughed on a bite of apple, while Dandin held his ribs tight to stop the laughter bubbling out.

'Aye, but give me the warrior with that devil-may-care look, one who can slay ruthlessly but still manage to laugh merrily, now that's the fellow for me!' Bowly's small face contorted as he tried to glare out of one eye whilst twinkling merrily with the other, and he brandished his two oatcakes as if ready to slay with them at a moment's notice, at the same time emitting a savage growl which he tried to couple with a merry laugh. Turning to his two companions, who were shaking with unexploded laugher, he sighed wearily.

'Phwaaw! It do take much 'ard work to look like a warrior!'

The two teasers laughed heartily, patting Bowly's

tender young prickled head. 'We think you'll make a splendid warrior, don't we Dandin?'

'Right! We'll be three warbeasts travelling south through thick and thin to wherever our adventures take us!'

Bowly's face lit up in a happy grin, and he clasped the paws of his two comrades firmly. 'Aye, an' never fear, I'll take care of ee both!'

3

Queen Serena watched her little son Truffen sadly as he sat alone in the centre of Castle Floret's banqueting chamber. Poor squirrelmite, forced to spend his days and nights in captivity, often separated from both parents, with only his old badger nurse Muta to protect him. Serena and her husband, Gael Squirrelking, sat together at one side of the chamber, with Truffen at his bench in the centre, whilst on the opposite side Nagru and Silvamord occupied the positions of honour at high table, surrounded by rodent Captains. Serena clutched Gael's paw tightly, and they fixed their eyes on the tiny hostage.

Serena let her mind wander over past events. Was it only a season ago that Nagru and Silvamord had arrived at their gates? It seemed as though they had been in Castle Floret for an eternity. She recalled the night they had allowed Nagru and his mate into their home. It was a windy, drizzling evening in early spring, and the two foxes had looked half-dead, starved and bedraggled. Her husband Gael ordered that they be admitted, fed and clothed warmly. Serena regretted that Gael had not heeded the urgent warnings of their friend Rab Streambattle. But the Squirrelking could be stubborn, and he would not hear of Castle Floret's hospitality being denied to any needy creature. Rab continued to oppose him and the argument escalated until the angry otter stormed out of the castle, taking his otter guard with him.

Within the space of two sunsets the foxes had taken over everything. It was done with fiendish simplicity. Silver-tongued Silvamord had lured Muta to a side chamber and locked her in. Nagru snatched little Truffen and held him breathless with fright, the fearsome hooked wolfclaws a hairsbreadth from the babe's throat. Gael was forced to lower the drawbridge, and in a trice the castle was teeming with rats, savage, dirty grey rodents, eager to maim, destroy or kill at a nod from their leaders, Nagru and Silvamord.

From that moment their lives had hung by a thread. All loyal friends and courtiers who resisted were slain or imprisoned in Floret's dungeons, while those who were not considered dangerous were forced to wait on the foxes and their officers. The far southern sun no longer shone over a peaceful and happy land. A new king and queen held sway, backed by a horde of murderers.

Nagru was big for a fox. Lean and powerful, he was mottled bluish grey from tip to tail, and his cruel eyes resembled chips of granite flake floating in a sea of carmine bloodflecks. His only clothing was the full pelt of a wolf, its head resting on top of his own like a cowl with eyeless sockets. The hide trailed down over his back with the front limbs covering his own. The wolfclaws had been replaced with sharp iron hooks, and when Nagru slid his own paws inside them they became awesome weapons.

His mate Silvamord was smaller in stature, but no less savage. Her fur was whitish grey with a silver-striped muzzle and back markings, and her eyes were dark obsidian green. Her regalia was a thick skirt of animal tails with glittering chips of crystal cunningly sewn into them. She moved sinuously to its strange tinkle, the equal of her mate in cunning and evil.

Now the barbaric pair sat side by side, sipping elderberry wine from Floret's cellars and sharing the gamey meat of a long-dead plover. Nagru spiked a damson with his claw and shot it viciously at a fat old rat who stood nearby holding a stringed lutelike instrument.

'Yoghul, play my song!'

The rat began playing, singing the dirge in an eerie, high-pitched voice.

'Where do you come from, where do you go to,
From tundras of white and bright sunrises few,
'Cross mountains and forests, o'er seas wide and
  blue,
The one they call Foxwolf, the Urgan Nagru.'

Yoghul was playing the verse over again when Nagru called across to Gael, 'Hey Squirrelking, d'you know why they call me Foxwolf?'

Gael sat silent, and Nagru answered his own question. 'Because I am the only fox that ever slew a wolf. This is his hide I am wearing. I'll wager you've never even seen a wolf, much less had to fight one. Well I did, and I won. Nobeast alive can stand against me!'

The Squirrelking ignored his captor, who continued boasting. 'I'll tell you something else, that wolf's name was Urgan. So I took it and turned it backward and made a name for myself, Urgan Nagru! Try saying it both ways, it comes out the same. That's to let my enemies know that I can come at them backward or forward, both ways. But I have no enemies, they're all dead. Only fools and dreamers are left, like you and your Queen. It's your own fault, squirrel, you let me in here. Aha! I see you are glaring at me. Good! You are wishing that the Foxwolf were dead, eh? The wishes of the weak are like raindrops on the face of the sea, they count for nothing. Play on, Yoghul!'

Whilst Nagru drank wine and tore at his meat, Silvamord had been staring fixedly at Muta the old badger nurse. Muta could not speak. Sometimes in peaks of joy or distress she would make hoarse barking noises, but it was unusual for her to make any sound at all. She crouched at little Truffen's side, always faithful to him. It irritated Silvamord to see the dumb badger's devotion to her small charge, and the vixen never missed an opportunity to humiliate or torment Muta. Calling Yoghul across to her, Silvamord divested him of his cloak, a small red thing trimmed with yellow. Then she snatched the cap from his head. It was floppy and conical with two tiny bells hanging from it. Flinging both hat and cloak at Muta, Silvamord called out derisively, 'Come on, up on your paws, stripedog. Put those on and do a dance for me. I command it, dance!'

The big badger did not move. She stood glaring at the vixen. Silvamord beckoned Riveneye, one of the Captains seated nearby. 'If that stupid beast doesn't start dancing right now,' she barked, 'I want you to take your sword to the squirrelbrat and tickle a dance out of him!'

Riveneye stood and drew his sword.

Muta had no choice. Rather than see Truffen hurt, she donned the small cloak and tied the ribbons of the ridiculous little hat beneath her chin. Slowly she commenced a shuffling dance.

Silvamord aimed a kick at the minstrel rat. 'Play, Yoghul – play faster. I want to see the big fool dance!'

Round and round Muta shambled, trying to keep up with the speed of the music, the bells tinkling wildly on her silly hat. Silvamord and the rats jeered cruelly at the badger's stumbling efforts. A single teardrop spilled down Muta's face.

Queen Serena turned away, unable to watch the cruel

exhibition. Gael leaned in close as if sharing her sympathy, and began whispering so only she could hear. 'It's all right Serena, don't worry. Listen to me and try not to show any surprise. Remember our singing blackbird Relph? Rab has sent me a message through him. There will be otters waiting in the castle moat today. We will accompany Muta when she takes Truffen for his afternoon nap. Relph will hang a red cloth on the window nearest the drawbridge to tell Rab we are coming. When we leave here, watch for the window with the red cloth on the sill, that's the one we jump from. When we land in the moat the otters will take us to safety. Don't look around, just nod if you understand . . .' Muta's hoarse bark caused the Queen to turn.

Truffen could not understand that Muta was being made fun of – they had often played at dancing together. Seeing her dance now made the little fellow chuckle happily. It was a game! He began hopskipping alongside her, giggling as he clapped his paws together in time to the music.

Muta threw back her head and made happy barking sounds, and the two danced wildly, leaping and jigging back and forth. Truffen pulled the cap from Muta's head as she bowed to him and waved it about, jingling the bells and shouting uproariously, 'Fasta! Fasta! More!'

Nagru flicked a damson contemptuously at Silvamord. 'Well, I see you've managed to make them both happy, a prancing whelp and a jigging badger, good work! Tell me, who looks the bigger fool now, you or the badger?'

Silvamord flung a wooden bowl at Yoghul. 'Stop playing, you oaf!' she shrieked.

The music ground to a halt. Truffen jangled the cap bells. 'More dances 'Uta, want more dances!'

Taking advantage of the moment, Serena hurried over. Sweeping her little son up, she took Muta by the paw and began leaving the room. Gael joined them. 'Time for Muta to take you for your nap, Truffen. Come on, Mummy and Daddy will go with you.'

They were almost at the door when Silvamord called out, 'Halt! Who said you could leave without our permission?'

Nagru idly flicked another damson at his mate. 'Let them go, huh, they're not going anywhere.'

Silvamord leaped up, eyes blazing. 'Stop flicking damsons at me, spotblotch, I'll say when they can go! You just carry on slopping wine!'

Nagru was not one to be insulted. He rose in a hot temper, sending dishes spilling and clattering. 'You'll feel these claws if you talk to me like that, vixen! If I say they can go, my word is final! Don't try taking your sour mood out on me because your joke went wrong!'

All the time the little party were edging further out of the banqueting chamber. Silvamord grabbed a spear from a Captain named Hooktail and pointed it at the Foxwolf, screaming, 'Put those claws near me and I'll gut you! Stop those creatures leaving, now!'

Two more rats, Sourgall and Ragfen, drew swords and leaped up. As Gael pushed the others ahead of him into the hall outside, Serena forgot herself and cried out, 'Look on the windowsill, the red cloth!'

Gael felt Sourgall's claws clamp on his shoulder. He jumped backward, cannoning Sourgall into Ragfen as he called out to the badger, 'Muta, out of the window – jump for the moat! Help is waiting there. Save my family!'

Then Gael went down. He was trampled and knocked aside as other rats, led by Silvamord, came charging into the passage. Muta dashed to the window where the red cloth fluttered, sweeping Serena and Truffen with her. Thrusting the little squirrel into his mother's outstretched paws, the big badger lifted them both bodily over the sill. A spearshaft broke across

Muta's back. She grunted and flinched, then, gathering her mighty strength, she hurled mother and babe outward, so that they would not strike the castle walls in their descent to the moat. Turning, she ripped the dancing-cloak from her shoulders. Muta smashed two rats flat with a single blow and smothered another two with the cloak, shoving them roughly into those behind and causing a mêlée of confusion in the enclosed space.

Now the corridor was packed with rats. Muta could not reach Gael – it was death to try. There was only one way left open to her. Lifting her bulk on to the windowsill, the badger glanced down at the long drop to the moat. Suddenly, claws sunk into her lower back. Silvamord had climbed over the milling rats and seized her tight.

'Got you, stripehead! Now you'll die long and slooooooo . . . !' Without a second thought Muta had clamped her footpaws around the vixen and rolled off the windowsill, carrying her enemy through with her.

Rab's otters already had Serena and Truffen out on the bank as Muta and Silvamord came plummeting down and hit the water with a resounding boom. Locked together, they plunged beneath the surface. Muta rolled over, thrusting the vixen beneath her, then, stepping on Silvamord's head, she pushed up towards the surface. Seconds later Muta was hauling herself up on to the bank and scrambling off in pursuit of her friends and their rescuers.

Terror and panic gripped Silvamord – the badger's footpaws had pressed her down into the muddy moat bottom. The vixen's ears, nose and mouth filled with water as she kicked and scrabbled furiously, then, coming free with a dull sucking noise, she drifted upward.

Whump!

The drawbridge thudded down on to the moatbank, and the rat horde came pouring out intent on catching the escaped prisoners. Spitting water and mud, Silva-mord splashed up and down, screeching, 'Help! Save me, you fools . . . Glubble . . . I can't swim!'

The rats halted, fearful of ignoring the Foxwolf's mate. Several long pikes and spears were stretched out quickly into the water, one so hastily that it clouted the drowning fox, half stunning her.

Nagru came bounding out over the drawbridge in time to see Silvamord hauled dripping from the moat. Her bedraggled skirt of tails clung wetly as she buffeted the head of a rat called Crookneck, shouting, 'I said save me, you addlebrained toad, not brain me!'

As she sank exhausted to the grassy bank, Nagru berated her. 'Idiot, why did you let them escape?'

'Why did I let them escape?' she shrieked, spitting moatwater and mud at him venomously. 'Where were you, bogbrains? Still swilling wine and feeding your face?'

Nagru sighted the receding figures vanishing into the trees on the wooded hillside. He pointed to a group of twoscore or more rats standing on the bank. 'You lot, follow me, I'll catch them!'

Silvamord tottered upright at the water's edge, foot-paws seeking purchase in the wet grass. The Foxwolf could not resist giving her a hefty slap on the back. 'You stay here and dry off, vixen!'

She overbalanced and toppled back, screeching, into the moat.

The four otters rushed Serena along at a cracking pace. Truffen was seated on the sturdy shoulders of a young male called Troutlad. Muta followed up the rear; for all her seasons and girth she was still nimble and swift. Tree shadows threw alternating patterns of sun and shade over the Southswarders as they fled up the thick-timbered hillside.

Nagru halted at the bottom of the causeway steps

leading down from the castle plateau. His keen eyes picked up the movements of the small group racing up the wooded tor across the valley. A rat Captain named Gatchag stuck his sword into the ground and sank down on his haunches beside the quivering weapon, shaking his head knowingly. 'Huh, they're away like two brace o' woodpigeons. Nah! You won't catch 'em now, take my word fer it!'

Swift as a flash, the Urgan Nagru grabbed Gatchag's sword and slew him with a single, powerful slash. The shock that ran through the rats was registered in a single moan, like a sudden gale running through long wheat. Nagru threw the blade down on the lifeless body.

'Anybeast got more strong opinions to voice can join him! Up on your paws, slopmouths, before I let daylight into some of your skulls! Mingol, take twelve and circle right. Riveneye, take another twelve and circle in from the left. The rest of you follow me, we'll go straight up after them. If we shift fast enough they'll be cut off from three ways. In my horde, a slow rat is a dead one. Now move!'

Rab Streambattle and six of his otters watched anxiously as the fugitives toiled uphill. Rab's mate Iris fitted a stone to her sling. 'Those rats are coming on fast, Rab. They're going to pincer in front of our lot before they get here – what'll we do?'

The otter leader loosed an arrow, picking off one of Mingol's front runners. Laying another shaft on his bowstring he took aim, and said, 'We'll have to buy them some time by holding off the rats. Lay on and make every shot count!'

The otters attacked with a will. Arrows, slingstones and short javelins whipped skilfully down the wooded slope to left and right, peppering the horderats and harrying their pincer movement. Rab hurtled forward

29

and reached the fugitives. He ran past them, calling out, 'Keep going, there's help ahead mates. Hurry! Nagru's right behind you, I'll keep him busy!'

Rab Streambattle was a warrior who did not know the meaning of fear. The most skilled weaponbeast among otters, now he showed his mettle. Planting both foot-paws firmly, he threw off his quiver and with a speed born of desperation began zipping arrows into the ranks of Nagru's rats.

The Foxwolf was sorry he had not slain the fierce otter on first sight. Leaping to one side he dodged behind a scrub oak, leaving the rat immediately behind to die by the arrow that was meant for him. Another rat screamed and leapt high, transfixed by Rab's next shaft. Nagru cursed silently, wishing he had brought a bow and arrows along. Flailing his claws wildly, he shouted, 'Idiots! Move about, duck and dodge, use your arrows and spears – he's only one otter!'

A deadly shot from Rab pinned a rat to a rowan tree. Grim-faced, he called out as he strung another arrow, 'Aye, I'm only one otter, but here I stand, try an' pass, scum!'

Serena came gasping and stumbling into the out-stretched paws of Iris. The otter embraced her briefly before going back to slinging rocks. 'Serena, no time to chatter now, we must get you an' the liddle un to safety!'

'But Gael . . . and Rab, what about them?'

Keeping her eyes on the target, Iris bowled a rat over as her stone cracked his skull. 'If your Squirrelking doesn't escape there's nothin' we can do at the moment, Marm. As for my Rab, you know he'd swap his life for friends – that's what he's doin' now. I've got to get you away, that's my job!'

A spear had furrowed Rab's side. He ignored the searing pain and dropped a rat with an accurate snap shot. Then he counted his remaining arrows. Three.

Using bush and tree cover, Nagru's rats were surrounding Rab. Without turning his head, the brave otter roared, 'Get them out o' here, Iris. Go!'

Snuffling a tear aside, his courageous mate hustled Serena and her babe along with the otters. 'You heard my Rab, come on, move yourselves!'

They fled over the hilltop, zigzagging north through the trees. All but one.

A deep rumble shook Muta's huge frame; anger and hatred shone in the badger's dark eyes. With unbounded strength she seized the thick, overhanging limb of a dead whitebeam. Her sinews stood out like ropes as she tore it from the trunk with a resounding crack. Regardless of twigs and splinters, Muta swung the large limb above her head, and like a whirlwind she thundered forward, launching herself upon Nagru and his vermin. Keen as March wind through a storm-lashed forest, a high-pitched whine tore from her throat. The wide, twigged end of the bough caught Nagru, sending him muzzle over tail, soaring high into the air like a dead leaf. The Foxwolf thudded painfully against a hornbeam, his shocked eyes taking in the destruction Muta was wreaking on his hordebeasts as he fought to regain his breath. Finally he managed to shout: 'Kill them both! Mingol, Riveneye – surround them! Use arrows, cut them down with spears . . . Anything!'

Back to back, the otter and the badger stood, battering away madly, one with a broken bow, the other with a tree limb. Wounded in a dozen places, they fought like madbeasts as the grey vermin closed in on them.

4

Extract from the writings of Saxtus, Father Abbot of Redwall Abbey in Mossflower Country.

It occurs to me that small bees are as foolish as they are fat and fuzzy, take for example this fellow. Humming and bumbling around me as if I were a flower. Very disturbing when one is penning a chronicle. I think he wants this crumb of honey pudding, stuck to my whiskers. Here, take it, you rogue. No, the crumb, not my paw! Dearie me, are all bees as short sighted as this one?

What a Recorder I am, playing with bees when I should be writing. Alas, the summer is to blame. It makes me want to dash outside and play with the Dibbuns (our Abbey young ones). It is they who hold the hope of Redwall's future; our Abbey would not flourish without the young. Many old friends have passed on to quiet pastures: Abbot Bernard, Friar Cockleburr, Old Gabriel Quill and a few other dear companions have run their seasons peacefully to a close. But the earth and its creatures continue to be renewed. Please forgive my ramblings and reminiscences under the spell of a warm summer. Let me tell you what has taken place of late at Redwall Abbey.

It all started as I was strolling in the orchard with Mariel's father, Joseph the Bellmaker. We were enjoying the early morning peace together. Joseph told me that he had been thinking about Mariel a lot and worrying about her. More than four seasons have passed since she went off adventuring with that rogue Dandin, a friend of my young days. He is a wild mouse, but with a good heart. Mariel and Dandin are kindred spirits, both with a yearning to wander.

Joseph's main worry was the lack of information about his daughter. He had received no news of Mariel from anywhere. Travellers, visitors to Redwall, passing birds – no creature knew their whereabouts, or had heard anything at all concerning Mariel or Dandin.

However, honest ones with troubled minds are often reassured by the appearance of Martin the Warrior in their dreams. Martin is the champion and founder of Redwall Abbey, a great warrior mouse who lived countless seasons ago. His guidance is peerless, and his words, though often shrouded in mystery, always carry a message of hope and truth. Little wonder then that a stout-hearted beast like Joseph the Bellmaker should find Martin, the spirit of Redwall, appearing in his dreams. I must confess that I was full of curiosity to learn of the message Martin had imparted to Joseph as his mind wandered the realms of slumber. But my good friend the Bellmaker was not ready to speak. He had not yet understood the meaning of Martin's words.

A single loud knock on the gatehouse door disturbed Saxtus from his writing. Without looking up, he called out, 'I recognize that sound; only Joseph the Bellmaker has a paw like an oak club!'

There followed a deep chuckle from outside as Joseph replied, 'Saxtus, have you dozed off in there? Come on, dinnertime!'

Hitching up his robe, the Abbot hastened to open the door. 'Good afternoon, Bellmaker, or is it early evening? No matter, I cast aside the pen in favour of the spoon.'

Joseph was a strongly built mouse, with a neat grey beard and a cheerful manner. He patted the Abbot's stomach playfully. 'Aye, I think the spoon is your favourite weapon these days, great Father Abbot.'

Saxtus strode out ahead of the Bellmaker, to show him that a bit of extra weight had not slowed him down. 'Hah! Great Father Abbot indeed! I'm only slightly older than your daughter. As for you, greybeard, you're old enough to be my father!'

Joseph matched his stride, eyes twinkling mischievously. Walking across flower-bordered lawns, they headed towards the main Abbey building. It loomed massive against an early evening sky, ancient red sandstone tinged dusky rose, framing a harlequinade of stained glass windows by the glow of a lowering sun. The Bellmaker stepped up his pace, leaving Saxtus panting in his wake.

'I may be old enough to be your daddy, but I'm still spry enough to be your son. Come on, Father, keep up!'

'Enough, enough. Slow down, ageless one!' said Saxtus, catching hold of his friend's sleeve. 'Why is it that everybeast seems to be in a hurry today? Look, there's Foremole, going as if his tail were afire. Hallo Sir!'

The Redwall mole leader halted and, tugging his snout respectfully, he addressed them both in quaint mole dialect: 'Gudd eve to ee zurrs. Whurr be you uns a-rushen to?'

He fell in step with them as Joseph replied, 'We

34

weren't really rushing, just stepping out a bit on our way across to dinner.'

'We'm gotten guestbeasts furr dinner,' said Foremole, wrinkling his button nose sagely. 'Oak Tom an' Treerose cummed in from ee woodlands.'

Saxtus raised his eyebrows. 'Well, that is a pleasant surprise. We don't see enough of Tom and his wife at Redwall. Those squirrels spend most of their time in Mossflower Wood together, never know where they are from one season to the next. Any other guests?'

'Hurrhurrurr!' Foremole's dumpy frame shook with a deep chuckle. 'Oi'd say ee best step out fast agin zurrs, Missus Rosie an' Tarquin, they'm bringed all thurr h'infants to ee Abbey furr to stay awhoil.'

Saxtus threw up his paws in mock despair. 'Great seasons of famine! Tarquin and Rosie Woodworrel with their twelve young hares, that's fourteen walking stomachs altogether. They'll eat us out of house and home then pick their teeth with the doornails!'

'I don't mind not eating,' said Joseph, clapping the Abbot on his back happily. 'My dream is beginning to work out.'

Saxtus halted beneath a drooping lilac. 'What do you mean by that friend?'

'I can tell you this much,' the Bellmaker said, stroking his beard thoughtfully. 'Martin said some things to me in my dream last night of which I can only speak later on. But the first words he spoke I will repeat now. They went like this:

"With sixteen more faces at table,
Bellmaker recalls his quest.
At daylight's last gleam you'll remember
My words whilst you were at rest."

Foremole scratched his velvety head, saying, 'Wot do et all mean, zurr?'

35

Joseph shrugged, but Saxtus nodded wisely. 'It means that Martin will reveal all when the time is right.'

Joseph continued walking to the Abbey. 'I'm glad you said that, Saxtus,' he said, 'because beyond those few words the whole thing is very hazy. I can't remember anything else Martin said.'

The Father Abbot deliberately steered the conversation away from his friend's dream; knowing that, if Martin had spoken, all would be revealed in good time. He held up a paw. 'Listen, Joseph. I love to hear the sound of your bell!'

Scented orchard blossom fragrance lay heavy on the summer evening air as the great Joseph Bell boomed out its warm, brazen message. Calling all Redwallers to cease their chores and come to Great Hall, for the day's main meal.

A group of Dibbuns – small mice, moles, squirrels and hedgehogs – trooped round the south gable from the orchard. Singing lustily, they marched paw in paw.

'Give us dinner every eve,
Or we'll pack our bags and leave.
Where we'll go to we don't know,
Up the path a league or so.
If we don't find comfort there,
Back to Redwall we'll repair.
We'll eat pudden, pie and cake,
All the Abbey cooks can make!'

They stopped to let their elders pass indoors first. Bowing politely and scrubbing paws across strawberry-stained faces, they chanted dutifully: 'Good evenin' Father Abbot. Evenin', Joseph sir, evenin' to you, Foremole sir!'

Saxtus raised his eyebrows. Peering at them over the spectacles balanced on his nose, he said, 'Well, good evening to you, young sirs and ladies. Pray tell me, where are you all off to?'

Scrubbing furiously at her face, a little molemaid replied, 'Whoi, furr ee dinner zurr, us'n's worked 'ard all day.'

Joseph surveyed the guilty-looking band. Pursing his lips in mock severity, he said, 'Hmm, guarding the strawberry patch against robbers, no doubt. A very difficult job, I'd say, eh?'

A tiny mousebabe, covered from ear to tail in strawberry pulp and seeds, puffed out his chest and squeaked, 'Most 'ardest job I doo'd in all me life, sir!'

Foremole prodded the babe's swollen stomach gently. 'Burr, you'm sure ee can manage dinner arter all yon 'ard wurk ee dunn?'

An equally small mole patted the mousebabe heartily. 'Ho aye, ee surpintly can, zurr, ee be a growen choild an' needen lots o' dinner, doant ee matey?'

The mousebabe nodded vigorous agreement. Saxtus looked to Foremole and Joseph, giving them a quick wink. 'What do you think, sirs, do these warriors deserve dinner as a reward for guarding our strawberries?'

Foremole scratched his chin with a hefty digging claw. 'Aye, oi do berleev they'm do zurr, tho' they'm lukk in need o' a good scrubben furrst, hurr hurr!'

'Oh yes, we can't have em sitting at table like that,' the Bellmaker agreed judiciously. 'All stained and scarred from their long, hard duties. Right, line up here, all down to the shallow edge of the Abbey pond. First one back and cleanest washed gets the biggest dinner. Ready, steady, . . . Go!'

'Redwaaaaall! Chaaaaaarge!' The Dibbuns sped off helter-skelter. Shaking with laughter, the three friends strode in to dinner.

From time out of mind Redwall Abbey had been renowned as a haven of comradeship, good manners, and legendary food. All Redwallers met each evening to share the fruits of their toil. Saxtus entered the Great Hall, warm in the feeling of being Father Abbot to the creatures of his beloved Abbey. Early evening sunlight slanted down through the stained glass windows, casting rainbow hues over the laden tables. Young and old alike sat together, the hum of their chatter rising to hallowed timber roofbeams. Garlands of rose, stitchwort, sorrel, violet and anemone decked the inner table borders. Duty cooks and servers bustled about on the outer perimeters, pushing trolleys and carrying trays heaped with culinary delights. Hungry onlookers commented eagerly upon the delightful fare. The two hares, Tarquin L. Woodsorrel and his wife the Hon Rosie, together with their twelve leverets, wiggled their ears in delight.

'I say, I say, jolly old meadowcream pudden, wot?'

'Just lookit those button mushrooms fallin' out o' that leek an' onion pastie, m'dear. Absolutely spiffin'!'

Hon Rosie was known for her strident laugh, which it was said could curdle cream at great distances. 'Whoo-hahahooh! Woodland salad an' yellow nutcheese with Abbey dressing, top hole! They must've known we were comin', Tarkers, wot?'

Foremole took his seat, nudging a molefriend. 'Yurr, be that turnip'n'tater'n'beetroot deeper'n'ever pie oi sees, Rungle?'

'Ho aye, that et be, zurr, wi' damsoncream pudden t'foller,' said the other mole, as he polished a small wooden ladle eagerly. 'Boi 'okey, if'n moi mouth waters much more oi'm afeared oi'll be drownded, hurr!'

Blind Simeon, the ancient mouse Herbalist, and old Mother Mellus, the matriarch badger of Redwall, sat either side of Saxtus. The Bellmaker was seated next to Mellus – all four were close friends. Joseph leaned towards the badger as two hedgehogs passed, bearing a tray piled high with fresh baked scones.

'What a delightful aroma, Mellus. Honey and blackberry scones, with maple icing too. Splendid!'

A smile hovered about the badger's silver muzzle. 'You're nought but a flattering fraud, Joseph, you knew I baked them specially for you. They do smell nice though.'

'Those scones will taste twice as good as they smell,' said Saxtus, unfolding his table napkin.

The old badger smiled graciously. 'How gallant, thank you, Father Abbot!'

'How is it that I'm nought but a flattering fraud and Saxtus gets thanked for his gallantry?' grumbled the Bellmaker, as he attacked a salad busily.

Mellus ladled fragrant dark gravy over a carrot and scallion pastie and placed it in front of Joseph. 'Compliments are like clouds, my friend; very pretty, but if we had to dine on them we'd starve. Eat and be thankful.'

Looking rather guilty, Saxtus stayed the Bellmaker's paw. 'Oops. Forgot to say grace, 'scuse me please!'

He rang a small bell, specially made for table by Joseph. All chatter ceased; silence fell over Great Hall. The Father Abbot arose, solemn faced. He was about to speak when the newly washed orchard guard clattered in through the doorway. With a frown and a paw to her lips, Mellus beckoned them silently to her. They tippawed across, Saxtus holding his silence as the badger whispered, 'Late for dinner, my little Dibbuns?'

A mousebabe piped up indignantly. 'Norra our fault, we was sended for a wash after us worked 'ard inna orchard all day long!'

The Dibbuns nodded in unison, backing up their spokesmouse. Mellus's huge paws scooped two of them on to her lap. 'Now sit quietly the rest of you, not a word until Father Abbot has said grace.'

She nodded to Saxtus, who coughed importantly and began:

'Fate and seasons smile on all,
From sunrise to the dark nightfall,
This bounty from both earth and tree,
Was made to share, twixt you and me,
To Mother Nature let us say,
Our thanks, for life and health this day.'

There was a mighty Amen. The little bell sounded and dinner commenced in earnest.

It was a joyous meal for honest creatures. Dishes were passed to be shared, both sweet and savoury. October Ale and strawberry cordial, tarts, pies, flans and puddings, served out and replaced by fresh delights from Redwall's kitchens. Turnovers, trifles, breads, fondants, salads, pasties and cheeses, alternated with beakers of greensap milk, mint tea, rosehip cup and elderberry wine. Rufe Brush, the Abbey Bellringer, shared a heavy fruitcake with his friend Durry Quill, hedgehog Cellarkeeper and nephew of the late good old Gabe Quill, from whom he had inherited his duties.

The Abbot watched Joseph leaning back in his chair. 'What is it, Bellmaker,' he said, 'not hungry?'

'Saxtus, when will my dreams be revealed?'

'Eat first, talk later, it will happen in good time. Is that a hot scone I see lying on your plate?'

Joseph turned too late; the scone was claimed by the mousebabe sitting on Mellus's lap. Joseph blinked. 'You little scallywag! I suppose you'd like to guard the kitchen baking ovens tomorrow as a change from the strawberry patch.'

The mousebabe shook his head and winked furtively. 'No, but we guard the win'owsill, where cakes an' pies be;' he said.

Mellus tickled his ribs until he giggled and squirmed. 'Oh no you won't, bucko, my pies and cakes are quite safe cooling alone on the windowsills. Though I once recall a certain Abbot when he was a Dibbun, spent three days in sickbay after guarding those windowsills. The greedy little snip, do you remember him, Saxtus?'

The Father Abbot of all Redwall applied himself to a plate of summercream pudding, pretending he had not heard.

The evening wore on until the Dibbuns began yawning, one or two coming perilously close to falling face down upon their plates with drooping eyes. Saxtus stood and rang his little bell.

'Anybeast on dormitory duty, please take the Dibbuns up!'

Wails of protest arose from the fretful babes. 'Yaah, not fair, s'not fair, us allus 'ave t'go t'bed!'

'I wish us big uns could go off to bed right now,' said Oak Tom, pulling a long face of comic dismay. 'We have to stay up and wash pots'n'pans'n'dishes clean for morning.'

Tarquin L. Woodsorrel flapped his ears in agreement. 'Indeed scout, 'tis a rough old life bein' a big un, wot? P'raps the Dibbuns aren't really sleepy, what say they stay up an' help, bet they'd make jolly good potwashers, eh?'

There was a sudden clatter of chairs and benches as the panicked Dibbuns dashed for the stairs, yelling, 'Gu'night Father Abbot, night night everybeast, we goin' abed!' They scampered up the stairs amid peals of laughter.

Flooding evening sunlight had now dimmed to a golden filter, illuminating the tapestry depicting Martin the Warrior which hung upon the wall of Great Hall. Saxtus felt himself arise unbidden from his Abbot's chair. He went to stand behind the Bellmaker. A dreamy feeling he could not explain had cast its mantle over the Abbot; it was as if time and the earth were standing still. A great silence lay upon the big chamber: golden dust motes hung lazily on the still air, gleaming in the last faded yellow sunrays. Amidst the tangible hush Redwallers sat immobile, each in their place, like figures captured in eternity upon some vast canvas. Across the peace that lay over all, Saxtus heard his own voice. It was low, yet the sound carried from floor to roofbeam, reaching every shadowed corner of Great Hall.

'My friends, I have something to say to you. Of late Joseph our Bellmaker has been thinking deeply about his daughter Mariel and her companion Dandin. I know that all Redwallers remember both those mice with great fondness; I certainly do. Dandin and I were brought up together, like brothers, in this very Abbey. Scarce a day passes when I will not see somewhere we played together, and then I think of him, off on adventures with Mariel the Warriormaid. Alas, there has been no news of them for more than four seasons now. Where are they? I think Joseph may provide us with some help. Last night he was visited in a dream by Martin the Warrior.'

To Joseph, the Abbot's voice behind him sounded like a distant murmur. He had not heard a word that was said. Now Saxtus had finished speaking, every eye was turned upon the Bellmaker. He sat upright, staring hard at the likeness of Martin upon the tapestry. Saxtus watched him – Joseph's lips were moving slowly as if he were holding a conversation with somebeast. The room became dark; Saxtus watched as dusk heralded nightfall. The sun's final ray reflected through a high window, wreathing the form of Joseph in a fleeting nimbus of light. Saxtus recalled the lines of the rhyme: 'At daylight's last gleam you'll remember.'

Then the daylight was gone.

Candles and walltorches burned bright as Joseph stood and looked about him.

'Listen now and I will speak as Martin the Warrior told me!'

5

It was much cooler among the green hills of the scrubland. Mariel, Dandin and Bowly took a leisurely lunch from the supplies they had commandeered from the two weasels. The travellers rested, half napping as they lay back on a mossy hillock, listening to the high trill of a skylark backed by the drone of bees and the dry chirrup of grasshoppers. Dandin was first to hear other noises; shaking himself out of a semi-torpor he cupped an ear to the light breeze.

'Listen, can you hear it, Mariel? Sounds like somebeasts doing a bit of roaring and shouting somewhere.'

Mariel prodded the sleeping Bowly firmly on his snout. 'Stop snoring and do something useful, sit up and tell us what you can hear, come on dozybones!'

The young hedgehog sat up, snuffling and grumbling. 'Call y'selves friends? Huh, won't even let a young warrior 'ave 'is slumber, you'll stunt me growth wakin' me like that.' Bowly had very sharp hearing and he assessed the situation in a trice.

'Sounds like some creatures tormentin' a mole. See that big hill yonder, third one goin' south to the right. I reckons it's comin' from ahind of there.'

Moles were friendly. No one hesitated. Mariel readied her Gullwhacker and Dandin drew his dagger. Bowly sighed aloud, picking up his two hard oatcakes as he followed them on their way to the big hill. 'Time for trouble agin. Mercy me, somebeasts got no consideration at all. Goin' gittin' theirselves into distress jus' when it's warriors' nappin' time!'

Bowly was correct, it was a fat old mole in trouble. Six grey rats were trying to bind him with grass ropes. The old creature was giving a good account of himself, but the rats were overwhelming him, prodding him with spears as they looped the coils about him and struggled to get a halter round his neck. Nearby three small young moles were weeping in distress, closely guarded by a seventh rat.

The old mole pulled a paw loose as he roared, 'You'm vurmints, oi'll never tug moi snout to no foxerwulf, ee Squirrelyking be the oandly one oi bow to, hurr!'

They had not yet seen the three friends. 'Me and Mariel will take the six who have the old fellow,' Dandin whispered to Bowly. 'D'you reckon you could deal with that rat guarding the young uns?'

Not stopping to answer, Bowly hefted one of his oatcakes and flung it hard with amazing accuracy. It whacked the rat solidly across the jaw, dropping him in a heap. The young hedgehog grinned from ear to ear. 'I done that Dandy, wot next?'

All activity below ceased as the six rats turned to stare up at the intruders. Dandin sighed in resignation. 'Bowly, you might have waited until I gave the word – we've completely lost the element of surprise.'

Mariel had her Gullwhacker ready as they strode down to confront the rats. She addressed the one who looked like their captain. 'You, frognose, get your filthy paws off that mole!'

The rat leered crookedly at her. 'Well, well, what have we here, a little mouseymaid. What's your name, pretty one?'

The Gullwhacker belted him square in the mouth and he sat down hard, spitting out a broken fang. Mariel smiled. 'Should have whacked you over the ears, it would have cleared some of the muck from them. I never asked for compliments – I told you to let the mole go.'

'You've just signed your death warrant, mouse,' said the rat, wiping a trickle of blood from his mouth. 'There's more than seven of us, you'll see!' He blew several sharp blasts on a bone whistle which hung from his neck, but before he could blow more, a kick from the old mole felled him. Knowing reinforcements would be arriving promptly, Mariel and Dandin hurled themselves headlong at the remaining five rats.

'Redwaaaaaalllll!'

Sheathing his dagger, Dandin tripped the first rat and grabbed the spear from his claws as he fell. Using the spearbutt as a club he set about belabouring the grounded rat furiously. Mariel tangled the footpaws of another in the coils of her Gullwhacker, whipping it free to punish him with the hard knotted end. Bowly leapt on the back of a third rat, striking hard with his remaining oatcake.

Reinforcements arrived in the form of ten more rats dashing over the hill. Mariel saw them coming and rapped out a swift order: 'Form foursquare around the little moles. Quick!'

They dashed to obey, facing outward with the young moles at their centre. Dandin brandished the spear, jabbing. Mariel swung her rope in an arc, daring any rat to step within its range. Bowly and the old mole had picked up spear and sword; growling, they waved the weapons wildly. The rats who had been felled began to recover and rise, hopelessly outnumbering the four defenders. A rat leapt back, sneering, as Dandin jabbed out with his spear.

The Captain whose fang Mariel had knocked out

45

staggered upright, wiping blood from his chin. 'You'll wish you'd never interfered with Captain Bragglin of Nagru's horde. Hitting me with that rope was the biggest mistake of your life, mouse!'

Some of the rats had bows. They began fitting shafts to their bowstrings in readiness. Dandin shook his head. 'Bowly, I told you it was wrong to knock that rat down before we had a chance to size up the situation.'

Quivering with anticipation, the rats began slowly closing in on the little party. For the first time Bowly's swaggering attitude deserted him and his voice sounded small and frightened. 'T'aint much fun bein' a warrior, looks like we're nigh to gettin' ourselves slayed!'

Mariel knew Bowly's words to be true. But desperate situations call for reckless remedies: the mousemaid hurled herself into action with lightning ferocity.

Snatching the dagger from Dandin's belt she clamped it firmly between her teeth, then, thundering forward, she struck hard, left, right and centre with the Gull-whacker. Totally unprepared for such an aggressive move, several rats were floored by hefty blows. They fell, bumping into others and knocking arrows awry from bowstrings. For the second time in a short space Captain Bragglin found himself in the path of Mariel's weapon. She swung it in a vicious arc, thudding the knot into his stomach. His mouth gaped wide as the breath was belted from him in a loud whoosh. Before the rats had time to recover, Mariel had thrown herself upon their Captain. She held the dagger point at his trembling gullet, roaring wildly, 'Don't even think about moving or this scum dies!'

As the attackers froze in their tracks, Bragglin shouted, 'Be still, don't make any false moves! Grinj, cover her!'

The rat called Grinj was an experienced archer. As the rest stood stock-still he slid close to Mariel, an arrow straining against his taut bowstring. Bragglin managed to gasp against the daggertip tickling his throat, 'Kill her if she moves this blade a fraction!'

Dandin heaved a loud sigh of dismay. It was a stand-off. Noontide shimmered over the grass-topped sandhills as both parties stood poised in a silent tableau.

'This'n's a right ol' mess we be gotten into,' said Bowly, shooting Dandin a pleading glance. 'Wot's a warrior supposed to do now, Dandy?'

Dandin knew the situation rested on a daggertip and an arrowhead. Squinting up at the high hot orb of the sun he whispered calmly, 'Learn patience and obedience, that's the way of the warrior. Don't show fear, Bowly; stand up straight and wait for the next move – but be ready when it comes!'

'Hail the conquering Foxwolf – you drooling idiot!'

The Urgan Nagru ducked as a bowl clanged against the banqueting chamber door. Wincing with the pain of his injuries he hobbled to one side as Silvamord flung a three-branched candlestick.

'One day that poisoned tongue'll be the death of you, vixen!' the Foxwolf snarled dangerously. Limping to his chair he slumped down and began tugging gingerly with his teeth at a long whitebeam splinter embedded in his paw. Silvamord continued her tirade.

'I could have caught them, but what did you do, cleverbrush? Tried to drown me in the moat! Nagru the nitbrain, that's you, the fool who chases his own tail!'

Nagru spat the splinter at her venomously. 'Ahh, give your slobbering mouth a rest, clattergob, letting yourself be pulled out the window by a big dumb badger!'

The rat horde sat in the courtyard, some licking their wounds, others slaking their thirst from the dwindling cellars of the castle. Sounds of furious argument rang out from the banqueting chamber windows high above their heads.

Fillch, one of the rats, looked up from the honey-preserved chestnuts he was sharing with his companion Sourgall. 'Big dumb badger, eh? That one didn't *need* to talk, she slew eight of ours with a tree limb it'd take ten of us to lift!'

Sourgall had remained behind to fish Silvamord from the moat. He looked Fillch up and down slowly. 'Huh, she didn't 'urt yew matey, where were yer? Leadin' from be'ind, I'll bet.'

'Aye, an' so would yew 'ave been, bucko. We nearly 'ad the otter, that'd fought like a madbeast while the others escaped. Then that badger was in the middle of us, swingin' an 'arf of a tree! Where d'yer expect me t'be, eh? Drigg, Flokky, Big Bragtail an' five others got in the badger's way, and they ain't around t'tell the story no more. You ask Hooktail if y'don't believe me, ain't that right mate?'

The rat in question had lost an ear. He was using a poultice of dockleaves bound with earth and water to staunch the wound. 'Gaah!' he groaned. 'It's all right you sittin' there makin' clever remarks, Sourgall, you wasn't there. Even the Urgan Nagru took to 'is paws an' limped off like a flogged toad. I tell yer mate, you wouldn't 'ave thought it was the same stoopid badger that played nursemaid to the liddle squirrelbrat. That beast came after us with a full tree in 'er paws, even though we filled 'er with arrers like a pincushion!'

A rat named Flangor joined the conversation. 'Wot d'yew suppose Foxwolf'll do now, mates?'

The one called Riveneye put aside the cider he had been swilling and snorted, 'Hah, you should know the Urgan by now, mate. Nagru won't rest 'til their skulls are bleachin' in the sun. Ol' Foxwolf'll hunt 'em 'til 'e gets every last one in those iron claws. Then we know wot 'e'll do with 'em, don't we?'

A shudder ran through every rat within earshot. They had seen what Nagru did to his captured enemies.

Riveneye's guess was right. Nagru was preparing to hunt the fugitives down. As evening shades drew the hot day to a close, he sat wincing as he flexed his injured limbs. The wolfhide across his back was still littered with whitebeam splinters. Silvamord sat watching him, unmoved by his plight.

The Foxwolf glared at her. 'What're you staring at now, frogeyes? Make yourself useful, get me a beaker of wine!'

'Get it yourself, jellyfish!' said the vixen, curling her lip in disdain. 'So, an old badger and a single otter thrashed the living daylights out of you and your killers! Tell me again, how many did they slay?'

Nagru's eyes blazed pure hatred at her. 'They never defeated us, they staggered off so full of arrows and covered in wounds that they're long dead now. If I hadn't been injured I'd have followed them and skinned their hides off to bring back and show you!'

Silvamord laughed humourlessly. 'Just like you skinned the wolf that had been frozen dead half a season so that you could take its skin and name? Oh, don't act surprised, I saw you. I'll wager your horde wouldn't be so quick in following you if they knew the truth about the great Urgan Nagru.'

The iron claws of the Foxwolf shot out, pointing at her. 'One word from you, blabbermouth, and I'll rip the tongue from your head and make you eat it, that's a promise!'

'You don't scare me,' sneered Silvamord, pouring wine for herself and sipping daintily. 'I know you too well. What does bother me is that Queen and her brat – they're still free. You'd do better to get out there and capture them before they raise the whole of Southsward up in arms against us.'

Nagru walked carefully over to the table. Pouring himself a beaker of wine he brought his face close to the vixen's. His voice dripped sarcasm. 'That's what I fully intend doing, my beautiful and beloved one. Meanwhile, you can sit here, where you are safe and comfortable. Oh, keep an eye on Gael Squirrelking, will you? I presume you weren't silly enough to have killed him in my absence?'

Silvamord eyed him levelly. 'Gael is not the problem. I had him tossed into one of his own dungeons – he could be dead or alive, I don't care. Now, are you going to hang about here until we both grow old, or are you going to do something about Serena and her little Truffen?'

They remained for a moment a hairsbreadth apart, eyes locked. Then, as if on an impulse, Nagru strode off to the window. He stared down at the horderats who were lying slumped on the stone courtyard, still warm from the day's heat. The Foxwolf brought them scurrying upright as he howled down at them: 'Sourgall, you and forty others stay behind on guard! Bladenose, Riveneye, get the rest ready for a hunt! Mingol, Vengro, get my Dirgecallers ready!'

The horde kept silent, mentally thanking the fates that they had not been chosen to be in charge of the fearsome Dirgecallers, the Foxwolf's legendary trackers. Mingol and Vengro were speechless, their mouths dry with fear.

Serena and Truffen rested beneath a willow on the streambank, the infant sitting in his mother's lap. Their food lay untouched. Together they watched a comet streaking its brilliant tail across the soft dark night. Otter patrols swam, sleek and silent, back and forth on the broad stream, alert for any strange sound in their territory. Greenbeck, a big male, slid smoothly on to the bank beside the squirrels. Dipping a bowl into the steaming pot of hotroot and watershrimp soup, beloved of otters, he offered it with an encouraging smile. 'C'mon marm, try some, it's good!'

Serena averted her eyes from the food. 'No, thank you, friend, I cannot bring myself to eat, not knowing if King Gael is alive or dead.'

'Good vittles marm, eat an' the liddle feller will too. You must take care o' him,' Greenbeck persisted, nudging the bowl forward. 'Lookit Iris, she don't know what's become o' Rab, but she eats to keep up 'er strength. Iris won't give up 'ope, an' neither should you, if y'll excuse me sayin', marm.'

Serena smiled wanly at the loyal otter. Taking the soup, she broke fresh barleybread and dipped it in, saying, 'Look, Truffen, supper, make you big and strong!'

The little fellow ate, staring up at his mother's face. 'Where Papa an' 'Uta?'

Serena ate to avoid answering the question, but the good food stuck in her throat as tears overflowed on her face. Iris appeared at the Queen's side, patting her gently.

'Hush now, don't let the babe see you upset. It's hard, I know, though I hope that my Rab and your Muta took lots of those murderers with them. Be like your son, Serena, eat and grow strong. Someday we will return to Castle Floret and avenge our loved ones.'

The Squirrelqueen ate, staring into the nightdark stream. 'I am not leaving Southsward country. I will stay to stand against Nagru and Silvamord.'

Iris sat beside Serena, a worried look on her kind face. 'We must leave Southsward now – we are too few, my friend. One day we shall come back in force; at the moment we would sacrifice our lives needlessly against the Foxwolf's great horde.'

Serena remained adamant. 'Some help will come to us, I feel it. We must stay and get others in Southsward to support our cause.'

'My Rab wanted you and Truffen out of this land,' said Iris, shrugging hopelessly. 'It has become a place of evil. But if you are determined to stay then the otters will stay also. I will not desert you – we have always been loyal to your family. Though if we stay I fear that only death awaits us.'

Truffen looked up from his soup. 'Stay an' make Nag'u dead!'

Iris settled down to rest. 'Aye, make Nagru dead, little one. Who knows, maybe you an' your mama are right, perhaps there may be warriors we have yet to meet who can help us do just that. I hope they show up soon, whoever they are.'

Peace fell over the otter camp. Gently lapping water and the still-warm night had cast its spell over the weary fugitives. Serena and Iris lay side by side with Truffen between them, all three mercifully deep in slumber after the day's harrowing events. Truffen would not remember his dream next morning, and even if he did the squirrelbabe was far too young to explain it. A mousemaid who carried a knotted rope, a strong old greybearded mouse carrying a stout stave . . . And a great bell tolling aloud the sound of freedom.

6

Both Mariel and the rat Captain Bragglin were in a perilous position. Dandin and his friends stood ready to
give up their lives protecting the little moles, whilst the
rat patrol crouched, willing to pounce at their captain's
word. Mid-noon heat caused both parties much discomfort; their paws shifted dangerously in the loose sand.

'If anything happens to me make the moles die
slowly!' Bragglin called out to his rats.

Mariel kept up her deadly bluff, cutting off further
words as she pressed the dagger meaningfully at his
throat. 'Won't do your Captain much good, he'll be
wormbait, and we'll take at least half of you with us if
you touch those little moles, be warned!' The mousemaid could feel the hot sand shifting under her
footpaws and she moved to gain a firmer position.

At that instant Bragglin made his move. He wriggled
away from the knife, kicking at Mariel and giving a
swift nod to Grinj. The rat had been standing over
Mariel, his bowpaw slackened slightly from the long
standoff, but he took the hint immediately and
stretched the bowstring taut to fire the arrow.

Zzzzz. Clunk!

Grinj fell pole-axed by a smooth round rock with a

hole through its centre. It was attached to a thin, toughened line. Grinj's arrow buried itself in the sand alongside the mousemaid's eye as a deep drawling voice called from the hilltop behind her.

'Paws still in the blinkin' ranks thah! If any of you longtails have half a bally brain I'll drop you before you can use it! You showah listenin'? That's not just a bloomin' order, it's a fact!'

Mariel watched in amazement as the stone was reeled swiftly in by a hare carrying a long, whippy fishing rod. He caught the stone skilfully as it swung back to him, his hooded eyes never once leaving the scene below. Holding the slack of the line in check, he whipped the slender rod back and forth, and the air hummed to its vibrations. Suddenly Bragglin's paw grasped that of Mariel as he tried to wrest the dagger from her.

Zzzzzz. Thonk!

With a swift, vicious flick the hare cast the stone deftly. The breath caught in Mariel's throat. Bragglin lay slain, the flying rock squarely between his eyes.

'You chaps never learn do yeh, didn't believe me, eh? Right, who's next?'

The rats dropped their weapons as they gaped up at the curious hare. Young Bowly Pintips' mouth hung wide; he had never witnessed such a splendid looking beast.

The hare was old and overweight, but obviously every inch a veteran warrior; his regalia proclaimed it proudly for all to see. On his head he wore a tricorn hat, with holes cut to allow his ears to pop out. It was surmounted by the most elaborate white drooping plume. Though his cheeks were pouched and baggy, the eyes that shone above them were hooded and sharp. His whiskers had been waxed and curled into a perfect handlebar moustache. He wore a faded but gaudy pink mess jacket, decorated with arrays of medallions and ribbons. He had epauletted shoulders and a front twinkling with polished silver buttons. Stowing the rod away like an elongated pace stick, he gave a cough and a nod. Four young leveret hares in quaint green uniforms nipped smartly out of the surrounding grass and saluted him. He acknowledged them with a wave of one ear.

'Righto, quick as y'like now squad, pick up all weapons an' lay those rats face down where they're no bother to anybeast . . .'

One of the leverets sprang forward but skidded to a halt at a fierce glare from his superior.

'What've I told you, laddie buck, wait for it, wait for it. Right, go to it, squad . . . Move!'

The young hares scurried about gathering up all weapons. One was about to relieve Dandin of his spear when he caught the stern eye of his elder.

'Tch, tch! Can't y'tell the good chaps from the rotters, Runtwold? Leave that mouse's weapon alone, sah!'

Pulling off his hat, he strode ponderously down the hill. Making a leg in front of Mariel, he bowed with a totally overdone flourish. 'Field Marshal Meldrum Fallowthorn at y'service, Marm. Though me reputation oft precedes me, no doubt you've heard m'name bandied about hither and yon, wot?'

Mariel could only shake her head.

'What's this, there's a thing!' said the hare, raising his eyebrows. 'Never heard of old Meldrum the Magnificent, astoundin'! Never mind m'dear, you will!'

Introductions were in order all around. The moles thanked their rescuers profusely, the old one tugging his snout respectfully to the warriors who had saved them.

'Burrhurr, thankee koindly guddbeasts, oi be Furpp Straightfurrer, an' these yurr h'infants be moi daughter's lot – Burdill, Grumbee an' Porgoo, Straightfurrers all. Bid ee gennelbeasts good day, moles.'

The three little ones tugged thier snouts politely. 'Good arternoon zurrs, foin day Marm!'

Meldrum turned his attention to the rats lying with their noses pressed into the sand. 'Now then y'blaggards, up on those paws smartlike. One, two, hup!'

The rats did as they were bidden with alacrity. Meldrum prodded one in the stomach with his rod butt. 'Now listen hard y'great stinker, I'm promotin' you *pro tem* otlisah of this mob. See that hill yonder, well, if you ain't all over it an' gone in two flicks of me eye, I'll make rat pudden with the lot of yah, understand?'

The rat nodded, knowing his life depended on it.

Meldrum signalled to his leveret squad and Mariel's group. 'Weapons at the ready, shoot at will if they don't move quick enough, aim for between the shoulderblades. Righto, attention vermin, on my command of run, you'll flippin' well run for y'lives. Got it? Good, ready . . . Run!'

Sand scattered in all directions as the terrified rats fled, stumbling helter-skelter over the hill. In an amazingly short time they were gone from sight. Field Marshal Meldrum Fallowthorn sniffed disdainfully. 'Rats! Nevah could abide the rotters, nasty, sly, an' not a scrap of guts or discipline in any of 'em!'

Bowly stood goggling at the array of decorations jingling and rattling on the Field Marshal's tunic. 'Gwaw! A real live warrior, wot d'yew get all those medals for, Sir?'

Meldrum's chest swelled, and he gave Bowly a swift wink. 'Battles, young hog m'lad, that's what a chap earns these gongs for. This'n was the Eastern Campaign, an' the big star here I got for subduin' a stoat uprisin', hah, made those blighters jump I can tell yeh! See these coloured bars, earned 'em for wallopin' weasels up north. This here special silver shield was for biffin' the daylights out of a snake, most arrogant adder I ever met, a real boundah! Now, about this golden crescent with a ferret straddlin' it . . .'

The young leveret Runtwold whispered to Mariel and

Dandin. 'Good ol' Uncle Mel, we're his nephews, y'know. He makes all those medals an' awards 'em to himself, but only when he thoroughly earns 'em. The old fellah's a top-hole warrior an' a real toff!'

Furpp gestured in the direction of a hill to the west. 'Burr, c'n oi offer ee guddbeasts summ afreshment, b'aint much, tho' you'm be welcumm t'moi dwellin' t'share et.'

Meldrum donned his hat and, pulling his ears through the holes, he signalled his squad into line. 'Refreshments! I say, that's rather civil of you, old molechap. Bib'n'tucker's me favourite exercise. Lead on!'

Furpp's dwelling was actually a hill, hollowed out and shored up with rock and timber, dark and cool after the hot noon sun. An entire mole colony lived there. Furpp was obviously the tribal patriarch. He gave them drinking bowls, brimming with a cold cordial of pennycloud and wild barley sweetened with honey. The leveret squad – Runtwold, Coltvine, Thurdale and Foghill – drank deeply, shuffling with anticipation as they watched wood platters being piled high with cold sliced deeper'n'ever pie, garnished with hogweed and dandelion salad dressed with crowfoot and garlic mustard. Meldrum the Magnificent shifted huge quantities as he planned his next decoration.

'Hmm, two rats slain an' about sixteen vanquished, lemme see. I think maybe two small silver rats, rampant over a black ribbon with sixteen yellow stripes should fill the bill. Foghill, pour some of that cordial for my chum Bowly.'

The young hare saluted casually. 'Right ho, Uncle Mel!'

The Field Marshal's ears shot up stiffly. 'Improper form, sah, you're on a fizzer, young Foghill! I charge you with addressin' a superior offisah as uncle. Penalty, polish all me medals before y'bunk down tonight! You know the regulations, laddie buck, I'm either Sir, or Field Marshal, or Meldrum the Magnificent. Next one I catch callin' me Uncle Mel or Nunky, I'll have his ears for breakfast an' his tail for tea, that clear, squad? Good, as y'were, carry on victuallin' up!'

There were so many moles introduced to the visitors that they soon gave up trying to remember names. The dwelling was very homely and every comfort was lavished upon them. Furpp invited the rescuers to stay for the night and they gladly accepted, though later Mariel slightly regretted her decision. Every nook and cranny of the dwelling, throughout its various side chambers and alcoves, was packed with multitudes of sleeping moles. They snored and snuffled, sleep-walked, and some of them even argued or sang in their slumbers. The dwelling became oppressively close. Mariel and Dandin, stepping carefully over the sleepers, made their way outside to sleep in the fresh air.

They strolled around the hill, noticing how the dwelling entrance was carefully concealed between a large rock and some thick bush. The gentle breezes constantly shifted the dry sand and smoothed over any traces of pawprints leading to Furpp's home. They came upon Furpp and Meldrum lounging outside, they too having deserted the packed chambers for the soft starred outdoors. The four sat down in the warm sand, discussing the day's events in low tones. Meldrum had already been appraised of the situation by Furpp and he was not happy.

'Too many of those confounded rats in Southsward now. I got back from me campaignin' an' travellin' too late, the bally place is swarmin' with 'em. That lot today aren't the only ones I've run into, I've seen patrols everywhere. Now Furpp tells me that me old friends Gael Squirrelking an' his good ladywife had the very throne pulled out from under 'em by invaders an' villains. Couple of foxbeasts, I hear, one's said to be half wolf. Tchah! The ruffian'll be half dead if he ever crosses my trail. Actually I was on me way to Castle Floret with the squad when I bumped into you chaps. What d'ye say, care to join us?'

Mariel exchanged a grim nod with Dandin before answering, 'We're with you! After what we saw today of those filthy rats, Dandin and I are game for anything that will rid the land of them and their evil kind!'

'B'aint that easy zurrs,' said Furpp Straightfurrer, shaking his head. 'You'm oanly see'd but a few of Foxenwolfer's 'orde. Gurt boatloads of ee vurmints came to this land, more'n ee leaves in autumn winds. Ho urr, they'm be too aplenty furr the loikes of us'n's to cope wi'.'

Meldrum the Magnificent sniffed as he twirled his waxed mustachios. 'Balderdash! Quality counts, old lad, not quantity, proved it meself many a time. What d'you think these medals are for, cleanin' me porridge bowl an' goin' to bed early?'

'Not so hasty, Meldrum,' Dandin spoke up on Furpp's side. 'Dashing deeds and dead heroes would be a sad fact in the face of a horde such as our friend Furpp described. Mayhap we should be a bit careful and take a closer look before rushing madly in.'

'Indeed!' Meldrum said, wiggling his ears huffily. 'Took the very words out o' me mouth, young feller. Proceed with extreme caution, then wallop 'em when the time's ripe, that's what I always say!'

Mariel could see Meldrum was in a touchy mood. She ended the meeting by yawning and stretching. 'I suggest we sleep on it, we're all tired and need a rest.'

Meldrum loosened off his tunic buttons. 'Of course, tucker first, shuteye next, then action! Eat, sleep 'n' fight in that order, always been me motto. Glad I thought of it, wot?'

Suppressing a giggle Mariel lay down, saying, 'I don't know where we'd be without your wise counsel, sir.'

Meldrum peered hard at her in the darkness. 'Tell you somethin' else, missie. Better off sleepin' out here under the stars, wot? Dreadful fellers for snorin' these moles, an' those young neph, er, troops of mine, sound like a pack of hogs in a truffle patch. Advise beddin' down outside, earth for y'bed, sky for a blanket an' all that. Capital stuff!'

Dandin yawned and closed his eyes. 'We'll take your word for it, Meldrum.'

The old hare hit the ground with a resounding thud, nestling his head into a grass tussock. 'Sensible creature, I can see we're goin' to get on well t'gether. G'night chaps!'

He was instantly asleep. After suffering an hour of his stentorian snores, Mariel, Dandin and Furpp crept around to the other side of the hill. The old mole stuffed grass into his ears as he commented, 'Hurr, oi c'n 'ear Meldum a snoren from yurr, ee could win a gurt fat medal furr snorin', that'n be a champiun, burr aye!'

Dandin drifted off to sleep, wondering how his old friend Saxtus was coping as Abbot of Redwall, and his companions, Durry, Rufe and the other good Abbey comrades, Mother Mellus and Simeon. Were they still well and happy, enjoying a long peaceful Mossflower summer? A wave of longing for his old home swept over him. What was he doing here, four seasons away from the Abbey he had been brought up in, going off to fight some other beasts' war? Then he thought of Mariel, the truest mousemaid he had ever stood alongside, through thick and thin over many adventures, trekking, eating, thinking and fighting together in all manner of strange places, making new friends and fighting many enemies.

A smile passed across the face of the sleeping mouse warrior. This was the life, he would not have had it any other way.

7

Candles cast their warm flickering glow over the tables, sending long shadows into the corners of Great Hall. Father Abbot Saxtus dipped his quill pen in the ink; a long bark parchment lay on the table before him. Though the night was late, his duties as Recorder were required. Every Redwaller sat silent, the food at table forgotten, as Joseph the Bellmaker stood to relate his dream of the previous night. The words sprang unbidden to his lips.

'All day I have been struggling to recall the message Martin the Warrior gave to me as I slept, but I could remember nothing until now. So friends, I will tell you about the dream as it happened.

'Martin guided my mind through a far country. It looked peaceful and warm, but I could feel fear, the fear of the creatures who live there. I also felt the presence of evil, a shadow loomed, like that of a big animal, a large fox maybe, or even a wolf! Then I heard Martin speak.

"Birds of cloth that fly o'er water,
Guide trees of the forest through the sea,
Where a snake begins, find thy daughter,
Go now, turn thou, due to my plea."'

Joseph paused. The only sound to be heard was the scratch of Saxtus's pen, who then said, 'Thank you, Joseph, I've got that. Is there more?'

The Bellmaker continued to narrate what he had dreamed. 'Oh yes, there is much more. Martin faded from my mind and I saw Mariel and Dandin, as clear as I can see you, my friends. They were repeating a verse together.

"Five will ride the Roaringburn,
But only four will e'er return.
Urgan sits in Gael's Royal House,
Warriormaid and Warriormouse,
Say hasten, and give aid."'

Immediately a murmur arose from the assembled Red-wallers.

'Five are to go, which five?'

'The rhyme never said?'

'Aye, but only four will come back, that's what he said!'

Simeon's stick rapped the tabletop sharply. 'Silence, please, friends!' he said. 'You must wait until Joseph has finished speaking.'

The Bellmaker bowed slightly to the blind Herbalist. 'Thank you, Simeon, I have not much more to say now. My dream ended with many images, swirling water, flames, the sounds of battle, and above all the voice of Martin calling aloud.

"Bellringer who'd love to stay,
Go! With cellarhog, I say,
Laughing flow'r with eye of hawk,
Digger who would rather walk,
Fathermouse with beard of grey,
Five from Redwall go, away!"

Saxtus stopped writing and looked over his spectacles. 'There! I feel that you have finished, Bellmaker?'

'I can remember no more, Father Abbot!' said Joseph as he took his seat. He looked tired.

Tarquin L. Woodsorrel loaded up his platter with salad and a mushroom turnover, then, pouring himself a beaker of October Ale he smiled brightly, and said, 'Righty ho! Well done sir! Now let's get down to solving the mystery an' unravellin' those riddles, wot?'

Mother Mellus shook her grizzled head. 'You'd stay up all night as long as there was food on the table, wouldn't you?'

'Mmf snnch glomff, 'scuse me!' the gluttonous hare spoke around a mouthful of food. 'An' what's wrong with that may I ask, chap needs his nosebag y'know!'

Sister Sage wagged a reproving paw at him. 'Can't you see Joseph is tired, Father Abbot too? No consideration for otherbeasts, that's your trouble!'

Simeon could not help smiling as he tapped gently on the table with his stick. 'Now now, I think we are all tired, the hour grows late. Perhaps it would be best if we slept on Joseph's words.'

'Wise counsel my friend,' said Saxtus, seconding Simeon's suggestion. 'Tomorrow our minds will be refreshed, when we have had rest and time to think.'

The Redwallers rose from their seats in a body, all save Tarquin, who carried on with his extended dinner. His wife, the Hon Rosie, ruffled his ears fondly. 'You carry on old lad, save a lot of clearing up, wot?'

Tarquin rescued the remains of a heavy fruit cake. 'Thank you, m'dear, beautiful and jolly understandin' too, made a wise decision when I chose you. Snch grmff mmm! Must've had a good meal before I met you, eh!'

Rosie allowed Simeon to lean on her paw as they went upstairs to the dormitories. 'That's my Tarkers for you, always payin' me compliments,' she said. 'Er, that was a compliment, wasn't it?'

Dawn was up and a beaming sun was drying the dew from lawn and orchard. It promised the Abbey dwellers another fine, long summer day. Breakfast was a picnic affair, set out on the west wallsteps by the main gate. Brother Fingle and Durry Quill set hot apple scones and cool mint tea on the grass at the foot of the steps. Sister Sage and Brother Mallen wheeled a trolley up the path, its small log wheels almost buckling under the weight of bowls piled with fresh fruit salad. They were surrounded by whooping Dibbuns. Sage waved a ladle threatening the little invaders and they dodged around, grabbing a slice of the fresh cut fruit whenever chance presented itself.

Mother Mellus intervened. 'Get out of it, you scamps! Listen, if you all go up on the wall and guard the battlements I'll have breakfast sent up to you. How does that sound?'

A mousebabe thought for a moment, narrowing his eyes fiercely as he weighed the proposition. 'Wanna lotta brekkist, it be 'ard work up there!'

A deal was struck and the Dibbuns fled, yelling warcries, to the west walltop. Brother Mallen shook with laughter. 'Guard the wall? Hahaha! They'd have to get ladders to see over the battlements!'

Saxtus sat on the grass with his back to the wall, noting the excited faces of those around him.

'Well, good morning, Redwallers, I see that some of you have already solved a puzzle or two. No doubt you may know the names of the five whom Martin chose.'

Durry Quill came dashing up and, throwing himself flat, he kicked all four paws in the air. 'Me! Me! I'm the cellarhog in the rhyme, I'm goin'!'

Joseph merely smiled and shrugged. 'Me too, unless there's another Fathermouse with beard of grey in our Abbey.'

Mellus ambled up and sat beside him. 'Nobeast has

more right to go than you, Bellmaker, your daughter is one of the two all the fuss is about,' she said. 'I only wish I were spry and young enough to go with you, I'd seek out Dandin. I brought that young rogue up from the time he was a Dibbun, huh, I'd still scrub his ears if he were here today. Rufe Brush, what's wrong?' Mellus had been watching the young squirrel closely.

Rufe blinked back a tear which was threatening to fall. 'Bellringer who'd love to stay', couldn't be nobeast but me, could it? I've never been outside of Redwall, really, don't want to either, the Abbey's my home an' I love it here.'

Durry threw a comforting paw around his friend. 'Cheer up, Rufey, it'll be a great adventure. I've been on adventures before, you'll enjoy it. I'm your matey, ain't I? We'll stick together, me'n you. Rufe'n'Durry, Durry'n'Rufe, eh!'

The young squirrel scrubbed a paw across his eyes and sat close to Durry. 'And we'll come back home to Redwall together, too!'

Mellus turned her attentions to Foremole. He was shaking his velvety head to and fro, murmuring to himself, 'Ho urr, lack a day, zurr Marthen ee said oi'm t'go.'

Joseph looked with surprise at the mole. 'Of course! Digger who would rather walk, that's you!'

Foremole continued shaking his head. 'Oi wishes et wurrn't, zurr. We'm be goin' aboard a boat, oi feels et in moi diggen clawn. Bohurr, oi'd rather walk anywhurre than sail on ee boat, oi'm gurtly afeared o' drownen. But if Marthen says et, then oi'm bound t'go!'

Joseph smiled as he took the heavy digging claw Foremole extended to him. 'Bravely said, we will need your logic and strength. Now, I wonder who the fifth one is, laughing flower with eye of hawk. Perhaps it is Treerose?'

Oak Tom's pretty wife shook her head. 'Not me. But I can tell you who I think it is, watch!' She crept over to the bottom step where Hon Rosie was sitting. Stealing up behind her, Treerose tickled the hare's long eartips. Rosie exploded. 'Whoohahahooh! I say, stoppit! Whoohahahooh!'

Treerose stopped. 'There she is, Rose Woodsorrel, the laughing flower! Though I don't know about her having an eye like a hawk.'

Hon Rosie stiffened her ears indignantly. 'Eye of hawk? Hawkeye! I say, that's what old Colonel Clary used to call me when I was in the Long Patrol. I'm absolutely top hole with any sort of weapon y'know, bow'n'arrows, slings, javelins, hit anythin' you name. Dead on target, first time!'

Recognition suddenly dawned on Rosie and she burst out afresh. 'Whoohahahooh! Oh I say, the thingummy, the rhyme, it meant me! What a wheeze, you chaps, I'm goin' with you!'

Rosie's husband Tarquin drew himself up huffily. 'Steady on there, old gel! Do I take it that you intend swannin' off an' leavin' me here with our young uns?'

Rosie was an excellent mother and she loved Tarquin dearly. But being caught up in the throes of an adventure appealed to her wild spirit. 'Got to do what Martin the bally Warrior commands, old lad!' She saw Tarquin's ears droop miserably and relented. 'But if you're against it m'dear, then I won't go!'

Knowing both hares well, Joseph came up with a ploy. 'You're right Tarquin, here at Redwall with the young ones and your goodself, that's the proper place for Rosie! Of course, this changes everything. I was thinking of giving my duties as menu setter and food taster to you, Tarquin. Mellus would look after your young leverets, give them a bit of Abbey schooling, they'd make friends and get a good education. Right, Mellus?'

The badger caught Joseph's wink and agreed. 'Indeed it is. Oh, then there's also the temporary Cellarkeeper's duties. I'm sure Durry needs some reliable beast to check on all his cellar stock. October Ale, strawberry fizz, got to be tasted each day and kept at the right temperature. Isn't that right, Durry?'

The hedgehog caught on to the ruse and he nodded firmly. 'Need somebeast with a good stomach for samplin' an' checkin'. Cellar should be cool'n'quiet in the summer.'

Tarquin L. Woodsorrel set his jaw in a decisive jut. 'Who said you couldn't go m'dear, eh? Show me the curmudgeon an' I'll give him two pieces of me mind! Our young uns need schoolin', never hurt anybeast. Now not another blinkin' word, Rosie, you're goin'! Oh I know it's a jolly hard sacrifice, but I'll stay right here. Samplin' ale'n'cordial, tastin' grub an' makin' menus. Don't you fret, my beautiful gigglin' blossom, I'll keep m'self busy. You nip off, the break'll do you good!'

Laughter and applause greeted Tarquin's noble offer.

Saxtus tapped the parchment whereon he had recorded all.

'Listen to this and see if anybeast can make it clear.

Birds of cloth that fly o'er water,
Guide trees of the forest through the sea . . .'

Simeon interrupted the poem. 'I solved that last night – it's simple to a blind one who has had to have things described to him all his life. Trees of the forest going through the sea – that's a ship; the white birds of cloth are its sails, they guide and propel the ship through water.'

Joseph shook his head in admiration. 'Well done, Simeon! Read the other two lines, Saxtus.'

'Where a snake begins, find thy daughter,
Go now, turn thou, due to my plea.'

The Abbot looked at the Bellmaker. 'Turn thou Joseph!'

Joseph did as he was bid; standing up, he turned around. 'Done that, now what do I do?'

Simeon shook with silent laughter. The Abbot glared in his direction. 'This is no laughing matter, my friend!'

The blind mouse took a little time to compose himself. 'Sorry Saxtus, but I did hear Joseph actually stand and turn then, that's what I was laughing at. You've got it all wrong, the rhyme means that you turn the word thou.'

Saxtus thought about it for a moment, then he tried. 'Uoth! What's that supposed to mean?'

'Try turning it a bit more, switch the letters O and U around.'

'Outh? Still means nothing?'

Simeon took a sip of his mint tea. 'It won't until you find where a snake begins.'

The Abbot looked puzzled. 'At its tail I suppose, that's where all snakes begin.'

'Oh really!' the blind herbalist snorted impatiently. 'I'm Simeon, that begins with S. You're Saxtus, that begins with S. Now what does snake begin with? An S!'

Saxtus still looked blank. 'I'm sorry Simeon, you've lost me. Could you explain it all?'

Simeon spoke in a slow and patient tone. 'Put the letter S with the word outh and you have South. Due South! Martin is pleading with you to sail Due South!'

Saxtus swept the cup from Simeon's paw and gave it to Rufe. 'Mint tea is no fitting drink for a genius, Rufe – take this to the cellars and fill it with the finest old blackberry wine, for a blind mouse who can see further than anybeast in Redwall Abbey. Simeon, accept my humble congratulations!'

Long into the afternoon they laboured at the final verse, Joseph reading it over and over:

'Five will ride the Roaringburn,
But only four will e'er return,
Urgan sits in Gael's Royal House,
Warriormaid and Warriormouse,
Say hasten, and give aid.'

Rufe Brush repeated the second line. 'But only four will e'er return? Will one of us die, Durry?'

The hedgehog shook his spiky head. 'Pay it no 'eed Rufey, we'll take care o' each other. Besides, it may be a trick line, Martin the Warrior always says one thing an' means another. Don't you worry, mate.'

'Durry's right, no use wondering how a journey will finish before you start it,' said Mellus, as she passed Rufe a cup of cider. 'Warriormaid and Warriormouse must be Mariel and Dandin, as you said Joseph, and you must hasten and give aid to them. But what do the other lines mean?'

Hon Rosie gave a careless shrug. 'Five riding the Roaringburn and Urgan sittin' in Gael's Royal House, wot? What's a Roaringthingy and what's an Urgan or a Gael, even if they do have a Royal bally House? We either know or we don't, an' take it from me, chaps, I certainly don't! Never was much good in the brainbox department, but I'm frightened of nothin'. So why worry about it, eh?'

Simeon rose slowly, straightening up his old frame with a grimace. 'That's the wisest thing I've heard all day, Rosie.'

Joseph stood and offered his paw for Simeon to lean on. 'Right! We've got the five and we know which direction to travel. That's good enough for me! Tomorrow at first light we set out, to find Mariel and Dandin!'

8

The dead heat of a still summer night was rudely broken. Columns of grey rats, armed to the fangs with all manner of weaponry, flooded out of Castle Floret. Nagru was abroad with his horde, out to hunt down Serena, her son and their otter allies. The Foxwolf and his Captains led the army out across the valley floor, speeding their trot to a run as they raced up the wooded tor. Bringing up the rear was a cage. Six rats with cross-hilted pikes pushed it from behind, whilst up front, sweaty with fear, Mingol and Vengro pulled on the towing ropes. The wheeled cage rattled forward with the two rats tugging in panic, keeping the ropes taut to put as much distance as possible between themselves and the occupants of the close-barred prison cage.

Thrusting his paws into the metal-sheathed wolf claws, Nagru threw back his head, baying a hunting call to the night sky.

'Owwwooooorrrr!'

Like an icy wind it chilled the blood of every horde-rat. The Urgan Nagru, their master the Foxwolf, was out with his Dirgecallers to taste blood. Stumbling and clanking amid weapons and arms, the lead platoons crested the hill, grinding to a breathless, quivering halt

70

at their Captains' signals. Leaving the escape trail of
Serena and the otters clear, they dispersed into the surrounding woodland. There they concealed themselves
in many places, some even climbing up into the trees.
Trembling with terror and exertion, Mingol and Vengro
arrived with the cage. Nagru dismissed them with a
growl, and they fled thankfully into the thickets with
the others.

The Foxwolf drew two scraps of cloth from his belt.
One was a torn kerchief which had belonged to Queen
Serena, the other a feeding bib of Truffen's. The barred
cage door faced head-on to the path taken by the fugitives. Nagru dangled the pitiful rags against the cage
door, chanting in a singsong voice:

'Ho Dirgecallers, swift and sleek,
You shall have your share.
Fangs will rip and blood will leak,
Scent your victims. There!'

He jumped back laughing as the bits of fabric were
snatched inside the bars. The cage began reverberating;
eerie screamlike growls mingled with the rake of
scratching claws and grinding teeth. Shreds of ripped
cloth flew from the madly buffeting pen. Fascinated and
fearful, the horderats peeked from their hiding places at
the spectacle. The Urgan Nagru gave a throaty chuckle,
enjoying the sight of his Dirgecallers working themselves into a blood frenzy as they took the scent of their
quarry. The wolfhide swirled out, starlight pinpointing
Nagru's metal claws. He called to his horde:

'What is black and what is red?'
The answer echoed back from the trees and bushes.
'Night is black and blood is red!'
Placing a claw on the cage latch he shouted:
'What is the colour of death?'
The reply rang out to the dark skies.

'Foxwolf and his Dirgecallers know the colour of death!'

The cage door sprang open with a clang and the Dirgecallers came bounding out.

Brought across seasons of heaving seas from the lands of ice by Nagru, maddened through a life of confinement, crazed from lack of live prey, two fully grown female ermine snuffled and wailed. Sleek maniac killers both, glazed red eyes shining against the dull brown of summer coats, teeth white as snow and sharp as spikes. Flexing claws as black as their tailtips, the two predators intertwined sinuously, weaving together into a perilous blur of teeth, claws and eyes. The Dirgecallers suddenly went rigid, then with an earsplitting wail they sped off down the trail into the darkness. Nagru charged after them, his whole being suffused by their bloodlust.

'They've found the scent, the hunt is on! Ooow-wooorrr!'

Bush, shrub and flower were trampled underpaw as the horde chased their savage master and his trackers; masses of armed rats thundered out along the trail. Then their cries died into the distance. The scene that moments ago had echoed to chaos, regained its silence and the lonely tor slipped back into the deep of night.

In the hour before dawn Serena found herself shaken into wakefulness by Iris. She picked Truffen up as the otter hustled them both to the streambank.

'Hurry, Serena, it will not be safe here soon, get aboard this log!'

The Squirrelqueen and her son hopped aboard the broad trunk of a dead fir laying in the shallows. Faint noises from afar floated on the pre-dawn breeze. Serena rubbed sleep from her eyes, asking, 'Iris, what is it, where are we going?'

Greenbeck's strong head broke the surface by the log. 'The Foxwolf is comin' this way marm, huntin' with a full pack. He'll find this place by dawn, but don't fret yoreself, we'll take you somewheres safe by water. That'll put 'is foul snout off the scent, stream water don't leave many tracks to follow, otters know that!'

Truffen was still asleep aboard the broad log. Serena covered him with her cloak, lying alongside him as the quiet waters rippled by. Powered by a small contingent of otters, the fir trunk swept onward smoothly. Greenbeck and his friend Troutlad held a murmured conversation as they swam with the log.

'Squirrelqueen's goin' t'get 'erself an' the liddle un captured if'n she don't leave Southsward, mark my words matey. That scum Nagru won't rest 'til they're both slain.'

'Aye, that's true, but you 'eard 'er, she's stayin' put. Trouble is, where's a good cove to 'ide 'em?'

'If'n we puts Nagru off their scent Iris should take 'em to ole Furpp's dwellin' in the mounds by the wastelands. They'll be snug'n'safe enough there, I reckons.'

Iris's head popped up between them. 'Stow the gab and save your energy for pushin'. Hear that!'

Greenbeck blew stream water from his nostrils. 'Sounds like more'n rats in our wake . . .'

'Wonder what's makin' that awful wailin' din?' Troutlad said as he began shoving the trunk faster. 'Come on mate, put yore back into it an' let's get movin'!'

Serena stared anxiously back over her shoulder, pulling little Truffen close. Her teeth chattered with fright at the unearthly, dirgelike wails of the pack that were on the trail of her and the babe.

It was a bright blue summer morn when the questors and a party of wellwishers left Redwall Abbey. Above the breeze the sky was ridged with high white clouds, patterned like rippled sand after the tide leaves a beach. Many Redwallers had turned out to march along with the five to the River Moss. They lined the banks, passing supplies from paw to paw to the shrews aboard four logboats. Abbot Saxtus embraced the shrew Chieftain warmly.

'Log a Log, old friend, thank you for the warmth and help you have always shown to us.'

Log a Log brushed aside the compliment modestly. 'Aye, Guosim, the Guerilla Union of Shrews in Mossflower, that's us, always here to help our chums. But let's go over these plans again, Father Abbot. You say that I've got to take your five to the sea in our logboats. Fair enough, but what happens then?'

Saxtus hummed and hawed as he filled a beaker with October Ale for the shrew, knowing he was about to ask rather a lot from the Chieftain of the Guosim. 'Er, well, haha, hmmm, it's rather hard to explain . . .'

Log a Log sipped his ale, both eyes never leaving Saxtus. 'Come on, spit it out Saxtus, what d'you really want?'

Plucking up courage, the Abbot ventured forth on his tale, from the night of Joseph's dream. Log a Log sat swirling the ale in his beaker as he listened openmouthed to the strange story. When Saxtus had finished he looked hopefully at the shrew, asking, 'Well, my old friend, what do you say?'

Log a Log sat silent awhile, watching his quarrelsome tribe of Guosim shrews – small, spiky furred, each wearing a coloured headband, broad belt and short rapier. They argued and fought constantly, over who would sit where, which paddle was to be wielded by one or another, how best to stow the supplies and accommodate the passengers. Their gruff bass voices and aggressive manners marked them indelibly as Guosim shrews. Log a Log shook his head.

'Adventures, quests, battles and the seasons knows what! That's just what my tribe needs, they're gettin' too fat and argumentative sittin' on the riverbank fishin' their days away. But I'm afraid we don't have what you want, Saxtus. Let me explain. A shrew logboat is fine

for rivers, streams and big lakes, but you couldn't put to
sea in one, they're not built big or strong enough to
stand high seas, waves or gales. A good storm'd send
our logboats straight to the bottom, that's the truth,
friend.'

Saxtus was crestfallen. All the hopes and plans of
Redwall's five questors had been dashed by Log a Log's
announcement. Then the shrew's eyes twinkled merrily
and he slapped the Abbot's back soundly.

'Cheer up, old frogfeatures, I didn't say I wouldn't
help, did I? There's more'n one way of shellin' an acorn.
Hah! Imagine trying to leave the Guosim out of adventures an' battles and so on!'

Saxtus immediately brightened up. 'You're going to
help us,' he said. 'I knew we could count on you!'

Log a Log stood up, resting both paws on his large
belt. 'Aye, what we'll need is a real ship and I happen to
know just the creature who'll get us one. Bear in mind,
a ship needs a proper crew, watershrews, not landlub-
bers. Anyway, don't worry, me and the Guosim'll be
going along for the voyage. Now don't go pestering me
with more questions, I've got work to do before we get
underway. Hi Bandle! What d'you think yore doin' with
those casks, put 'em abaft of the bundles in the stern of
my boat. Fatch! Make that headrope secure or somebeast'll fall in the water trying to get aboard – tighten
the backspring too!'

He strode off issuing orders left and right, leaving
Saxtus to join the rest in bidding farewell to the five
travellers. Log a Log's shrews were getting more quarrelsome and impatient to be off, so most of the Redwallers' goodbyes were shouted as they ran along the
banks when the logboats paddled off.

'You'm taken gurt care of eeself zurrs, doant fall in ee
h'ocean, burr no, tis vurry wetten!'

'Have a super time, Rosie old gel, don't fret over the
young uns – I'll look after the blighters. Oh, an' try not

to laugh too much, those shrew chappies y'know, pretty short tempered an' not too jolly, wot?'

'I've packed October Ale aplenty for ye Durry, think of yore ole pals when you sup it!'

'Don't worry about the bellringing, Rufe, we'll all take turns. Be good and come home safe!'

'Joseph ole mate, next time I see that grizzly gob of yourn I'd like to see Mariel kissin' it. Good luck mate!'

'Cheerio mater, pip pip an' all that, bring us back somethin' tasty to eat, toodle pip!'

Blind Simeon spread both paws wide, his reedy voice carrying on the breeze. 'Fortune, fates and fair seasons be with you, may the spirit of Martin guide and guard you all!'

The cries grew fainter and dimmer as the logboats picked up the centre current and swept away, sped skilfully on by the paddles of Log a Log's tribe.

Joseph sat in the prow of Log a Log's boat, listening to the shrew Chieftain.

'Finnbarr Galedeep, there's a rogue for you, if anybeast can get us a ship he can. You ever met a sea otter, Joseph?'

'Never, though I've heard tell of them. What's this Finnbarr Galedeep like?'

Log a Log dug his paddle deep, chuckling. 'Oho, you'll find out soon enough my friend!'

Day turned into night and back again twice as the four logboats sped downstream travelling seaward. Overhanging trees, resounding with Mossflower birdsong, cast speckled shade and gave way to shimmering water meadows and silent green fields. The fields changed gradually into high, sunwarmed banks where yellow-horned poppy, purslane and pink-flowered thrift were visited by bees, as they danced gently with the breeze. Peaceful and ancient, the landscape skimmed quietly by. Guosim shrews were not so quarrelsome once they were waterborne and paddling awhile. Often they would break out into river shanties, gruff bass voices resounding into the countryside –

'I was born on a stream and fed from a paddle,
Shrum a doo rye 'ey, shrum a doo rye 'ey,
And here I'll stay 'til me tail don't waggle,
See longweeds grow where the currents flow,
Aye that's the way I like it sooooooooooooo.
Shrum a doo rye 'ey, shrum a doo rye 'ey,
Ho run you river, run my way,
Ho ummm, Ho ummmm, Ho ummmm!'

The final daybreak of their voyage found Hon Rosie wakened from a cramped position. 'Oohh! I feel like a jolly old frog in a jug, wot? I say though, the old foot-paws are rather warm'n'comfy.'

'Burr aye, they'm should be marm, ee be'n sticken 'em daown moi ears all noight long. Hurr!'

Foremole pulled himself up to enjoy the spectacle of dawn across the dunes. Powder-blue skies were barred by rollers of pearl-grey clouds, their tops tinged apricot and rose by a sun rising in the east. Sounds of waves and seabirds stirred Rufe from his slumber. He lay still as the logboats nosed aground in a sandy cove, twixt two high dunes at the shore edge. 'Are we in the sea, Durry?' he asked.

The hedgehog splashed over the side into the shal-lows. 'Bless yer 'cart no, Rufe, this 'ere's still the stream. We'll 'ave to trek across the shore to reach sea-water.'

Log a Log had jumped to land first. 'Don't show yourselves, stay here close by the boats until I return,' he cautioned them. 'Bandle, keep a lookout from the top of that dune, the rest of you keep your heads down. The seashore can be a dangerous place sometimes.' With that he was gone.

Rosie shrugged and started unpacking breakfast. 'I'm

bally well famished, what ho you lot, who's for nose-bags. Whoo . . .'

Foremole's paw clamped across her mouth, cutting off the strident laugh. 'Yurr naow marm, ee doant wants t'be oopsettin' everybeast do ee, koindly keep from larfin' thankee.'

The shrews lit a smokeless little fire from tinder-dry grass and charcoal. It burned low and red. Breakfast was a simple affair of honey, hot shrewbread and mint tea.

About halfway through the morning Bandle hopped down from his lookout perch high on the dune, crying 'Log a Log's back an' he's brought company!'

The Redwallers were quite taken aback by the appearance of the shrew Chieftain's companion. Log a Log introduced the newcomer briefly.

'Meet Finnbarr Galedeep, the sea otter.'

One time in the distant past the big malebeast might have been a handsome creature, but the long scars of old battles tracing a course over his muscular form, coupled with a musselshell eyepatch and a missing ear, gave him a fearsome look. A curved swordhilt protruded over each of his shoulders, carried in crossbelted sheaths strapped to his back. Grinning good naturedly at his wide-eyed audience, Finnbarr thrust forth a heavily tattooed limb. ''Ere's me flipper, it's as good as me true 'eart, the Galedeep's at y'service!'

Introductions were made all round and food was brought for the guest. He seated himself on the landward side of the dune, enjoying the mid-morning sun. Winking roguishly at the assemblage, Finnbarr went through pasties, salad and October Ale as though he had survived a seven-season famine. Then, wiping foam and crumbs from his mouth, the sea otter got right down to business.

'Belay mateys, as I sees it yore wantin' t'sail far south o'er deep seas. Well fer that you needs a good stout ship. Ole Log a Log's canoes wouldn't take ye a rough sea league out there on the waves.'

Joseph looked the sea otter directly in his good eye. 'Are we to take it that you have such a ship, Finnbarr?' he asked.

The big fellow laughed uproariously, as if at some private joke, clapping Joseph soundly on the back. 'Hohoho! Bless yer cockles, mouse, I ain't got so much as a waterlogged twig t'me name!'

Foremole wrinkled his nose in consternation. 'Burr, b'aint no larfen matter zurr, if'n you'm doant 'ave a gurt shipper, whurr'll us'n's get one?'

'We steals it o' course!'

A loud cry rang out from both shrews and Red-wallers. 'Steal a ship?'

'Quiet now and listen to Finnbarr's plan,' Log a Log silenced them curtly.

The sea otter gestured over his shoulder. 'Not 'arf a day's march round yon 'eadland lays two big searat galleons, the *Pearl Queen* is the best of the twain, she was my craft once, but that's another story. Now she belongs to a scurvy-backed bilgerat called Cap'n Slipp. The other vessel's the *Shalloo*, 'er master's Cap'n Strapp. They're brothers, Slipp'n'Strapp, Corsairs, dangerous an' sly, both of 'em, always fightin' among themselves.'

Hon Rosie could contain herself no longer, and she blurted out, 'Oh I say, pinchin' a ship off some rotten ol' searats, what a super wheeze. Whoohahahahoo!'

Finnbarr winced, waggling a paw in his good ear. 'A hare, eh, I likes hares, mad an' perilous beasts. Tho' I'd be beholden if ye'd stow the hootin' marm, sound carries round thisaways. Lissen now, the plan's simple. We sinks the *Shalloo* an' steals the *Pearl Queen* an' sails off in 'er, wot d'yer say, mates?'

Log a Log spoke for them all. 'It sounds like a desperate scheme, Finnbarr, but we're with you all the way, everybeast!'

The sea otter showed glittering white teeth in a swift grin. Whipping out one of his swords, he began outlining a map of his plan in the damp sand of the streambank.

'Hearken now, cullies, 'ere's where the two ships lie at anchor, in the shallows offshore. Both crews will be on the beach tonight, feastin' around a fire, so there should be only a few aboard each vessel keepin' watch. We wait 'til the swell of 'igh water when the tide's aturn after midnight, then 'tis quick'n'silent. In these 'ere shrewboats you lot sail seaward, come in on a curve to board *Pearl Queen* an' take 'er. Meself an' Log a Log'll swim o'er t'the *Shalloo* to bore some 'oles in 'er side an' scuttle 'er in the bay. Then it's out on to the wide blue briny fer us all!'

Joseph studied the plan, nodding solemnly. 'I like it, simple and straightforward, that's the best way!'

The remainder of that day they spent resting in the shelter of the dunes. Rufe Brush watched the lengthening shadows on the sand, confiding his worries to Durry in hushed whispers.

'I've never stolen anything before. Well, I suppose I filched a few candied chestnuts when I was a Dibbun, but never something as big as a ship!'

Durry Quill, an adventurer born, winked at Rufe. 'Don't you fret yoreself mate, we'll stick t'gether. Hah! Searats are all great big cowards, just show 'em a weapon an' growl, like this. Grr! That settles 'em!'

Rufe picked up the rapier given to him by one of the Guosim. Waving it half-heartedly, he tried a timid growl. 'Grr, how does that sound, Durry?'

'Garrooohaharroogurrrrr!' The twin blades of Finnbarr Galedeep's curved swords flashed in front of Rufe's startled eyes. Then, swiftly sheathing both blades, the big sea otter ruffled the young squirrel's ears playfully.

'Do it like that, matey, show 'em y'mean business an' don't be 'arf 'earted about it. You'll do all right.'

Darkness fell as they made a final cold meal of oat-scones, cheese and cider – no fires were allowed to pinpoint their position in the dunes at the shore edge. Sentries were posted whilst the rest lay trying to steal a quick nap, each with their thoughts of what awaited them where the two ships lay at anchor around the headland. Would it be a swift victory and a good ship, or a wrong plan ending in capture and death, or slavery at the cruel claws of searats? A three-quarter moon shimmered over the restless sea in the soft summerdark as the time drew closer to midnight.

9

Dawn had already broken over Southsward when Furpp called two of his grandchildren to assist him.

'Yurr Burdill, you an' Grumbee stir ee stumps, us'n's must take ee brekkist to our friends.'

Burdill shook his velvety head. 'Hurr granfer, they'm a'ready be gonned. Miz Mariel, she'm roused t'others long since, me an' Grumbee packed 'em a brekkist to eat on ee way.'

Furpp inspected his digging claws closely, in the way that some older moles will do when deep in thought. He nodded decisively, then patted the two small moles. 'Gudd gudd, ee did woisely, both o' you'm h'infants. Hurr, tho' oi wanders whurr they be agone to?'

'Oi did 'ear ee gurt rabbet Meld'n say as they wurr eckertoimerin,' Grumbee piped up.

Furpp blinked down at the youngster. 'Eckertoimerin, hoo arr, that sounds noice, tho' oi be wunderin' wot ee means, eckertoimerin?'

Had the moles been able to pronounce the word properly they would have known that Mariel, Dandin and Bowly had gone out on a reconnoitring trip with Meldrum and his leveret squad. Meldrum the Magnificent was familiar with the terrain, he explained as they strode south over the hills.

'Best route to Floret's this way, see a stream ahead soon, take that route, might meet some otters, wot? Useful coves, otters, may get some info from them about this confounded Foxwolf thingee. Reconnoitre an' gather information, that's what I always say, eh?'

Mariel, whose idea it had been in the first place, nodded agreement as they crested the brow of an immense sandhill. On an impulse she spread her paws, stopping them from continuing further. 'Hold it, did you feel the ground a bit shaky then? I did.'

Bowly crept under her outstretched paws, then after venturing a bit further on the hilltop, he tip-pawed gingerly back. 'Yore right, it's like a great over'angin' sandcliff we're stannin' on, best move back afore it collapses!'

Meldrum waggled his ears and sniffed. 'Don't remember it bein' like that before, bit of a while since I've been in this neck o' the woods, doncha know. Not an uncommon occurrence, though – erosion I think they call it. Side of the jolly ol' sandhill slips away one day an' leaves the grassy top like a big overhang. No matter, we'll go another way.'

They slid down the undamaged side of the hill and climbed to the top of another, safer, one. Dandin was first up, and he shot out a paw. 'Look, there's the stream. Something's happening down there, looks like trouble!'

Mariel and Meldrum joined him. The hilltop commanded a good view of the scene taking place some distance off downstream. Two creatures, a squirrel and her young one, clung to the broad surface of a treetrunk which was being propelled by a band of otters. Closing rapidly on them was a band of rats, headed by two ermine and Nagru. The Field Marshal hare peered down, recognizing the adult squirrel.

'Great seasons, it's Queen Serena. Looks like she needs help – form into skirmish line, troop!'

Mariel placed herself squarely in front of the impulsive hare, halting any further activity. Her mind raced madly as she tried reasoning with him. 'Field Marshal, sir, remember what you said, plan first, act later!'

'No time now missie, duty calls y'know, stand aside!' said Meldrum, as he adjusted the stone at the end of his rod.

Dandin joined Mariel. 'Sir, there's far too many of them for our small force to go up against. If you charge in now we'll all be killed. Your four young nephews, Bowly, do you want to see them massacred by hundreds of vermin? There'd be no point to it!'

Whilst Dandin was reasoning with Meldrum, a solution had formed swiftly in the mousemaid's agile mind. It was risky, but worth a try. She interrupted Dandin's pleas.

'Listen, I've just thought of a plan! Runtwold, Coltvine, we'll need your slings and stone pouches. Bowly, take these four young hares back to Furpp's dwelling, tell him to watch out for those creatures on the stream and shelter them. Go!'

Mariel's voice had such a ring of certainty to it that Bowly and the hares were gone in a flash. As she and Dandin armed themselves with slings and stones she turned to the slightly bemused Meldrum. 'Now, we need a beast of some weight and courage. Are you game for this, sir?'

Meldrum the Magnificent was caught up by Mariel's urgency and sureness. His ears stood straight as he said, 'Game? Hah, say on m'gel, there's none gamer than this hare!'

Mariel knotted the Gullwhacker securely about her waist. 'Good! Now here's what we'll do . . .'

Queen Serena hugged little Truffen to her. He was

weeping piteously, frightened by the sight and sounds of the horde led by the Dirgecallers and Nagru. They were in plain sight now, pouring along the streambank after the floating log. While the rest of the otters pushed the treetrunk through the water, Iris and Greenbeck, armed with javelins, climbed on to the log. Protecting the squirrels with their bodies, the two brave otters prepared to face the onslaught together.

Howling with triumph, the Foxwolf halted his horde on the streambank. The two ermine snuffled and wailed hideously. Eager to get at their prey but reluctant to venture into the deep stream, they wove back and forth at the water's edge. The otters had steered the log over to the far bank to distance themselves from attack. Some of the horderats were beginning to string their bows up and select arrows. Nagru turned on them with a snarl.

'Put those bows away, arrows would spoil the sport. I've got them now and I want them alive and unharmed. My Dirgecallers can have the otters, but I want those two squirrels alive. Stand ready and await my orders!'

Without warning the rat called Mingol shrieked as, grabbing his head in both paws, he fell senseless to the ground. His partner Vengro stared down in puzzlement at him.

'What's wrong with Mingol? He was just . . . Unhh!' Vengro slumped beside his companion. Nagru whirled about to see what the trouble was and a slingstone thudded hard into his back. One of the Dirgecallers yowled in anguish as another stone slammed into its ribs.

'Get down, we're being attacked!' the rat Captain Riveneye yelled.

More stones followed in quick succession, and a mocking laugh rang out from some bushes a short distance away.

'Hahaha! Keep those heads down, scum, there's a whole army of slingers ready to pick you off!'

The wolfhide had taken most of the impact of the stone that struck Nagru. He scrambled forward on all fours, peering into the bushes. Seeing he was not immediately hit, the Foxwolf ventured upright, ducking swiftly as a good-sized pebble lodged between the wolf skull and his brow. Grimacing with pain he plucked it out and hurled it back at the bush. A short yelp was followed by the sight of two mice retreating to the deep cover of thicker foliage. Nagru grabbed stones from the ground, throwing them at the place where the mice had hidden as he ran forward, calling, 'There's only two of 'em, it's no army. Charge!'

Dandin nudged Mariel urgently. 'The game's up, time we weren't here!'

They broke cover and began a mad dash, back the way they had come. Mariel risked a quick glance backward. 'Better shift, the whole pack's after us!' she yelled.

Footpaws thrumming madly against the earth, Mariel and Dandin ran for their lives, the breath rising ragged in their throats as the two Dirgecallers, heading the pack, sped on their tails, gaining by the moment. Nagru followed in the rear, hurling challenges and threats.

'Tear them to bits! Stop and fight, mice!'

Dandin stumbled. Mariel, catching his paw quickly, pulled him upright and they dashed on together, side by side, dust and sand flying, hearts pounding wildly, with the Dirgecallers, slightly ahead of the horde, closing fast. Mariel's head came up; she glimpsed the big eroded dune ahead, rearing up like a mighty wave of sand, the grassy crest projecting perilously over a huge inward curving hill. Through her blurred vision she could barely make out the ponderous form of Meldrum perched far out on the grassy top. Putting on a final spurt she tugged Dandin along. 'Not far . . . Come on . . . just a bit more!'

Meldrum the Magnificent watched the tableau below, gritting his teeth with suspense. It looked as if the two mice would surely be stopped by the ermine before they made the slope. No! They had put on an extra spurt and pulled away a bit; now they were on the final stretch and, calling up stamina from some deep reserve, they actually broke into a headlong sprint. As Meldrum stamped his footpaw down with delight the whole dunetop shuddered. He went still immediately, saving his move until the exact moment. Leaning out, he squinted downward – there they were! Mariel and Dandin had made it to the hill. Sand flew from beneath their paws as they battled upward into the curve with the ermine and about ten front runners of the horde beginning to close on them again. The two mice suddenly changed course, veering sideways to the right where the curve of the hill straightened, and Mariel shouted one word at the top of her voice.

'Now!!!'

Meldrum instinctively knew the pursuers were climbing the hill directly beneath him, but Mariel's voice confirmed it. The old hare jumped as high as he could into the air.

Whump!

The whole dunetop shook. He jumped again, harder.

Whump!

The earth trembled as he landed, grass roots tearing as they parted company with the sand. Gritting his teeth, Meldrum the Magnificent leapt high in the air a third time, yelling out the battlecry of hares and badgers.

'Eulaliaaaa!'

Whoooossssshhh! Whooomph!

The entire top curve of the high dune fell with an almighty avalanche of weeds, grass and sand. It seemed to hover in midair a fraction, then down it came like a thunderbolt, with the old warrior perched atop still yelling his warcry. The Dirgecallers and at least a score of the rat horde never knew what happened to them. Countless tons of sand wiped them out instantly.

Nagru came dashing up, pushing and kicking his way through the awestruck masses. He made his way to the front and gaped in amazement at the scene. Mariel and Dandin had escaped the worst, but they were trapped, buried almost to their necks in sand. Meldrum had fared little better; being immersed to his ample waist he could only struggle helplessly and hurl insults at his enemy.

'Good wheeze, eh, wished we could've got the crummy lot of you under there with your stinkin' rotten ermine and some of your other pals. Well, what're y'gawpin' at?'

The Foxwolf glared at the bold veteran. 'My Dirge-callers, you killed them!'

Mariel spat sand from her mouth and yelled defiantly. 'Aye, dig me out of here and I'll give you a run for your acorns too, you great two-headed, slop-mouthed, ringtailed excuse for a toad!'

Dandin joined in hurling imprecations. 'Now then scabbyskin, just imagine if we had been an army? Hah! You and those other grey slime wouldn't be around to tell the story. Dig us loose and you'll find out that we're not a couple of helpless squirrels!'

Nagru controlled his rage. 'Oh, we'll dig you out all right, but after a good spell of starvation in my dungeons you'll find yourselves dangling by your footpaws as target practice for my archers, then you'll wish you had been a couple of squirrels. Wetchops! Go and get those squirrels. Take fifty archers and finish those otters off, then bring the Queen and her brat to me. The rest of you, dig those three out and bind them tight!'

The three companions were dug out and tightly pinioned with ropes, though they continued their verbal abuse of Nagru and his horde.

'Hey, lily liver, tie my paws tighter, because if I get them around your filthy neck I'll throttle you!'

'Zounds! Takes six of yeh to truss me up, eh, so it should, you frog swampin', mud scoffin', fly wallopers!'

They were lugged down the hill and bound to carrying poles. All three lay in the sand as Nagru circled them, aiming the odd kick at their prostrate forms as he spoke.

'You'll wish you'd never crossed trails with the Urgan Nagru when I'm done with you. Two bold little mice, eh, maybe we'll give you to the cooks after my archers have finished with your carcasses. Hmm, and a big fat hare, I've never tasted hare. What d'you say, hare, will you be tasty enough to be served at a conqueror's banquet?'

Meldrum sniffed in disgust. 'If it's the last flippin' thing I do I'll stick in your rotten throat an' choke you. Blaggard!'

Wetchops came dashing back yelling, 'They've gone! There's not a sight nor sound of otters or squirrels anywhere! They've vanished into thin air!'

Mariel winked cheekily at the Foxwolf. 'Bit of good news, eh? How d'you feel about that, lumpbrain?'

Nagru kicked the mousemaid savagely. 'Not half as bad as you're going to feel, mousemaid!'

10

Sighing restlessly, the boundless sea broke large rollers into white cream which hissed hungrily up to the tideline. A sea breeze, with no clouds to chase around the moonlit vault of the skies, spun dry sand into dancing spirals. Midnight laid its cloak over the Mossflower coast. The four logboats, propelled on muffled paddles by Log a Log's Guosim shrews, slid silently out over the remainder of the stream that stretched across the shore from dune to sea.

Finnbarr Galedeep and Log a Log sat in the prow of the leading vessel. Between them lay a mallet and a broken sword which would serve well as hammer and chisel. Hon Rosie and Joseph perched in the stern, both armed with strong throwing slings and satchels of sturdy pebbles. The female hare wriggled her ears delightedly, scarcely able to contain her excitement.

'I say, what a jape! Whoo . . . Umff!'

Joseph clamped strong paws about Rosie's mouth, his voice stern and low. 'Not one single giggle, d'you hear me, Rosie Woodsorrel?'

Rufe, Durry and Foremole wielded paddles in the second boat, the mole muttering darkly to himself. 'Oi doant moinds liddle boaters an' streamwater, but those gurt shippers as sails on waves, boo hurr, no zurr!'

Rufe mispaddled and splashed himself. 'Wish I was back in Redwall,' he sighed. 'I'd kiss the grass an' never have ought to do with water again, not even to wash!'

Durry Quill smiled across at the timid squirrel. 'Acorns! By the end o' this voyage you'll be as big an old seadog as ever stood afore a mainmast. Keep yore tail up, Rufe, an' dip that paddle deep.'

The prows of all four boats bucked as they struck the first waves from the sea. Finnbarr turned to the crew sitting abaft of him, his single eye shining wildly, and shouted, 'Now dig those paddles strong'n'deep cullies, we're on blue water!'

Cap'n Slipp of the *Pearl Queen* sat alone on the shore beyond the headland, toasting whelks over an open fire. He had been arguing with his brother Cap'n Strapp again. Though Slipp was the larger and stronger of the two searats, he did not possess Strapp's eloquent tongue. Tonight they had argued over whether to sail north or south. Slipp wanted to sail north, but Strapp painted such a glowing picture of southern sun and easy pickings that both crews sided with him. They had all gone aboard his ship the *Shalloo* to celebrate, leaving Slipp alone to sulk over a small fire on the shore. Slipp was not worried; tomorrow he would continue the argument, escalating it into a fight, and he could always beat his brother hollow in a hard scrap. Then he would humiliate Strapp and regain command, perhaps he might even imprison him aboard the *Pearl Queen*, and have Rappsnout, his first mate, take over as Captain of the *Shalloo*. Slipp smiled to himself. Yes, that would teach Strapp to keep his high-flown opinions to himself.

Log a Log looked worried. He knew something was wrong with the plan as soon as he spotted the tiny fire on the shore, then his view was obscured as the hulks of the two ships loomed large in the dark.

'Finnbarr, did you see, there's hardly anybeast on shore?'

The sea otter thumped the prow with his paw. 'Barnacles'n'bilgewater! I shoulda knowed t'wouldn't be all plain sailin'. Hark though, mate, they must be all aboard the *Shalloo*, see the lights shinin' from 'er ports an' lissen to that racket. They're 'avin' some sort o'feast below decks. All the better for us, they won't 'ear the mallet.'

Log a Log stared at him incredulously. 'You're not still thinking of scuttling the *Shalloo*?'

Finnbarr was already slipping over the side into the inky seawater. 'Course I am messmate! I ain't leavin' no searat ship afloat to come chasin' after us. Pass me those tools,' he said as he stretched out a paw.

With a grunt of resignation, Log a Log grabbed the implements and dived over the side into the sea. He bobbed up beside Finnbarr and passed him the heavy mallet. 'You're right, of course. Let's get it done!'

As they swam off, the four boats hoved to on the seaward side of the *Pearl Queen*. Joseph seized hold of a rope that trailed down from the deck high above. 'Come on, let's steal ourselves a ship!'

Blaggut, boson of the *Pearl Queen*, was lying half asleep beside the mainmast, consoling himself with a flagon of seaweed grog. There were only himself and six crew left aboard whilst the others feasted and roistered aboard the *Shalloo*. Still, a ship had to have a watch and at least the bad-tempered Cap'n Slipp was ashore. He took a pull at the flagon. Wiping a grubby paw across his lips, he blinked twice – was that a mouse and a big rabbit just come aboard? Blaggut staggered upright. 'Ahoy you two, what'n the name of fishes are ye do . . .' Thunk!

Rosie's slingstone collided with his jaw, sending him

staggering backward. Tripping over the coaming, he fell into the hold with a loud bang. As the rest of the watch came pouring out on to the deck, disturbed by the shouting and the noise, Joseph shrugged. 'Good shot Rosie, pity you never dropped him where he sat.'

Hon Rosie fitted another stone to her sling. 'Sat? The blighter was standing. Look out!'

Joseph swung his loaded sling without letting go its stone, and caught a second rat neatly across the skull, dropping him like a log. Then the shrews swarmed aboard, rapiers clenched in their teeth, followed by Durry, Rufe and Foremole. Durry went down with a piercing yell as the flat of a searat cutlass smacked him across the back of his head. The rat stood over him, raising his weapon, about to strike when Rufe Brush came whistling through the air on a sailrope and booted him overboard. Rufe swung back and forth doing what the sea otter had told him to do – growl.

'Garrrooooaaarrreeeaaaarrrrgghh!'

As he careered to and fro, Rufe's bottom accidentally bumped another searat, who was perched on the ship's rail, ready to dive on Foremole. The rat was knocked overboard into the sea. Still growling in his most ferocious manner, Rufe slipped from the rope, rendering another rat senseless as he landed with a bump on the unfortunate creature's head. Throwing valour to the winds, the remaining two searats took one glance at the invaders and hurled themselves overboard.

Joseph sprang to the foredeck, gazing anxiously across the dark waters at the vessel *Shalloo*. Hon Rosie joined him.

'Hi ho and away we go on our very own stolen ship! Come on, Joseph, you old stick-in-the-mud, what's up?'

The Bellmaker nodded towards the *Shalloo*. 'Look, our noise must have roused the searats, the ship's swarming with 'em. Finnbarr and Log a Log are in trouble!'

Through the darkness the two creatures could barely be seen, swimming towards the *Pearl Queen* as searats hurled spears, arrows and slingstones at them. Joseph began shouting orders.

'Get some ropes, throw them out to Finnbarr and Log a Log as soon as they get close enough! Archers, slingers, give those searats something to think about, keep their heads down so they can't get our friends in the water! The rest of you, make ready to sail, stand by to slip anchor, get up in the rigging and loose the sails. Hurry!'

As the arrows and stones whined out over the sea, Rufe found himself scrambling up the rigging alongside Durry. They slashed at the ties holding the sails furled, both roaring. 'Groooaaarrgharrr!'

A slingstone bounced off Log a Log's head, stunning him. He was going down, his mouth and nostrils filling with seawater. Finnbarr dived and came up under him and, with the shrew lying across his back, the big sea otter struck out valiantly for the *Pearl Queen*.

'I say, Finn old lad, catch this!' Hon Rosie was her usual accurate self. She slung the rope, landing it neatly a pawsbreadth from Finnbarr. The otter latched on to it with powerful jaws. Next moment he was streaking through the waters like a great minnow, as Rosie and several others heaved the line in paw over paw.

'Whoohahahahoo! Up you come, you two. Great seasons, look at the bump on old Log a thing's bonce, righto, I've got him!' The sails were billowing, blown out taut by the wind. *Pearl Queen* strained against the anchor rope like a wild animal waiting to be unleashed. Joseph, aided by Finnbarr Galedeep, heaved against the tiller, forcing the rudder around until *Pearl Queen* was bowsprit out, facing the horizon. The tideswell was lifting at its peak when the sea otter bellowed, 'Cut loose your anchor cable!'

Foremole had found a ship's axe, perfectly suited to

the job. He struck the rope twice where it came through the for'ard port. Whack! Thwack!

Pearl Queen ran free, veering southwest into the heaving seas.

Cap'n Slipp was waist deep in the water, about to take the plunge and swim towards his ship, when he saw it buck from the anchor cable and begin heading out to sea. With a howl of dismay he hurtled forward into the waves and struck out for his brother's ship.

Dizzy from roistering in the close confines of a hot and well-lit cabin, Cap'n Strapp shivered on deck, rubbed his eyes and peered into the darkness, demanding, 'What'n the name o' burstin' bilges is goin' on?'

Rappsnout, mate of the *Pearl Queen*, explained as best he could. 'That bangin' amidships Cap'n, it was two h'animals, otter an' a shrew I fink, they musta been tryin' to bore an' 'ole in yer vessel, I reckon.'

Strapp peered anxiously over the side. 'An' did they?' he asked.

'Bless yer cockles, no, Cap'n, we chased 'em off,' Rappsnout said, brandishing his cutlass. 'But they swimmed o'er to yer brother's craft, looks like them'n their mates 'ave took off with it.'

'Avast the *Shalloo*, throw me a line!'

Strapp's eyes were now accustomed to the night. He saw his brother swimming towards the *Shalloo*, and shouted, 'Rappsnout, throw Cap'n Slipp a line.'

The dutiful mate grabbed a heaving line and hurled one end of it out to the figure in the water. Strapp chuckled wickedly. 'Now throw him the other end of it!'

Rappsnout blinked and scratched his head in bewilderment. 'Frow 'im the other end, Cap'n, are you sure?'

Strapp was already shouting orders to the two crews he had aboard. 'Hoist yer anchor! Bring 'er about souwest. Unfurl all sail smartlike! Nip to it!'

He turned to Rappsnout. 'Sure? Course I'm sure,

mate. That's if yer want to be Cap'n of the *Shalloo*. When we've captured the *Pearl Queen*, I'll be master of 'er, I've allus wanted that vessel for meself, now's the chance!'

A slow smile spread over Rappsnout's dull features. 'Ho I see! Yer a sly un, Cap'n. But wot about yore brother?'

Strapp felt the ship shudder as the anchor was hauled free of the water; he watched the sails billow out into the wind. 'My brother, that stinkin' bully! Cap'n of the seashore, that's wot 'e can be if'n 'e makes it back to land. Throw 'im the other end of the line, Cap'n Rappsnout!'

Proud of his new appointment, the former mate tossed the line to Slipp, sticking his snout in the air, and ignoring the swimmer's cries, in a dignified manner as befits a Captain. Slipp floundered in the creamy wake of the *Shalloo*, swallowing seawater as he watched the stern recede southwest.

'Strapp, ye double-dyed villain, come back! Rappsnout, stop 'im matey! I'll 'ave yore liver'n'lights fer this, d'you 'ear me! I'll saw off yer tail an 'ang yer by it, you scum!' Treading water and still grasping both ends of the useless line, the infuriated pirate shouted threats and insults until the *Shalloo* grew small in the distance.

Foremole thumped Log a Log's back as he spat out seawater, holding a wet cloth to the swollen lump between his ears.

'Thurr, you'm taken et easy naow zurr Log, we'm all safe!'

Finnbarr had relinquished the tiller to Durry and Rufe, whilst Joseph went below to check the ship's supplies and weaponry. The sea otter tucked Log a Log in a blanket. 'There now, shipmate, pity we never 'ad a chance to sink the *Shalloo*, but never mind, we got us the *Pearl Queen*. Our lads did a good job takin' over. I 'ear young Rufe accounted fer four searats single pawed. Haharr, we got us a prime crew, no mistake!'

Rufe and Durry clung bravely to the tiller, holding the ship on course until further orders. They grinned fearsomely at one another and growled like old seadogs.

'Gooarrarrarrurrgggg!'

Rosie found an unopened flagon at the foot of the mast, uncorked it and took a long pull.

'Pthoowah!'

It sprayed out over several shrews. Rosie held the flagon at paw's length, her face crinkled in disgust. 'Whoa corks, I say, is this the stuff they call bilgewater?'

Joseph was passing by. He took the flagon and sniffed it. 'No marm, this is the famous seaweed grog. It'll come in very useful for lighting the galley fires. Now I can get a decent supper cooked.'

Wiping her mouth on a kerchief, Hon Rosie muttered, 'That's about all the blinkin' stuff is any good for!'

The ship was well stocked and in excellent repair. Joseph discovered a good cache of cutlasses, knives, spears and archery equipment in her arms locker. A hot meal of biscuits and shrimp soup was dished out to the crew; they relieved each other in turns so they could all eat. Finnbarr sat under a stern awning with Joseph and Log a Log. The shrew was curious to know what course they were taking. Finnbarr licked a paw and tested the wind, saying, 'We're runnin' southwest as I ordered, mate.'

Joseph watched the first streaks of dawn over to the east. 'Southwest? I thought we were supposed to be heading south.'

The sea otter drank soup from the bowl, smacking his lips. 'So we will, Bellmaker, take my affydavit for it, mate, we'll be runnin' due south the moment we strike Roaringburn.'

Joseph and Log a Log repeated the name simultaneously. 'Roaringburn?'

'Aye, Roaringburn,' Finnbarr chuckled as he stretched out to take a nap. 'It's a current – narrow, deep an' very swift, only ever runs one way, south. Mind, it'll take some findin', but the moment we hit it, we'll shift like the wind!'

The shrew Bandle poked his head around the awning. 'Then we'd best find it quick, the *Shalloo*'s hard on our paws an' bearin' down on us fast!'

They dashed out from under the cover and sure enough, there was the *Shalloo* with every scrap of canvas piled on, double crewed and coming after them like a hungry, windblown hawk.

Dawn also found Cap'n Slipp wandering the shoreline in a daze, completely unsure of how he had ever got back to land. Stumbling back to his position of the previous night he found the ashes of his fire. He crouched in the windtossed sand and blew on a glowing ember, adding sticks and dry grass to it until a small fire flickered. Miserably he perched by it, drying off and waiting for the sun to get up. Cursing and muttering the most dreadful oaths to himself, he scanned the stretch of beach left by the ebbing waves of the outgoing tide. The corpses of six drowned crewrats who had been his ship's watch lay still, washed up with the jetsam of the previous night's encounter.

Shivering and damp, Slipp stood up, turning his back to warm it by the fire. Then he saw it.

Blaggut, bosun of the *Pearl Queen*, was seated in a shrewboat paddling inshore. Slipp leapt up and down, waving to attract the other's attention.

'Ahoy there, Blaggut! Matey, it's me, yer good ole Cap'n!'

Blaggut heard and acknowledged with a wave of his paddle. Leaping out into the shallows, he dragged the boat ashore and beached it, smiling and waving joyfully. 'Cap'n, Cap'n Slipp, matey, 'tis yerself!'

Laughing happily he ran towards Slipp, paws out-stretched. 'Ho Cap'n, y'don't know 'ow good it does me 'eart t'see yore face, an' a fire too! There's a stroke o' luck, I'm froze to the marrow an' starvin'.'

When they met, instead of embracing his bosun, Slipp leapt upon him and began punching and kicking him. 'Bosun eh? 'Ead of the watch? Keepin' me vessel safe from invaders, was you! You . . . you . . . useless, gutless, brainless, spineless jellyfish!'

Blaggut pranced about on the sand trying to avoid Slipp, who punctuated each word with a hard kick to the bosun's rear.

'Leave a ship with you, lardbottom! I wouldn't leave you in charge of a tadpole's tail! I'll wager you was full o' grog an' snorin' when those shiprobbers came aboard! Brainless, bumblin', bulbnosed buffoon!' Slipp had Blaggut tight by the ear and his seaboot squelched every time he booted the bosun's bottom. Blaggut howled.

'Owowowow, Cap'n! Mercy, spare me! There was 'undreds of em, I was wide awake an' at me post, I swear it. Ouchooch! They ganged up on me! Ow stoppit please! I fought like a madbeast! Aagh that 'urts! But they overwhelmed me. Honest, ouch! I remembers shoutin', 'elp I'm bein' whelmed over!'

Slipp flung the blubbering bosun face down in the sand. 'What's that thing yore paddlin' about in, dogs-bottom?'

Blaggut kept alternately covering his head and his rear with both paws, in case the Captain felt like kicking again. 'It's a sorta liddle boat, Cap'n, I was paddlin' up an' down searchin' for you, cross me 'eart I was. I found a big stream back yonder with fresh drinkin' water, nice'n'sweet 'tis. D'you want me to show it ye, you can drink yore fill!'

Slipp drew his cutlass and whacked the bosun's back, hard. 'Up on yore paws, bubblebrains. Take me to it.'

Blaggut paddled the tideline with Slipp lying back in the boat, giving him the occasional cutlass prod. 'C'mon, put yore back into it! Where's this stream, or does it just run through yore empty 'ead?'

Blaggut paddled harder. 'Yowch! There it is up ahead Cap'n, see the sun glintin' on it, good'n'sweet, just like I said.'

The morning sun warmed Slipp's back as he bent and lapped streamwater. Blaggut brightened up.

'You'll like it 'ere, Cap'n, there's dunes an' probly fruit growin' nearby, I can fish for us an' we'll live 'ere snug as two bugs in a rug. I'll . . . Yaagh!' Slipp gave the bosun a smack that sent him sprawling into the stream.

'Froghead! Get in that boat an' start paddlin' upstream. It must lead somewheres, maybe there's good pickin's up there. Come on bulgebelly, stir yer stumps.'

By noon Blaggut had paddled the shrewboat into the fringes of Mossflower Wood.

11

Dandin was first to regain his senses. He wished fervently that he had not – his entire body was a mass of pain. The last thing he recalled was the three of them being dragged along the ground all the way to Castle Floret. Kicked, buffeted, bumped and scratched, until they lost consciousness. Somewhere in the background he heard voices.

'Sourgall, look, one of 'em's comin' around.'

'C'mon Fillch, we'd better go an' report back.'

As the voices died away in the distance, Dandin sat up, trying to ignore his discomfort. One of his eyes was swollen shut; through the other he took stock of his surroundings. Mariel and Meldrum lay on either side of him, still senseless. All of their footpaws had been bound together by a thick rope. They were in a prison cell, its floor strewn with dry rushes and old straw. Four stout stone walls surrounded them; there was one high, barred window and a heavily timbered door, with iron studding and a small spyhole grill. Sunlight flooded in from the wide-barred window, lighting up the grimness of their dungeon.

Mariel stirred, her voice a hoarse croak. 'Water!'

Dandin winced as, cradling her head on his lap, he

scoured the cell with his one good eye. 'Sorry, there's not a drop in the place. Are you all right?'

'I'm thirsty, that's how I know I'm still alive. How're you?'

'Still here, I suppose. Meldrum looks very still.'

The old hare lay prostrate with both eyes shut. He began muttering half to himself. 'Want a full military burial, lots of fuss, medals, sad music an' tears, that'll do. Hmm, at the foot of a good oak tree, nice an' shady, they can carve somethin' fittin' on it too. Now, me effects, let me see. I leave a nice mess jacket to Thurdale, hope he wears it with pride. About me rod'n'line, young Foghill gets that, blighter's always had his eye on it anyway . . .' The Field Marshal's finely attuned ears waggled. 'There's somebeast comin', steady in the ranks thah. Lie doggo, make 'em think we're still out.'

Locks squealed and bolts clanked as they were withdrawn, and the door creaked open. Nagru and Silvamord swept in, flanked by a dozen rats. One of them stirred Meldrum with his footpaw.

'This is the beast who slew Captain Bragglin. We had the two mice cornered when he butted in. There were four, no five others, four young hares and a hedgepig.'

Nagru shoved the rat aside contemptuously, saying, 'And they vanquished a full patrol of you!'

'You should talk,' said Silvamord, her voice heavy with scorn. 'These three between them slew your wonderful Dirgecallers and more than a score of hordebeasts. Tell us about that again!'

The Foxwolf ignored her, but took his spite out by kicking Mariel. 'I thought you said they were coming around, Sourgall. This one's still senseless. Look!'

He kicked Mariel again and her eyes snapped open. 'I'll remember your face when the time comes for me to slay you, ugly one!' she spat.

Nagru stood over her, smiling evily. 'Well, well, tough words for a mousemaid who's hardly in a position to slay anybeast. Listen fool, I am the Urgan Nagru,

I could squash all three of you like so many bothersome gnats, and I will if you don't answer my questions. What are you doing in Southsward? Where did the squirrels and otters go to? Tell me!'

From his position on the cell floor Meldrum the Magnificent blew a long sigh of boredom. 'Somebeasts love t'hear the sound of their own voice, don't they. Tell that wallah to buzz off, will you, I'm takin' me noon nap!'

Silvamord drew a dagger and leapt at the hare. Nagru restrained her as she snapped at him, 'Dolt! Can't you see they're not going to tell you anything? Kill them now, I say!'

Nagru placed himself between Silvamord and the captives 'I want them kept alive for the moment. Leave this to me.'

The three friends sat up facing Nagru, conscious of the vixen prowling back and forth behind him. The Foxwolf crouched, letting his metal claws show ominously.

'You'd do well to listen to my words. Make it a lot easier on yourselves and just tell me where Serena and that brat of hers are hiding.'

Dandin eyed him coolly. 'Or?'

Silvamord leaned over Nagru's shoulder, brandishing her dagger lovingly as she hissed, 'Or you won't be able to talk for screaming!'

The Foxwolf shook his head pityingly. 'She'll get to you sooner or later, probably after you've rotted in here awhile from hunger and thirst. So give me your answer now and we'll reach an agreement. I could do with three warriors such as you, it would spare you all this.'

The trio looked from one to another. Mariel nodded. They lay back down, with Meldrum yawning. 'Close the door on your way out, will you, it gets quite draughty in here with it open.'

Surprisingly Nagru kept his temper, though he had to signal the guards to restrain Silvamord. She was struggling to get at them, spittle and foam ringing her lips as she shouted wildly, 'Leave me an hour with them, just an hour, I'll have them talking so fast they won't be able to stop!' The guards hustled her out. Nagru stood framed in the doorway, a thin smile on his lips.

'Fine words from warriors, but think on this. You are no longer warriors free to do battle. You are my prisoners, to do with as I please. Without liberty, food or drink. Soon you will begin to feel weak, thin and hungry, sick and thirsty. I have seen it before. You will be reduced to whining, cringing wretches who will betray each other for a cup of water or a crust of bread.'

Meldrum raised his head, careful not to show how painful the effort was. 'Hard luck laddie, fear won't work on us, we've faced death too many times taking felons like y'self down a peg or two. Y'see, there's a world of difference twixt warriors'n'windbags, between real fighters an' jumped-up johnnies who go around wearin' the skins of other creatures – bad form, y'know! Quick as y'like now, toddle off an' close the door quietly!'

The cell door slammed shut with an ear-splitting bang. Nagru shouted through the spyhole as he left, 'Bravado won't feed you and stupidity will kill you!'

In the silence that followed Mariel untied the rope that bound their footpaws together. Standing up carefully, she gave an agonized groan. 'Ooahh! That villain's right, you know, we're hardly in a fit state to stand on our own paws, let alone defy him.'

Supporting each other they staggered over to the window. It was not as high as it had first looked. They scrambled up on to the broad sill and Mariel pulled herself forward, craning her neck to peer between the bars.

'Oh my giddy paws! It feels like sitting in the clouds looking down from here, it's a sheer drop down to the valley. The trees look like tiny blobs of green moss!'

Meldrum crawled over to join her. 'Right m'dear,

we're at the rear of Castle Floret, straight drop, no moat round this side, no need for one y'see. If I'm not mistaken we're on the third floor, north wing. Nice view across the valley, wot? Pity we ain't got nothin' t'do but sit here an' admire it.'

Dandin took a look and then sat back, resting against the sunwarmed stone. 'Don't you wish you were a bird?'

The garrulous old campaigner flexed a stiffened paw. 'Wish I were any flippin' thing but a three-quarter dead hare at the moment, young feller, 'deed I do!'

Mariel felt her back, raw, through the holes that had been made in her tunic with being dragged along. 'Injured, imprisoned, hungry, thirsty. There's only one way for us to go now, up!'

'We're already up old gel, how much further up would you like us t'be, eh?' said Meldrum, probing gingerly at a loose tooth. 'Listen to a veteran, you two, best thing to do in a case like this is sleep. Calms the nerves, clears the brain, an' helps nature heal the body, wot? Bit of shuteye, that's the ticket!'

He received no arguments on that score, and within moments the three of them were dozing on the broad windowsill in the noontide sun. Deep sleep overtook the trio of battered warriors immediately.

A search party scoured the collapsed sand dune, sifting through the sand. Furpp straightened up, unable to find anything. He shook his head at Bowly, saying, 'You'm sure they'm been round boi yurr, maister?'

Iris waved a paw at the upset state of the wrecked sandhill. 'They must have been, look at all the activity that's taken place round here – prints, tracks, holes. I'd say some sort of fight took place. Whoops, careful there!' The female otter had been standing on one end of Meldrum's rod, and she toppled backward downhill as Coltvine unearthed the other end vigorously. He gave a whoop.

'What ho! Lookie here, Uncle Mel's fishin' weapon!'

'Aha! The Gullwhacker, I was right!' said Bowly as he tugged Mariel's rope from the sand.

Greenbeck shook his head in admiration as he unearthed the paw of a dead horderat. Letting it go limp, he kicked sand back over it. 'Sink me, wot a tussle they must've put up!'

'Aye, just like Muta an' my Rab, brave creatures!' Iris said as she blinked back a tear.

Furpp patted her with his huge digging claws. 'Roight marm, they uns gived us toim to rescue ee Queen an' ee babby, leastways they'm safe naow.'

Greenbeck sat down between them, keeping his voice low and out of earshot of Bowly and the leverets. 'Furpp, get yore moles to dig round 'ere,' he said. 'If they ain't buried under this lot then they've been taken by the Foxwolf an' that 'orde.'

'Fate and seasons have mercy on the poor brave beasts,' Iris shuddered. 'If they're in the cells at Floret no creatures can help them, even supposing that they are still alive!'

12

'Up in the riggin', out on those yardarms, crew!'

Finnbarr Galedeep fought with the tiller to keep the *Pearl Queen* ploughing southwest as he roared orders.

'Pile on every scrap o' sail, buckoes! Log a Log, search the lockers, we need more canvas! Joseph, lash that boom on the same course we're runnin', sou'west an' keel down! I'll show the scurvy flotsam, with me own paw on me own tiller there's not even the seagulls kin outsail the ole *Pearl Queen*!'

Out on the yards, lashing down sheets like two old salts, Durry and Rufe roared into the blasting winds, whilst at the same time comforting a thoroughly seasick Foremole.

'Foremole, forget that your stomach's heavin', just roar like we do, you'll feel better right away, promise!'

The good mole tried, but he was not convinced, roaring fitfully as he glanced backward to the *Shalloo*. 'Hooourrrarrruurrg! Oi wishes oi wurr back 'ome, 'stead o' bein' chased by a gurt boatload o' vurmints. Hooarrurg!'

*

Strapp was perched high on the prow of *Shalloo*, clinging to the wet lines as the bow dipped and heaved. He
howled encouragement at his double crew.

'Bend yer louse-ridden backs, cullies, I said we'd be
sailin' south, didn't I? Keep yore glims on the prize
ahead, the *Pearl Queen*, me new ship! If I can't catch 'er
wid two crews to speed us on, nobeast can!'

Rappsnout joined him, shouting to be heard above
the shrieking gale and hissing spray. 'Don't fret yer
'eart Cap'n, they got a few lengths start on us, but we'll
overhaul 'er soon!'

'Yer right there mate,' Strapp said as he wiped bow-
spray from his eyes. 'Get some archers up 'ere, an'
some grapplin' 'ooks. When we gets close enough then
we'll clap grapplers an 'old 'er close, while the archers
picks 'em off. Tell 'em t'get that rogue Galedeep first!'

Rappsnout cackled happily as he leapt down to obey
Strapp's orders. He spat on his paw and patted a bulk-
head. 'Haharr, that's fer luck, *Shalloo*, ole Rappsnout'll
soon be yer new master. Ahoy Snicker, get below an'
break out bows'n'arrers. Sharkoe, lay yer paws on some
grapplin' irons an' lines. Jump to it, messmates, we're
lucky rats this day, a ship'n'crew an' plunder too!'

Finnbarr knew his old ship like the hairs on the back of
his paw. He ordered triangle sails to be set between the
bowsprit and the cable from the topmast, and two
square sails sitting low amidships to port and starboard.
It worked like a charm, lifting the for'ard end, and sending *Pearl Queen* skimming. Log a Log smiled at the sight
of many searats crammed into the bows of *Shalloo*, sending her head deeper down and slowing her.

'Hoho, look at that, Finnbarr, *Shalloo*'s starting to wal-
low like an old leaky bucket!'

Joseph came dashing up. 'Finnbarr, what's that roaring noise I hear?' he shouted.

The big sea otter grasped Joseph's paw. 'Come aloft
with the Galedeep, Bellmaker, and I'll show ye!'

Together they climbed into the rigging, and Finnbarr pointed direct on the course they were heading. 'There's a sight ye can tell yore grandmice about. Look at the hole in the sea, Joseph!'

The sight took Joseph's breath away. Less than a sea league southwest was a gigantic whirlpool, more than ten shiplengths wide, a complete circle, whirling around like a tornado, with a massive hole at its centre. The roaring noise increased until it filled the air for miles around. Finnbarr's single eye watched it impassively.

'Few creatures 'ave ever seen it an' lived. 'Tis called the Green Maelstrom. See there, it spins off south creatin' the fastest part of the current they call Roaringburn!'

Redoubtable as he was, Joseph found himself trembling with fear of the unknown hole in the deep. 'But we're heading straight for it,' he said. 'We'll be sucked in!'

Finnbarr's scarred face was grim as he grabbed Joseph's paw. 'Trust me, the Galedeep knows wot 'e's about! It's not my ship that'll be pulled over the edge o' the Green Maelstrom, no, that's where *Shalloo*'s bound for!'

Joseph was horrorstricken. '*Shalloo* has two crews aboard her!' he cried.

The sea otter's face quivered with emotion. Joseph was not sure whether it was seaspray or tears he saw running down from Finnbarr's single eye.

'Aye, two crews of murderin', torturin', fate-forsaken searats. I was the only one escaped when they captured *Pearl Queen* – they killed my 'ole crew, wife an' two sons as well. Left me fer dead, but it takes more'n searats to finish Finnbarr Galedeep, you can lay t'that! Now git below an' foller me orders to the word, or we'll all find out what the earth below the 'igh seas looks like!'

Cap'n Strapp was laying about with the flat of his cutlass at the rats crowding the bows. 'Git back, yer shellbrained slackers, wait'll I gives the word, go an' shove on more sail, yore slowin' the vessel by all pilin' up 'ere. Belay an' git back, I say!'

Rappsnout came scurrying forward, still grinning. 'Cap'n, Cap'n, looks like *Pearl Queen*'s flounderin', she's limpin' like a lame duck with all sails on the starboard side slack!'

Strapp was jubilant at this sudden stroke of luck. 'Hararr, she ain't goin' nowheres. Ahoy, where are you lot off to? Git back up for'ard 'ere, stan' by with weapons an' grapplin' 'ooks! Runnin' with this gale we'll hove alongside 'er in no time!'

A rat in the rigging on lookout began shrieking, 'Waaah Cap'n! There's a big 'ole in the seas!'

Strapp shook his head in mock despair. 'You bin up there too long, Drangle, come on down.'

But the lookout persisted. 'I never seen nothin' like it, Cap'n, off t'the sou'west, can't you 'ear the noise it's makin'?'

Strapp could ignore the warning no longer, even though *Shalloo* was upwind of the maelstrom. At first he thought the roaring of the vortex was thunder, but there had been no lightning flashes. The Corsair Captain hauled himself high into the forepeak rigging to take a look. Most of the crew did too, and the sight of the colossal whirlpool caused chaos.

'Drangle's right, 'tis a pit in the waters!'

'Put about or we're all deadbeasts!'

'We'll be sucked down into it, mates!'

'Bring 'er round, Cap'n, afore we perish!'

Strapp gritted his teeth – he was determined to have the *Pearl Queen*. Luck had been with him so far; he had rid himself of his brother and gained another crew. Now after chasing the prize halfway across the main he was not about to give up and turn tail. Booting the closest rats down to the deck, he railed at them.

'Down an' stand ready, every rat jack of ye! I ain't

goin' back empty clawed! Are you searats or land-swabs? Wherever *Pearl Queen* goes, we can follow. Anybeast not with me is agin me, an' it's over the side with the cowards! Now look lively an' jump to my bid-din'!'

Spume and roaring water were everywhere, enveloping the crew of *Pearl Queen*. Log a Log and Finnbarr fought against the tiller as it bucked and yawed. The shrew Chieftain had to shout at the sea otter to be heard above the gale. 'Are y'sure you know what you're doin', Gale-deep?'

Finnbarr laughed like a madbeast. 'Yahaharr! I've wrung more salt water out o' me whiskers than that lot 'ave sailed on. Leave it t'me! Keep those starboard sails slack an' this rudder 'ard over. When I gives the word then pile the starboard sail back on an' slack off the lar-board sail, an' swing this tiller over for all yore worth, matey. Joseph, get our crew up in the riggin', tell 'em to stand by. Rosie, marm, 'ow far off is *Shalloo* now?'

Hon Rosie sloshed her way up to the high stern. 'Less than forty shiplengths, bearing down fast, old thing!' Her voice was cut off as Durry and Rufe fell from the rigging and clung tight to her neck, wailing.

'We'll never see Redwall again!'

'We're goin' t'fall off the sea's edge into that pit!'

Foremole and Joseph untangled them, the mole unable to tear his eyes from the maelstrom, which was hardly more than six shiplengths off now.

'Boi okey, ee must've be'd a gurt seabeast to dig an' 'ole loik that'n, whurr, lookit 'er!'

Pearl Queen seemed to be almost tottering on the brink of the whirling water tunnel now. The terrifying greeny-grey walls revolved at a breathtaking speed, a gaping hole reaching down, down, into mysterious darkness.

Joseph boosted Rufe and Durry aloft. 'Come on, you

two, I'll climb up there with you. Try not to look at the whirlpool and keep your ears pinned back for Galedeep's orders. Up you go!'

'Finnbarr, here she comes,' Rosie's voice rose above the mêlée. 'Shalloo's sailin' straight at us, she'll strike the centre of our ship soon. Look out!' Expertly Rosie caught the first grappling hook that shot out from Shalloo's bows and hurled it back, ducking a volley of arrows. Cap'n Strapp's jubilant roars rang above the thunder of the Green Maelstrom.

'Lay on, buckoes, she's ours, she's ours!'

Suddenly Finnbarr was swinging the tiller over, calling out his orders: 'Lash those starboard sails tight, let the wind catch 'er. Rosie, lend a paw on this tiller with me'n Log a Log! You shrews up there, look smart, slack off the sails on the larboard side. Move yerselves!'

Durry laboured furiously, trying to get his cold, spray-soaked paws to work on the ropes. Joseph toiled alongside him.

Rufe's footpaws left the yardarm momentarily as a sail caught the wind and billowed out. 'What's the sea otter doin', Joseph sir,' he cried, 'larboard, starboard, slack off an' tighten up, pushin' that tiller thing here an' there, I don't unnerstand none of it.'

The Bellmaker's weatherbeaten face creased into a grim smile. 'Nor do I, young un. That's the thing about being crew, we're not here to understand, just to obey orders. Though I think Finnbarr has left it too late. Duck!' Arrows hissed viciously overhead as the three ducked.

The searats of the Shalloo were only a boatslength away. They crowded the bows of their ship, snarling as they fired arrows and whirled grappling hooks. Finnbarr held the tiller hard over as Rosie and Log a Log secured it in position with a rope halter. The larboard sails fluttered loose as Guosim shrews slacked them off.

Shalloo's bowsprit was a fraction from striking the *Pearl Queen* amidships when Finnbarr's seaskills paid off. The first six grappling hooks caught as it happened.

With a groaning of timber and creaking of rigging the *Pearl Queen* turned sideways! Finnbarr drew both the swords from their back scabbards, tossing one to Log a Log. Both creatures sprang to the rail, shearing the taut grappling lines with single strokes of the finely honed swords. Durry and Rufe stared wordlessly as *Shalloo* shot by them, her decks crowded with silent searats, numbed with shock as their ship caught the spinning edge of the Green Maelstrom. Halfway round the whirlpool it spun, hanging a split second in midair with its entire keel visible, then it tippled head first into the dark abyss. The *Shalloo* was gone into the depths, never to be seen again by living eyes.

A gasp of horror arose from the crew of the *Pearl Queen*. Then Finnbarr was in the midst of them shouting, 'Save yer pity for the ones they murdered! They've gone where all searats should go, mates! Stand by, we ain't safe yet by a long chalk!'

Pearl Queen travelled sideways around the far outer rim of the whirlpool, seemingly helpless, until they jumped to obey Finnbarr's next commands.

'Pile on all sail agin, crew!'

Slashing the rope that held the tiller he centred it and held it level with Log a Log and Rosie's help. When she saw what was happening the Hon Rosie's natural exuberance returned in full force.

'Whoohahahooh! I say chaps, the jolly old ship's sailin' straight again, an' goin' like the clappers. Whoohahahahoo!'

Joseph looked behind him. The Green Maelstrom was rapidly disappearing in the distance as *Pearl Queen* rushed due south like a great sea eagle. He scrambled down from the rigging and ran to Finnbarr. Grasping the sea otter's paw in both of his own, the Bellmaker shook it strongly.

'Roaringburn, you found it, we're sailing south!'

The whole crew gave a great cheer, and Finnbarr grinned crookedly as he turned to acknowledge the compliment.

Boom!

The sea otter was knocked flat on his tail as the vessel shuddered from stem to stern. He scrambled upright, shouting, 'What is it, what's happenin'?'

The shrew Bandle leaned out over the starboard rail. 'Look, we've just passed a rock stickin' up out the water, we musta struck it!'

There was an instant flurry of activity; the crew scattered in all directions to inspect the vessel for damage. Finnbarr held the tiller, calling anxiously, 'Is everythin' shipshape?'

There was a chorus of 'ayes'. Then Foremole's head appeared from the for'ard rope locker.

'Zurr, thurr'm a gurt 'ole in ee shipper 'ere. Hurr, ee watter be a pouren in, oi'm afeared us'n's a sinken!'

BOOK TWO

The *Pearl Queen*

13

It was still an hour before afternoon tea at Redwall Abbey. Sister Sage put the finishing touches to a raspberry and apple pie and, wiping her paws on a flour-dusted apron, the old mouse stood back and watched Simeon, the blind Herbalist. He was lining hot vegetable pasties on the window ledge to cool, his experienced paws selecting the ones that were ready and replacing them with those fresh from the ovens. Sage poured out two beakers of the cold oatmeal and pennycloud water she had brewed early that morning.

'Come and have a break, Simeon, I've got something here for you.'

The blind mouse felt his way over to the table. 'Ah, oatmeal and pennycloud, how thoughtful of you, Sage.'

They sat listing the fare they had made, sipping slowly. 'Raspberry and apple pie, strawberry tarts, nutbread, vegetable pasties and a mixed fruit cake, that should be enough, Simeon. Oh, my mint tea – where is it?'

The blind ancient restrained Sage from rising. 'I took it off the stove while you were baking, it's cooling off in the big pottery jar.'

Sage smiled, patting her friend's paw. 'Simeon, I don't know what I'd do without you!'

Gesturing for silence, Simeon turned his ear towards the window ledge and, as if speaking to nobeast, he said, 'If those paws touch a single pastie they'll be washing greasy pots for two seasons!'

There was a gasp of surprise from the other side of the window ledge, followed by a scurry of paws running off. Again Simeon restrained Sage from rising. 'No problem, I heard those Dibbuns sneaking up on our pasties a while back, little rascals. Though my ears tell me we've got a bigger problem coming our way.'

Sage was about to enquire what it was, when the kitchen door swung open and Tarquin L. Woodsorrel breezed in.

'Phew, it's a scorcher today! Afternoon chaps, how're things comin' along on the jolly old caterin' front, wot?'

Sister Sage coughed politely. 'Very well, thank you, Mr Woodsorrel. Is anything the matter?'

Tarquin's smile would have melted butter. 'Matter? Why, no, my charming Queen of the Kitchens, matter o' fact I'm just here in me official capacity as sampler.'

Simeon nodded knowingly. 'I thought you might be. There's a carrot and onion flan right behind you, perhaps you'd like to sample that.'

The hungry hare spun around and turned his attentions to an oversized golden pastried creation. He wolfed down a huge mouthful as he spoke. 'Mmf snch! My very, very favourite. I say, are we havin' carrot 'n'onion flan for tea, chaps?'

Simeon chuckled, shaking his head. 'No, I made that specially for you, so you wouldn't sample the entire tea-time menu down to empty plates.'

Tarquin ignored the remark and continued bolting hastily. 'Grrurrph! 'Scuse me. What a considerate cove you are, Simeon.'

Sage sniffed distantly as she watched Tarquin eating,

then rose and went to the kitchen door. Striking a small triangle that hung over the doorway, she remarked pointedly, 'I think we should get the servers in to take all this temptation out of your way, Mr Woodsorrel. I'm training some of the Dibbuns to take up table serving, you know.'

At the sound of the triangle several Dibbuns trooped in and stood waiting for the trolleys to be loaded. Tarquin congratulated three of his own brood heartily. 'Excellent! Learnin' a bit of waitin' on; your mater will be proud of you when she gets back, wot?'

Sage counted the number of Dibbun serving trainees. 'Eight? There's two missing.'

'Right, paws up all those who aren't here!' Tarquin chortled.

Sister Sage turned on him severely. 'Mr Woodsorrel, it's no joking matter! These young ones have got to learn their responsibilities to others!'

Tarquin swallowed the last of his flan apologetically. 'Oh, er, right you are, marm, buckle down, do a bit of thingeeyin', does 'em the world of good. Now then, you sprogs, which two are absent? Speak up!'

A small squirrel held up his paw. 'Fink it's the mousebabe an' Furrtil the mole, sir,' he said.

The hare picked crumbs from his whiskers. 'Mousebabe an' Furrtil, eh, where would they be at?'

'If we knew, then we could tell you, Daddy!' one of the little leverets replied.

Tarquin blinked and twitched his ears. 'Hmm, quite. What d'you think, Simeon, you know as much about bally Dibbuns as the next chap?'

Simeon put aside his beaker and stood up. 'Come on, Tarquin, we'd best go and check all the gates. If they're locked then nobeast has been out today and they should be somewhere inside the Abbey walls.'

'But apposin' a gate's unlockered, Sir?' the small squirrel tugging Simeon's robe asked.

The ancient mouse patted the Dibbun's bushy tail. 'If a gate's unlocked that means a major search in Mossflower after tea, my little friend.'

Afternoon tea was taken in the orchard. Mother Mellus sat beneath a gnarled pear tree with Saxtus. The old badger was plainly worried; her pastie lay untouched as she confided to the Father Abbot.

'It's always that small wicker gate in the east wall, the one which leads straight into Mossflower Wood. I've often said that the lock should be placed higher, so that tiny paws can't reach it. Ooh! That mousebabe, he's the one who's led Furrtil astray, she's always been a splendid little molemaid, not a moment's trouble until the mousebabe comes along with one of his wild ideas.'

Saxtus took her paw and squeezed it reassuringly. 'Brother Fingle and some others are searching upstairs right now, so stop worrying, Mellus. Remember last week when the mousebabe and three others were found sleeping under the Abbot's bed in the dormitories?'

Mellus took a half-hearted bite of her pastie. 'I suppose you're right, friend. Let's wait and see. I wish we could contact Oak Tom and Treerose, but nobeast ever seems to know what part of the woodlands they're living in. They have a spring house, a summer residence . . .'

Saxtus squeezed her paw tighter. 'They'll be found, now stop worrying and eat!'

But the two Dibbuns were not found anywhere inside the Abbey walls. Afternoon shadows were beginning to lengthen, tea was long finished. Tarquin lined up a score of Redwallers, then, pacing up and down in front of them, he gave his orders.

'Right, listen up in the ranks now! Proceed out of the east wallgate into the forest, spread out in line an' comb the area. Leave no stone unturned. No questions? Good, let's make a start then. By the left, quick march!'

High sun lanced down through the leafy greenery of still woodland depths, while somewhere in the distance a cuckoo call echoed through glade and copse. River Moss had many tributaries. One of them, a small, slow-flowing stream, had two small visitors on its bank that afternoon. A purloined dormitory sheet from Redwall Abbey was draped over a low willow bough to form a tent, and inside sat the mousebabe and the little mole-maid Furrtil, unaware of the upset they had caused, playing at Dibbun games. The mousebabe carried a stick, which he fondly imagined was the sword of Martin the Warrior, while Furrtil was armed with a knotted length of twine, obviously Mariel's Gullwhacker

She swiped at an inquisitive gnat with it. 'Oi be gurtly 'ungered, Marthen, us'n's missed tea.'

Martin, alias the mousebabe, tied a thread to his stick. 'Nev mind, Mariel, I catch us a big fish inna river.'

'Hurr, whurr ee be getten fires to cook'n et?'

The mousebabe thought about this a moment, then tossing aside the thread he lay down. 'We goin' asleep then, warriors got to 'ave sleep!'

'Hurr, but oi doant bee toired.'

'Course you're tired,' the mousebabe snorted impatiently. 'All a beasts gets tired!'

'Oi dearly loikes t'go back to ee Abbey furr supper, then oi be sleepen in moi own bed if'n oi toired.'

The mousebabe sat up, throwing a comforting paw about Furrtil's neck as they both watched the stream drifting by. 'Mm, I wanna go back to the Abbey too. We sit 'ere 'til they comes'n finds us, eh?'

Furrtil shook her head despairingly at this announcement. 'O gurt seasons! You'm gotten uz lost, b'aint you?'

Her companion fidgeted moodily with a dandelion. 'Not lost, just don' know a way back, s'all. They always come an' find us, you see, always come an' say, "Likkle rogues, worry us a death, very naughty!"'

The molemaid giggled at the mousebabe's imitation of Mother Mellus. 'Hurr hurr, ee sounden same as owd badgermum.'

Slipp and Blaggut were lost too. They had strayed from the main course of River Moss in the shrewboat and now lay becalmed up a tributary. Slipp had decided the blame lay with Blaggut.

'Yew arf-baked barnacle, what did yer bring us up this 'ere backwater for?'

The searat knew he dare not argue with his Captain, so he shrugged with an injured air. 'Cap'n?'

Slipp was working himself up into a fine temper, and drawing his cutlass slowly he imitated Blaggut's voice. 'Cap'n, Cap'n, is that all y'can say, Cap'n, Cap'n? I'll Cap'n yer, you useless lump o' seaslop, now over the side with yer carcass an' get pullin' on that 'eadrope afore I carves yer into crabmeat!'

Stifling a sigh of resignation, Blaggut heaved his bulk over the bows, drawing in a swift gasping breath at the stream's chill. Shouldering the headrope he began towing the shrewboat behind him, but not without protest.

'I'd be better off paddlin', Cap'n, s'pose there was h'eels an' those 'ungry pikefishes swimmin' in these 'ere waters, I could get meself et up, an' you'd 'ave t'go it alone . . .'

Slipp snorted at the idea. 'Pikes'n'eels got more sense than to try an' eat a big, fat, poison blubbergut like you. Just keep 'eavin' on that rope 'til I tells yer t'stop!'

The searat heaved, but kept up his complaints. 'The bottom's all muddy an' squishy Cap'n, s'pose I sinks outer sight, sucked under like . . .'

Slipp lay back in the boat, letting sun patterns play over him as the trees went by. 'No such luck, barrel-bum, this stream's got too much respect fer itself than to 'ave the likes of you layin' in the mud like a dirty great porpoise. Pull, ye swab!'

*

The sun was beginning to dip low as Tarquin halted his searchers. He squinted up at the sky before nodding decisively.

'That's as far as we go in this direction, chaps – two little uns like those couldn't have got further than this.'

Brother Mallen, a young mouse, who himself had been a Dibbun until four seasons ago, held up his paw. 'Mr Tarquin, sir, you'd be surprised at how far two Dibbuns can go in one afternoon. Maybe we should press on to the River Moss and search over that way.'

'You're barkin' up the wrong tree, laddie,' said the hare, staring down his nose for a moment at the Brother. 'Take m'word for it, I know about these things. When y've got a few seasons under y'belt, like me, you'll know how to track an' search expertly. Meanwhile, I suggest we spread out further apart an' comb the bally old country t'the east, makin' a sweep down south towards old Saint Ninian's church. Righto troop, as y'were, thrash the jolly bushes an' shrubs with your staves, call out the names loud, Furrthingee an' wotsismouse, no slackin', be dark before y'know it!'

The Redwallers moved off into the undergrowth, shaking bushes and calling aloud as they moved in a southeastward sweep. Off in the opposite direction to the lost Dibbuns.

Slipp yanked at the headrope impatiently, sending Blaggut sprawling backward into the water. 'Take me into the bank, over there by that big tree!' he barked.

Coughing streamwater, Blaggut obediently pulled until the shrewboat was banked, then he looped the headrope round the three-topped oak his Captain had indicated.

'Cap'n?'

The searat Captain ambled ashore and slumped against the oak as if wearied after a hard day's toil. 'Cap'n, Cap'n, there you go again! Now lissen hard, cocklebrains, mark this tree, remember where it is an' don't get lost. Take yore mouldy carcass off into these woods an' get me some vittles.'

Blaggut stared hopefully at Slipp. 'Vittles, Cap'n?'

'Aye, vittles, Cap'n! You know wot vittles is, don't yer? Food to shove in yore face; berries, nuts, fruit, there must be stuff aplenty to eat in this jungle. Get goin'!'

Blaggut's dull features brightened.

'Aye, aye, Cap'n, vittles! I'll bring yer all I kin lay claws on, an' water to drink as well.'

Slipp glared at the westering sun as if it were partly to blame, then he smiled disarmingly at his servant. 'We've been surrounded by fresh streamwater all day, nitbrains, wot would we need more for? Look, just go an' get the vittles, will yer, an' remember the way back.'

Blaggut stumbled off into the woodland muttering to himself. 'No water, jus' vittles, an' remember the way back, got it. No vittles jus' remember an' water if y'come back, or was it don't remember water an' no vittles on the way back . . .'

Slipp covered his head with both paws and slept.

Mother Mellus and Saxtus, with several of the old and very young, stood on the path outside Redwall Abbey's west side. They held lanterns high, even though there was a full moon to give good light.

Blind Simeon turned his face south. 'Is that the search party coming from the direction of Saint Ninian's?' he asked.

'It is indeed,' said Sister Sage, peering down the path. 'Though I don't see the Dibbuns with them.'

'Have they been eaten by wildbeasts, Mellus?' one of the leverets piped up.

The old badger cuffed the young hare's ears gently. 'Of course not, and don't let me hear you spreading horrible stories around, by rights you should be in bed!'

Weary and paw-sore, the search party halted in front of the main gate. Tarquin threw the reception committee a tired salute. 'No sign of the little uns at all, I'm afraid; we covered a wide area, north, east and south, no joy whatsoever.'

The Abbot studied his paws in the moonlight. 'You did all you could. Come in now, we've held supper over for you. Tomorrow we'll start the search again at first light. Inside, you Dibbuns, come on now, bedtime.'

The Redwallers drifted into the Abbey grounds. Tarquin stayed back with Blind Simeon to secure the main gate for the night.

'Perhaps we'd better post sentries on the wall, they might wander home during the night,' said the blind sage as he felt about for the bar-lock. 'Dearie me, I can't help wishing that Joseph were here, he'd know what to do.'

Blaggut made his way back to the oak on the streambank, more by luck than judgement. He shook the sleeping form of his Captain vigorously. 'Cap'n, Cap'n, guess wot I found?'

Slipp yawned and blinked in the darkness. 'Don't tell me, a cask of seaweed grog and a roasted gull!'

'O, that's a good un, yer a one you are, Cap'n!' Blaggut chuckled heartily.

Slipp grabbed hold of the slow-witted scarat. 'I'm an 'ungry one right now, flop'ead, where's those vittles?'

'O er, vittles, er, there wasn't none,' Blaggut's voice rattled on with excitement. 'But I found two liddle beasts asleep, they're livin' in a tent jus' a stroll further up the bank, Cap'n!'

'You didn't wake 'em, did yer?'

'No, Cap'n, bless their liddle 'earts, they looked so peaceful. I came right back 'ere t'let you know.'

Slipp released Blaggut and shook his paw. 'That's the first sensible thing you've done today, mate. Now you lead me to 'em, nice an' quiet like!'

14

The onset of night in the dungeons of Castle Floret weighed deeply on Mariel and Dandin. They sat on the wide window ledge, tired, hungry and sore, watching the moon hanging like a buttered disc over the valley. Mariel was using the rope which had bound their foot-paws to fashion a new Gullwhacker. As she worked she wondered dolefully if she would ever get a chance to use it.

Dandin, half awake and half asleep, was imagining himself back at his beloved Redwall, strolling through the moonlit orchard with his friend Saxtus after supper, as the great Joseph bell softly boomed out the quarter; hearing the distant voice of Mother Mellus from the dormitory windows as she shooed Dibbuns off to bed; sensing the odours of apple, plum, strawberry and pear on the still, fragrant air. He was roused from his reverie by Mariel's voice.

'How does he do it? That old Field Marshal will sleep through anything – look at him.'

Meldrum the Magnificent was lying full stretch, his weighty stomach rising and falling to each snore. Dandin watched him, envious of the hare's capacity to recede into slumber at the wink of an eye.

Mariel stared up at the moon, speaking her thoughts aloud. 'That same moon will be shining over the Abbey now. I'll bet my Dad has taken himself off to bed, he's another one who can sleep anytime, night or day, it makes no difference to him.'

Dandin looked away from the window to the stark, hostile interior of their cell. 'Makes you wonder if we'll ever see Redwall again,' he said, his voice wistful. 'Though at the moment a beaker of water and a crust of bread would be a welcome sight.'

To take her friend's mind off food, Mariel climbed down from the window ledge, and said, 'We haven't explored this cell yet. Come on – let's see if we can find a weak spot to escape from.'

Dandin slid from the window ledge to join her. 'It all looks pretty solid and secure to me; they didn't build this place with a view to letting anyone break out.'

Together they inspected the dungeon. Walls and floor alike were heavy, close-jointed stone. Dandin tried probing the narrow cracks with his paws but soon gave up. 'Hammer and chisel'd help, know anywhere we could borrow 'em?' he said.

Mariel was staring upward. 'Hmm, ceiling's the same, rock solid. Let's take a look at the window bars.'

Meldrum was lying in their way, and they had to move him. The old hare opened one eye and muttered, 'What'n the name of flattened frogs are you chaps up to? Disturbin' my nocturnal repose, wot, no respect for age at all, that's the trouble with this young generation!'

'We're sounding the place out, looking for ways of escape,' said Mariel suppressing a smile. 'D'you mind moving away from the bars, sir?'

Meldrum moved, rather huffily. 'Whatcha goin' t'do, rip the bars out an' fly away?'

Dandin was kicking the bars with his footpaws. 'A chance is a chance, no matter how slim. Huh, it's no chance here though – creature who put these bars in knew what he was doing. They're bedded tight, set in the stone with molten lead, deep too, I imagine.'

Meldrum sat up, he stretched and yawned. 'Ah well, no rest for the righteous, I s'pose. So then, escape y'say, let's see. How did we get into this lockup?'

'How did we get in here?' said Mariel, looking at him quizzically. 'Obviously by way of the door!'

The hare wiggled his ears so that they rubbed together. 'Full marks, young mouseygel, now you're startin' to think properly, wot! Stands to reason, don't it, if the door is the entrance it's also the bally exit. Doors were made to close . . . and open, so let's inspect the jolly old portal!'

Together the three captives moved to the door. Mariel and Dandin, bowing to Meldrum's seniority, let him take over. 'Righty ho, young Dandin, bang loudly on this door, please.'

Without question Dandin started thumping as hard as he could. Nothing happened for a moment, then there was a sound of footpaws and a drowsy, irritable guard's voice rasped out, 'Stop that bangin' in there, prisoners!'

Meldrum adopted a whimpering tone. 'Please sir, we want a drink of water.'

His plea was followed by a harsh laugh from the guard. 'Water? You three ain't allowed no water, huh, only water you'll get is when they fling yer dead bodies inter the moat, now be quiet or you'll get a taste of me spearpoint. Shurrup, d'yer 'ear?'

This was followed by footpaws receding along the outside corridor. Meldrum winked, signalling them to keep their voices low. 'Number one, we've established that there's a sentry on duty, out there night an' day if I'm not mistaken. Two, the villain's armed with a spear, that'll come in useful when the time comes.'

'What time, and how can a guard with a spear be useful to us?' said Dandin.

The hare frowned. 'Don't interrupt laddie, unless y've got somethin' useful t'say. Now, about this door, I'm willin' to wager it's got a simple dungeon lock, see if you can take a quick peek.'

Dandin boosted Mariel up to the spyhole. By pushing her face hard sideways into it she strained her eye downward and was able to view the contrivance. 'You're right sir,' she said. 'It's just a long bolt that pushes through a staple driven into the side wall, no real locks or keys.'

'Good, good, exactly as I thought!' Meldrum snorted with satisfaction.

Dandin let Mariel down quietly. She shrugged, saying, 'It's a very strong bolt though, and we've no chance at all of reaching it.'

Meldrum was busily scanning the other side of the door. 'Why should we want t'reach it? Lock's prob'ly the strongest part of the door, we're lookin' for the weakest.'

'And what part is that, sir?' Mariel enquired.

The hare smiled craftily. 'The hinges, of course! This is better'n I thought, just look at these hinges, stupid things! The buffer who erected this door placed the hinges on the inside. Weakest part of a door, hinges, y'know, and these are no exception. Simple pin flattened both ends is the only thing holding this top one together, bottom's the same. Half rusted too I shouldn't wonder. There y'go, young warriors, remove two hingepins an' the door can be shoved outward!'

Dandin rubbed his paws delightedly. 'Aye, and if we shove hard enough the staple holding the bolt will be torn out of the wall by a big heavy door like this. The whole thing will fall flat into the corridor!'

'I hate to put a damper on things,' said Mariel, interrupting his jubilation, 'but how are we going to cut through the hingepins with no tools?'

Meldrum stroked his twirling mustachio thoughtfully. 'Good question, good question. Ah well, a chap's got to make sacrifices, only one thing for it.'

He inspected the medals left on his tunic – some of them had been lost as they were dragged along. Choosing carefully, he selected a huge, silver-coloured orb with serrated edges. 'See this, order of the shining sun, presented t'me by moles, can't recall exactly what it was for, jolly pretty though, doncha think. Very hard metal, made by mole craftbeasts, should do the job.'

Mariel tore a strip from the edge of her tunic and wound it around the bar which held the medal. 'Dandin, we'll work on the hingepins together. Meldrum sir, keep an eye to the spyhole in case the guard comes.'

Dandin took first try. Grunting with exertion, he scraped and sawed with the medal. He rewound the strip of cloth around it often, as his paws got scratched and tender.

A quarter of the way through the bottom hingepin, Mariel relieved him, hacking and sawing busily. 'We're not making too much noise are we, sir? Can you see the guard?'

Meldrum kept his eye glued to the spyhole. 'No, not really, but I think the blighter's kippin'. I can hear him snore every now an' then. How's it goin'?'

'It's hard, but I'm making good progress,' said Mariel, groaning as she changed position. 'Just a bit more on this one. Dandin, shove your footpaw against my back so I can lean harder on the medal. That's it!' A moment later she straightened up, holding a small length of rusty iron in her paw. 'There it is, the bottom hingepin!'

Heartened by the sight, Meldrum spat on his paws and took the medal from them. 'You two take turns at the spyhole, leave the top hinge t'me, wot?'

Using his considerable weight and strength the hare went at the hingepin with a good deal of brute force.

His sizeable stomach wobbled back and forth as he sawed, talking all the time to the remaining pin. 'Hah! Think y'can stand against the strongest hare alive, eh? Let me tell you, m'little feller, I've picked bigger than you out o' me molars after a good dinner!'

Gritting his teeth, Meldrum braced long hindpaws against the floor as he worried and tugged the hinge-pin. 'Come out! Out, I say sir! Gotcha, you rusty blighter!' The door stood free of its hinges, held only by the bolt staple. Meldrum the Magnificent winked at his comrades. 'Stage one completed! Stage two, how to proceed with a simple escape, lissen carefully in the ranks thah!'

The rat on guard was rudely awakened by panicked cries from the new prisoners.

'Guard, help, help! Aagh! Look what's in our cell! Help!'

Grumbling to himself, he shouldered his spear and lurched dozily along the corridor. 'Wot is it now? Will you three in there give your gobs a rest! Soon as I can, I'm goin' to 'ave yous gagged!' He appeared at the spy-hole waving his spear. 'Shut that noise up, wot's the matter . . .?'

Dashing from the far side of the cell the three prisoners hurled themselves bodily at the door.

Crash!

The staple holding the bolt flew from the wall as the door thudded flat into the corridor with the guard beneath it. Reaching under the door, Meldrum retrieved the guard's spear and unfastened the keys from his belt. Mariel twirled her new Gullwhacker.

Dandin motioned them to be silent. 'Sshh! Let's wait a moment to see if the noise has alerted anybeast . . .'

They stood stock-still for a short while. There was no response or indication that anyone had heard. Meldrum stole softly down the corridor, spear poised, to see if rats were on their way. As he passed one cell, a hoarse voice called him. 'Meldrum the Magnificent, is it really you?'

The hare had to look twice through the spyhole before he recognized the cell's occupant. 'Seasons of slaughter! King Gael!'

Swiftly unlocking the door, he hauled forth a squirrel, thin to the point of emaciation. Mariel and Dandin hurried forward to help support the frail figure of the Squirrelking.

A raucous cackle issued from the next cell. 'Gwaw! Norra nuff to mayka dinna thirr!'

Dandin peered through the spyhole, but withdrew hastily as the tip of a pointed beak sought his eye. Meldrum drew him to one side and, using the spearbutt, the hare rapped the beak sharply until it withdrew. Standing a cautious distance away, he looked through the spyhole.

Mariel was filled with curiosity. 'What is it, what's in there?' she said.

'Kchakchakcha! Glokkpod inna hirr!'

'By the ancient ears of me grandsires,' said Meldrum, turning to Mariel and Dandin. 'It's a shrike!'

'What's a shrike?' both mice chorused together.

The hare pointed to the cell with his spear. 'A maniac killer, that's what a shrike is. Butcher Birds some call 'em! Not as big as some owls, bigger'n most hawks hereabouts, but more dangerous than the lot of 'em! Stab y'to death with that beak an' hang you out on a thornbush like some cob o' meat, that's why they're known as Butcher Birds. Very rare, 'stremely dangerous!'

There was a flap on the bottom of the door to allow food to be pushed in. Meldrum held it up to let his friends see the shrike.

Gael sat against the far wall of the corridor breathing heavily.

'He's called Glokkpod,' said the Squirrelking. 'He

flew in there when they were replacing the old bars, and they blocked the window. Poor bird's been living in the dark – they torment it with spears just for fun.'

Mariel and Dandin could see the strange bird. It was indeed a great, red-backed shrike. The mousemaid murmured in a kindly tone to it, 'Hello there, don't be afraid of us. I'm Mariel and this is Dandin, Meldrum and Gael.'

Obviously crazed through captivity, the shrike laughed. 'Kchakchakcha! I Glokkpod, 'fraida nothin, Glokkpod killa! Watcha me alltime, badbird!'

Dandin looked away from the wild glittering eyes. 'Whew! Wouldn't like to meet him on a dark night.'

Glokkpod inched closer to the flap. 'Wouldan like meet me anytime, mousa!'

Meldrum shoved the shrike back with his spearbutt, saying, 'This is gettin' us nowhere, chaps. We've got to make good our escape an' take poor ol' Gael with us. I say there, Glukkpuddle, or whatever y'call y'self, listen! If you ain't with us you're against us, 'fraid I haven't time t'bandy words with you, understand?'

He received a swift reply. 'Openna door longears, Glokkpod witcha, killa rats, lotsa rats!'

The hare unlocked the cell and, standing to one side, he shoved the door open with his speartip. Glokkpod hopped out, eyes glittering, beak flicking from side to side. 'Glokkpod badbird, killa anybist!'

Mariel whispered to Dandin, 'Looks like we've caught a whirlwind by the tail!' Swinging her Gull-whacker she brought it within a hairsbreadth of the shrike's eye. 'Try killing this bist and you're on a loser!'

Completely unafraid, Glokkpod winked one beady eye at her. 'Glokkpod make jokah, kchakchakcha! On'y killa rats!'

'Help! Help! Murder! Escapin' prisoners, rouse the guard!' The rat sentry had crawled out from under the fallen door – he scampered off down the corridor in the opposite direction of the escapers, shrieking full blast. He was too far away to be caught – Meldrum's spear bounced harmlessly off the wall and he threw up his paws in disgust.

'Tchah! That's blown it, they'll be on us in force soon. Which way now, we can't go down, they'll be comin' up!'

Mariel shouldered her Gullwhacker. 'Like I said yesterday, there's only one way to go. Up!'

The sound of masses of hordebeasts dashing towards them clinched the issue. Supporting Gael, the three friends sped along the corridor and up the flight of stairs at the far end. Glokkpod brought up the rear.

It was a stone spiral staircase and it did not take them long to realize they were in a narrow round tower. The stairs seemed to continue endlessly upward, terminating in a small circular chamber. Sounds of guards pounding their way upwards reached them. Dandin shut the door and barred it from the inside. Crossing to a narrow slit window he looked out.

'We're twice as high up as we were before, it makes me dizzy just looking down. We're as high up as anybeast can go in this castle. Let's face it, we've trapped ourselves good and proper this time!'

As he spoke the first spearblades and axeheads came crashing through the door.

15

Late afternoon found *Pearl Queen* riding dangerously low in the water. Heavy swelling seas and an overcast sky were causing Finnbarr Galedeep problems. He muttered from between clenched teeth to Joseph as they fought to push the tiller hard over. 'We're shippin' too much water, mate, got to get 'er out o' this Roarin'burn current an' find land where we can make the *Queen* shipshape agin!'

A fork of lightning crackled across the western horizon. Joseph glanced up at the storm-bruised clouds. 'Aye, and we'd better make land soon, Finnbarr.'

Durry and Rufe stood in line, passing basins, bowls and buckets, anything the crew could lay their paws on to pass down the for'ard locker, where Log a Log and Rosie were baling out furiously.

Foremole felt useless. Stricken by a severe attack of seasickness, he sat in the scuppers moaning softly. 'Hurr, oi must be the furst ever green mole t'put t'sea. Burr, shame on oi! 'Ow be it goin' maister Quill?'

Durry staggered on the bucking deck as he emptied a bucket over the side. 'Not good at all, Foremole, the water's coming in so fast an' the sea's so heavy that it's

135

making the hole bigger!' Thunder boomed directly overhead, causing the crew to jump.

Finnbarr yelled orders as he clung gamely to the tiller. 'Slack sail afore we're driven under, slack sail! Keep balin' below decks there messmates ... Whooooooooaaah!' *Pearl Queen* lurched mightily as she slewed out of the Roaringburn current to eastward. Rain came in torrents, lashing and stinging, wind-driven curtains of it, until it was difficult for the crew to see each other. Night set in without warning, aided by the dark stormy skies. *Pearl Queen* was driven scudding sideways across the face of the deeps, sails torn and flapping, lines and ropes whipping viciously and masts creaking as she settled lower in the water.

'Belay the balin','' Finnbarr bellowed, ''tis doin' no good, we're in the paws o' fate now, mateys. Lash yerselves fast to anythin' that won't be washed overboard!'

Rosie and Log a Log were hauled out of the locker. They grabbed ropes and made themselves fast to the rails with the rest of the crew. Several of the shrews trapped Foremole as he came rolling past, a wet, furred ball of misery. 'Wohurr, let oi be drownded zurrs, loif b'aint gudd no mores furr the loikes of oi. Buhurr!'

Drenched as he was, Durry could see that Rufe was weeping from the way his body shook in the ropes that held him fast. The good hedgehog clutched his friend tightly. 'Bad luck fer us all, Rufey, but you stick by me and we'll go down t'gether. I won't leave ye to sink alone, Rufe Brush.'

The young squirrel buried his head against Durry's chest where the spines gave way to softer fur. 'Will they remember us for a long time at Redwall, Durry?' he wept.

The hedgehog gagged as he spat salt spray from his mouth. 'Always Rufe, that's how long they'll recall us. Father Abbot'll put up a marker stone with our names on, an' Mother Mellus'll teach young Dibbuns about us an' how bravely we perished. We'll be famous, I bet.'

Chain lightning lit up the whole eastern horizon as Joseph looked up. Suddenly he smiled through the torrential gale and cried out, 'Land ho!'

Finnbarr Galedeep grabbed Joseph's paw in a vicelike grip. 'Land ye say, Bellmaker – where away?'

'Due east, we're headed straight for it, that's if we don't fill up and sink first. Keep looking east, Finnbarr, next lightning flash will light it up.'

All the sea otter could see was black night, rain and spray in front of him. Suddenly there was a roll of thunder and sheet lightning illuminated everywhere, revealing a rocky coastline jutting up less than a league away! The realization that he could save his ship and crew sent Finnbarr roaring out commands again. 'Untie yerselves mates, start balin' agin! Log a Log, get yoreself in the bows an' watch out for reefs! Hoist for'ard sails to keep 'er stem up! Lively now, jump to it, me lucky buckoes!'

Pearl Queen became a hive of activity amidst the storm. Even Foremole picked himself up at the mention of land and began baling furiously. Whilst Joseph supervised deck operations, Rosie took several creatures up into the for'ard rigging to set the sails. Rufe and Durry scurried upward to the highest sails, Rosie ahead of them. The vessel heeled perilously as a towering wave struck her broadside on, and there was a piercing squeal.

The shrew named Fatch had been swept from a lower yardarm, and now he hung upside down, one footpaw snarled in a rope line. Rufe Brush was the only one who could see Fatch, dangling wrong way up, his head dipping under every time the ship swayed to port. Leaving Durry and Rosie to deal with the topsails, Rufe climbed back down to help the shrew. Battered by the blinding spray Rufe inched out along the low yardarm, calling to the shrew, 'Hang on, matey, I'm comin'!'

The entire yardarm dipped deep below the sea's boiling surface. Rufe locked both footpaws and tail around the timbers and reached out, catching Fatch by his ears. He pulled and hauled, the shrew alternately screeching in pain and swallowing water, but Rufe tugged savagely, knowing if he let go, Fatch was lost. With a mighty effort he hauled the shrew right side up, draping him across the yardarm. Rufe snatched the rapier from Fatch's belt, and hacked loose the rope that had trapped the shrew's footpaw. Then, fastening the unconscious shrew close to him with his own belt, Rufe clambered down into Finnbarr's waiting paws and collapsed with Fatch in a heap on the deck.

The sea otter blew stormwater from his whiskers, shaking his head in admiration at the plucky rescue. 'Yore a brave liddle beast Rufe, I never seen a creature so game in all me born days, an' that's a fact!'

Suddenly a single clap of thunder rang out directly above *Pearl Queen*, followed by an immense lightning bolt that struck the ship. An eerie blue light enveloped every creature aboard, as their fur stood out straight from their bodies. There was a rending crack; the foremast snapped like a twig and was hurled off into the darkness.

'Durry! Rosie! They've gone!' Rufe Brush screamed. 'They were up the mast!'

Joseph had to grab Rufe – the young squirrel was about to dive over the side and swim to find his friends. The Bellmaker held the kicking, struggling squirrel fast. 'Rufe, Rufe, have y'gone mad? You'd be drowned in a trice out there, we can't even see where the mast went!'

But there was no reasoning with the squirrel. He fought Joseph wildly, striking him with all paws. 'Let me go! I've got to save Durry, he's all I've got!'

Joseph flinched as Rufe's paws battered his face. He held on grimly until there was nothing else for it.

Whack!

The sturdy Bellmaker laid Rufe senseless with a single blow to the squirrel's jaw, then he laid him down safe. 'Poor Rufe, I wish you hadn't made me do that.'

For what seemed endless hours the crew of the *Pearl Queen* battled with the elements, fighting to bring their vessel to the land, which now appeared temptingly close, but so difficult to reach. Windblown and soaked they moved with frozen paws and numbed minds, automatically forcing themselves to go about their tasks. Log a Log was standing far out on the prow, watching for hidden rock shoals, and he did not have time to brace himself when *Pearl Queen* shuddered and ground to a halt. The shrew Chieftain was thrown overboard. Foremole saw him go; he ran to the bows yelling, 'Shrew overbooooooard!'

The crew dashed for'ard in Log a Log's wake, stopping sharply as they reached the bows.

'Hohohoho, lookit me!' It was Log a Log, standing only waist deep in the water.

Finnbarr Galedeep drew both his swords, brandishing them at the storm and the heaving seas. 'Haharr, we beat yer, you never got Galedeep an' the *Queen* that time!'

Carrying Rufe on his back, Joseph called everybeast to abandon ship and make their way to shore. Foremole moved with a speed not associated with his kind – he fairly scooted through the shallows to the dry land, where, lying flat on the beach, he kissed it fervently. 'Oo urr, oi luvs ee gudd furm urth!'

The remainder of the night the crew spent miserably, crouching behind a rocky outcrop, as the storm spent its fury over the heaving seas, driving *Pearl Queen* even further up on to the tideline. Without food or drink they huddled together, utterly spent and fatigued. Through the grey dawn they slept, unaware that the storm had abated, and the tide had slipped silently out leaving *Pearl Queen* high and dry, listed over at a crazy angle. High rolling clouds drifted westward on a calming breeze while the skies turned deep blue.

The warm sun beating down on his back, mingled with the plaintive cry of seabirds, gradually brought Joseph awake. He sat up stiffly and looked around. They were on a wide sandy beach, backed by huge brown cliffs dotted with greenery. *Pearl Queen* had been washed up only paces away from where the Bellmaker sat. Sometime before dawn Rufe Brush had regained consciousness, only to cry himself back to sleep with the realization that Durry had been lost at sea. Joseph drew quietly away from his slumbering form, seeing Finnbarr up and about.

The sea otter had boarded his vessel and found food for breakfast, and now he was busy building a fire from dry driftwood he had gathered above the tideline. Smiling kindly, he greeted Joseph. 'Mornin' t'ye, Bellmaker, lend a paw 'ere. We'll get vittles goin' fer the crew atween us.'

They mixed oatmeal with dried fruit and a little fresh water to make flat moist cakes, which they laid on a metal shield from the ship's armoury and placed over the fire. Taking dried mint leaves and honey, Joseph put them in a pan Finnbarr had brought from the ship and soon had a fine brew of mint tea boiling.

'Mmm, is that mint tea an' oat scones I smell?' Log a Log came to squat by the fire, followed by the others as the rest of the crew came awake.

Breakfast was taken thankfully. They sat on the sun-warmed sands, glad to be alive after their ordeal on the deep. Finnbarr retrieved a batch of fresh-baked scones from the shield, nodding towards his ship. 'Straight after brekkist we'd best take a look at the *Queen*, she's in need of a new foremast an' a repair job to 'er hull fer starters, no tellin' wot else needs doin'.'

Joseph sat with a comforting paw about Rufe. The young squirrel was eating: hunger and thirst had driven him, with the Bellmaker's urging, to take some breakfast.

Joseph indicated Rufe with a nod of his head. 'Finnbarr, the first thing we must do is to remember our two friends who were lost in last night's storm.'

'Aye, right you are mate,' said the sea otter, putting aside his breakfast. 'Let's do that here an' now!'

A small stone cairn was built on the shore above the tideline soon afterwards. With Joseph's help, Rufe had taken a piece of flat timber and burned a message upon it with a heated knife. The crew of *Pearl Queen* stood around the neat heap of stones as Rufe fixed the wood securely between the top stones facing seaward. Log a Log read the simple message.

'To the memory of Rosie Woodsorrel, warrior and mother. Also Durry Quill, Cellarmaster. Two Redwall friends.'

Still with his paw about Rufe's shoulder, Joseph recited some words he had put together for the ceremony.

'Friend is a very small word,
A little sound we make,
For one who is true, one who will do,
Great deeds for friendship's sake.
So while I grieve for you, my friends,
Who gave all that you could give,
You'll be my friends in memory,
For all the days I'll live.'

Tears ran openly down Foremole's honest face. 'Oi doan't be knowen wot zurr Tarquin an' ee liddle uns be a doin' wi'out miz Rose, they'm be gurtly sad!'

Log a Log patted the stones. 'I know it sounds funny, but I miss that laugh of Rosie's.'

The shrew Fatch took Rufe earnestly by his paw. 'Lissen, young un, some good always comes out o' misfortune. If'n you'd been up that mast then you'd have been lost with 'em. But you ain't lost, an' I ain't neither, cos you risked your life an' saved mine. Rufe, I'm your friend for life now!'

Though Finnbarr Galedeep was a tough-looking otter, he was deeply touched at the sight of Rufe and Fatch shaking paws together over the cairn. The sea otter turned away, gazing at the high cliffs to forestall a tear dropping. But he soon forgot his sorrow.

'Stand by crew, git yoreselves armed! We've got visitors an' they're a-comin' fast!'

Loud war whoops split the summer morning air as masses of creatures poured down from the cliffs, heading straight for the crew of *Pearl Queen*.

16

The two Dibbuns huddled together in terror as the ugly heads of Slipp and Blaggut poked into their makeshift tent. The searat Captain snarled at them. 'Give us vittles or we'll eat yer!'

Blaggut was horrified by Slipp's pronouncement. 'O Cap'n, you wouldn't eat two pretty liddle babbies like them, would yer?'

Slipp bit Blaggut's ear and punched his snout. 'Will you shuttup an' let me do the talkin', doodlenose!'

Despite his smarting ear and throbbing nose, Blaggut winked chummily at the Dibbuns. 'Never fear, me liddle chicks, ole Cap'n Slipp won't eat yer, he's got an 'eart of gold!'

Slipp yanked Blaggut out of the tent and began booting his rump soundly. 'I told yer once already, scrummitchops, keep yer stupid mouth shut until I tells yer to speak . . . Yowch!'

The mousebabe had regained his confidence and was jabbing his 'sword' stick in Slipp's back. 'You leava 'im alone, big bully!' he squeaked.

'Ooh, me liver'n'kidneys!'

Slipp sat down nursing his back. Blaggut was all concern. 'Aye aye, liddle feller, that was a naughty thing ter do, you've gone an' 'urted the pore Cap'n's livers'n'kidney. 'Ere, let me 'elp yer up, Cap'n. Are you shipshape?'

Slipp drew his cutlass, raging, 'I'll slice that cheeky snippet in arf afore 'e's much older, let me at the swab!'

Blaggut placed himself between the mousebabe and Slipp. 'You kin cut me in three arfs if'n yer like Cap'n, but don't yew lay a blade near that there h'infant!'

Furrtil had regained her composure by now. She attached herself to Blaggut's leg, chuckling, 'Oi loik ee zurr, you'm a funny vurmint!'

'D'yer 'ear that, Cap'n? The liddle molemaid likes me!' The searat's face was a picture of delight.

Slipp's voice dripped sarcasm that was lost on the un-witting Blaggut. 'Ho, she likes yer, does she, well ain't that nice. Why don't we all siddown an' 'ave a pick-ernick?'

The big, slow searat patted his Captain affectionately, nearly knocking him flat. 'Arr that's the spirit, Cap'n, I knew you'd see things my way.'

Slipp's seabooted footpaw began moving in the direc-tion of Blaggut's behind. The mousebabe brandished his stick, squeaking, 'You kickim an' I stick your livers'a-'kiddies . . . !'

Slipp stamped his foot down and glared at the mousebabe. 'Don't yew 'ave no vittles at all?'

The mousebabe thought about this for a moment, then replied, 'Wot's vikkles?'

Blaggut sat down next to the Dibbun, chuckling, 'Hoho, bless yer liddle 'eart matey, vittles is food!'

'Hurr, food!' Furrtil nodded understandingly. 'Loik pudden an' pie an' cakes an' soop?'

'Yes, yes, that's the stuff,' Slipp said, nodding eagerly. 'Pudden'pie'cake an' soup, where is it, 'ave you got any?'

The mousebabe thought quite deeply about the question then stated matter-of-factly, 'No!'

Blaggut laughed until tears rolled down his ugly face. 'That babbie mouse is a cool un, Cap'n!'

Furrtil trundled off into the woodland. Slipp looked after the molemaid curiously. 'Where does she think she's off to?' he asked.

The mousebabe curled his lip scornfully at Slipp's ignorance. 'Vurmint your size shoulda know tha', she gone to get food vikkles for ya, shoopid!'

The searat Captain brought his face close to the Dibbun, sneering nastily. 'Don't call me stupid, and I'm a rat, not a vurmint!'

The mousebabe sat himself on Blaggut's lap in a business-like manner and explained patiently to Slipp, 'Rats *is* vurmints. Anybeast know tha', an' if you not shoopid then don' ask shoopid questions.'

Slipp began drawing his cutlass, then thought better of it, blew a snort of exasperation and glared at Blaggut. 'Why did yer 'ave t'go an' find this wisemouth, why didn't yer just bring back vittles like I told yer to?' he growled.

Blaggut stroked his new friend's head fondly. ''E don't mean nothin', Cap'n. You leave the liddle tyke t'me, I wager we kin chat like ole messmates. Avast, 'ere's the molemaid back wid vittles.'

Furrtil ambled up and emptied her apron. Two apples, some wild plums and a small pile of blackberries tumbled out. The searats began wolfing the fruit.

'Tsk tsk, you'm maken eeselfs sick piggen et all daown,' she chided them. 'Chew ten toimes an' swaller more slow, ee Muther Mellus allus sayin' that to Dibbuns.'

Slipp spat out a plumstone. 'Wot's a Dibble?' he asked.

'Hurr, us'n's Dibbuns zurr, b'aint Diddles.'

Blaggut polished an apple on his stomach, saying, 'An' where does Dibbuns live, in liddle tents like yonder one?'

The mousebabe popped a blackberry into his friend's mouth. 'Norra tent, on'y a blanket. We come from a h'abbey, name a Redwall, bigga place than this high.' He held a tiny paw as far over his head as he could, to indicate the size of the Abbey.

Slipp whispered to Blaggut, 'Find out where it is.'

The mousebabe shook his head despairingly and pointed an accusing paw at Slipp. 'No whisp'rin', s'bad manners. We take you to Redwall inna mornin', if we c'n find it.'

An hour later the two Dibbuns were sound asleep in their tent. Slipp scoffed at Blaggut who sat at the entrance watching them. 'Ahoy nurseymaid, d'yew reckon they'll want a drink o' water in the night?'

The searat took off his tattered jerkin and carefully covered the two small creatures. 'Aye, well, if they do, Cap'n, I'll get it for 'em!'

Slipp tossed an apple core at Blaggut. 'Well lookit yew, the bold searat, yew butterbrained brute, 'ave y'gone soft all of a sudden?'

'Don't cost nothin' t'be nice to babes,' Blaggut shrugged. 'May'ap if somebeast'd been nice to me when I was a liddle shrimp I wouldn't 'ave growed up t'be no searat, might've been good an' respectable, who c'n tell, Cap'n?'

Slip leapt up and grabbed Blaggut by the throat. 'You 'ave gone soft!' he snarled. 'Well lissen, softrat, when we gets ter this Redwall place there might be plunder an' killin' so don't yew go soft on me then, or else y'll feel my cutlass across yore gizzard, do y'hear?'

Blaggut gulped and nodded. He knew only too well what his Captain was capable of. When there was loot to be had, murder and treachery became a mere formality to avaricious searats like Slipp. Blaggut took one last look at the two Dibbuns before settling himself down to sleep at the tent entrance, hoping in his heart that the tiny pair were so lost that they would not know the way back to Redwall Abbey on the morrow.

Early sunrays filtered through the slitted windows of the high tower room on to the besieged friends. Nagru's grey rats packed the narrow winding stairway outside, with the Foxwolf exhorting them on to slaughter. 'Come on – there's enough of you! Hack that door to splinters and finish them off. Sourgall, you and Wet-chops go and fetch a battering ram, that'll speed things up!'

The chamber was home to one piece of furniture, an old wooden bench. Meldrum and Dandin held it wedged against the door as a temporary measure. The old hare looked worried.

'Hear that, the blaggards have gone t'get a batterin' ram. They'll smash this door t'smithereens! Look out!'

Dandin hopped to one side at Meldrum's warning, as a spear ploughed through the damaged woodwork, protruding almost half its length. Nipping in smartly, Mariel grabbed the haft and tugged the weapon through, then began jabbing through the slits in the door at the enemy outside.

'If I've got to go I'm taking a few with me!' she shouted.

Gael Squirrelking stared despairingly round the small tower chamber. 'There's nowhere else for us to go, once they're through that door we're finished!'

The red-backed shrike Glokkpod had been hopping about excitedly, waiting to give good account of himself when the rats came through the door. At Gael's announcement he ceased his dance, flicking hither and thither with his head as he searched for an avenue of escape. 'Good littil nest uppa thirr!' he croaked.

Gael followed the shrike's eyes upward. 'Of course!' he cried out. 'This is a tower with a pointed top, there's a small cone-shaped attic up there!'

Meldrum the Magnificent grabbed the crosshilts of a long pike that came thrusting through the door, wrenching it forcibly from its owner. 'Any port in a storm, wot, let's give it a try!'

It was a simple crossplanked ceiling, resting on thick wooden beams. Using the butt of the pike, the hare soon knocked two of the centre planks loose. 'C'mon birdie, do your stuff, up there an' push those planks t'one side!' he shouted.

There came a cry from Nagru out on the stairway. 'Out the way, you four, get on that battering ram with Sourgall an' Wetchops! Give them space there!'

Anxiously, Mariel watched Glokkpod flap awkwardly upward, calling, 'Hurry, bird – there's not a moment to lose. They're going to start battering the door!'

The shrike shoved and pulled until he had moved one plank aside. Wedging himself in the narrow space he had created, Glokkpod used both talons and beak to shift the other ceiling plank. Suddenly it shot aside with a clatter, and he disappeared through the opening, cackling, 'Kchakcha, eazy, wassa eazy, good nest uppa hirr!'

Meldrum shot an irate glance at the attic. 'Glad you've found yourself a good nest, old chap, now d'you mind hoppin' down here an' helpin' out?'

Surprisingly the shrike did hop down. Flashing his bright savage eyes at the hare, he demanded, 'Wharra want, longirrz?'

'I say, less of the longears. See if y'can help our friends up into the attic, mattressback!'

The shrike's feathers bristled dangerously as he glared at Meldrum. 'Don'ta call Glokkpod matrissback!'

With a boom and a crack the battering ram struck the door, sending splinters flying. Mariel placed herself between Meldrum and Glokkpod. 'Are you two going to stand here insulting one another,' she said, her voice tight with anger, 'or do you feel like helping out round here before we're all killed?'

The shrike made a circular movement with his beak. 'All uppa thirr, leave thizz ta me!'

The ram thudded against the door a second time. Meldrum took the now-useless bench and, laying it ladder-fashion against the wall, he scrambled ponderously up into the attic. Leaning out, Meldrum thrust both paws down to assist the other three. Helped by Dandin and Mariel, Gael climbed quickly into the small conical room.

The ram struck the door a third time, creating a gaping hole at its centre. Backing out of spearthrust range, the great red-backed shrike stood in full view of the rats outside. Glokkpod's mad eyes shone with joy as he gave vent to his battlecry.

'Kachakachakiiirrrrr! Hirrs a butcha bird, ratzz!'

There was an immediate scramble as the horderats retreated from the door at the sight of the Butcher Bird. Nagru was almost knocked flat. He pulled himself upright, raking wildly with his metal wolfclaws, and screaming, 'Charge the door or I'll flay you alive. Charge!'

Urged on by the claws of Nagru they rushed the door. Riveneye kicked aside the loose door timbers; swinging a sword he rushed into the tower room. Death was on him in a blur of feathers, talons and stabbing beak. Nagru pushed two more rats through immediately – they were slain before they had time to draw breath. Glokkpod's talons rattled against the floor as he spread his pinion feathers in a war dance. One wing had been badly torn by a rat's spear and several feathers were missing. Glokkpod was infuriated by this injury.

'Kirrchakkachirrr izza good day to fearrrrr me!'

Silvamord pushed her way through the rats on the spiral staircase. She whirled on Nagru, berating him. 'Fool! Can't you see that bird can hold the doorway as long as it likes while you send in hordebeasts a few at a time?'

'Well, there's the Butcher Bird, my dear,' said the Foxwolf, his voice dripping condescension. 'What's your bright idea?'

Ignoring his patronizing tones, Silvamord gave her orders. 'Back out of sight, all of you. Hooktail, pick out ten good archers, get on the third and fourth steps down and keep firing heavy volleys until you've made a pincushion of that bird!'

The friends in the attic had heard Silvamord's commands. Mariel called out urgently to Glokkpod, 'Quickly, fly up here before they start shooting!'

But the shrike continued his dance, challenging the rats. 'Kirrchakachirrr! Glokkpod fear no ratzz!'

'It's no good talking to that one,' Dandin sighed wearily. 'He's going to get himself killed. Save your breath.'

Meldrum solved the problem with a few barbed insults. 'I say there, y'great flyin' featherbed, d'you keep your brains in your beak or your bottom, nestnoddle!'

With a lurch and a flapping leap the shrike was up in the attic with them, standing eye-to-eye with Meldrum. Quickly, Mariel and Dandin slammed the attic floorboards back in place. Not a second too soon – the planking quivered to the thud of arrows.

'Hullo, that's a bit much,' Meldrum called out to them moodily, 'leavin' a chap in the dark with a bally Butcher Bird. Shed a bit o' light on the subject someone, it's pitch black in here!'

Dandin had brought a spear up with him. Using the butt he knocked a few of the rooftiles aside, dodging as they fell in. Sunlight streamed in, flooding the attic. Mariel looked round at their refuge. It was the inside of a conically tiled towertop and through the broken roof she could see a tiny flagpole flying a gaily coloured pennant.

The commanding voice of a rat sounded from the room below. 'My Lord and Master Urgan Nagru, King of all Southsward, Foxwolf Supreme and his Queen Silvamord send this message to you! Be it known that if you surrender yourselves to his mercy, the Urgan Nagru will spare your lives, all save that of the Butcher Bird – the creature is too dangerous to live. Hear this and know these are the words of the Urgan Nagru, all powerful in battle and ruler of all he sees!'

Hefting one of the red pottery rooftiles, Meldrum shifted aside a floorplank. He flung the tile accurately, laying the rat low.

'All merciful indeed. Poppycock! Did y'hear that, Glokko?'

The shrike bowed, deferentially. 'Nize shot Melderrin!'

'Oh I dunno, you could've prob'ly done as well y'self, old lad,' the hare shrugged modestly. 'By the way, it's Mel-drum, as in boom boom. Drum!'

The shrike nodded understandingly. 'Derrin, bum bum, like in drim!'

Gael stared up at the cloudless patch of blue sky that could be seen through the hole in the roof. 'Well, we're free in a way I suppose,' he said, 'free to stay up here and starve until the Foxwolf and Silvamord find a way of winkling us out and killing us all.'

Mariel removed a few more tiles until she could see further outside. 'If we could only find a way of getting down there,' she mused.

Meldrum took a peek and covered his eyes. 'Great seasons, it makes me go all of a dither just thinkin' about it. Now I know why birds always look dizzy!'

'Birds, there's a bird here, he could do it!' They all turned to look at the Squirrelking, pointing at Glokkpod as if seeing him for the first time. 'There's the bird!'

Dandin shook his head, totally nonplussed. 'But what use is Glokkpod to us?'

Gael was shaking with excitement. 'Maybe he can't fly us down with that injured wing, but he can go and get help for us! He can find the otters, they'll be able to help us!'

Silvamord had tired of watching Nagru commanding archers to shoot ceaseless arrows into the tower room ceiling. She wandered off to her chamber, which was on the same floor as the banqueting room. There she sat discussing the situation with Sicant, a female horderat who often doubled as the vixen's maid. They took wine and a roasted fish together, and Sicant was careful to agree with all Silvamord's views.

'You're right, of course, my Lady. Sooner or later those escaped prisoners will be starved down from there.'

Silvamord tapped her chin knowingly. 'Malebeasts, they're all the same, not happy unless they're fighting. Nagru will keep those archers firing arrows into the ceiling, and for what? A waste of arrows, that's all. Now as for me, I prefer to fight when the time is right. It's brains that win in the end.'

She smiled as a paw rapped gently on the door. 'Watch and I'll show you what I mean, Sicant. Come in!'

A small, furtive-looking rat stole into the room and bowed, saying, 'Majesty, you were right, the Butcher Bird flew off a short while ago. It headed north and east slightly, I watched until it was out of sight.'

Pouring a beaker of wine, the vixen pushed it towards the rat. 'You did well, Bluebane. Go now and say nothing of this to anybeast.' Taking the beaker of wine with him, Bluebane slunk away.

The vixen turned to Sicant. 'Your mate, Graywort, he's willing to serve me?'

Sicant nodded eagerly. 'To the death, my Lady. He is like me, he knows that you are the real power on the throne of Southsward.'

Silvamord took a dainty sip of wine. 'Good! Riveneye was slain today and we need a new horde Captain. I'll see that Graywort is promoted. Now, tell him to post six lookouts around the castle and keep one full squad in readiness night and day. The Butcher Bird is bound to bring help for the prisoners in the tower attic. When the lookouts spot them coming, tell them to report to your Graywort. As soon as he hears that help is arriving he must come directly to me and no other, is that understood?'

Sicant knelt and kissed the vixen's paw gratefully. 'I understand, Majesty.'

17

A small mole almost bowled Furpp over as he dashed into the mole dwelling. The old fellow kept himself upright by catching hold of the youngster, and said, 'Yurr Bruggit, whurr be ee 'astenin' off to?'

Bruggit saluted the oldster hurriedly. 'Zurr, thurr be a gurt burd out yon, ee'm be a-callen sumthen fearful furr ee otter an' maister Bowly!'

Furpp took Bruggit outside. 'Naow, whurr be ee burd?'

Bruggit tugged on Furpp's digging claw. 'O'er this way zurr, you'm can 'ear 'im, 'earken!'

Furpp listened carefully. On the mid-morning air the sounds of Glokkpod came drifting clearly over a dune.

'Kcha kcha! Irriz otter, Bowly Pintip, whirr are yirr?' The Butcher Bird hove into view over the hilltop, walking with his customary swagger as he called out the names. Furpp had seen Butcher Birds before. Carefully stowing Bruggit behind him, out of the bird's view, he called, 'A mornen to ee zurr burd, whurr cum ye frum?'

The shrike cocked a bright eye towards the mole. 'I, Glokkpod, come from Miriel and Dindin, Meldrin and Squirrelking, they say find otters.'

'Burr, you'm foller an oi'll take ee to otterfolk,' said

Furpp, turning towards his dwelling. 'Us'll feed ee too, if'n you'm promise not to go an eaten of uz.'

There were mixed emotions inside the cavernous mole dwelling. The Squirrelqueen and her little son were overjoyed at the news that Gael was still alive. However, the feeling swiftly changed to one of anxiety when they were told of the peril that Gael and their friends were in. Iris soon took command of the meeting.

'We'll go to Castle Floret tonight, as soon as it gets close to dark. If they haven't been recaptured we'll see what's the best way to get them out of there. Glokkpod, how long do you think they can hold out?'

The Butcher Bird was hastily gobbling cold turnip'n' tater pie, and he shrugged as he explained between beakfuls, 'Don't know, mibbee long time, mibbee not so long. Lotsa ratz, lotsa weaponz!'

Bowly Pintips, who had placed himself in command of the four leverets, hefted his two hard scones. 'Rats don't bother us, we be warriors!'

Glokkpod choked on a piece of pie as he laughed, 'Kchakcha kcha! Yirr only infints!' The young hedgehog ignored the jibe, but the leverets were indignant.

'Steady on there an' have a care sir!'
'Aye, you wouldn't like to tangle with these infants!'
'Infants indeed, infant y'self sir!'
'Great feathered windbag!'

The shrike's bright eye rested on Foghill, the last one to speak. 'Meldrin yirr father?'

Foghill treated the question with the contempt he thought it deserved. 'Tchah, old uncle Mel my pater? I should think not!'

Iris ignored the interchange as she started arrangements. 'Troutlad, Greenbeck, get the others together, we'd best start out now. Bring all the ropes you can find.'

Bowly insisted that he and the hares go along too. Iris refused flatly, but softened the blow by telling him that he and the hares should stay behind to protect the Squirrelqueen and her young one.

Firgan was a big tough rat; he patrolled silently around the east side of Castle Floret, as Greywort had told him to. Confidently he strode the valley floor, poking and prodding at bushes with his spear. It was early evening, still light, when Firgan sat down to take his food. Tilting a flask of water the rat drank deeply, unaware of the huge paws that came silently from behind his neck. He managed one startled gurgle before the flask slipped from his lifeless claws. The huge paws receded, accompanied by a cracking snap as the broken spear was tossed carelessly aside into the bushes.

On the south side another of the rat patrol heard a noise behind a nearby rock. Padding stealthily forward he went to investigate, a long curved sword held ready. A large slingstone hit him at the base of his skull – he fell poleaxed by the missile. A smaller, sleeker pair of paws took the sword and, wedging it between two rocks, they snapped the blade effortlessly.

Night was starting to set in when Silvamord grew impatient. She snarled at Sicant, 'There should be some news by now of rescuers coming. What's Graywort doing out there, dreaming?'

The female horderat went to the door and looked out. 'Here he comes, my Lady,' she said, relieved.

Graywort entered the chamber carrying a ruined pike and a snapped sword. He was frightened, breathless, glancing back over his shoulder as if he were being followed. 'M'lady, they're dead, Firgan, Gringol, and the rest of them, slain!'

Silvamord sprang up, knocking the useless weapons from the horderat's dithering paws. 'Stop babbling and talk sense, you fool! Here, sit down, drink this and pull yourself together!'

Elderberry wine slopped down Graywort's chin as he drank greedily. Having finished, he told his story.

'I posted the six guards, just as you commanded, told them t'watch for a party of otters. Later I went out to see if they had anything to report . . .'

Silvamord leaned closer, staring hard at Graywort. 'And?'

'Majesty, they were all dead, the six of them! First I found Gringol – his neck had been snapped like a twig! Look at this pike, it's shattered, broken in two places. What sort of wild beast had the strength to do that? Then I ran to find the others, they were either killed by slingstones or their necks had been busted like Gringol and Firgan's. I heard a noise in the bushes, a rumble and growling, and I ran for my life. Somebeast was tryin' to track me down – I never stopped to look back, just dashed straight into the castle!'

The vixen hastily armed herself from a wall cupboard, buckling on a sword and grabbing a bow and arrows. 'Where's that special squad I told you to have standing by? Get them up on their paws! I'll find out what sort of beast is at the bottom of all this!'

Meldrum leapt to one side as a pikehead came smashing through the floorboards. Gael had taken to sitting on the upper beams where the rooftiles had been removed and staring down at the steadily deteriorating floor, and the arrowheads, spearblades, pikeshafts and swords that were reducing it to splinters. Dandin tapped the Squirrelking's paw lightly.

'Move over Sire, I'm coming up there with you, it's safer!' Mariel followed suit shortly, then between them they hauled Meldrum up to the relative safety of the sloping roof.

Meldrum pulled a tile loose and aimed it between a rift in the floorboards. 'Take that y'blighters!' He was rewarded by the sound of an agonized rat squeal.

Mariel watched gathering cloud masses being swept in from westward, and she groaned, 'Oh no, rain, that's all we need! Still, I suppose it'll provide us with a drink. No sign of Glokkpod yet?'

Dandin scoured the sky to the north. 'No, I wish he'd hurry up. D'you suppose he's found the otters yet? He could be completely lost.'

'Wouldn't surprise me,' Meldrum the Magnificent snorted. 'I'll wager the rogue's flown off someplace to fill his stomach. Never met any Butcher Birds before, but if that'n is a specimen then they're a pretty shabby lot, if y'ask me.'

Nagru stood in the doorway of the tower room, out of the range of roof tiles. The Foxwolf was confident that he would recapture his prisoners. 'Wetchops, Ragfen, keep 'em stabbing upward. That ceiling won't last much longer, then we can bring them down with arrows. Don't kill them, just wound them a mite, I want our friends alive for a bit of fun.'

Bluebane came scurrying up the stairs and tugged at Urgan's wolfhide. The Foxwolf smiled. 'Ah, my little eyes and ears, what is your lovely Queen up to now that I should know about?'

They held a short whispered conversation together. Nagru patted his informant's back, saying, 'Well done, Bluebane. Now go and find Graywort, tell him I want to see him up here, right away.'

Bluebane stood on the lower stair as if waiting for something. Nagru looked at him curiously. 'What are you waiting for, my little spy?'

Bluebane fidgeted with his tattered tunic. 'Sire, Queen Silvamord rewarded me with a beaker of elderberry wine.'

The Foxwolf smiled understandingly. 'Ah, I see, you'd like a reward from me too, is that it?'

The spy nodded eagerly. Nagru spoke softly, dangerously.

'Life is the highest reward of all, my friend. Double dealers and traitors often receive death as their payment. But I will not slay you for your treachery to me and my Queen – I give you your life as a reward, you are spared. Now go and do my bidding.' Without another word Bluebane sped gratefully away.

18

It was late afternoon. Rain began falling in large spots, slowly at first, then it gathered force into a major downpour. On a wooded slope of Castle Floret's valley a score of otters threaded their way through the undergrowth. The quick eyes of Greenbeck picked up a movement close by; a sharp wave of his paw sent Iris and the rest of the troop into a crouch, wary and silent. They held their breath, watching keenly as Silvamord and her horderats tramped by, hardly a pawlength from them.

When they had passed, Troutlad stood up hefting a javelin.

Iris pulled him down, saying, 'Not yet, we don't want them to know we're here, and besides, we don't know if there's more of 'em patrolling. Where's the Butcher Bird?'

Glokkpod poked his head out of a wet swathe of feathers. 'Hirr I am, Glokkpod not like thiz ryne!'

Iris blew rainwater from her muzzle enjoyably. 'Nothing wrong with a bit of clean rain! Now, show me the tower our friends are trapped in.'

Not being airborne, it took the shrike a little while to find the exact location. The otter troop hid among the trees as Glokkpod pointed his beak upward at the highest point of Floret, crying, 'Thirr, up thirr they are.'

Iris looked up. From where she was, the tower was a mere pinpoint, almost invisible in the rain. 'Butcher Bird, fly up there and tell our friends we've arrived,' she said. 'Ask them what they want us to do. It looks impossible to help anybeast trapped that high up.'

The four escaped prisoners were sitting out on the roofbeams, open-mouthed as they caught raindrops to drink. Glokkpod landed alongside them; settling himself on a beam he stared down at the weapons chopping through the splintered floor of the attic. 'Ratz gonna gitcha soon if you notta 'scape hirr.'

Mariel wiped a paw across her mouth. 'You're here at last! Have you brought help?'

The shrike dipped his beak towards the valley floor. 'Down thirr, otters, Irriz say how they gonna help, whatcha want them to do?'

'Hmph! Should've thought that was jolly obvious,' said Meldrum, twitching his ears in annoyance. 'A whacking great long rope'll do the trick, wot!'

'Kchakcha kcha! No rope that big, longirrs!'

The hare shot the Butcher Bird a murderous glance. 'I've warned you once about calling me longears, you great puffed up windbag!' But he was speaking to empty space, the shrike had flown down to the otters.

Greenbeck shook his head. 'A long rope, mate? There's never been a rope that long in the history of seasons. What d'you think, Iris?'

The female otter leader moved this way and that, viewing the Castle from different angles. 'You're right, there's no such thing as a rope that long, but I think they could do it with a shorter rope. Greenbeck, what d'you think of this as an idea . . .'

All four prisoners were now ripping tiles from the roof and hurling them through the sizeable hole which hordebeast weapons had created in the attic floor. Their attack was so ferocious it had driven the rats from the tower room out on to the spiral staircase. Even Gael Squirrelking was throwing tiles with every ounce of strength he could muster. Dandin took his time, waiting until he could see a venturesome rat poke its head into view before he hurled a tile.

'We'll only keep them at bay for as long as these tiles last, then Nagru will send his archers in to pick us off,' he said.

Mariel struggled to loosen a tile from a crossbeam. 'That's true, make each shot count. Glokkpod, what news?'

The Butcher Bird landed almost sideways, gripping the small flagpole at the apex of the tower.

'Lissin t'thiz silly idea, it's yirr only hope.' He explained Iris's scheme to them. Meldrum looked positively crestfallen at the wild notion.

'Let me get this straight, you chaps. The otters can send us a rope up that's not very long. Right, then we double it over a beam and one of us swarms down it and swings to and fro until he can reach the battlements at the end of the west wall. He lands on the battlements then one by one the rest of us shimmy down the blinkin' rope an' swing like bloomin' pendulums until we're all on the bally battlements.'

Dandin continued, 'Then we loose the rope, hitch it round the battlement and swarm down into the moat, out of the moat and climb down the rest of the plateau. Sounds dangerous, but I'll risk it! What about you Meldrum?'

'Outbloominrageous! Fiddlesticks, totally impossible!'

Glokkpod sneered at the hare. 'You frightinned, longirrs?'

The old hare flung a tile which took another rat out of commission. 'Frightened, I'd be an idiot not t'be, you befeathered buffoon, but it's the only way, so Meldrum Fallowthorn will do it, frightened or not, sir!'

Sourgall trotted down the stairs on Nagru's orders, to where Graywort was waiting nervously.

'Foxwolf says he'll see yer now.'

Graywort followed Sourgall, probing nervously. 'Did he say what he wants me for, mate?'

Sourgall shrugged. 'Dunno, but you'll soon find out.'

The Urgan Nagru smiled at Graywort cordially as he ushered him forward. 'I've been hearing good reports about you, rat. Been out helping Queen Silvamord search for intruders, have you?'

Graywort was slightly bewildered but happy that he was receiving complimentary attention from the horde leader. 'I was just about to, Sire, when Bluebane said you wanted to see me. Is there any service I can perform for you?'

Nagru stopped him two stairs short of the tower room. 'On the contrary, Silvamord tells me that you are a good trustworthy beast capable of giving orders. Of course you heard what happened to poor Riveneye. He's dead, unfortunately, my best Captain. So, there's a small service I can perform for you, my friend. I'm promoting you to Captain in Riveneye's place.'

Graywort's chest swelled and he trembled with delight. 'Thank you Sire, I am yours to command!'

Nagru's smile widened. 'Well, that is nice to know. May I give you your first command now . . . Captain Graywort?'

The newly promoted Captain threw an extra smart salute. 'I'd be proud to carry out your orders, Sire!'

Nagru retreated one step, his smile practically extending to the wolf skull perched on top of his head. 'Right, go and tell those escaped prisoners that it's useless to resist, they must surrender immediately.'

The Foxwolf turned his back on Graywort, who strode smartly off into the very centre of the tower room. Standing amid the wreckage of fallen rats and broken tiles he glanced about nervously, then summoning up his courage he coughed and called out in officious tones, 'I am Captain Graywort of Urgan Nagru's horde and I order you to come down from there and surr . . .'

Graywort's voice was cut off abruptly, as was his existence, by four well-aimed tiles.

Nagru sat upon the stairs, changing his smile to an expression of heartfelt pity. 'Sourgall,' he said, 'is it still raining heavily?'

'Yes Sire, it shows no sign of slacking.'

'Hmm, I think we'll leave the prisoners to soak until morning, I'm getting tired. Mount a guard on these stairs, will you? Oh, and when you've done that would you be so kind as to convey some sad news to Queen Silvamord?'

'Aye Sire, what shall I say?'

'Tell her that our brave new Captain Graywort was cruelly slain by the escaped prisoners. You'll do that for me, won't you? I can't stand being the bearer of sad tidings.'

Silvamord was at that moment regretting her decision to venture outside Castle Floret into the downpour of a rapidly darkening evening. The squad of horderats was diminished by four and some beast, or beasts, were stalking her and the patrol through the rising mists that curtaining rain was releasing from the warm ground. The vixen could not see her assailants, and she was rapidly of the opinion that she did not want to see them. Her one desire now was to get back inside the safety of Floret's walls. To save losing face in front of her command she ranted at them, 'Stop pushing from behind there, what's the matter with you? Frightened of a bit of rain and mist?'

Beside her a rat gurgled and fell, transfixed by an arrow. She dodged behind a tree, calling out to the rat Fillch, 'Where's Graywort? Why isn't he here?'

She jumped, startled as Fillch's voice came close to her ear, 'I dunno m'Lady, gone off to see the Urgan Nagru, I think.'

'You think? Who said he could, I never did? Who's second in command to Graywort?'

Fillch knew what was coming, but he answered truthfully. 'I am y'Majesty, d'you want t'go back to the Castle now?'

'Well of course I do, oaf!' Silvamord's voice was shrill with fear and frustration. 'Didn't you hear me give the order to return? I can't see a thing with all this mist and rain, we'll be picked off one by one if we don't move.'

Fillch's voice held a note of justifiable complaint in it. 'But you was shoutin' that order to Graywort, not me!'

The vixen kicked out savagely, relishing the squeal of pain that issued from Fillch. 'I didn't know Graywort was not here then, idiot. Why didn't you tell me at the time, you're useless!'

But Fillch was not answering. Silvamord turned on him, only to find the horderat pinned to the tree, slain by a barbed shaft from out of the misty deluge. Any vestige of boldness or courage deserted the vixen then, and she turned and ran headlong for the castle.

Her beaded skirt of tails swished wetly against her as, gasping for breath, she pounded on to the woodwork of the lowered drawbridge. Urging each other on, the horderats ploughed up the steps to the plateau after her.

'Inside, come on, move yourselves, get inside!' Fillch shouted.

The last rats hurried past Silvamord as Sourgall ran out, holding a scrap of sacking over his head to keep dry. 'Majesty, I have a report from Urgan Nagru for you, he says that he regrets to tell you Captain Graywort . . .'

Silvamord did not hear the rest. She stood rigid, unable to tear her eyes away from the causeway steps up to the plateau. There, standing in a patch of pale watery moonlight, were two creatures returned from the dead.

Rab Streambattle and the badger Muta!

Moonlight glimmered whitely on the terrible scars and lacerations on the bare skin where new fur had not grown. She saw the otter's paws rise as he stretched a shaft on his tautened bowstring, and acting instinctively Silvamord threw herself flat. Sourgall was still finishing his message as the arrow took his life.

Then Silvamord was dashing into Floret screaming, 'Raise the drawbridge! Raise the drawbridge!'

As the heavy wooden drawbridge creaked upward the vixen peered around the side of it at the plateau steps. Rab Streambattle and Muta were gone, vanished into the mist and rain like two wraiths out of a nightmare.

19

Finnbarr Galedeep drew his two swords as he watched the swarming masses approaching. Log a Log stood at his side, rapier at the ready, assessing the oncoming foe. 'Giant marshtoads, big uns, there must be thousands of 'em!' he yelled.

'Everybeast to the *Pearl Queen*, use her as a fort, we'll stand a better chance of fighting them off!' shouted Joseph as he grabbed a long driftwood spar.

It was a sensible idea and the crew rushed to do his bidding. The shrew Fatch pulled Rufe Brush away from the memorial cairn, hurrying him along. 'C'mon mate, said I'd look after you, didn't I?'

Rufe found himself pushed aboard, and he took up his position with Fatch on the aft gallery of the crazily listed stern. 'I dearly wish Rosie Woodsorrel was here, Fatch,' he said, 'she was as good as ten warriors!'

Long green banners streamed out above the hordes of giant marshtoads as they came on in their hundreds – huge, horrible wart-studded creatures, armed with what appeared to be big curved scythe blades mounted on poles. Rufe swallowed hard, his paws trembling. 'I'll wager they could inflict awful damage with those things, d'you think they'll attack us, Fatch?'

The brave shrew tested the point of a boarding pike. 'They ain't here for a party, Rufe, you stick close t'me!'

Finnbarr grinned with anticipation. His lust for battle rising hotly, he spoke out of the side of his mouth to Joseph, 'Well, it was nice knowin' ye, Bellmaker. Let's go out with a bang. D'you creatures 'ave a battle cry?'

The toads were almost upon them as Joseph shouted out, 'Give 'em a good roar, come on crew – where's our war shout?'

Wild cries ripped from the throats of everybeast aboard: 'Redwall! Redwall! Logalogalog! Redwaaaaallll!!!'

The toads halted dead in their tracks.

An eerie silence fell over shore and cliff. Joseph looked quizzically at Finnbarr. 'Great seasons of plenty! That seemed to do the trick – look at 'em, you'd think they were frozen!'

The sea otter was stupefied for a moment, then his love of battle took over. Clashing his twin sword blades in the face of the massed toad army, he bellowed defiantly, 'What're ye waitin' for, ya blisterin' mudsuckers? 'Ere's the Galedeep, fightin' fit an' rarin' t'go. I'll take on any number of ye, pot-bellied marshspawn, web-brained cowards! Do ye use those weapons fer eatin' yore vittles or diggin' 'oles to 'ide in?'

Joseph restrained the impetuous sea otter. 'Steady on there, Finnbarr, no use forcing a fight with this lot. There's too many of 'em, we'd be slaughtered. Let's wait and see what they do next.'

The marshtoads raised their weapons and began chanting: 'Glogalog! Hoolya, hugg hugg! Glogalog!'

The massed ranks parted, leaving a long aisle. From the foot of the cliffs came a procession of toads, carrying a canopied hammock on a wooden frame. Laying in the hammock was a massive old toad, far bigger than all the others. Across his stupendous stomach rested a bulrush sceptre with a sun-bleached lizard skull fixed to its top.

Fatch nudged Rufe, whispering, 'Looks like the big boss wants to visit us.'

The bearers let the framed hammock rest on the sand. The marshtoad ruler pointed to himself and uttered a guttural sound. 'Glogalog, Bulgum Glogalog!'

'What d'you think he's saying?' Joseph murmured to Finnbarr.

The shrew Chieftain came to stand with them. 'I think he's telling us his name, Glogalog. Sounds very like mine, Log a Log.'

The marshtoad pointed to himself again. 'Glogalog, Bulgum! Bulgum!'

The vast army of marshtoads bowed low, their voices almost a moan as they chorused, 'Bulgum! Bulguuuuummmmm!'

Finnbarr sheathed his swords. 'What d'yer suppose a Bulgum is mates?' he said.

A familiar ear-splitting laugh rent the air. 'Whooha-hahooh! I say, you chaps, d'you need a jolly old interpreter, wot?'

Fatch had to restrain Rufe from leaping over the stern. 'It's Rosie an' Durry,' he yelled. 'They're not dead! Oh look, Fatch! Rosie an' Durry, they're alive!'

The Hon Rosie Woodsorrel and Durry Quill stepped from behind the canopied frame and waved merrily to their friends aboard the *Pearl Queen*. Both looked none the worse for their ordeal of being lost at sea. A great gasp of delight and astonishment came from the animals massed on the deck. Rosie and Durry crossed the sand, while the toads stood watching silently. They reached the ship, and dozens of hands leant out to help them on board. Rufe threw himself happily on Durry.

'What the . . .? How did . . .?' spluttered the Bell-maker.

Rosie gave Joseph a huge wink. 'Toodle pip, old sport – listen carefully an' don't ask silly questions. Young Durry an m'self have got to keep up our image as Bulgums, sort of greatbeasts who come flyin' out of the sky an' all that. Have you got any of that absolutely foul sea-weed grog that those searats left aboard?'

Log a Log scratched his head in bewilderment. 'There's jugs an' jugs of it in the galley, why?'

'Never mind why, old thing, just go and get a jug, please.'

While Log a Log went to the galley Durry and Rufe carried on hugging each other. The young squirrel seemed lost for words, all he could do was weep. Durry hugged him tighter. 'There, there now Rufey, don't you cry no more, I'm back!'

Fatch could not help chuckling. 'He'd prob'ly weep a lot less if you didn't 'ug so tight, matey, the pore beast gets spiked worse every time y'do!'

Durry immediately let go and Rufe giggled helplessly as he pulled hedgehog spines from his paws. 'Oh haha-heehee, I'll never let you out of my sight hahaheehee again, Durry Quill. Hahaheehee!'

Fatch and Durry joined in the laughter, three friends together. Log a Log had returned with a jug of seaweed grog and Rosie took it from him.

'Come on, young Quill, stop that laffin' an' conduct y'self like a proper Bulgum. Leave those two a moment, they'll still be here when y'get back. We've got a bit of magic to do for old Glogalog.'

Log a Log gave Rosie a sceptical look. 'Can you really understand the marshtoad language?'

Hon Rosie jumped down to the sand, carefully catching the jug of grog as Durry lowered it to her. 'I s'pose so, though not all of it, just the main bits,' she said. 'A Bulgum is a high-up sort of chap, chief or magician, that kind of rot, and Glogalog is the podgy feller in the ham-mock. He's the King of all marshtoads, we saved his life – but I'll tell y'more about that later. Oh by the way, I'd change my name if I were you, just for the time we're here. The mighty King wouldn't like havin' somebeast around with a name that sounded too much like his. Well cheerio, see you later, Glug a Bag!'

The shrew Chieftain looked at her indignantly. 'Glug a Bag?'

The breakfast fire was reduced to a few smouldering twigs and ashes. Glogalog and the marshtoads formed a circle around it. Rosie instructed Durry as to what they should do, and the performance began. As the hare and the hedgehog went into a wild dance, jigging and prancing madly, the toad circle moved back to give them more space. At intervals Rosie and Durry would point to each other and shout out in deep impressive voices, 'Bulgum hoolya hugg hugg Bulgum!'

Still cavorting crazily, they passed the jug of seaweed grog, each taking a quantity and holding it in their mouths. Rosie's ears stood up stiff – that was the signal.

Ppphhhssssstt!

Durry and Rosie squirted the grog from their mouths over the smouldering ashes of the breakfast fire.

Whoof! Red and blue flames shot up high, as the embers ignited by the grog took fresh light. All the marshtoads, even Glogalog, fell flat on their faces in the sand, moaning, 'Bulgum, Bulguuummmm!'

Pulling a wry face, Durry spat out, again. 'Pthooey! 'orrible stuff, my ole nuncle Gabe would've had it all buried in a hole far out in the woodlands!'

Rosie pointed to the prostrate toad masses. 'Whooha-hahooh! 'twas worth it though, Durry, we're a right old pair of Bulgums now and no mistake!'

With the threat of a marshtoad invasion now gone, the crew set about making a ceremonial lunch aboard the *Pearl Queen*, with Glogalog and several of his lieutenants as guests. Food was prepared and spread on the hatch covers. The Guosim cooks did it up proud: October Ale, heavy fruit cake, hot plum scones, mint tea and a superb apple and blackberry flan. Whilst Rosie held disjointed conversations with the marshtoad King, Durry related their strange story to the crew.

'When the mast broke off in the storm, me and Rosie hung on to it like limpets, and we were swept off by the winds, high up in the sky. I was never more frightened in me life, but Rosie there, she laughed an' laughed fit to bust. Up an' up we went, whirlin' an' twirlin', drenched through by the rain an' clingin' on for dear life. Next thing I knew the wind dropped an' so did we, straight out the sky like an arrow, down! We landed on the far side of yonder cliffs in a great swamp, an' guess what? That mast came down smack on the skull of a fearful great hissin' adder, a serpent! It was just about to make supper of King Glogalog when me'n Mrs Rosie an' the mast landed on its 'ead, whacko!'

Joseph selected a slab of heavy fruit cake. 'So that's how you became a Bulgum, eh Durry, by saving Glogalog's life? But how did you figure out the language?'

'I never, that was Rosie,' shrugged Durry, sipping his October Ale. 'It weren't two ticks before 'er an' the King was Bulgummin' an' Blogalogin' an' hoolyahoyin' together. She picks things up very quick y'know – ain't that right, Mrs Rosie?'

Hon Rosie Woodsorrel gave up ravaging the apple and blackberry flan momentarily. 'Right you are, us Bulgum types are pretty sharp in the lingo business, wot? Woohahahooh!'

King Glogalog winced and stuffed a webbed claw in one ear. When the laughter had subsided he pointed to Rosie, saying, 'Bulgum umutcha Glogalog, umutcha kug yettayur!'

Rosie shook her head and pointed seaward. 'Numutch Bulgum Glogalog, Bulgum yuggafurr yur yur!'

Joseph put aside his fruit cake. 'What's going on Rosie?' he said. 'I don't like his tone.'

The hare translated. 'It seems the old King gets a bit cheesed off bein' the only Bulgum in this neck o' the woods, he wants me to stay here forever as official Bulgum to the jolly old toads. But I've just told him that

172

this particular Bulgum has other plans – I'm sailin' off with you lot when we've patched the *Pearl Queen* up. You'll notice he doesn't look too happy about it.'

Glogalog shook his lizard skull sceptre at Rosie and the crew. 'Yutcha slugg! Bulgum yuggafurr!'

Rosie took a dainty sip of mint tea. 'Says he'll kill us all before he'll let me sail away, I've got to stay here forever. I say, this is all gettin' a bit tiresome, wot? Very basic chaps, marshtoads.'

'Look, I'll stay here as Bulgum if Glogalog lets you all sail away without any trouble,' said Durry glumly.

Rufe picked up a jug of seaweed grog. 'No, you won't mate. Come on Rosie, I'll need an interpreter. Tell Glogalog to come with me to the galley. The fire is still lit there – I'll teach him to be the greatest fire raisin' Bulgum these toads have ever seen!'

20

Late that night Joseph took delivery of the broken fore-mast from a squad of toads who had lugged it back from the marshes to the *Pearl Queen*. Finnbarr had rigged a block and tackle to haul it aboard, and Joseph, Rosie and some others stood by with rope lashings, metal pins, wooden splints and spars to fix the mast firm when it was hoisted. Durry and Rufe helped the Guosim to patch the hole in the for'ard locker – the shrews were expert boat repairers and worked well under Log a Log's direction. With melted pitch, rope caulking and planks, they soon had the gap sealed and the hull seaworthy again.

A fire had been built further along the shore. Fatch tended it carefully until it was reduced to glowing embers. Countless fireflies, trapped inside lanterns, glimmered and twinkled as the marshtoads surrounded the nearly extinct fire. Fatch hailed the ship. 'Ahoy, *Pearl Queen*, if this fire gets any lower Glogalog won't be able to do his magic. You'd best fetch him now!'

Rosie left the mast repair gang to supervise the loading of the King, together with ten jugs of seaweed grog, on to the framed hammock. Finnbarr nodded to her.

'You an' Fatch git back aboard sharpish, miz, the tide's arisin' an' waits for nobeast.'

Marshtoads moved aside to let the hammock be set down beside the fire. Glogalog grunted as they heaved him out of his comfortable bed. Rosie gave him a swig of seaweed grog; his bulging eyes popped out further as he held it without swallowing. Skipping around the edge of the circle Rosie began singing in a serious baritone voice, a song she had made up for the occasion.

'Stand back and watch this Bulgum toad,
He's goin' to do some magic,
But if young Rufe has taught him wrong,
It could turn out quite tragic.
Get back to the ship now, Fatch,
I'll be right behind you,
Glogalog oh please don't sneeze,
Or they will never find you.
Careful when you spit that grog,
Don't stand near the venue,
Or you'll end up crispy fried,
On the marshtoad menu!'

With a twitch of her ears, Rosie signalled to Glogalog, who spat the grog over the embers, causing a sheet of flame to flare skyward. The marshtoads hopped about croaking with fright and excitement at their King's magical skill. Glogalog took another swig and, swallowing half, he spat out the rest, causing another upburst of flame. Rosie took advantage of the jubilant mêlée to make good her escape.

Smiling foolishly, Glogalog continued to swig great quantities of the lethal seaweed grog. Some he spat at the fire, but for the most part he was happy to guzzle the grog, now that he had a taste for it. Spraying and spitting the stuff at random he soon had several marshtoads croaking in distress as they hurled wet sand on their smouldering webs and beat out threads of flame racing round their gills.

Pearl Queen righted herself on the incoming tide, and bobbed in the water with her keel free of the sand. Joseph watched anxiously as the large rollers started to crash along the tideline, rapidly eating up the land. The breeze was springing up stiffly as he helped Durry and Rufe to haul their friend Fatch aboard.

Finnbarr stood ready with a heaving line. 'Where's Rosie? We can't wait, even with slack sails!' he shouted.

Out of the darkness Rosie made herself heard. 'Whoohahahooh! Over here chaps, comin' aboard, ahoy an' all that nautical nonsense!'

The sea otter shot the line out to the long-limbed figure pounding through the surf towards his vessel. Rosie caught it with her usual accuracy and was soon pulled aboard. She lay on the deck chortling helplessly. 'Whooha! Better pile on all sail Finn, the way old Glogathing was performin' back there, I think it's all goin' to end in tears. Whoohahahooh!'

Directly she had finished speaking there was a loud bang from the shore, and sheets of flame shot up high into the night sky. Finnbarr took Rosie's advice quickly.

'Hoist all sail mates, sharp now, jump to it, on to those yardarms an' loose every stitch of canvas on 'er!'

By the light of following explosions masses of angry marshtoads could be seen, hopping across the beach towards *Pearl Queen*. Having unfurled the sails, the crew took boarding pikes and any long timbers they could find, and pushing hard, they punted the vessel, trying their best to get her into deep water, away from the hordes of maddened toads speeding over the shore towards them.

Pearl Queen bobbed on the incoming waves, slow and stately, despite the frantic pushing of her crew. Rufe, Durry and Fatch sweated and struggled at the stern. Then there was a massive bang as the jugs of grog and the canopied hammock rose skyward in a searing column of flame. The three friends felt a blast of heat from the explosion. Marshtoads threw themselves flat across the sand and in the shallows of the tideline. Finnbarr slammed the tiller hard over, sending *Pearl Queen* listing perilously as she turned side on to the shore.

Rosie was propelled across the deck; she cannoned into the rail glaring at the sea otter. 'I say, what'n the name of seasons are you up to?'

Finnbarr Galedeep kept an experienced eye on the sails. 'You leave it to an able-bodied seabeast, marm, we're goin' to run the rollers!'

The toads had begun clambering up the stern now. Striking out with their long spars and pikes, the defenders knocked them off into the water. Other toads climbed on the heads of their floundering companions to leap at the ship.

The sea otter gave a triumphant shout. 'Avast cullies, 'ang on tight, we're away!'

A prolonged gust of wind howling down out of the north clouted *Pearl Queen's* sails and she took off like a javelin. Bows lifting high, the great ship scudded free on the roller crests, speeding along parallel to the shore. Finnbarr played the tiller deftly, skipping her from one wavetop to the next, veering and tacking out to open sea in a dainty sidestepping dance.

Behind on the shore a scorched and blackened Glogalog sat smouldering in helpless rage, watching his marshtoads flopping helplessly in the waves, as the ship carrying his former Bulgums sailed off into the night. Struggling upright, he shook his sceptre at the receding vessel and croaked venomously, 'Yurrg Golchukkum furgalumm Boolawugg!' A combination of marshtoad curse and insult that would have caused any interpreter to blush deeply.

*

Dawn light reflected twinkling greengold across the restless waves. Finnbarr yawned aloud as he relinquished the tiller to Joseph. 'I don't knows wot I want first, matey, a good sleep or a decent breakfast, 'twas a long 'ard night.'

The Bellmaker shoved his sea otter friend playfully. 'Get along with you, go on, I'll hold her head south. The shrews are making you a victory breakfast for sailing us out of that scrape last night – only a Galedeep like yourself could have done it.'

Finnbarr was instantly revived as he sniffed the delicious aromas wafting from the galley. Guosim shrews laid the food out on the hatch covers amidships; there was October Ale, raspberry cordial and hot mint tea, a plum and pear pudding, meadowcheese, and fresh farls of shrewbread, piping hot from the oven. *Pearl Queen's* crew cheered their skipper until the summer morning air rang to their cries.

Finnbarr bowed modestly before launching himself at the food with a formidable appetite. 'Fall to messmates, 'elp an ole seadog to clear these vittles! Ahoy there, Foremole, wot's that thing yore carryin'?'

'Oi found et zurr, 'twurr 'idden in ee for'ard cabin!' Reverently the sea otter took the small melodeon that Foremole presented to him.

'Wallopin' clamshells, 'tis me ole ottercordion, I thought it were lost. Wonder if she still works?'

Twiddling his paws across the buttons, he expanded the instrument's ribbed bellows and it produced a melodic chord. Much to the delight of everybeast Finnbarr threw back his head and began singing a merry sea otter ditty. Durry, Rufe and Fatch stamped their paws on the deck rhythmically in time to the comic song. It was a happy release for them all after the perils they had endured, and Finnbarr could play as well as he could sing.

'Whoa there was an ole lobster who married a cod,
Boggle me barnacles, sail off t'sea,
And tho' all the cockles an' clams thought it odd,
Boggle me barnacles, over the brine,
I knows yer a codfish but darlin' yore mine!

For a weddin' brekkfist the pair 'ad to feed,
Boggle me barnacles, sail off t'sea,
On rootybag cake an' the best of seaweed,
Boggle me barnacles, over the brine,
I knows yer a lobster but I loves yer fine!

They was married offshore by a little fat whale,
Boggle me barnacles, sail off t'sea,
An' the guests drank barrels of deepwater ale,
Boggle me barnacles over the brine,
Pass me that flagon of green ocean wine!

The party went on 'til an hour before dark,
Boggle me barnacles, sail off t'sea,
An' they were ate up by an iggerant shark,
Boggle me barnacles over the brine,
A shark don't 'ave manners when he's out to dine!'

Amid hoots of laughter and loud applause Finnbarr did
an encore, with Rosie and Foremole dancing the parts
of lobster and cod. They breakfasted until mid-morning, the weather being calm and the seas mild. Joseph
lashed the tiller straight south. Having missed a full
night's sleep, the entire crew lay about on the sun-
warmed decks to take a few hours of much needed rest.

In the heat of mid-noon Rufe woke parched. Bleary-
eyed he drew a dipper of water from the ship's drinking
cask and drank half, pouring the rest over his head to
waken himself properly. Blinking water from his eyes, the
young squirrel stared out over the gently swelling deep.

Finnbarr was wakened by Rufe shaking him. 'Eh, wot
time is it, mate? Musta been asleep 'alf o' the day! Rufey
– somethin' the matter, young un?'

179

The squirrel tried to keep his voice calm. 'Er, this morning, Mr Finnbarr, you sang a song about cods an' lobsters being eaten up by a shark . . .'

The sea otter stretched luxuriously. 'Aye, so I did Rufey, d'ye want me to teach ye the words?'

'No sir, I'd just like to know what a shark looks like.'

'Bless yer 'eart matey, you don't sees much of em, an' you don't wants to neither. Mainly all you'll see is a great dark fin stickin' up out o' the water.'

Rufe took the sea otter's tattooed paw and led him to the rail. 'Does it look like this one circling our ship, sir?'

21

In the same noontide Tarquin L. Woodsorrel was beginning to get really worried. Since dawn he had headed a major search party in Mossflower Wood. Without stopping to rest or eat, they had combed copse and thicket alike with no success – the two Dibbuns were still missing. Brother Mallen poked fruitlessly at the undergrowth, his staff clacking against that of Sister Sage. He shook his head. 'I'm beginning to think this is a complete waste of time, Sage. Are there any deep swamps hereabouts?'

The Sister dropped her staff. 'Mallen, how could you even think that!'

'Hearken, silence in the ranks there, somebeast comin'!' At Tarquin's low warning the search party became still.

The pretty squirrel Treerose dropped from the boughs of an elm, directly in front of Tarquin. 'Are you looking for two Dibbuns, a mouse and molemaid?' she asked.

The hare perked up considerably. 'Indeed we are, Treerose, d'you know where the little blighters are at?'

Treerose pointed east and slightly south. 'Over that way. My Tom's with them, follow me.'

Slipp and Blaggut did not like the look of Oak Tom. The big sturdy squirrel stood perched on a bough, an arrow notched meaningfully on his bowstring.

'Dibbuns, come over here to this tree,' he ordered. 'You rats, stay where you are or I'll let daylight into you.'

The pair did as they were told, though Slipp was figuring the odds of either seizing the Dibbuns as a shield, or attempting a rush attack on the stern squirrel. Blaggut heard the search party approaching and whispered, 'Psst Cap'n, there's more of 'em comin'.'

In a moment they were surrounded by Redwallers armed with stout ash staves. Slipp gave Blaggut a swift vicious kick. 'See wot you've got us into now, leave the talkin' t'me.'

Tarquin thought Slipp was talking to him and he leaned closer, asking 'Eh, what's that y'say?'

The searat Captain put on his best oily smile. 'Good noontide to ye sir, I 'ope yore not 'ere to rob 'onest travellers like us.'

'Fiddlesticks,' said the hare, waggling his ears indignantly. 'The very idea of it, we're Redwallers sir, but more t'the point, where d'you think you're takin' those two Dibbuns off to, eh?'

The mousebabe avoided Sister Sage's paws and piped up, 'Wazzen taken us nowhere, huh! Me an' Furrtil was takin' them to the h'abbey, they's losted, like us!'

Sage was of the old-fashioned school. She caught the mousebabe by his ear, saying, 'What've you been told? Don't interrupt your elders, even if they are searats!'

Blaggut was unsure what the proper protocol was, so he held his coat edges and dropped an elaborate curtsey. 'Don't be 'ard on the liddle un marm, 'tis the truth 'e's tellin' yer. Bless their liddle paws, they was takin' me an' me mate 'ere back to Redwalls h'abbey, we're lost yer see.'

Sage was sceptical. 'Lost? What are two searats doing this far inland?'

Slipp adopted his look of injured dignity. 'Beggin' yer pardon marm, but we're not searats, ho no, my name's Slipp an' I'm a cook, this 'ere's me mate Blaggut an' e's a, er, er, carpenter, aye, that's wot 'e is, a carpenter!'

Tarquin took over from Sister Sage. 'You still haven't told us what you're doin' round here.'

Slipp wrung the tails of his coat in both claws, as if the tale was too harrowing for him to tell. 'Well y'see, yer Lordship, we're the only two beasts left alive from the wreck of the *Muddy Duck*, that was our ship, she was sunken by a storm an' all our mates was drownded, ain't that right messmate?' He gave Blaggut a sly kick.

'Oh er, that's right Cap'n,' the searat stammered, 'the ole *Dirty Swan* was lost at sea right enough, there's on'y me 'n' the Cap'n left alive to tell the tale.'

'Why does that one keep calling you Captain?' said Brother Mallen, smartly relieving Slipp of his cutlass.

'You'll 'ave ter forgive ole Blaggy sir, 'e's a bit slow in the 'ead, Cap'n is his nickname fer me.' Slipp gave Blaggut a playful buffet, as hard as he could.

Mallen inspected the chipped cutlass blade. 'One of you said your ship was the *Muddy Duck*, but the other said it was the *Dirty Swan*, now which is it?'

Both searats started contradicting each other. 'The *Muddy Swan*, er, the *Dirty Duck*, er, the *Mucky Dud*, er, er, the *Swanny Duck*, the *Dirty Mud* . . .'

'You mean you can't remember the name of your own ship?' Sage interrupted sharply.

Slipp collapsed to the ground, covering both eyes with his claws as he made weeping noises. 'It's the shock an' 'unger! O it was awful. Awful!'

Blaggut produced a grubby kerchief and began comforting Slipp. 'Don't go gittin' upsetted now Cap'n, 'ere, blow yer snout an' you'll feel better.'

Blaggut performed a silent dance of agony as Slipp bit

savagely on his paw. Tarquin separated them. 'Steady on there chaps, that's enough of that. Well, we've got our young uns back no worse for wear an' I s'pose it's you two we've got to thank. S'pose you'd better come back to the Abbey with us. Tom, Treerose, will you follow up the rear in case anybeast gets lost again? Tom, Treerose?' But the two reclusive squirrels had vanished into the fastnesses of Mossflower.

Supper that evening was served in Cavern Hole, a smaller, less decorated venue than the Great Hall. Blind Simeon sat next to Mother Mellus. 'So Mellus, your two Dibbuns are back safe and sound,' he said.

The badger nodded as she helped herself to blueberry tart and meadowcream. 'Aye, a bowl of soup apiece, a sound scrubbing in the bath and sent off to bed straight away, as an example to the others.'

Simeon smiled as he poured her a beaker of maple cordial. 'Little rascals. Dibbuns seem to live in a world of their own. I don't suppose they meant any real harm.'

Saxtus peered over his spectacles across a summer salad. 'I agree with Mellus, they must learn their lesson. It's lucky the two rats found them. What d'you make of those two?'

Mellus stared hard at the pair who were bolting everything in sight ravenously. 'I don't like them or trust them. Cook and a carpenter indeed – got searat stamped all over their scurvy hides!'

'Again I agree with you, my friend,' said Saxtus as he broke a fresh oat farl to have with his salad, 'but without them the little ones might have come to harm. They haven't showed badwill to anybeast so far, and with that in mind we cannot refuse them the hospitality of Redwall. They must be treated as harmless lost travellers.'

Simeon smiled broadly at Mellus's answer. 'Harmless lost travellers my left footpaw!'

Blaggut dug his spoon into a bowl of mixed fruits with honey. 'This is the life, eh Cap'n,' he said as he shovelled it down with gusto, 'these is the fanciest vittles I ever et in me life. Pass me that fizzy strawb'rry stuff.'

Slipp was forging hastily through a wedge of yellow cheese studded with beechnuts, but he could not resist a sarcastic dig at the former bosun of the *Pearl Queen*. 'Fanciest vittles you ever et, eh, didn't they 'ave stuff like this at Blaggut Mansions?'

Blaggut grabbed two hot blackberry scones from a passing tray. 'Blaggut Mansions, where's that? Pity they ain't got no seaweed grog. Yowch!' He jumped sharply as Slipp's claws nipped his stomach.

The searat Captain saw Mellus watching them, so he pasted a smile on his face as he muttered threateningly, 'Lissen, onionbonce, one more mention of seaweed grog an' I'll rip yer nose off, see? If'n they 'ears you blatherin' on about seaweed grog they'll know fer sure we're searats!'

But Blaggut was enjoying himself. He bit deep into a plumcake, spraying crumbs across the table as he addressed Mellus, 'Ahoy there, stripedog, where's me two liddle mateys? You shoulda invited them to the party!'

The old badger glared dangerously at him. 'They're fast asleep in bed. And my name is not stripedog, it's Mellus, is that clear?'

Blissfully unaware of the wrath he had nearly brought down on his own head, the searat answered, 'Clear as a fat merchantship, pleased t'meet yer Mellers. My name's Blaggut, but the Cap'n 'ere calls me fat'ead an' lazypaws an' baggybum an' suchlike names. Hoho, 'e's a one fer the names is the Cap'n!' He was jolted by repeated kicks from Slipp beneath the table.

'Will you stow all that Cap'n, Cap'n! Yer an addle-nosed, bottlebrained, butterbellied barnacle!'

Blaggut winced until the kicking stopped. 'Aye aye, Cap'n! Ooh look, they got trifle, Cap'n!'

The bad manners of the two searats were tolerated with great patience by most of the Redwallers, though Mellus and Sister Sage were forced to stifle stern comments when Abbot Saxtus looked reprovingly over his spectacle tops at them. Slipp and Blaggut continued grabbing and gorging, with scant regard to the other diners. After the meal most of the Abbey creatures took themselves off to the dormitories with sighs of relief. Brother Mallen was heard to murmur as he and Mellus helped to clear tables, 'Huh, I suppose we'll have the pleasure of those two at breakfast tomorrow morning. If I had my way I'd sit them both outside the gate to share a trough!'

The old badger nodded in agreement as she folded a cloth. 'There's no excuse for bad manners. I wish that I'd had charge of those two rats when they were Dibbuns, I'd have made them sit up straight and behave, indeed I would!'

Moonlight beamed through the guest room window, bathing the walls in a soft radiance. Warm summer night cast its drowsy spell over the Abbey, not a breeze stirred the leaves of the orchard, and peace lay over all. Slipp lay staring at the ceiling, listening to the silence and formulating plans in his mind. He was still fully dressed and in possession of a carving knife he had stolen from the table. In the next bed, Blaggut snuffled noisily, then turning on to his back he began to snore uproariously. Slipp flung a pillow which caught Blaggut in the face, enveloping his head. The former bosun of *Pearl Queen* came awake, thrashing about as he was tangled by bedlinen.

'Whuhhh mainsail's fallen, up the riggin' mates!'

Rising hastily, Slipp tweaked his companion's ear. 'Stow that noise y'great oaf, you'll wake everybeast!'

Blaggut sat up scratching his head. 'Wot's up, Cap'n? You woke me out o' the middle of a good ol' sleep there.'

Slipp looked contemptuously at his bosun's comical figure. 'Get yerself out o' that daft nightgown, y'look like a jollyboat with a floppy sail. Do it quietly an' keep yer voice down. Now listen t'me, I've got plans.'

For the short time he had been acquainted with it, Blaggut liked his little truckle bed very much. As he dressed he sat on the edge of it, bouncing happily. Slipp, fast running out of patience, aimed a kick at Blaggut, hissing, 'Will you keep still, bucketbelly, I'm talkin' t'you!'

Blaggut pulled a face and continued bouncing. 'I kin 'ear you, Cap'n. Hoho, this is the life, better'n some ole 'ammock or deckplank this bed is. I never 'ad me own liddle bed. If we're goin' to steal things I'm gonna pinch this an' take it wid me when we go . . .' His voice trailed off as Slipp drew the carving knife menacingly.

'Let's git somethin' straight, I didn't pick you t'come with me, but yore 'ere whether I like it or not. I'm still Cap'n though, an' if yore not still an' quiet rightaway I'll see to it that yore silenced fer good!'

Miserably Blaggut stopped bouncing and listened to his Captain's scheme.

'All this fancy vittles, nice rooms an' whatnot, stands to reason a place o' this size must 'ave a great store of treasure 'idden away somewheres. Right?'

Blaggut nodded dumbly as Slipp continued. 'So we looks fer it by night an' keeps our noses clean durin' the day. Come on, foller me.'

'Where are we goin', Cap'n?'

'Where d'you think, cloth'ead, pickin' daisies? We're startin' our treasure search, now come on, an' stop callin' me Cap'n!'

'Righto Cap'n, but what'll I call yer?'

'Call me Slipp, that's me name.'

'Righto Cap . . er Slipp. Sounds funny, me callin' you Slipp. Nice name though, Slipp, I likes it. Righto, let's go Slippy!'

The carving knife pricked Blaggut's nose as the irate Captain snarled at him, 'I'll Slippy yer, I'll slip this blade between yer ribs if yer calls me that once more, understand?'

The searats found a candle and lit it from a walltorch in Great Hall. They crept about searching the alcoves and crannies. 'What're we searchin' for, Cap'n?' Blaggut whispered as Slipp lifted the edge of the great tapestry.

The Captain rapped lightly on the wall. 'Some 'idden door or secret panel, that's where I'd stow me loot if'n I owned a place like this.'

Blaggut held the candle up to the tapestry, illuminating the figure of Martin the Warrior. 'Lookit this feller, Cap'n, I wouldn't like to cross swords with that mouse, looks a right tough un!'

'It's only a picture, stupid, 'old that light down 'ere.'

They continued searching Great Hall without success. From there the two searats progressed to Cavern Hole and again, they found nothing. Blaggut smelt food.

'No treasure 'ere, Cap'n. Let's try that place where the nice smells are comin' from.'

'What, you mean the kitchens? Who 'ides treasure in kitchens?'

Blaggut shrugged. 'I dunno, who does?'

Slipp stared strangely at him in the candlelight. 'May'ap you got somethin' there. A good place to 'ide loot would be a place nobeast'd think of looking fer it. Come on!'

The kitchens were in darkness save for a dim, red glow from the ovens, and the candle cast a dancing light laced with flickering shadows. Nervously Blaggut grabbed a warm loaf from a baking tray and began munching on it.

'Blisterin' barnacles!' Slipp cursed softly as he scorched his paw on an oven door. He plunged the limb into what he imagined was a jar of water, only to find it was warm honey. As was customary with the searat Captain, he began blaming his bosun. 'Now see wot you've made me do, gimme that candle!' Snatching at the candle he knocked it from Blaggut's paw, and the light went out. Slipp was searching the floor with sticky paws when his companion began hugging him tightly.

'We're bein' watched, Cap'n. Look!'

In the red ovens' glow a black caped figure swept silently by them. Both rats gave a gasp of horror. The mysterious shape paused a moment in the doorway; it appeared to be looking in their direction. Slipp and Blaggut crouched paralyzed by nameless terror, then, as suddenly as it had appeared, the black caped form was gone!

Blaggut leapt up with a strangled yelp, knocking the honey jar from its perch – it smashed on the floorstones. Slipp was already up and pushing the bosun to one side. He dashed off, tripped and crashed into a rack of pots and pans which clattered noisily to the floor. Both rats fled the kitchens, hearts pounding madly as they tore through Cavern Hole, across Great Hall and up the stairs. They reached the guest bedroom not a second too soon. Sounds of Redwallers coming out of the dormitories to investigate the noises echoed along the corridors. Slipp closed the door as quietly as his shaking limbs would allow him to.

'Quick, get inter yer bed an' snore!' he croaked.

Blaggut needed no second bidding. He hurled himself into bed, swept the sheets over his head and began snoring. Slipp followed suit. A moment later he heard the door open carefully and the voice of Abbot Saxtus.

'Well, whatever it was it wasn't these two, they're snoring like a pair of stuffed hogs.'

His voice was followed by that of Brother Fingle. 'Aye

Father Abbot, hogs at the table and hogs in bed. We'd best go and check on the Dibbuns.'

The door closed and their pawsteps receded down the passage. Slipp sat up in bed, about to make some indignant comment on being called a hog when he remembered something odd. 'Blaggut,' he said, 'when you jumped in bed just then, was yore bedlinen all upset, the way you left it?'

'Upset, no Cap'n, it was all tidy an' shipshape.'

Slipp ran a trembling paw across the neat counterpane. While he and Blaggut had been downstairs, somebeast, or something, had visited their room and remade the beds!

22

Glokkpod took off from the valley floor again, flapping wearily upward into the raindashed night. Iris watched him go, shaking her head doubtfully.

'That's the fourth try now. The rope is heavy, maybe too heavy. Each time the Butcher Bird gets more tired.'

Troutlad peered into the mist, watching for any sign of hordebeasts. 'The Bird's their only hope up there, if he can't get the rope to 'em they're deadbeasts.'

Mariel leaned out over the ruined attic beams. She watched the shrike's painful efforts, thumping her paws on the beams. 'Come on! Oh, come on Glokkpod, you can do it!'

The Butcher Bird was almost halfway up to the tower top when he seemed to run short of energy. The wings flapped awkwardly, he hovered and dropped slightly, hampered by three ropes knotted into one coiled about his neck. Struggling gallantly the shrike sought to pick up his wing action.

Dandin bit his lip anxiously. 'The ropes are too heavy, they're pulling him down!' he said.

Gael Squirrelking had given up hope. 'He's never going to do it, it's too high.'

Heaving his ponderous stomach across a roofbeam,

Meldrum the Magnificent watched Glokkpod. 'I've just had an idea, super wheeze really, you chaps keep silent now, no matter what I say.'

Raising his voice, the old hare began insulting the shrike. 'Call y'self a bird? You're a disgrace t'the species, sah! I've seen worms do better at flyin' than you! Hah! Butcher Bird, I'll bet y'father was a dead duck an' your mother was a half-shot cuckoo! Go on, give it up, you'll never make it, you useless lump of pillow stuffin', you great blatherin', bobblewinged, bandy-beaked blowbag!'

'Rakachakk! I kill yirr Mildrin!'

Pure murder shone from the eyes of the red-backed shrike as he began powering his wings upwards. Meldrum twitched his rainsoaked mustachios cheekily, and carried on. 'Kill me? You must be jestin', featherface, you couldn't damage cream on top of a hot scone, let alone kill me. If I had wings I'd fly circles round you, you eggwalloper!'

'Kiiirrrr! I do mirdir on yirr, you fat hirr!' Regardless of rain, tired wings and the weight of the rope, the Butcher Bird punished its body into mad upward flight, screaming challenges all the way.

'Mildrin yirr a dead hirr! Kiiiirrrakachak!'

In a wet flurry of wings Glokkpod landed among them.

Mariel, Dandin and Gael had to throw themselves between Glokkpod and Meldrum – the Butcher Bird was intent on killing the hare. Meldrum kept his distance, trying to pacify the shrike.

'Calm down, old lad, I was only chivvyin' you on a bit so you'd get the rope up here, didn't really mean it, wot?'

But Glokkpod would not be satisfied, he strained towards Meldrum, stabbing with his fearsome beak. 'Yirr deadnow Mildrin longirzz, I killyirr!'

Mariel did the only thing she could do in the circumstances. Pulling the rope from the shrike's neck she shoved hard, overbalancing Glokkpod so that he fell from the tower. The Butcher Bird spread his wings and, soaring in an upward arc, he circled the towertop, screeching, 'Yirr cowwid longirzz, cowwid! Nofight, yirr all mouth!'

Mariel swung the coiled rope, warning Glokkpod off. 'Don't be a silly bird, can't you see Meldrum was only doing it so you could fly up here? If he hadn't called you those names you'd never have made it!'

But there was no reasoning with the maddened bird. 'Kiiiirrr! Nobeast live after 'sultin' thissbird! Glokkpod go now, I finished with yizz. Lissin longirzz, we ever meet again, I kill yirr, frien's not save yirr. Kiiirrrra-kachakiiiiirrrr!'

Glokkpod winged off into the rainsplashed darkness and was gone from sight.

Meldrum uncoiled the rope. 'Strange feller, no sense of humour at all. Ah well, who's for a spot of jolly old escapin', wot?'

The rope had to be doubled, so it could be freed to get them down from the west-wall battlements. Dandin draped it over the stoutest of the roof support beams, checking to see both ends were level. Gael Squirrelking surprised them all by grasping the twin sides of the rope and lowering himself away. 'Let me go first, weak as I am. If a squirrel can't do it, nobeast can!'

Bluebane knocked timidly on the Foxwolf's bed-chamber door. There was no answer, so he knocked louder, starting slightly as Nagru shouted, 'Stop that knocking and get in here!'

Bluebane scurried in and crouched by the mound of cushions which formed his master's resting place. Nagru's head appeared over the top of them, close to Bluebane's. 'So, what is it this time, tittletattle?'

'Lord, I stayed by the tower door listening carefully. The Butcher Bird brought them a rope. They plan on swinging across to the west wing edge, where they can land on the battlements. From there they'll be able to get down to the moat. Gael is already on the rope. The Butcher Bird quarrelled with the hare and he has flown off. I don't think he will come back, Sire.'

Nagru slid from the mound of cushions. 'Tell the Lady Silvamord I wish to speak with her.'

Gael had not climbed since his younger days. He was older and slower now, but his natural squirrel skills aided him in clambering down. Soon he was hanging from both ends of the doubled rope. He began swinging himself back and forth. To and fro he urged his body on the rope ends, each arc of his swing getting wider, until he saw the west wall through the mist and rain, its battlemented top getting closer with each fresh swing.

Down below, Iris was banking on the success of the plan. The escapers would need good backup and covering fire.

'Troutlad, take half the crew, get to the top of the plateau steps and watch for the drawbridge being lowered. If any try to come out, stop them. Greenbeck, stay here and see they get down safe. Give any help you can. I'll go to the steps with Troutlad, that's where the main action should come if Nagru finds out they're trying to escape.'

Nagru told Silvamord of the escape, and she affected an air of disdain. 'So, what do you want me to do? You're the Warlord.'

The Foxwolf's tone was reasonable. 'I thought we might work together for a change, stop fighting each other and fight the enemy.'

The vixen too kept a level tone, though her quick mind was watching for double dealing. 'Yes, that sounds sensible. As I said, what do you want me to do?'

'I thought you might want to take a patrol down to

194

the valley floor and catch them as they climb down the plateau.'

Silvamord's reply was definitely cool. 'That's more your style. I have a better idea. Why don't we take a good squad up to the west battlements and grab them one by one as they swing in?'

'Good idea!' the Foxwolf said, smiling thinly. 'Though why you don't want to go down to the valley floor puzzles me. Have you had trouble out there already?'

The vixen shot a sly glance at Bluebane, then turned to Nagru. 'You should know, your eyes and ears are everywhere, Foxwolf.'

As they walked to the horde barracks to pick out a squad, Sicant caught up with Silvamord. The vixen whispered to her, 'It was Bluebane who had your mate Graywort slain.'

Gael's footpaws had touched the battlements once, then on his return swing he made it. Clamping footpaws and tail firmly over the protruding stones he let go of the rope. Mariel's voice came to him faintly from above, 'Gael, are you safe?'

Cupping paws around his mouth the Squirrelking called back, 'Yes, I'm on the battlements. Mariel, I don't need the rope to go the rest of the way, I can climb down the wall, the plateau side too, once I've got across the moat.'

Mariel's answer came back immediately. 'Good, then don't wait about there, escape while you can. We'll be down right after you. Go, your wife and babe need you.' Gael started scaling the walls down to the moat, sure pawed and nimble now that freedom was within his reach.

Mariel nodded to Dandin. 'You're next, mate.'

'No, after you, miss. I'll go last!'

'I'm the senior officer here, I go last, m'lad!' huffed Meldrum.

Mariel spread her paws in despair. 'We can't all go last. Look, who's going now?'

Dandin and Meldrum pointed firmly at her. 'You!'

Mariel let herself down on to the ropes, muttering, 'Well, if somebeast doesn't go we'll be stuck up here all season. Here goes!'

Armed with pikes and archery equipment, thirty horderats, led by Nagru and Silvamord, sneaked furtively along the ramparts until they were at the west battlement edge. Crouching down in the shadows, Silvamord whispered to Nagru, 'We catch them one by one as they land, right?'

Pulling the wolfhide about him to shelter from the rain, Nagru neatly sidestepped any responsibility. 'Your idea, my Lady. Make your move.'

Silvamord crawled forward armed with a pike that was double hooked below its blade. She thrust it at Bluebane. 'Hook them in by the footpaws,' she hissed. 'We'll be waiting to grab them.'

The vixen winked at the spy. 'Do it well and I'll reward you!'

Mariel had reached the rope's end. Kicking against the wall, she began swinging herself. Rain beat on her face as she pendulumed back and forth, widening the arc each time. Blinking water from her eyes, she peered into the mist each time she sailed west.

Bluebane recognized her as she swung into view and vanished back into the night again. 'My Lady, it's not the Squirrelking, it's the mousemaid!'

Nagru growled out of his wolfhide shelter. 'I don't care who it is, yank them in. Do it!'

Bluebane timed it nicely. He stood erect, holding the battlement with one paw, and swung the barbed end of the pike towards the mousemaid on the rope.

Mariel could not stop herself. She saw the rat strike out towards her with the pike as she sped towards the battlement on the rope. Kicking her paws hard against the wall, she shot outward. The kick gave her extra impetus – she avoided the pike and shot over Bluebane's head. The rope struck the gable of the wall and was torn from her paws. From behind came the sound of a vicious hiss; an arrow stood out between Bluebane's eyes. He fell backward into the hordebeasts as Mariel landed heavily on top of Nagru. Pandemonium broke out – stamping hard on the wolfskull, the mousemaid leapt free and went dashing along the ramparts. The dead wolf's fangs had cut two furrows on Nagru's brow. Lying flat out, he roared, 'Get her, kill the mousemaid!'

The first rat who jumped upright to obey met with another arrow. Silvamord scrambled on all fours after Mariel. Taking her lead and keeping safe, the other rats followed. Nagru sat up, tenderly feeling his head where the fangs had pierced. Looking around, he realized that he was alone. An arrow zipped by overhead, and instinctively the Foxwolf ducked and scurried off on all fours, shouting, 'Come back here, you deserters, wait for me!'

Dandin leaned over the rafters, staring down into the mist, his vision hampered by the night-time rain. 'There's something gone wrong down there. Mariel may need help, I must go to her!'

Without wasting further words he grasped the ropes and vanished over the edge of the tower top. Meldrum wrung rainwater from his ears as he called after Dandin, 'As y'were! I gave no orders for you to go shimmyin' off down that rope, sah! Come back, d'ye hear me?' The hare watched the rope begin swinging from side to side and straightened his jacket resolutely. 'Hmph, mustn't have heard me, not like that young feller to disobey an order! Right, you're next, Fallowthorn.'

23

Mariel was far too quick to catch. Vaulting battlements, cutting corners and slamming doors behind her, she dashed off into the rambling passages of Castle Floret. The mousemaid could hear her pursuers behind her, tripping and stumbling as they hastened to catch her. Skipping nimbly down the dizzying stone steps of a spiral staircase, she ran full-tilt into a horderat coming the other way. The mousemaid could not stop herself barging into the rat; he was taken completely off guard, and with a panicked squeak he toppled backwards, hurtling tip over tail down the stairs. Bruising her paws on the rough-hewn stones, the mousemaid managed to stay upright. She slowed her pace as she approached the rat. He lay crumpled at the bottom of the stairwell, completely senseless.

Mariel paused momentarily to relieve him of a sharp, double-headed axe he had thrust in his belt. The sounds of Silvamord and her troop pattering down the stairs kept the mousemaid on the move. Hurtling out down a corridor she cut left and then right, looking wildly about for somewhere to hide.

Nagru had travelled down by a different route, ordering horderats to follow him as he went. 'Leave what you're doing, come on, bring your weapons!' Threading his way through chamber and hall he rushed onward, with more than a score in his wake. Now Mariel could hear her enemies coming from both sides, still some distance away, but getting closer by the moment. She brandished the axe, looking left and right desperately. There was only one way left to go. Lifting the latch of a door in front of her, she entered. It was a small inner chamber, devoid of windows. Mariel closed the door, noting that it had neither lock nor bolt to protect her. She had run herself into a cul de sac and it was too late to escape now. Taking up a warrior's stance, she gripped the axe handle tight, prepared to go down fighting.

Safely on the battlements, Dandin reached out with the pike that Bluebane had been carrying. Meldrum wobbled and swayed as he clung for dear life to the swinging rope. The young mouse called encouragingly to him, 'Just a bit more, sir, come on, swing yourself forward another fraction.'

With both eyes shut tight the hare did as he was bidden.

'Gotcha!' Dandin hooked the curved pike crosstree into the hem of Meldrum's pink mess jacket and pulled him to the battlement. Seizing both the old hare's footpaws, Dandin stretched him over the stone top and took the weight. 'You can let go of the rope now, Meldrum! Let go of the rope and open your eyes, that's an order!'

The old hare opened one eye, saw he was safe and clambered down on to the rampart with as much dignity as he could muster. 'Incorrect procedure, laddie buck, a subordinate can't give orders to a rankin' offisah. We'll let it go this time, well done, well done. Now, what's been goin' on round here, where've all the bally vermin gone?'

Dandin gazed at the rat carcasses and the empty rain-swept walltop. 'More important, where's Mariel gone?' he said.

The rope was caught on a niche of the battlement. Meldrum began pulling it in and coiling it. 'Where d'you think she's gone, bright little gel like that, escaped of course, bally well scarpered!'

Dandin however was not convinced. 'Escaped, how could she have escaped?'

'Don't ask me m'lad, I'm no expert in these matters,' Meldrum said as he fussed with the torn hem of his tunic, 'but I'll lay you an acorn to an apple they've not captured her. She'd have yelled out an' warned us.'

Dandin peered down, he could barely make out the moat below. 'I suppose you're right, sir. Wonder how she got to the moat without the rope, though?'

Meldrum the Magnificent snorted through his mustachios. 'Jumped, of course, a young rip like her wouldn't think twice about takin' a leap. Good job we don't have to, wot? Wouldn't chance it at my age, lucky for us we've got the jolly old rope to swarm down, eh!'

Dandin still looked doubtful, so Meldrum took command. 'Mariel will be furious if she thinks we're standin' up here twiddlin' our paws all night. Situation calls for decision. I'm givin' the orders now. Get that rope round this battlement, look sharp now, you're first down!' Realizing there was no other sensible course to follow, but still beset by doubts, Dandin doubled the rope about the stones and began his descent to the moat.

A voice startled Mariel as she stood alone in the darkened chamber. 'A mouse that fights and runs away, lives to fight another day!'

Barely visible in the dim light from under the door, a fat mole clad in a belted shagreen tunic stood watching the mousemaid. 'Twittering is for the birds, but earthly creatures heed wise words. Follow me mousemaid,' he said, nodding sociably at her.

The exit appeared to Mariel as a small black hole in a corner, but as she crawled through and watched the mole close it behind them, she realized it was a cunningly hinged stone door, which blended perfectly with the walls about it. Feeling completely safe she followed the mole down dark dusty tunnels, keeping one paw against his back in case she lost him in the gloom. They travelled downward, twisting and turning in the strange mole's silent world. Sometimes they passed through cellars and caves, other times they had to bend double and crawl along. They halted at a small, stout-timbered door, whereupon the mole produced a key and opened it.

'This humble abode doth suit me fine,
a simple homely place, 'tis mine.'

He turned up the flame on an oil lamp, and yellow light flooded the room. It had a couch which served as a bed, a table, and a big, elm-planked larder cupboard. The whole place was littered with books, scrolls and parchments. The fat mole bobbed his head politely to her, extending well-groomed digging claws. 'I am Egbert the Scholar, and you, I take it, are the escaped prisoner, Mariel.'

Questions flooded to Mariel's lips as she took Egbert's paw and shook it. 'Pleased to meet you, Egbert, but how do you know my name, and why do you not speak like other moles?'

Egbert sat her down on his sofa bed, then taking a thin tin plate, he placed it on a bracket above the oil lamp and began warming two plump vegetable turnovers. Filling a beaker, he offered it to Mariel. 'Dandelion cordial, I brew it myself. Drink up, food will soon be ready. As to your questions, Mariel, I know your name and your companions too, nothing goes on in Floret that escapes my notice. You were very clever to escape the way you did, extricating yourself from a dire predicament – ah, long words, I love the sound of them! As to why I am, who I am, that is a complicated narration, a long story.

'Egbert the Scholar is a name I gave myself. I was once a mole like others, humming and urring and much given to bucolic speech forms. I had a mole name too, something very moleish, Soilburr it was, as I recall. I lived a happy and simple existence with my tribe, east of here, but I thirsted for learning and the ways of the scholar. So I left home and came here, tunnelled in and set myself up. Nobeast ever knew I was inside Floret, not Gael or Serena, or that pair of barbarian vermin, Nagru and Silvamord.'

Mariel accepted the hot turnover, biting into the pastry and eating ravenously, regardless of the dark aromatic warm gravy that dribbled on to her paws. She spoke around mouthfuls of hot tender vegetables and pastry crust. 'Mmm, s'lovely! But what do you do here with your life?'

Egbert gestured at the files of books and scrolls lining the walls of his little home. 'I study to better my knowledge, to improve my powers of learning, one can never have sufficient education. Did you know that the Squirrelking and his family were heirs to an extensive library? Oh yes, a veritable palace of literature, all in one great room. My life's work is dedicated now to saving it. Those dreadful rats use rare manuscripts and valuable books to light their fires, can you believe it!

'Fortunately I come and go in Floret by my own secret routes. I pop up in the library whenever I can and take away material, though I fear my little abode is getting too small to hold it all. Just look at these scrolls I retrieved today, a treatise on autumn-cloud formations in the south – invaluable!'

Egbert paused and smiled apologetically. 'Mariel, forgive me for prattling on ceaselessly, I must be boring you to death with my lengthy discourses. Being alone one tends to talk to oneself a lot, but twice as much to visitors like yourself. Is there anything you want? Would you like to take a nap – you look tired – or is there any way at all I can help you?'

Mariel finished the turnover, washing it down with refreshing dandelion cordial. She stood and picked up her axe. 'I must go and help my friends now. They are trapped at the top of the north tower.'

Egbert clipped a quaint pair of spectacles to his nose and studied a blueprint of Floret pinned on the wall. 'Ah yes, the north tower, very high, extremely perilous. So that's where you got to; I thought you were all lost or slain when you escaped the dungeons. North tower, hmm, not a lot we can do up there, I'm afraid. Maybe if you created a diversion in another part of this castle, that would give your comrades time to escape without interference.'

Mariel hefted the axe eagerly. 'That sounds good Egbert, what do you suggest?'

'Let me apply logic to this problem,' the scholar said as he sat on his bed and nibbled at his turnover. 'Now, let me see. If you have allies outside, some of the otters, say . . . Ah yes, that's it! The drawbridge, find your way into the gatehouse and mess up the mechanism, cut the ropes. Then the drawbridge will fall open, giving easy access to your allies, and Foxwolf will have to defend it with his horde. I should think the last thing he'll be worrying about in a case like that is a few escaped prisoners stranded on a towertop . . .'

Mariel was already holding the door open. 'What a great idea! Lead on Egbert – where's this gatehouse?'

'A creature of action I see, a warrior!' The scholar put aside his food and arose. 'But you cannot do it alone and I am not a fighter. Follow me and I will take you to where there are other warriors.'

Again they were off, Mariel hurrying in Egbert's

wake, through a succession of tunnels and underground chambers where daylight had never shone. The mousemaid sensed they were moving in a downward direction, she felt a coolness across her nostrils, which she knew could only be the air from outside. After rounding a few more bends and climbing over a blockage of rubble and rock, they emerged into a sizeable cavern. The rain outside could be heard pattering and splashing; half the chamber was thick with mist that had rolled in from the valley floor. Egbert sat on a rock, nodding with satisfaction. 'Ah, here we are. Hello my friends . . . anybeast at home?'

A lightning-swift form snatched the axe from Mariel, bowling her over. The mousemaid's cry of surprise was squashed from her as two huge paws swept her off the ground, crushing and squeezing unmercifully. Mariel found herself dangling helplessly in the air, staring into a pair of maddened bloodshot eyes . . .

24

Finnbarr Galedeep watched anxiously as the triangular grey-blue fin sailed in close to the midships of *Pearl Queen*. Rufe tugged at the sea otter's paw. 'Well, is it a shark, Mr Finnbarr?'

Finnbarr nodded unhappily. 'Aye, liddle Rufey, 'tis a shark all right. Big monster too, lookit that, 'e's watchin' us, the villain.'

The shark had turned slightly on its side. Above the crescent-gashed mouth with its rows of ripping teeth a small circular eye stared at them. Finnbarr kept his good eye on the monster. 'Don't call out loud or make sudden movements, Rufey,' he murmured quietly. 'We don't wants ter excite this fish – they've been known to wreck vessels, just to git at the crew an' eat 'em.'

Rufe stole silently away. Finnbarr called after him in a loud whisper, 'Rufey, mate, where are ye goin'?'

'To keep miz Rosie quiet – if she starts laffin' we're all done for!'

Rufe was knocked from his feet as *Pearl Queen* shook from stem to stern. He crawled over to Finnbarr. 'Is the shark attackin' our ship now?' he said.

The sea otter watched the manoeuvres of the great shark. 'No, 'e's only playin' with us, scrapin' his hide along the ship's sides, scratchin' hisself, y'might say. Sharks likes to do that now an' agin. Lookout, 'ere comes the other sleepin' beauties, all waked up an' fit fer a fright.'

The vessel juddered again under the impact of the shark's rubbing. Rosie Woodsorrel was knocked in a heap with the rest. She sat on the deck giggling aloud. 'Whoohahahooh! I say, bit bumpy t'day, wot? Whooha . . .' Rufe effectively gagged her by throwing himself bodily across her face.

'Miz Rosie, hush, please hush!'

Log a Log lifted Rufe off Rosie. 'What's the matter, young un?'

Rufe seized hold of Durry and Fatch, pulling them to the rail. 'It's a shark monster attackin' our ship!'

They grabbed the rail alongside Finnbarr as the vessel quivered under a heavy swipe from the shark's blunt snout. Finnbarr slapped the rail, exhaling loudly. 'Well 'e wasn't attackin' us afore, jus' bein' playful an' nosy. That was 'til you started laffin', marm!'

Rosie leaned over amidships to view the massive bulk of the shark. It could be seen clearly now by all the crew. From tip to tail it was nearly as long as *Pearl Queen*, a true monster of the deep, with rows of slitted gills either side of the huge evil head, a white underbelly and bluey-black back markings. With a powerful flick of its sickle-shaped tail it sped away from the ship.

Rosie waved. 'Oh look, he's going, good show, wot? Whoohahahooh!'

Finnbarr gritted his teeth as he looked at Joseph. 'Will yew stuff a gag down that long-eared foghorn's mouth, mate, that shark ain't goin', 'e's just takin' a run so 'e kin charge us proper. All crew 'ang on tight!'

The shark came back like a juggernaut, spray flying from its fin as it headed straight at *Pearl Queen's* bows. Finnbarr leaped to the tiller, shoving it hard over in the same direction as the shark was travelling. It hit for'ard.

Whummmm!

Log a Log ran to Finnbarr's assistance, shouting, 'Well done, Finn, you took most of the force out of that blow, goin' the same way the shark did!'

Durry had run for'ard. He shouted from the bowsprit, 'The shark's gone under the water now, I can't see him!'

Pearl Queen shuddered fitfully. 'It's underneath now, scraping along the keel,' said Joseph, pointing down.

Finnbarr made ready with the tiller. 'Tell me where 'e comes up agin an' 'ow 'e's comin' at us!'

Durry stayed for'ard, Joseph took the stern, whilst Rufe and Fatch climbed into the lower rigging to port and starboard. Late afternoon shadows lengthened on deck, sails flapped gently and rigging creaked, as the four lookouts scanned the sea around them. Suddenly Durry called, 'Here it comes again, dead on for'ard!'

Finnbarr and Log a Log were quick this time; they shot the tiller hard aport and were rewarded by Durry's cheer. 'Hurray! The shark never touched us that time!'

Silence again . . .

Rosie sat with a towel in her mouth, eyes travelling back and forth. Joseph's paws gripped the rail; he shouted, 'Look out, it's coming at us from astern . . . No wait! . . . It's gone down again. Rufe! Over by you!'

Rufe Brush anchored his tail around a spar, screaming, 'The shark, the shark! Comin' starboard side amidships!'

Again the sea otter and the shrew threw the tiller aport, Finnbarr muttering as they did, 'Can't git outta the way much if the rogue belts us amidships!'

Boooommmm!

The entire ship shook sickeningly under the impact. 'Hog overboard, Durry's in the water!' somebeast yelled.

The shark was a short distance away. Feeling the agitation caused by Durry's thrashing paws, it homed in on him, heading straight and swift as an arrow. Durry was being swept along level with the midships as Joseph yelled out, 'Get a line, somebeast throw him a line!'

Already the Bellmaker was dashing to the rail. He saw it would be too late for Durry in a very short time. Without thinking he grabbed the nearest thing – Foremole. Grasping the mole's footpaws firmly, Joseph shot him out through a gap in the rails, shouting aloud, 'Stretch out, Foremole! Durry, get hold of him quick!' The hedgehog practically leapt from the sea to grab Foremole's digging claws and he held on like a leech.

'Oo urr yurr cumms zurr shark!'

The vicious head lifted clear of the waves, mouth agape as it hurled itself at Durry. Joseph's grip on Foremole was like a vice. The powerful Bellmaker lifted back his head, roaring at the sky as he gave an almighty heave.

'Redwaaaalll!'

Thokk!

Foremole and Durry shot over Joseph's head, so great was the strength he put into his effort. All three collapsed in a heap on the deck, Joseph wriggling backward calling, 'Look out, the shark – stay clear!'

The shark's head was stuck between the midship rails. *Pearl Queen* listed heavily as the giant brute thrashed and pulled. Log a Log grabbed a boarding pike, Finnbarr unsheathed his swords, and together they charged the shark. Jumping from side to side, avoiding the snapping jaws and slashing teeth, Finnbarr Galedeep attacked ferociously with both swords, hacking and thrusting at the monstrous head. The ship began heeling perilously as it pushed forward, wriggling its body, thrusting to get at its tormentor.

Log a Log saw Finnbarr slip and fall to the water-slicked deck, and with a wild cry he charged the shark.

'Logalogalogalogalog!'

The shrew Chieftain drove the pike hard into the fleshy area above the shark's mouth. With a dreadful rattling, hissing noise it recoiled sharply and fell free of the smashed rails into the sea. *Pearl Queen* bobbed upright, freed of the great weight, water running from her gunwales in torrents. The crew's mighty cheer was overshadowed by Fatch shouting from the rigging, 'Finnbarr! Another shark, coming from astern!'

Sure enough, there was the deadly triangular fin of yet another sea monster ploughing steadily towards *Pearl Queen*.

To the amazement of the crew, Finnbarr Galedeep began a little jig around the tiller. 'Hahaharr, we're saved, hohoho, good ole shark!'

Rosie took the towel from her mouth. 'The poor chap's gone cuckoo, what's he laughin' at?'

Finnbarr sat on the tiller, swinging to and fro. 'Haharr, you'll see marm, mad am I? Watch that other shark!'

The other shark ignored the ship completely and headed right for the injured monster, scenting its blood in the water. The sea thrashed up red foam as predator attacked predator.

Joseph turned away from the sickening sight. 'Now I know what you were laughing at, Finnbarr. The sharks are cannibals, they'll eat each other.'

The otter resumed his position at the tiller. 'Aye, they're scavengers, they'll attack anythin' that's bleedin' an' injured. Seabeasts don't know about pity. So now, Bellmaker, ask the fates'n'fortunes t'be good an' sail us inter land soon.'

'Sail into land, what for?' Joseph appeared puzzled by the request.

The sea otter gave a rueful grin. 'I knew the tiller wasn't workin' right, it didn't budge the *Queen* last time yon shark charged us amidships. Now I knows why, that scurvy seabeast snapped our rudder clean off when it was attackin' us.'

Joseph tested the tiller; it swung limply back and forth. 'You mean that you can't control the vessel?'

'Aye, that's about the size of it, Joseph. We're at the mercy of the 'igh seas, matey, an' 'tis comin' on night too. I'll post lookouts in the riggin', and if they sights land we might be able to row an' scull, so's we kin 'elp pore ole *Pearl Queen* inter shore. Then I kin fix 'er up.'

Fortunately the night seas lay calm, with little wind or breeze to carry the vessel one way or another. Rosie and Foremole took first watch aft, with two shrews standing for'ard. Foremole turned his gaze up to the star-strewn skies. After a lengthy spell, in which he attempted a star count, he turned to his companion.

'You'm be vurry soilent marm, be ee thinken?' he asked.

Rosie tossed an apple core overboard; it bobbed on the surface aimlessly. 'What, er, oh yes, thinkin'. Hmm, can't help wonderin' how Tarquin is coping with the family back at Redwall. I'm a dreadful creature really, wot? Goin' off harum scarum, sailin' and questin', while poor old Tarkers is prob'ly workin' his paws to the bone lookin' after the family. There must be a lot of butterfly in me somewhere.'

Foremole scanned the dark horizon, his chin resting on both paws. 'You'm b'aint no butterflyer marm, us'n's are only a doin' our dooty, 'elpin' friends and fol-lowin' Martin's request. Zurr Tarquin an' ee liddle uns, hurr, oanly danger they be in is frumm eatin' too much. Yore fam'ly be a gurt lot safer at ee Abbey than us'n's out 'ere on ee gurt sea wi' no rudder to steer us.'

The optimistic hare pulled another apple from her tunic and began munching happily. 'You're right of course old thing, I'll bet Tarquin and the family will be so bally tubby I won't recognize 'em when we return. Bunch of gluttons, scoffin' away at all that lovely food, without a thought of their poor mater starvin' out here on the deep. Wot?'

Foremole smiled as another apple core went sailing over the stern rail and plopped into the sea. 'Hurr, you'm roight thurr marm!'

25

Joseph roused Durry, Rufe and Fatch for the dogwatch in the two hours before dawn. Rufe yawned and stretched mightily, saying, 'Looks like we've been bobbing up'n down in the same place all night to me.'

Fatch cast a weighted line over the side, noting its progress. 'No, mate, we've been movin' all right, only slow, but steady.'

Durry sniffed the still air appreciatively. 'Wood burnin' in the galley, soon be breakfast time. I'm fair starved an' that's a fact!'

They had not long to wait. Finnbarr appeared with a tray. 'Some early vittles fer me gallant watchbeasts. Come on, mates, there's a bowl of 'ot veggible soup apiece an' some fresh baked bread. Tuck in!'

While they ate, Finnbarr's keen eyes spotted the telltale signs to the east in the early dawn light. 'There 'tis, land ho, buckoes!'

Durry ran to the rail, bowl in paw. 'Land – where? I can't see anything.'

The sea otter chided him merrily. 'That's cos yer a cellar 'og from an Abbey, but we'll make a sailor of yer yet, young Quill. Ahoy, Fatch, yore a waterbeast, show Durry the landfall.'

The Guosim shrew pointed with a fresh bread crust. 'East. See that bundle of grey cloud, matey, well it ain't cloud, that's land, though it don't look like much.'

Finnbarr climbed into the rigging for a better view. 'Aye, yer right, all rock an' cliff, but any ole port'll do fer rudderless ducks like us. Rufey, rouse all paws, we'll set sail fer any breeze t'carry us to it.'

Under Finnbarr Galedeep's skilful navigation *Pearl Queen* hove alongside the high grim rocks in bright morning sunlight. Log a Log stared up at the grey forbidding cliffs, saying, 'No place we can berth her around here, Finn!'

The sea otter took up a boarding pike. 'That's a fact. Come on crew, git pikes'n'spars, we'll push 'er round these rocks until we finds a landing!'

Striving and sweating under the eye of the hot morning sun, the crew pushed at the rock face with pikes and spars. It was high noon when they found a landfall on the island. A rocky cove opening out into a forest-fringed beach, the high cliffs rearing either side of the entrance, it gave *Pearl Queen* scant leeway. Finnbarr winced as the vessel scraped through the opening with barely a splinter to spare; he called out orders to guide them through.

'Joseph, Durry, Rosie, git rope fenders o'er the sides to protect 'er. You aloft, turn those mast spars sideways or they'll be smashed. Fatch, sound the depth with a lead!'

Rufe had the best view of the incoming shore from his perch in the bows, and he could not believe his eyes. 'Ships! Look, there's ships in here, Finnbarr!'

And ships there were, but none of them in any fit state to sail on the sea. They were all wrecks. Finnbarr cast an experienced eye over the hulks that littered the shoreline where beach met cliff on both sides. 'Harr, that's a sad sight, messmates! That'n there is a merchantship, t'other side of it looks like a searat galley, an' lookit that, an' ole otter fishin' smack, 'tis long seasons since I clapped eyes on one o' those!'

Joseph came up to stand beside Finnbarr. 'But they're all wrecked beyond repair. What d'you suppose happened here, Finn?' he asked.

'Happened? Nothin', mate, they've all been thrown up 'ere by the sea, blown towards this island durin' storms an' forced through that gap in the rocks on floodtides. Ah well, mates, one beast's ill wind is another's good fortune. We'll soon find us a spankin' good rudder in this cove!'

Joseph scouted out a good axe, Log a Log took a broken and chipped sword to serve as a saw and Finnbarr found his heavy mallet. *Pearl Queen* nosed into the soft sands of the shallows and the trio of rudder finders prepared to wade ashore. Rosie pouted a little. 'Bit of a bore, wot, all of us cooped up here on board, we could be off into those woods lookin' for fresh water and provisions.'

The Bellmaker wagged a warning paw at her. 'Stay where you are, Rosie Woodsorrel, and pay attention to Finnbarr. We don't want the crew wandering loose about this island, you never know what beasts may be lurking inland.'

A rudder was found sticking from the stern of a high-beached wreck. They got to work immediately, and, using the mallet and the axe, Log a Log and Joseph unpinned it from its moorings. Finnbarr stood on the deck of the wreck. 'This'n's been a fast Corsair craft in 'er day, single masted an' flat bottomed for coastal raidin'. Aye aye, why don't we use 'er mainmast to replace our broken one?'

Rufe and his two friends attached themselves to a party of shrews who came aboard to remove the mast. It was hard and heavy work under the hot noonday sun. Rosie had given up sulking and appointed herself cook. She and Foremole were in the galley inventing a huge mixed fruit and honey pudding for the evening meal.

'Where's the candied chestnuts got to? Foremole, you villain, stop nibblin' them an' pass them here!'

The mole relinquished the nuts with a guilty smile. 'Burr, they'm good uns, me an' ee Abbot picked 'em last autumn, they'm been soakin' in ee cask of hunny ever since. Ho urr, oi dearly do luv a good candy chesknutter, hoo aye!'

Rosie stuffed several in her mouth and spoke around them. 'So do I, d'you think it's worth savin' any for the crew?'

Pearl Queen's crew worked late into the evening on Finnbarr's urging. 'Fix 'er t'day, sail away tomorrer, mates, that's the ticket! Besides, I don't like 'angin' around on this island, I got a funny feelin' in me stummick about the place, 'tis too nice.'

Joseph wielded the mallet, hammering home the last copper spikes that held the rudder brackets in place. He tested the tiller, and found it swung well. 'There, a good job well done! How's the mast coming along, Log a Log, nearly there?'

'Aye, almost ready,' the shrew Chieftain called up from the for'ard hold. 'I'm seatin' it in pitch an' caulkin' it tight with oakum so it'll be waterproof and stand firm.'

Foremole and Rosie poked their heads from the galley. 'We'm gotten noice cool 'tober ale yurr for ee!'

'And a *Pearl Queen* Pudden, though you chaps best hurry or it'll start stickin' to the stove!'

The rudder workers joined the mast riggers, and with the added help of willing paws they had the foremast rigged as the sun dipped below the western horizon and night set in.

The *Pearl Queen* Pudden was voted a huge success by all the crew, who went back licking their spoons for second helpings. Rosie undid her apron with a flourish, winking at Foremole. 'Y'know, it wouldn't hurt old Finnbarr to appoint me permanent cook aboard this vessel, jolly wise choice!'

Foremole heaped two bowls with pudding for himself and Rosie. 'Ee must amember, miz Rose, that cookers be potwashers too, hurr.'

Rosie threw the apron to a nearby shrew. 'Hmph! I've just resigned!'

Sheltered by the high rocks, the cove was snug from wind and weather. With no anxiety and the prospect of sailing on the morrow, *Pearl Queen's* crew lay about on the hatch covers, eating, drinking and singing. Rosie was prevailed upon to perform her laughing song. With Finnbarr twiddling the keys of his ottercordion she braced herself and launched into it.

The crew found themselves sorry they had asked her to start. Rosie stood demurely, paws clasped, eyelids aflutter, and began singing in a piercing soprano voice, outrageously twisting and elongating the words:

'There is nought on this earth to com-pa-a-a-are,
With a comely young fee-hee-male ha-a-a-a-are,
He-er beauty is winsome to see-e-ee-e-e-ee-ee,
She will smile and she'll larff pri-ti-lee-eeeeeeee!
Whoohahahahooh haha, whoohahahahooh ha ha
ha.'

She smiled coyly at her stunned audience. 'Tarquin wrote this for me, y'know – there's another six verses. Shall I sing them for you, chaps?'

There followed a joint unplugging of paws from ears as the entire crew yelled in a single voice, 'No thank you!'

The Hon Rosie sniffed airily as she launched herself at a bowl of pudding. 'Rotten lot, somebeasts have no appreciation at all of life's finer things, wot?'

However, her indignation soon vanished as she clapped paws with the rest, in time to Joseph's rendition of an old favourite. Finnbarr twiddled an accompaniment as the Bellmaker's strong baritone voice echoed round the cove.

'O Willyum mole to his father said,
"Why don't I hear daybreak?
And why can't I hear the nightfall?
No noise does either make.
O riddle me diddle me riddle me ree,
Silly old father tell to me,
Why doesn't a fish nest in a tree,
Or a bird fly under the sea?"
"O wise little son," said his father,
"You never hear daybreak,
And you're never awake to hear nightfall,
You're asleep for goodness sake!
So riddle you diddle you fiddle you do,
Your silly old father loves you true,
If you're good I'll tell you something more,
A beech is a tree and a beach is a shore,
And if sky is blue and wind blew too,
Your silly old father is wiser than you,
So weigh my words as you go on your way,
Tomorrow's today when the nightfalls away!"'

Amid the applause that followed Finnbarr slipped back into the darkness, fading away like a shadow. Log a Log followed him, rapier at the ready. Rufe noticed them going and said in a loud voice to Fatch, 'Where are those two going, mate?'

'Keep yer voice down, Rufey, an' act normal like,' the Guosim shrew cautioned him.

There followed a squeal and a scuffle. Joseph reached for a boarding pike as he whispered, 'Stay calm every-beast, keep your weapons close to paw and wait until Finnbarr or Log a Log calls us. There's been something or someone out there since dusk!'

'Owow lemme go, get y'paws off me, searat!'

Durry was startled by the shrill voice. He turned to see Finnbarr hauling a struggling young squirrel over the rail. 'Be still, yer liddle rogue, or I'll tan yer 'ide. Ouch! 'E bit me!'

Log a Log materialized out of the gloom, tugging a small sobbing mousemaid behind him. 'Here's another one, I reckon there's more out there!'

The mousemaid broke free; throwing herself down in front of Joseph she pleaded brokenly, 'Oh, please don't slay us sir. Please!'

The young squirrel attempted to bite Finnbarr Galedeep again; he struggled and kicked viciously, shouting, 'Save your breath Wincey, they're pirates, you won't get mercy from this scummy lot!'

Rosie Woodsorrel confronted him. 'Now see here, young thingummybob, mind your manners, do we look like pirates?'

Squirming hard to get free of the sea otter's iron grip, the young squirrel bared his teeth. 'If you're not pirates then tell this big searat to let go of me!' he snarled.

Joseph filled two platters with *Pearl Queen* Pudden, then taking the mousemaid's paw gently, he signalled Finnbarr to release the young squirrel. 'Don't be frightened of Finnbarr,' he said to them, 'he's just a great big old sea otter. What's your name, young un?'

'My name's Benjy an' I'm not afraid of you or anybeast!'

'Of course you're not. Come and have something to eat, Benjy.' Joseph placed the plates of pudding in front of Benjy and Wincey, speaking softly to allay their fears. 'Rosie, is there any raspberry cordial in the galley? Bring our guests a beaker each. Come on, young uns, eat up, you look as if a plate of pudding apiece would cheer you up. Oh come on now, we're not going to hurt you.'

They ate hungrily, grunting and snuffling in their haste to get the pudding down. Rosie brought their cordial.

'My word, has there been a seven-season famine round here?' she laughed.

With his whiskers coated in fruit and pastry, Benjy shot her a quick glance. 'You don't look like no searat,' he said.

'I should hope not, and don't speak with y'mouth full,' Rosie said as she refilled the two plates. 'We're honest voyagers from Redwall Abbey and we don't go about slayin' and whatnot. Just look at you two! A good bath, some more food an' clean clothes is what y'need.'

Joseph took the little mousemaid on his lap. 'I had a little one like you, though she's quite big now. Tell me Wincey, how did you come to this place?'

She took a great sucking gulp of raspberry cordial and shrugged. 'Always been here, I think.'

The squirrel called Benjy had moved closer until he was leaning against Joseph. 'Aye, always, me an' Wincey an' Figgs.'

'Figgs, who's that?' said the Bellmaker, ruffling Benjy's ears fondly.

Benjy smiled secretly as he licked his pudding plate. 'Figgs is Figgs, she's our sister. Want me to call her?'

Before Joseph could reply Benjy was crying out, 'Figgs, Figgs, come out wherever y'are! Hurry up, they've got nice pudden an' drinks an' they're not searats!'

A tiny ottermaid popped her head shyly over the rail. 'Pudden's nice, Figgs wants some!' she squeaked.

Shaking with laughter, Foremole lifted her over the rail. 'Ee liddle raggymuffin choild, you'm can 'ave pudden 'til ee bursters, you'm a needen et t'be growen gurt!'

Figgs was so tiny that she had to pick up the wooden spoon in both paws, but there was nothing tiny about her appetite.

Finnbarr shook his head in wonderment at her. 'She could go to sea in a clamshell with a sail! Ahoy there, Figgs matey, is that the full crew of ye, or is there any more giants out there 'idin' silentlike?'

Figgs paused a moment as if thinking hard. 'No, only our father, Benjy knows where our father is.'

The young squirrel took Joseph, Finnbarr and Rosie a short walk into the hinterland of the island. Holding torches they followed him through thick undergrowth to a tattered sailcloth rigged askew of a fallen aspen. Benjy stopped short of it, pointing as if ashamed to go near. 'Our father's in there,' he said.

Finnbarr strode forward and went into the tent. He came out swiftly, shaking his head at Rosie and Joseph. 'You don't want ter go in there, t'aint a nice sight!' Tears were rolling silently down Benjy's face as the sea otter placed a tattooed paw about his shoulders. 'Hush now, matey, yore a big feller now, don't weep.' The young squirrel snuffled, wiping tearstained eyes on his tail. For one so fierce and scarred the sea otter spoke surprisingly softly.

'Who was that 'edge'og in there,' he asked, 'and 'ow did you all come t'this isle, tell me, young un?'

Benjy sniffed several times before explaining. 'Ship was wrecked t'pieces out on the sea at the start of summer. Burrom the hedgehog was hurted bad by a falling mast, but she clung to it an' pulled us aboard with her. Figgs too, though she was just born; don't know what happened to Figgs's mother. We got washed through the rocks into the cove; been living here all through summer. Poor Burrom never really got over that mast falling on her. She was mixed up all the time, talking strange.' Benjy shuddered hugely as if fighting back more tears. Finnbarr kept him talking as a distraction.

'How long's she been like that . . . I mean . . .' The young squirrel pulled himself together gallantly. 'You mean dead? Since last full moon, though I couldn't tell Wincey and Figgs. They kept wanting to see her but I told them she was sleeping.'

'But you said father,' Joseph interrupted. 'Burrom was a female?'

The young squirrel smiled through his tears. 'That was Wincey's idea. She never knew her father, so she thought it would be nice to call Burrom father. I told Figgs we were her family, brothers and sisters, she's too small to know any different.'

To cheer him up Rosie chuckled, 'Well I'm a mother and you can count on me, though you'll have lots of fathers aboard *Pearl Queen*, brothers too. Hmm, should've brought more sisters along with us!'

When they got back to the ship Foremole had made beds up for Wincey and Figgs in the crew's accommodation. Joseph settled down on the hatch covers with Benjy close by, and they lay watching the stars, like silver pins, holding up the dark velvet canopy of the night sky. Joseph outlined his plans for them. 'We're sailing in the morning, right after breakfast. I think you and your sisters would be better coming along with us, Benjy, what d'you think?'

'I think that's the best thing too, sir. I'll have to tell Wincey and Figgs that Burrom won't be coming along, it'll be difficult, 'specially for little Figgs.'

The Bellmaker nodded understandingly. 'You're growing up well, Benjy. You stay aboard with the others and Finnbarr and I will go ashore early and give Burrom a decent burial.'

The young squirrel sat upright. 'No, please, leave our father in the tent. I couldn't bear thinking about Burrom buried there all alone. Besides, she might get better and wake up someday . . .'

'So be it, Benjy,' said Joseph, smiling sadly, 'but don't grieve, Burrom will be glad that you three are safe and with friends now. Goodnight.'

'Goodnight sir. Oh, may I ask where we're going on your ship?'

'It's not my ship, *Pearl Queen* belongs to Finnbarr. We're bound for Southsward to search for my daughter Mariel and her friend Dandin. It's a long story.'

Benjy's eyes shone bright in the darkness. 'Southsward, that's my home!'

Now it was Joseph's turn to sit up. 'You come from Southsward?'

'Yes sir, every creature on the ship did. We were driven out of there by Urgan Nagru the Foxwolf – his rats killed both my parents. I want to go back to Southsward!'

'I'll bet you do, Benjy!' said Joseph, looking steadily at the youngster. 'Come to the galley with me, there's food and drink there. We have a lot to discuss.'

BOOK THREE

Southsward

26

Rosy-hued dawn flooded through the guest room window at Redwall Abbey as Mellus and Tarquin stirred the snoring searat Captain from a tangle of sheets.

'C'mon, Slipp, rise and shine, old rat. Let's see if you were bluffin' when you said you could cook.'

Slipp tried burrowing deeper into the bedlinen, as Tarquin turned him none-too-gently on to the floor. 'Go 'way, s'only just dawn, beat it!' he grumbled.

The hefty paw of Mother Mellus scooped the searat up on to his paws. 'Less of your insolence! You said you were a cook, so let's see you up and cooking!'

Blaggut poked his head from beneath the pillow, giggling dozily as he watched the proceedings. 'Show 'em what yore made of, Cap'n. Burn up a mess o'skilly an' duff, that'll warm the cockles of their 'earts, hahaharr!'

The badger turned as she propelled Slipp through the doorway. 'I wouldn't laugh too much if I were you, Blaggut, there's two friends outside want to see you. Go in and wake the nice rat up, my Dibbuns!'

The mousebabe and the molemaid came dashing in and threw themselves upon Blaggut, buffeting him unmercifully with Slipp's pillow. 'Cummon mista

Blackguts, Ma Mellus said you was a carpenter, we wanna see you carp!'

'Carp y'say, well I dunno,' said Blaggut as he sat up and scratched himself absently. 'Let's see mates, wot d'yer want ole Blaggy ter carp for ye?'

Furrtil the molemaid was in no doubt at all. ''Ee lickle boat to sail on ee Abbey pond zurr, so's us'n's can set in it. Can ee carp a boat, zurr Blackguts?'

Blaggut sensed a chance to help Slipp achieve his desire. 'Mebbe I kin, mebbe I cain't, boats don't git carped fer nothin', mates. D'you know where the secret treasure of this 'ere Redwall H'abbey is 'idden?'

The mousebabe looked furtively about, then drawing close he whispered in Blaggut's ear, 'A' course we does!'

The searat brightened up, his ruse was working. 'Right then, you show me the treasure an' I'll make ee an' 'andsome liddle boat t'sail round the pond in, eh?'

'No Zurr,' said the molemaid, stroking her digging claws solemnly. 'Furst you carp ee boat fer us'n's, then we tell ee whurr secret treasure be 'idden, hurr!'

Blaggut considered the offer, peering closely at the two well-scrubbed faces radiating honesty and trust at him. 'Haharr, you drive an 'ard bargain, but it's a deal, buckoes. One thing though, swear you won't tell anybeast about this?'

The mousebabe shook his paw vigorously in Blaggut's face. 'We don' swear, s'not nice t'swear, y'get sent t'bed.'

'Bless yer 'eart, messmate,' the dullard searat grinned. 'I don't mean swear'n'curse, I means we gotta take a vow t'gether, a solemn oath.'

The three conspirators placed their paws together and the Dibbuns repeated the words that Blaggut recited:

'I take this oath.'

'We take an oaf.'

'That me liver'n'lights be ripped out if'n any of us breathes a word of our secret to anybeast, so 'elp me!'

'Hurr e liver be gripped when ee lights be out an' ee secret breathin' of anybeasters to 'elp ee!'

Blaggut scratched his head as both Dibbuns smiled at him.

'I never 'eard it said like that afore, but I s'pose it'll 'ave ter do mates!'

An air of gloom hung over the breakfast tables in Cavern Hole. Blind Simeon wrinkled his whiskers in disgust as he took his seat.

'Phew! Has somebeast moved the orchard compost heap into here, Father Abbot?' he complained.

Saxtus prodded the mess on his plate glumly. 'Evidently you haven't heard of an old seagoing dish that Slipp our new cook has served up, it's called skilly an'duff. Like to try some?'

'Stick to plain honest bread, my friend, you'll live longer,' said Mother Mellus as she broke a fresh-baked farl and passed half to Simeon. 'Dearie me, no wonder searats are so wicked and wild, I'd be like that too if I had to live on a diet of the dreaded skilly an'duff!'

Slipp forestalled further conversation by pushing in a trolley piled high with platters of his creation. The searat captain was quite proud of his new-found cooking skills. Clad in a clean white smock and a tall chef's hat, several sizes too small for him, he swaggered up to a table. 'Skilly an'duff, that's the stuff t'put a curl in yer whiskers, made by me own fair paws. Anybeast want some more?'

Suddenly a lot of Redwallers left the tables, claiming that they felt the need for fresh fruit from the orchard. Ladle in paw, Slipp looked from the empty places to his few remaining victims left sitting at the main table. 'Fruit from the orchard? That'll never put a back on ye like velvet an' a twinkle in yer eye. Skilly an'duff, now that's a real brekkist for ye! C'mon Father H'abbot, yew ain't touched yores yet, it'll be gone cold. 'Ere, let ole Slipp freshen it up with some that's fresh cooked.'

Saxtus averted his head from the foul-smelling mess that Slipp was piling on to the cold contents of his plate. 'You'll excuse me asking, Slipp, but what do you put into this, er, skilly an'duff?' he asked.

Slipp licked the ladle and winked.

'Haharr, that's an ole seadog's secret, a bit o' this an' a touch o' that, lashin's of wild garlic, white dead nettle, some cleavers an' just a smidgeon o' dogwort.'

Saxtus clapped a paw to his mouth and hurried from the table.

Slipp hooked a clawful of the steaming concoction from Saxtus's plate, straight into his mouth. 'Wot's wrong with 'im, tastes fine t'me?'

Mellus's huge paw crashed down on the table. 'Enough is enough! The only thing you've ever cooked up is roguish schemes. Clear this . . . this . . . *garbage* away, and bury it somewhere deep to let nature take care of it. Now!'

Slipp drew himself up haughtily, about to protest when the badger seized him by one ear and shook him. 'You are a cheat and a liar! You've never cooked in your life! When you've cleared this lot up I want to see you out in the kitchens. Scrub all the pots and pans and spread rosewater round until every trace of skilly an'duff, sight or smell, is gone!'

'Yowowow, lemme go, stripedog! Ooch ouch!'

Brothers Fingle and Mallen took over cooking duties and a satisfactory lunch of summer salad, cheeses and apple pie with meadowcream brought the Abbey back on to an even keel. The day wore on, warm, sunny and still; bees droned lazily from flower to flower. Redwallers went on with their daily chores, tending crop and orchard, harvesting honey, reading and studying, or helping with the upkeep of Abbey buildings. Tranquillity was the keynote, with the high green mantle of Mossflower shading the outer walls on three sides, leaving the west ramparts open to sunny flatlands where larks sang and grasshoppers chirruped.

Towards mid-noon Blaggut put the finishing touches to a pair of boats he had made by halving an old cider barrel lengthways. The searat was proud of a previously unknown skill he had discovered that day – boatbuilding. He had sawed the barrel neatly from top to bottom, making two butt-ended little vessels. A cask lid cut in half provided two keels for balance. Inside the boats he wedged short flat planks for seats. Two big ash staves served as masts, with a third, cut in half, completing the cross spars, from which hung twin, much-patched sails. They had done sterling service as tablecloths and were donated by Sister Sage. The mousebabe and Furrtil the molemaid scurried round the searat's footpaws, squeaking excitedly.

'Which un's mine, Blackguts sir?'

'Hurr, they'm bootiful ships!'

'Can us 'ave rowers to row with?'

'Oi'm callen moi ship ee Daffydil!'

'Mine be called Watermousey!'

Blaggut sat down on the pond edge, sipping cider that he had drained from the barrel into a bowl before construction began. The searat was as happy as the two Dibbuns.

'Haharr mates, I'm a boatbuilder! All me life I've been called stoopid an' clumsy an' thick as two short planks. But I ain't, I got clever paws, I kin make boats, good 'uns!'

'Write our ships' names on 'em, Blackguts sir. Oh please!'

Blaggut had hoped they would not ask him this. 'Er, well, mebbe Sister Sage oughter do that, shipmates. I never learned no writin', bein' a seara . . . er, carpenter, there wasn't no need fer such things. Aye, we'll ask the Sister, 'sides, she prob'ly kin write proper fancy, I bet good ole mouseladies like 'er does writin' a lot. But 'old 'ard mateys, wot about our bargain, you know, the secret treasure you was gonna show me?'

The mousebabe planted his paws on tiny fat hips. 'Nono, first we wanna sail, see if these ships work right!'

Blaggut finished his cider. 'Yore an 'ard master, mousebabe. Come on then, let's launch 'em.'

The boats were an instant success. They sailed wonderfully on the slightest breeze and in the absence of any wind could be rowed easily with the paddles Blaggut had made. All the Abbey Dibbuns gathered at the pond's edge, anxious to take their turn being ferried about on the Abbey pond. Both mousebabe and molemaid were in their element, sailing, paddling and roaring orders.

'Hurr, you'm sit yurr an' ee sit thurr, 'old on naow!'

'Two atta time, on'y two atta time, who's next?'

'Oi'll take ee round yon bullyrushers!'

'Watch out for big fishes an' pirates!'

Blaggut lounged on the bank, proudly watching his two new boats on their maiden voyages. After a while, Slipp came shuffling wearily along and slumped down beside his former bosun. 'Enjoyin' yerself are yer, 'avin' a good time?' he asked.

'Aye thankee Cap'n, see the boats I made fer my Dibbuns!'

Slipp cast a weary eye over the two sleek little craft. 'So that's 'ow you been fritterin' the day away, I mighta known, you great lazy loaf'ead!'

Blaggut had not expected Slipp to make any nice comments on his achievements. 'Buildin' boats ain't fritterin' time away, Cap'n. Wot 'ave you been up to all day?'

Slipp waved airily as if it were no big thing. 'Oh, they

made me 'ead cook, I'm in charge of all the kitchens. Did yer taste my skilly an'duff at brekkfist?'

'Aye Cap'n, it was 'orrible. Yew make a better Cap'n than a cook. The bread was nice though, did y'make that?'

Slipp was no stranger to fibbing. 'Baked the bread meself,' he lied glibly, 'it was those Abbey mice who made the skilly'an'duff, they ignored me instructions.'

Blaggut leaned close to Slipp's ear and whispered, 'Cap'n, we don't 'ave to go 'untin' fer booty tonight, so don't you worry about that black shadder we saw.'

Slipp felt the hairs on his nape rise with fear. 'Shur-rup y'fool. Shut yer mouth! I tol' you never to mention that black shadow again long as you live. It didn't 'appen, d'ye hear me? There's no such thing as black shadows. Any'ow, why don't we 'ave to go lookin' fer booty tonight?'

Blaggut told his Captain all, from the boatbuilding to the oath he had taken with the Dibbuns. He smiled slyly at Slipp and winked. Slipp cuffed him roughly on the nose. 'Y'mean to tell me that those two Dibthings know where there's secret treasure 'idden, an' yore sittin' 'ere like a loungin' lobster watchin' em sail round a pond?'

'Bargain's a bargain, Cap'n,' said Blaggut, rubbing his nose tenderly. 'They gotta try out their new boats. Besides, I got to stay 'ere an' keep an eye on the liddle rascals in case one falls in.'

Tarquin L. Woodsorrel came strolling up and wagged an ear at Slipp curtly. 'C'mon Slippy ol' rat, back to work wot? Lots of sticky pots t'be washed, they've been making honey pudden an' maple toffee apples. Sticks the pots'n'pans up frightfully y'know. Mellus sent me, said if y'don't come she'll be down here an' fetch you herself, y'don't want that, wot?'

Blaggut stared nonplussed at his companion. 'But Cap'n, I thought you said you was the cook in charge?'

Tarquin chuckled at the thought of Slipp ruling the kitchens. 'Oh he's in charge all right, Lord of all the greasy dishwater, King of the pots'n'pans. Well old thing, are you comin'?'

Slipp gnawed a sticky claw, his bravado shattered by the thought of the Fearsome Mellus standing over him, inspecting each dish to see it was clean. He clung to Blaggut, whimpering, 'Don't let'im take me mate, you wouldn't let them crooly use yer ole Cap'n as a galley slave, would yer?'

'Leave the Cap'n 'ere sir,' Blaggut appealed to Tarquin. 'Those young uns need watchin'. I've gotta take the molemaid an' the mousebabe fer their afternoon stroll. Ahoy there you two, come on now.'

Tarquin winked at Slipp. 'Righto, but don't forget those pots and pans or Mellus will remind you with a ladle, wot?'

The two Dibbuns held Blaggut's paws as they guided him round the back of the main Abbey building. As they went he questioned them. 'You shore that it's the real secret 'idden treasure of Redwall's h'Abbey?'

The mousebabe gave an exasperated sigh at Blaggut's ignorance. 'Phwaw! Course we sure, it's the mos' secretest treasure in alla world, innit Furrtil?'

The molemaid smiled and tapped her nose knowingly. 'Yurr, that et be, an' oanly us'n's know whurr et be buried.'

At the southeast gable of the Abbey the mousebabe planted his back firmly against the wall and began striding out in measured steps, counting. Blaggut and Furrtil followed.

'One, two, three, five, seven, six, twennyfour, eleventeen . . .'

The molemaid nodded her head in admiration. 'Burr, oi wished oi knowed 'ow to count in numbers loik ee mousebaby do, ee'm turrible clever!'

Blaggut watched the little figure striding boldly out.

'Twennyfifty, sixfortyeight, two again, leventy-twelve . . .'

'Bless me, eddication's a wunnerful thing, look at 'im go!'

The mousebabe halted at the southeast corner of the outer wall and he pointed down.

'There, you has to dig now!'

Blaggut looked at the spot. 'Who dug the 'ole in the first place?'

Furrtil pointed a digging claw at herself. 'Oi did zurr, ho t'wurr 'ard wurk, oi tell ee!'

Blaggut leaned up against the wall. 'Yore a mole, why can't you dig the treasure up?'

The mousebabe looked at him as if he had taken leave of his senses. 'Cos she messed up 'er frock diggin' it inna first place, d'you want to get 'er sended off t'bed again, silly!'

With a look of long suffering Blaggut knelt down to dig.

The black shadow fell over him.

Startled, he looked up in time to see the hooded figure on the walltop draw back out of sight. Grabbing the Dibbuns' paws the searat rushed them off across the Abbey grounds. Suddenly the quiet summer afternoon was laden with unspeakable dread for him.

The molemaid held on to her mob cap as he whisked them along. 'Whurr be ee rushen us'n's off to, zurr?'

'Save yer breath, little un – keep runnin'!'

'But wot about ee gurt secret treasure?'

'Ferget it, c'mon, back to the pond.'

The mousebabe broke away and sped off yelling, 'Ahoy ahoy, back to our boats!'

They made it back to the pond when the Joseph bell tolled out a single boom. Teatime. Trestles had been set up for a summer orchard tea. Strawberries and cream, toffee apples, yellow dandelion bread and dark, fizzy elderberry cordial.

Tarquin placed a slab of white celery cheese on some dandelion bread, took a bite, chewed critically, ears flapping slowly, then washed it down with a beaker of the cordial. 'First rate, top hole! All in order, compliments to the cook, couldn't ask for nicer, grade one tuck!'

'Keep talking, while you're spouting you aren't scoffing!'

Tarquin wrinkled his nose at Sister Rose's remark. 'So beautiful, yet so cruel, marm. Pray be seated, I'll join you presently if I may.'

He turned and stalked to where Blaggut and Slipp were seated side by side, both scrubbed and wearing clean tunics. The hare wagged a warning paw at them. 'Best behaviour now, you chaps, mind y'manners an' don't go piggin' everything in sight.'

Mellus murmured quietly to Simeon, 'That's rich coming from Woodsorrel the walloper; don't go pigging everything in sight, did you hear him?'

'A case of glutton shall speak unto glutton I'd say!' smiled Simeon as he nodded.

Saxtus rang his table bell and everybeast folded paws and lowered their eyes. Brother Mallen nudged the two searats to do likewise. Then Father Abbot of Redwall said grace.

'Thanks to seasons, praise the fates,
For this peace within our gates.
Welcome, friends, who gladly toil,
In our fertile Redwall soil.
May we never famine fear,
Mid the summer's goodness here.'

Mother Mellus inspected the mousebabe's paws approvingly. 'My, my, these are very clean indeed!'

Mousebabe rolled his eyes skyward, impatient to be eating. 'Hmm, should be clean paws, losed me paddle an' I been rowin' my ship rounda pond wiv them.'

Slipp kicked Blaggut under the table. 'Well, where's the treasure, did yer get it?' he whispered.

Keeping his eyes straight ahead, Blaggut applied himself to the business of strawberries and cream. 'Uh uh, Cap'n, sorry. You told me never t'mention it as long as I lives.'

'Never t'mention wot? Tell me!' said Slipp, and he bit a slice of cheese savagely.

Blaggut chose a strawberry, dipping it in the rich golden tinged cream. It vanished into his mouth. 'Mmmm, wunnerful! No Cap'n, I'm only obeyin' orders, you told me never to mention that black shadder as long as I lives, so I can't tell yer.'

Slipp felt the hair rise at the nape of his neck again. 'Black shadow, was the black shadow there?' he croaked.

Blaggut sorted through his bowl of strawberries until he found the biggest of all. 'Can't tell yer Cap'n, you said black shadders don't 'appen an' I was to ferget it all, so I'm fergettin' it, Cap'n!'

Slipp was trying hard to keep his claws away from Blaggut's obstinate neck. He tried another ploy. 'Yore right mate, don't mention that other shadow thing, just tell me about the treasure, or the place it's buried in.'

Blaggut piled cream on to his big strawberry until it was completely covered and held it near his mouth. "Ang on a tick, Cap'n. Glopp! Mmmff, mmmff!'

The infuriated Slipp had to sit waiting whilst his former bosun munched away with a look of delight pasted on his oafish face. Blaggut finished and licked the cream from his lips. 'Aaahhh, never 'ad more prime vittles in me life! Oh, now, where was I? The secret treasure of Redwall h'Abbey, aye, that's where I was. It's buried at the corner of the southeast wall, eleventynine steps from the buildin' itself . . .'

'Eleventynine steps y'say?' The Captain managed to keep a straight face.

'Aye, that's 'ow the mouseybabe measured it out, an' that liddle cove knows 'ow to count, take my affydavit on it. I knows the h'exact spot where it lies, truth to tell, I was startin' to dig it up when . . . Oho, but I promised I wouldn't mention that, beggin' yer pardon, Cap'n.'

Slipp relaxed and began searching his own bowl for big strawberries to dip in the cream. 'I've got it now,' he said, 'yore tellin' me that you knows where the treasure is buried, the very spot. Now, you was just goin' t'dig it up when wot we vowed never to mention again came an' scared you off, is that right?'

Blaggut poured himself cordial, watching it fizz.

'Eddication's a great thing, Cap'n, 'ow do they put the liddle bubbles in this grog. Yowch! I told you I knows where the treasure lies, Cap'n, no need ter keep kickin' me!'

Further conversation was halted by the tinkle of the Abbot's bell. A smile hovered about the face of Saxtus as he made his announcement.

'Attention friends, tonight at dusk we will gather by the pond for a concert. Everybeast is allowed to take part, but I beg you to keep any songs and dances brief, so that all may have a chance to perform. There will be a number of prizes, the main one being a silver cup donated by Mellus. Dibbuns can stay up late to take part. Thank you!'

There was a rousing cheer from the Redwallers, then they left the tables to go about any remaining chores, discussing with each other what they would do at the concert.

Slipp murmured out of the corner of his mouth to Blaggut, 'Perfect! While they're singin' an' jiggin' we'll be diggin' the treasure up.'

Blaggut was about to raise an objection when a large black shadow fell over them both. He covered his face with both paws and tried to hide beneath the table, but it was only Mellus.

'Slipp, haven't you got work to finish in the kitchens?' she asked. 'Blaggut, come from under that table, you'll be needed to gather wood for the fire by the pond. Come on you two, look lively or you won't get a chance to do your bit at the concert this evening.'

Blaggut and Slipp looked at each other nonplussed. 'Do our bit?' groaned Slipp.

The searat Captain snorted as he gathered up dishes. 'Huh, the only bit we'll be doin' is robbin' the treasure from this place an' makin' a run fer it, an' 'tis woe betide anybeast who gets in the way!'

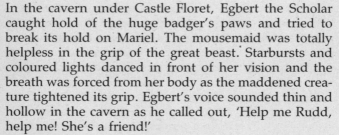

27

In the cavern under Castle Floret, Egbert the Scholar caught hold of the huge badger's paws and tried to break its hold on Mariel. The mousemaid was totally helpless in the grip of the great beast. Starbursts and coloured lights danced in front of her vision and the breath was forced from her body as the maddened creature tightened its grip. Egbert's voice sounded thin and hollow in the cavern as he called out, 'Help me Rudd, help me! She's a friend!'

An otter bounded out of the mist. He stood before the badger and made a swift motion with a javelin he was carrying. Instantly the badger dropped Mariel, who fell to the rocky floor gasping for breath. Egbert ministered to Mariel as he spoke soothingly to the badger.

'This is our friend Mariel – she will not harm us, Muta. She is an enemy of Foxwolf, you and Rudd can help her.'

The otter dipped a beaker into a pool among the rocks and, holding it to the mousemaid's lips, he allowed her to drink.

Aside from a few aching ribs, Mariel was not badly injured. She regained her breath and sat among the rocks with Egbert. The badger and the otter sat a short distance away. She watched them. Both were completely still as if awaiting an order from Egbert. The mousemaid could not help but notice the dreadful scars tracing the fur of both creatures. Egbert explained their story.

'They staggered in here one night, virtually ripped to pieces and nearly dead. I took care of them both. It was no easy task. I learned most of my healing skills from books and scrolls, and luckily they worked, though not completely – I cannot heal minds. It was Nagru and his horde who tried to kill them – see the way they bare their teeth at the mention of his name. The badger I know is called Muta, she used to be nursemaid to the son of Gael, here at Floret. I do not know the otter so I call him Rudd. Strange, but neither beast talks, nor do they appear to have any memory of things that went on before I found them here that night. They are both mighty warriors. I think Muta has taken the way of the Berserk – I have read of badgers being like this, nobeast can stop them when a bloodlust is upon them. Rudd has become like her.'

Mariel interrupted Egbert. 'I think I know more about these two than you do, friend. The otter is called Rab Streambattle. I was told about them at the dwelling of Furpp the mole; they were believed to be dead, both killed when Serena and Truffen made their escape. I will tell you the full story when we get time. Meanwhile let me try something.'

Mariel approached the two silent beasts, as they sat motionless. The mousemaid spoke first to Muta and then to Rab, repeating the names of their loved ones.

'Muta, I come from Gael, I have news of Serena and little Truffen. They are safe. Rab, you are alive, yet Iris thinks you are dead. Your mate, Iris!'

There was no response. The two battle-scarred warriors stared blankly at Mariel as if she were talking in a strange language. Egbert drew her aside.

'It is no use,' he said, 'I have tried similar things with them. Whatever was done to those two has changed them, they are inseparable and live only to kill their enemies.'

Mariel felt a great wave of pity for the two dumb beasts. She too had known what it was to be like them; seasons before she came to Redwall a similar thing had happened to her. She clasped their paws in hers – Muta's, huge and forbidding, Rab's, sinewy and dangerous.

'Listen friends,' she said, earnestly. 'I am Mariel of Redwall. Together we will rid Southsward of Urgan Nagru and his scum, this I promise you! Egbert, where is the gatehouse that works the drawbridge?'

The scholarly mole squinted over his glasses. 'Follow me, but be careful!'

Greenbeck bowed low as Gael Squirrelking materialized out of the mist to meet the rescuers on the plateau.

'Your Majesty, fates be thanked!'

Gael clasped Greenbeck's paw, saying, 'Do not bow to a fool like me. There are others following – send your scouts to guide them here.'

On Greenbeck's order, two otters, Ruckal and Cresseye, trotted off into the rainspattering mists and returned leading Meldrum and Dandin.

Silvamord had given up searching for Mariel. She sat kicking her paws on a windowledge, shaking her head in mock pity at Nagru.

'What are you going to do, mighty conqueror – tear the castle apart to find one mousemaid? She's long gone!'

The Foxwolf had been roaring orders, tearing down wall hangings, smashing doors and generally abusing his searchers. With his chest heaving from exertion, he slumped down and sat on the cold stone floor.

'Catch them as they swing into the battlements,' he sneered. 'That wasn't my idea, that was your bright scheme, vixen!'

Wetchops and Mingol came scurrying up from opposite ends of the corridor. Before they could speak, Silvamord pointed at Mingol. 'You first, what's your good news?'

The rat shuffled nervously, keeping out of range of Nagru. 'The prisoners have all escaped, Sire. We finally broke into the attic of the tower, but there was nobeast there!'

'Leave them up there in the rain, I'll deal with them tomorrow after a good sleep,' said Silvamord, mimicking Nagru's voice. 'That's what you said – *Sire!*'

Nagru shot her a swift, murderous glare before turning his attention to Wetchops. 'Well, what have you got to say for yourself? Speak!'

'Sire, the drawbridge is being attacked!'

'By who?'

'Dunno, Sire, too much rain an' mist outside, but they're firin' arrows, throwin' lances an' slingstones.'

Silvamord eased herself off the windowledge. 'Well, they're wasting their time,' she said. 'That drawbridge gate won't budge for arrows or stones and lances. I wonder what they're really up to?'

Nagru stood up slowly, saying, 'A diversion maybe, what d'you think?'

Silvamord raised her eyebrows approvingly. 'I think you're right, for once. Better double the guards on the walls and in the turrets, they may try a surprise attack from another part of the valley.'

Iris loosed an arrow off into the mist. She heard it thud into the drawbridge gate.

Troutlad fitted a shaft to his bowstring. 'Rain's gone off,' he said. 'But I think we're wastin' arrows and lances here, that keep door is too sturdy.'

'Oh, I don't know old chap,' came a voice from in front of them. 'You may've kept 'em off our backs while we escaped!'

Greenbeck's party emerged from the mist, Dandin, Meldrum and Gael striding along with them. Iris waved her bow. 'Cease fire! Dandin, Meldrum, welcome! Your Majesty!'

Egbert emerged from a dark tunnel and held out a cautionary paw to his friends. 'That's as close as I can get you by hidden ways,' he said.

They came out into a long hallway broken in parts by broad flights of steps. Mariel let the wall tapestry drop back into place across the tunnel mouth. 'Which way to the gatehouse, Egbert?' she asked.

The mole scholar pointed. 'As far as you can go, through the banqueting chamber, down another flight of stairs and first left. Er, it's not that I'm afraid or anything, but I'm a scholar, not a warrior – wouldn't I be in the way?'

Mariel patted the mole's paw understandingly. 'Of course, you'd be a liability if fighting broke out, we'd have to look out for you. Besides, you must have other business to attend to.'

Egbert pushed aside the tapestry that hid the tunnel. 'Thank you, Mariel. I'm sure I'll be around should you need me.'

Muta and Rab waved goodbye as Mariel called softly, 'Good luck and fortune go with you, Egbert the Scholar!'

The mole poked his head back around the tapestry. 'Through extensive research I have found that luck and fortune have little to do with anything. It is brains like mine and a warrior mentality like yours, combined with the element of surprise, that invariably wins the day!'

The three warriors trod lightly down the first flight of steps, looking from left to right, ready for anything.

Mariel peeked through a partially opened door, and saw horderats sleeping on a straw-littered floor, a chamber full of them. Without a word to her berserk companions she gently removed a spear from the claws of a slumbering rat. Closing the door, the mousemaid slid the spearhaft through the ring in the latch, effectively imprisoning the sleepers in their own barracks. Muta looked at her questioningly. Mariel smiled. 'It's nothing, just making sure we're not followed.'

Voices came from further down the darkened hallway. 'Well, *you* go an' tell Nagru that you ain't stannin' out on no walls all night, I'm not!'

'But I don't 'ave a cloak like you, s'pose it's still raining', I'll catch me death of cold out there!'

'Aye, mate, and you'll catch yer death a lot faster if you tell Foxwolf that you don't fancy obeyin' his orders!'

'Huh, if it wasn't for those mangy escaped prisoners we'd be in our barracks n . . .' The rat never finished the sentence he was speaking; neither he nor his companion would ever have to worry about going out on guard again. Muta and Rab carried on down the next flight of stairs as if nothing had happened. Mariel took a curved sword from one of the dead rats and hastened to catch up with the silent slayers.

The banqueting chamber had a torch alight on one wall. The three warriors moved through, silent as the flickering shadows that played over tables and chairs.

Six horderats were seated round a table in the gatehouse, playing a game with three shells and an acorn. A flagon of wine stood on the table, a prize for the winner. A draught flickered round the wall torches as the door swung open. One rat looked up, and squealed with fright at the sight of Mariel and her two silent allies entering the room. Muta charged, her relentless energy taking her crashing into the nearest two rats, then all became confusion.

The table went crashing end over end, knocking the wall torches from their sconces and plunging the gatehouse into darkness. In the onslaught, amid the screaming, clattering, grunting and banging, five of the rats met their doom. One rat, more nimble than the rest, slipped by Rab. He fled through the doorway and up the stairs before anybeast could stop him. Mariel struggled with the otter in the doorway as he tried to give chase. 'No, Rab, leave the rat, we've got what we want – the gatehouse is ours!'

Slamming the door and securing it, the mousemaid found the torches and blew on them until they flared into light. A huge wooden drum with turning handles attached and a crude block brake held the thick ropes that controlled the drawbridge. Muta finished tipping the last of the slain enemies from the gatehouse window, smiling grimly as the carcasses hit the moat below with a splash. Taking Mariel's sword, the badger swung it high over the coils of rope wound around the drum, ready to slice them through to lower the bridge. Mariel shook her head. 'No need for that, my friend. We control the drawbridge now – besides, the time may arrive when we'll need to have it closed!'

Silvamord was frightened; Nagru was furious. They had both listened to the terrified recitation of the rat who had escaped alive from the gatehouse. The Foxwolf watched sunny daylight dispersing the valley mist from his chamber window, then banged the ledge so hard that his paw hurt. 'They double-bluffed us! So that was how their decoy worked, fooling us into thinking they were attacking the drawbridge, drawing our guards away on to the walltops to forestall another trick, when all the time they really were attacking the drawbridge, from the inside! Now they have control over our very front door! Come on, vixen, where's all your crafty ideas? Why are you sitting there trembling like a pile of frogspawn?'

Silvamord was not looking at Nagru. She stared at the wall blankly, her voice atremble as she said, 'The badger and the otter, you couldn't have killed them right, they've come back from the dead and they're inside this place now!'

The Urgan Nagru shook his head until the teeth of the wolfskull rattled. 'I can't believe those two aren't dead. We left them like pincushions, they were ripped to bits . . .'

A loud bump from below interrupted him. It startled Silvamord from her trance, and she dashed to the window. 'They've lowered the drawbridge!'

Watching from the wooded slopes on the opposite valley side, Dandin's sharp eyes caught sight of a small figure in the gatehouse window. It was gone in a second, but almost at once the drawbridge fell open and spanned the moat. He turned to Iris, his eyes shining happily. 'Now I know where Mariel is, in the gatehouse! There's only one warrior maid could've pulled off a trick like that. Haha, escaping's not good enough for that one, she's got to capture the drawbridge as well!'

Meldrum tore himself away from the impromptu breakfast he had scrounged. 'Brains eh, that gel will control her own regiment one day, mark m'words. Righto, up on y'paws you lot, we've got to jolly well help her!'

Amid the jubilation it was left for Iris to provide the voice of reason. 'Hold hard, you two, we're only a small rescue party. I don't think you've grasped just how large the Foxwolf's horde is. We'd be committing suicide trying to attack Floret, even with the drawbridge down.'

Meldrum stroked berry stains from his mustachios. 'You're right, of course,' he admitted. 'So, what action d'you propose we take? Can't leave the brave mousey there on her own t'be winkled out an' slain by those foul creatures, can we?'

Gael had been listening to the conversation. An idea was forming in the Squirrelking's mind. 'I suggest that you send word to Mariel telling her we are here. If you stay in the valley and harass the foe to keep their attention off Mariel it will go a long way towards helping her. Meanwhile, I will go to Furpp's dwelling, and from there I must try to raise up the whole of Southsward in arms to march upon Floret. Mariel has opened up a golden opportunity for us; the time is ripe. I think we will never get a better chance to rid the land of Foxwolf and his horde. The sooner we strike the better!'

Mariel and her two silent friends had shared the flagon of wine and eaten what small amount of food there was to be had in the gatehouse. Rats had gathered on the stairs outside, but so far they had made no move to try and recapture the room. Nagru knew that he would only lose valuable hordebeasts by trying to charge the door, for in such a small space the badger and the otter could hold the doorway against all comers. The mousemaid was making herself a new Gullwhacker with a thick length of spare drawbridge rope; she sat at the window, working at the complicated knots known only to herself. The valley was fresh and green under bright morning sun, deceptively peaceful and calm. The mousemaid's quick eyes took in a slight movement on the wooded slope opposite. 'Look Muta, Rab, see, we have friends close by!' she cried.

The badger and the otter joined her at the window. Mariel gave out a piercing whistle, swinging her half-completed Gullwhacker out of the open window. 'If they can't hear me maybe they'll see this rope.'

A moment later she glimpsed a small figure climbing to the lower branches of a sycamore. It was waving what appeared to be a long dagger. The mousemaid waved back, saying, 'That's got to be Dandin. I can't see properly from here but I'll wager anything it's him!'

Dandin climbed down from his perch to where Meldrum and Iris were waiting.

'Aye, that's my Mariel all right,' he said. 'She's got herself a new Gullwhacker. Do you think you could put an arrow through that window, Iris?'

The otter shouldered her bow and quiver busily. 'Get me close enough and I know I can, third shot!'

As Mariel watched the three figures duck and weave across the valley floor, she commentated on their movements to Muta and Rab. 'Here they come, there's three of them, I think one is Meldrum but I can't be sure. They're holding a great chunk of bark in front of them as a shield. They must have been sighted by Nagru's rats – arrows are being shot at them, one or two have struck the bark shield, but they're still coming forward. Oh come on, come on friends!'

Meldrum the Magnificent pulled his twitching ears in below the top of the bark. 'The blighters are shootin' at us, nearly had my bally ears pierced just then. Much further t'go chaps?'

Dandin held tight to the sheet of bark, sidestepping as an arrow thudded into the earth close to his paw. 'What d'you think Iris, is this far enough?' he asked.

The otter squinted through a knothole at the castle. 'This will do, here goes number one!'

She ran from behind the shield, a shaft already strung tight on her bowstring. Taking quick aim, Iris fired and nipped back behind the shield as a volley of arrows zipped from the battlements at her.

'Too high,' she said, 'it hit the stones above the gatehouse window, but Mariel knows what we're up to now. She's pulled back out of sight and put a table upright in the windowspace. Right, here goes my second shot – it won't hit, it's only a rangefinder.'

Notching another arrow on her string, the otter leapt

out and fired. She watched the arrow in flight for a brief moment before diving back under cover. 'Thought so, too low! Give me the arrow with the message tied to it, Dandin, I've got the range now.'

Fitting the third arrow to her bow, Iris waited a moment as a hail of arrows passed overhead.

'One . . . Two . . . Now!'

She sprang into the open, bowstring taut against her cheek, and squinting one eye along the arrow she released it.

Sssssst thunk!

Muta and Rab stood guarding the door against any sudden attack as Mariel tugged at the arrow buried in the tabletop. 'Whew, whoever shot that one knew what they were doing!' she said, admiringly.

Nagru and Silvamord had both been in line with the rats on the battlements, shooting arrows for all they were worth. The Foxwolf put aside his bow as the three figures retreated behind their shield.

'Stop shooting,' he ordered. 'They're out of range now. All down to the drawbridge. Come on, you fumble-pawed lot, shift yourselves!'

A big grey rat named Grutch was in charge of the ranks that stood six deep blocking the open drawbridge entrance. He saluted Nagru smartly. 'All quiet here, Lord, no sign of any attack yet.'

The Foxwolf glanced up at the gatehouse window high above. 'It will come, though. Grutch, I want this entrance guarded night and day. No lapses – stay alert. Those three in the gatehouse have received a message from their friends.'

Mariel unrolled the thin strip of cloth from around the arrowshaft and read aloud the charcoal scrawl to the badger and the otter. 'Hold gatehouse long as you can. Gael gone to raise an army. It is war!'

28

Pearl Queen skimmed the summer seas like a great bird, ever southward, cutting white-crested rollers, with webs of sunlit water patterns racing along her hull above the seashadows. Finnbarr and Joseph leaned over the stern rail, watching their vessel's creamy wake trail out until it merged with the distant main. The sea otter squinted at the feathery clouds being chased across the sky by playful breezes.

'We're makin' good headway, Joseph, let's 'ope our luck stays with us, mate,' he said.

The Bellmaker could not resist smiling at this remark. 'Luck? We've been holed by rocks, attacked by toads, fought off a shark, lost our rudder, had a mast snapped off like a twig and been chased by a double-crewed shipload of searats and that's *beside* losing the Roaringburn current that was supposed to take us to Southsward. What more luck do we need, you puddle-headed old seadog?'

Finnbarr threw a tattooed paw about the Bellmaker's shoulders, hugging him fondly.

'Yew mizzuble ole bellbonger, I never said 'twas goin' t'be easy, did I? We ain't sittin' on the bottom o' the briny with a sunken ship, that's lucky. May'aps those three liddle orphans we took aboard at the island are our lucky charms, eh?'

Joseph turned and watched the three young ones. They were playing skip the rope on the hatch covers with Rufe, Durry and Fatch. 'Poor little mites, they could do with a bit of luck themselves. We're the only ones they've got left in this world now. Benjy will be useful to us, he knows Southsward.'

'Wot about the other two young coves?' Finnbarr nodded towards Wincey and Figgs.

'Fortunately they have no memory of Southsward, or if they do it's never mentioned. From what Benjy told me it was a terrible place to be once the creature called Foxwolf came there. He rules the land by terror; there's none to stand against him and his rat horde. The Urgan Nagru is his other name and he has a mate called Silvamord. Benjy's not sure whether they're wolves or foxes. They murdered and tricked their way into power – have you ever heard of them, Finn?'

The sea otter touched his twin sword hilts ominously. 'No, but when we meet I'm sure the pleasure'll be all mine, matey. I've allus been a freebeast, an' I never could take to tyrants an' conquerors, 'specially those who'd make orphans of liddle uns. Bad fortune to 'em says I, an' I'm the beast who'll bring it to 'em!'

Figgs was not built for rope skipping. She attached herself to Rosie, knowing that the hare was a good food provider.

'Figgs wants pudden, Rosie, more pudden!'

Rosie Woodsorrel gave a gusty whoop. 'Whoohaha-hooh! I say, what a good idea, Figgs, so do I. Come on, old scout, let's chuck those shrews out the galley and see what we can jolly well cook up between us, wot?'

Foremole stumped about, opening supply lockers and searching the galley cupboards gloomily. 'B'aint much vittles left, miz Rose, we'm should've taked on more supplies at ee island. Burr, soon us'n's be a drinken ee sea an' cooken ee sails furr zoop!'

Rosie frowned as she turned a few withered apples out of a drawer. 'Well lack a day, you mean there's no tucker left?'

Log a Log crawled out of an empty locker, saying, 'There's a bit, but not much. I've just been sounding the water casks, we're going to have to ration the drinking water from now on. If we don't sight land soon I think fish would be a good idea, eh, Foremole?'

'Burr, nay zurr Log, we'm 'ad one gurt fish aboard, that wurr enuff furr oi, thankee!'

Figgs followed Rosie about, throwing her paws in the air and repeating over and over, 'Lack a day, no tucker's left, lack a day!'

A meeting of the crew was called. Joseph faced them across a small heap of supplies, all that was left aboard *Pearl Queen*. The Bellmaker's face was grave as he addressed the assembly.

'This is the sum total of our food, and from now on the water is rationed. We must go carefully.'

Rosie watched Figgs toddling about repeating her lament. 'Lack a day, no tucker's left, no tucker, lack a day!'

The kindly hare gathered the little otter to her. 'Well, I'm not really hungry, doncha know. Give my share to young Figgs here.'

Finnbarr shook his head, saying, 'O no, marm, an' all you others who volunteered t'give their vittles t'the young uns. No, it can't be done. We'd all starve an' they'd be left alone agin. Everybeast must take their rations an' eat 'em t'keep up strength, that's an order!'

Lookouts were posted in the rigging to watch out for land. Benjy sat up on the bowsprit with Durry, Rufe and Fatch. They scanned the horizon constantly with no success. Mid-noon became hot, and the breeze dropped until *Pearl Queen* was practically lying becalmed. Joseph filled a water dipper from a pail to give the sea otter his ration.

'Looks like that luck you were talking about has run out,' he said.

Finnbarr sipped steadily, his single eye roving the sea. 'Keep yer chin up, Bellmaker, bit o' a breeze is all we needs to shift us on t'fresh fortune.'

Benjy was the youngest of the four who sat on the bowsprit. He stared unhappily at the empty wastes of water stretching as far as his eye could see.

'Fatch, what'll happen if we don't get food?' he asked. The shrew was the eldest by a season. He winked at Durry, saying, 'If we don't get food we'll prob'ly have to eat one o' the crew, that's what they do at sea, ain't it mates?'

Durry and Rufe went along with the joke. 'Aye, that's right. Wonder who Mr Finnbarr will pick to cook for supper tonight?'

Benjy stood up, paws clenched. 'He'd better not choose Wincey or Figgs!'

'Nah, they're too liddle.' Fatch dismissed the idea airily. 'Us young uns are safe, there ain't enough on us t'make a decent pan o' soup.'

Benjy was completely taken in; wide eyed, he asked, 'Does that mean we'll have to eat one of the big uns? Hope it's not Mr Joseph, I like him!'

Rufe thought for a moment. 'Hmm, Foremole might taste all right, or maybe one of the shrews – Log a Log, he's plump enough.'

'I couldn't eat them, they're nice creatures!' Benjy said, horrified.

Rosie and Figgs were parading round the deck. Rosie was so amused by the little ottermaid that she had joined her in the game. They both went about waving their paws, calling aloud together, 'Lack a day, no tucker, tucker's gone, lack a day!'

Passing by the four on the bowsprit, Rosie gave them a wave. 'Toodle pip chaps! Whew, this is hot work. Lack a day . . .'

Fatch cast a sly glance at Rosie and rubbed his paws gleefully. 'At least we wouldn't have to put up with Mrs Woodsorrel laughin' all the time,' he said.

Rufe had not really taken part in the grisly joke, and now, unable to stand any more of it, he put a comforting paw around Benjy. 'Don't worry mate, there'll be nobeast cooked aboard this ship. Huh, I'd like to see anyone try to eat Miz Rosie!'

Figgs heard the remark and thought it was the signal for a new game. She grabbed the hare's footpaw, crying, 'Lack a day, eat Miz Rosie, lack a day!'

Rosie Woodsorrel was highly amused, at first. 'Whoohoohahahooh! I say, that's a good un young Figgs, eat Miz Rosie, wot? Yowch, y'little villain, she bit me!'

The four youngsters nearly fell off the bowsprit laughing. Benjy stood up and grasped a rope to steady himself. When the laughter subsided, he pointed west. 'Look, what's that? The water's all ripply out there.'

In a trice Finnbarr was across the deck and up on the bowsprit alongside the squirrel. 'Show me, Benjy, mate?'

'There, see Mr Finnbarr, the sun glitters on it!'

'Aye, I sees it, messmate. Joseph! Bring that tiller about, it could be a shoal of small fishes. You young uns, go an' 'elp Log a Log rig up some nets. Mebbe our luck is back. Well done Benjy!'

Joseph and Log a Log watched the strange rippling water as *Pearl Queen* sailed towards it. The shrew Chieftain was plainly puzzled. 'Never seen nothin' like that before, hope it's not rocks under the surface or anythin' dangerous. What d'you s'pose it is, Joseph?'

'I don't know enough about the sea to say, friend. It certainly is odd though. Our best bet is to follow orders and trust Finnbarr. Are the nets ready?'

'Aye, I've posted Fatch an' the rest at the stern. We'll do a spot of trawling if it is small fish.'

Figgs had given up trying to eat Rosie. Now she sat on the hare's shoulders, gazing out over the flurrying, rippling strip of sea that came out of nowhere and vanished into the distance. It was about twenty boat-lengths wide.

The nets were cast over as soon as *Pearl Queen* entered the disturbed patch of water. Finnbarr Galedeep hung over the stern peering into the meshes at the grey wriggling swarms trapped in them. Pulling himself back on deck, he clapped Log a Log's back with a paw that was hearty as it was heavy, and shouted, 'Shrimp! We sailed into shoals of shrimp!'

A cheer went up from the crew. Rosie and Figgs headed swiftly for the galley. 'Whoohahahooh! D'you hear that Figgs, shrimp! Now, I'm sure I spotted some mushrooms and spring onions. Aha, leeks! It's shrimp stew all round for tea, what d'you say Figgs?'

'Thrimps? Lack a day, tucker gone, Figgs want thrimps!'

Finnbarr helped the crew pull in the nets that bulged with grey wriggling shrimps. 'Haharr, they'll soon be all pink an' tender when they gits cooked,' the sea otter chortled. 'I wonder, is there any pepper about? Great seasons, there's a dish t'warm the cockles of yer 'eart, shrimp stew with hotroot pepper aplenty. Ahoy there, Bandle, steer us out o' this lot now, we got enough!'

A panicked cry rang out from the shrew at the tiller. 'I can't hold 'er, Finnbarr. We're bein' pulled into the ripplin' water, I can't get 'er out!'

Finnbarr dropped the nets and dashed to the tiller. 'Give it 'ere mate, this ship ain't goin' nowhere I don't want it to. Come over, *Pearl*!' The sea otter fought with all his strength against the tiller, trying to get the vessel back into calm seas.

Joseph strolled up and stood grinning at him. Finnbarr Galedeep's face was a picture of disbelief. 'Joseph, what ails yer, matey? Don't stan' there grinnin' like a witless woodypecker, lend a paw 'ere an' quick!'

The Bellmaker shook his grizzled head, saying, 'Seems like your luck is back, Finn, you old wavedog. Shrimp stew for supper and you've found Roaringburn again.'

The sea otter's jaw dropped in amazement. 'Roarin-'burn?'

Joseph flung out a paw at the rippling waters. 'Aye, Roaringburn, look at the speed we're travelling and headed due south too. What else could it be?'

Finnbarr gave over trying to control the tiller; he put it on a rope holder, due south. 'Well, swoggle me whiskers an' rot me rudder, if I ain't a bottle-nosed son of a barnacle. Roarin'burn! Come 'ere, young Wincey, an' give yer ole uncle Finn a great big kiss fer more luck!'

Wincey obliged, then ran off scrubbing at her lips. 'Phtooh! Sea otter's whiskers, yukk, tough an' salty!'

As evening fell, Rosie wiped a paw across her brow, weary of serving up helpings of Figg'n'Rosie shrimp-stew. She filled Foremole's bowl, saying, 'Mercy me, Figgs, how many more to come?'

The tiny ottermaid was seated on a stool, helping out. She glared at a shrew who was shuffling in in a guilty manner. 'Lack a day, Figgs seen you afore, two times – no more f'you! Mercy me, lots more wants more, miz Rosie.'

Figgs was a proper little tyrant, she rapped Finnbarr with a ladle as he held out his bowl. 'None f'you 'til you singasong. Figgs wants a song!'

The sea otter shook his ottercordion at her. 'If you wasn't so lucky I'd a cooked ye along with those shrimps, young Figgs.'

Figgs narrowed her eyes and brandished the ladle. 'I cook you if you don't singasong young Finnbars!'

Finnbarr Galedeep riffled off a jaunty chord. 'I'm too young t'be cooked. I'll sing for ye Figgs.'

Pearl Queen sped south into the night with the merry

strains of singing hovering in her wake. The small galley was packed with crew, firelight from the stove
flickering on their faces as they ate supper and listened
to Finnbarr's song.

'Well there ain't a dish in all the world,
As good as ole shrimp stew,
An' this is the best I've ever 'ad,
An' I've 'ad quite a few,
You kin keep yore big sea biscuits,
That duff an' skilly too,
I'll scrape me bowl an' lick me spoon,
An' sing to you by the light o' the moon,
There's better days a comin' soon,
But none quite like tonight!'

It was still dark when Wincey shook Joseph. He sat up
on the hatch covers rubbing sleep from his eyes.
'What's the matter, little one?' he asked.

'The ship's stopped, Joseph.' The Bellmaker sat quite
still, holding his head to one side as he listened for the
familiar noise of rigging, sail and wind. Taking Wincey's paw he rose. 'You're right, the ship has stopped. I
wonder why?'

Together they made their way up to the prow. Joseph
lifted her on to the bowsprit as he peered over the
for'ard end. The *Pearl Queen* lay in shallow water, nosed
deep into a broad sandbank. To the west the Roaringburn current could be seen, running off into a distant
arc. A movement close by caused Joseph to turn – it was
Finnbarr.

'Looks like the current don't want us no more, matey.
She's drifted us off on to this 'ere sandbank, we've run
out o' luck again.'

Joseph lifted Wincey down. 'Go and get Benjy, little
maid, and bring him here, quickly. Hold hard a

moment, Finn. I think our luck may still be running good.'

Benjy came pattering along paw in paw with Wincey. Joseph boosted him up so he could see over the rail. 'Tell me, Benjy, these sandbanks, those little islands yonder and that shoreline behind them, do you recognize them?'

The young squirrel nodded vigorously and spoke only one word – 'Southsward.'

Joseph lowered him to the deck. 'That's what I thought. I've seen this coast once before from the deck of a ship some seasons ago, though I've never been ashore here. As soon as I saw it I had a feeling inside that this was Southsward. We made it, Finnbarr!'

The Bellmaker and the sea otter shook paws firmly.

Dawn came gently. A slight inshore mist lifting under the sun's warmth revealed a verdant coast fringed with silver sand and backed by luxuriant woodland. As the last of the ship's food and water was issued for breakfast, Log a Log joined Finnbarr and Joseph on the forecastle. Below on the hatch covers, *Pearl Queen*'s crew sat waiting for orders. Finnbarr gestured in the direction of land.

'That's Southsward mates, the place we set out t'find,' he said. 'It might look peaceable right now, but don't let that fool ye. First we got to git ole *Pearl Queen* on an even keel in a safe cove; we kin manage that with a bit o' tuggin' an' shovin' when y've finished yer vittles, Joseph.'

The Bellmaker stood forward to speak his piece. 'Then we choose our weapons and strike inland. No cooking fires, and sentries and lookouts at all times. Listen to me carefully – if you don't it may cost you your life. Benjy knows this country and he will be our guide. Log a Log, have your Guosim protect our sides and rear wherever we go. Fatch, Durry, Rufe, you will scout ahead with Benjy. Take care of him, only he knows the way.

Rosie, you and Foremole will be in charge of the armoury – make sure everybeast is kitted out with the weapons that suit them best. If what Benjy has told me is correct, we are up against a large horde, far larger than we could ever imagine facing. So we must act as a guerrilla unit, hit and run all the time, and weaken the enemy by chipping away at their numbers. Most of you know Mariel and Dandin. We are searching for them, so look before you loose arrows or slingstones. I have my own ideas where we will find my daughter and her friend – right in the middle of any trouble we come across, so be prepared. Log a Log, have you anything to add?'

The shrew Chieftain drew his short rapier and showed it, blade foremost, to his tribe. 'Guosim, you know how to use these, swift and quiet. Protect our friends at all times and make them proud to fight by your side in battle.'

It took half the morning to prise *Pearl Queen* off the sandbank. The crew strove, waist deep in seawater, levering and using log rollers. Once the ship was back afloat she was towed on two stout ropes by the crew. Panting and struggling they pulled her through the shallows to a wooded cove. There she was made fast to three trees on slacked ropes that allowed room for the tide's rise and fall.

The afternoon was taken up with the issue of weapons. Rosie Woodsorrel tested would-be archers before giving them bows and arrows. She had a good eye for slingers, javelin throwers and spearbeasts too. Beside their chosen weapon every crew member was given a knife or sword from the searats' well-stocked armoury. Wincey, Benjy and Figgs, accompanied by Durry, Rufe and Fatch, collected buckets of hard, round seawashed pebbles from the tideline for slingstones.

Evening shades fell as the sun started to dip below

the western sea. Joseph stood on the cove bank with his little army, watching Finnbarr say goodbye to his ship. The sea otter had personally checked that all the sails were reefed tight under their mast spars; every piece of rigging he inspected, carefully coiling each rope and line. After battening down the hatches and securing galley and cabin doors he leapt ashore.

'Take a good rest, *Queen*,' he said, 'y've earned it. We'll see yer when we gets back off this trip if our luck stays with us.' All the crew raised their weapons in a salute to the good ship they had come to love so well.

Then they turned inland to whatever fate and fortune would bring them. Death or victory.

29

Warm dusk stole through the twilight at the pond's edge in Redwall Abbey's grounds; moths fluttered softly over shimmering firelight reflections upon the still waters. Scarlet and gold flames flickered upward from the fire, their light forming a cave in the encroaching dark of night. Oak Tom and his pretty wife Treerose had temporarily deserted their Mossflower seclusion to be at the festivities. Tom tended the fire whilst Treerose supervised the roasting of wheat ears.

Tarquin L. Woodsorrel was in fine form. He had taken command of his leveret family, who were laying out the food. 'You there, thingummy, stop paddlin' in the water an' give y'sister some assistance to fill up the plates – and wipe y'paws.'

'Got it pater, assist the sister, what's to be done?'

Tarquin sent young hares scurrying as he explained, 'Simple really, one small fruit pie to each plate, four candied chestnuts, three honeyed plums and a good ladle of meadowcream to dip 'em in, per plate, per creature.'

'But what about this scrummy cheese'n'celery dip, papa?'

'Oh, er, nip back t'the kitchens, you three, an' get the

small wooden bowls to put it in. You there, sir, what's y'name? Don't put the cheese'n'celery stuff on the plates with the fruit pies, not done, y'know.'

'Papa, shall I slice these oat farls an' put em round the salad in a nice pattern?'

'What? Er, yes, there's a good little haremaid. No! Give me that knife, I'll do the slicin'. You, whatsaname, will y'come out the water, please. Oh hares'n'horrors! Rosie, where are you? I can't control this bally brood of yours, mine, I mean ours. Stop scoffin' those honey-plums, you rip!'

Simeon and Mellus sat with their footpaws in the shallows, oblivious to the bustle around them.

'Ah, this is the life, Simeon, I haven't done this since I was a Dibbun. Nothing like it for cooling the paws after a hot day.'

'Indeed, it certainly is refreshing. The old Abbey pond, there was nothing like it when we were Dibbuns. Fished it in spring, swam around it in summer, sailed and skimmed pebbles over it in autumn and skated on it in winter. What a useful thing it is to be sure, Mellus. Listen, I can hear Oak Tom planning other uses for our pond.'

The sturdy squirrel had Blaggut and Slipp by their ears, shaking them sternly as he lectured on manners. 'It's share an' share alike at Redwall. If I catch either of you grabbing roasted wheat ears before the others I'll duck some courtesy into you in yonder pond, understand?'

The two searats were dancing a little jig of agony as Tom tugged their ears, when the mousebabe intervened. 'They 'ad enuff now, Tom. C'mon, Blackguts an' Slick, me'n Furrtil wants you to put lanterns in our boats.'

Oak Tom released the searats and watched them follow the mousebabe off to the boats, rubbing their ears and grumbling. The squirrel dusted his paws off reflectively. 'I don't like those two, they're trouble, you mark my words!'

Treerose pulled roasted wheat ears from the embers at the fire's edge and stacked them with others, ready to be dipped into the bowls of celery and cheese. 'Oh, give them a chance, Tom,' she said. 'They're not used to Abbey life like Redwallers are. Now, how many more wheat ears do I need?'

Benches and logs had been placed in a circle not far from the fire. Everybeast found a seat, and the food was served. As Abbot Saxtus shared a bowl of dip and wheat ears with Brother Fingle he looked around at the happy faces in the firelight, Dibbuns and old alike, enjoying themselves hugely.

Fingle watched his Abbot. 'An acorn for your thoughts Father,' he said.

Saxtus licked dip from his whiskers pensively. 'My thoughts, Brother? You may have them for free. I was wishing that Joseph and his party were with us here to enjoy this evening, Mariel and Dandin too. May the fates be kind to them wherever they are. You know, Fingle, nothing gives me more pleasure than to see my Redwallers happy and well fed. Contentment, it is a thing I love dearly. I was never one for dashing off on quests and adventures. The Abbey and its life is sufficient for an old stay-at-home like me. I'm glad I thought of this concert. Look at them – did you ever see a merrier, more peaceful bunch? That's my adventure, the quest for contentment and happiness for all in my Redwall.'

Brother Fingle accepted a fresh bowl of dip and wheat ears from a well-mannered Dibbun. 'Here, Father Abbot, get some of this inside you before you content yourself off to sleep, you're starting to nod.'

Tarquin produced his harolina, a cherished though slightly battered instrument. He tuned it, plucking the strings lightly, ears close to it. 'There, good as the day I first serenaded Rosie and won her bally heart, wot? Righto, line up chaps, two to each corner, maids in the middle, bow to the centre. Good, here we go with the mousemole reel!'

Blaggut and Slipp found themselves hauled up among whooping and cheering Redwallers as Tarquin raised his voice:

'One, two, let me bow to you,
Away we go from the centre through.
Oh there was a mouse in Mossflower,
And he was plump and cheery,
Lived right next to a mole so fair,
A little dark-eyed dearie.
Three, four, I'll tell you more,
Whirl your partner round the floor!
She baked a pie, oh my, oh my,
And said, "I've got no cherries,
Sir mouse when you go out abroad,
Will you bring back some berries?"
Five, six, here's a fix,
Curtsy maids and gather sticks!
The mouse roved out into the woods,
And came back heavy laden,
With cherries and ripe fruit to boot,
To give unto the maiden.
Seven, eight, stand and wait,
Clap your paws, it's very late!
The mole took up a wooden bowl,
The mouse he grabbed a ladle,
And as they ate that lovely pie,
They danced around the table.
Nine, ten and back to one,
Bow to your partners for the dance is done!'

Laughing and panting, the dancers retired breathless to

their seats. Blaggut whispered to Slipp, 'We goin' fer the treasure now, Cap'n?' He was rewarded with a swift kick.

'We ain't goin' nowheres 'til I gets me wind back, bladderbrain. Whew, that dancin' takes it outta a beast!'

Tarquin cleared his throat officiously and took centre stage. 'Errahem! Father Abbot, Mellus marm, good creatures all, it is my singular honour to open the concert singin' competition, wot? I have with me the jolly old prize for the winner, it is right here . . . somewhere?' The hare beckoned hastily to one of his leverets. 'You there, thingybob, it's under me seat, bring the blinkin' thing here, will you? Ah yes, as I was sayin', I have here with me the winner's prize. As you can see, it is a badger drinkin' vessel, hmm, chalice in fact, silver mounted, gold lined, with lots of rather jolly stones studded around it, precious gems I'd say. Now, who's goin' t'be the first to get up an' warble off a song? Oh, by the way, we must thank our good chum Mellus for donatin' this prize. Cheer for Mellus, thank you!'

When the cheering died down, Mellus stood up, a grin of mischief on her broad face. 'Thank you one and all. Now, as for the first singer, or singers, I think I have the privilege of choosing them. As is our custom at Redwall, guests first. Mr Blaggut and Mr Slipp would you be so kind as to oblige us?'

Willing paws seized the unwilling searats, who were hustled into the centre of the circle, where they stood nervously shuffling from paw to paw. Slipp was not amused.

'O no, mates, we ain't no singers, seara . . . er, travellers like us ain't much good at singin', are we Blaggut?'

'I likes singin', Cap'n. Couldn't we sing 'em the Slaughter of the Crew of the Rusty Chain, that's a good 'un?'

Slipp's furious protests withered under Oak Tom's stern proclamation, 'If you're too shy to sing there's always the pots to be washed!'

That seemed to decide the issue. Taking up searat performing stances, the pair stood straddle-legged with paws clenched above their heads, and began singing in hoarse, off-key voices:

'Whoa, the Cap'n of the Rusty Chain,
Ain't feelin' much surprise,
'E's deader'n a duck on the ocean floor,
While the fish nibble out 'is eyes.
An' the crew of the Rusty Chain,
Ain't feelin' too much pain,
O y'can't wipe yer nose when yer 'ead's chopped
    off,
An' they'll never see their tails again . . .'

There was a pause as they consulted together, arguing over forgotten verses. Some of the gentler Redwallers closed their eyes and covered their ears as the song continued in the same bloodthirsty mode:

'O the bosun's got a spear in 'is liver,
An' the mate's got a spear through 'is throat,
An' they're usin' the fat off an' ole searat,
To set alight to the boat.'

Distressed cries began issuing from some of the Dibbuns, and a dispute arose with Slipp and Blaggut as to the next line.

'Ho they've gone an' skinned the cook . . .'

Slipp cuffed Blaggut's ears soundly. 'Puddenbrains, that's not 'til the next verse, I knows the line, it goes like this . . .

'O they carved off the lookout's ears,
An' stuffed em up 'is no—'

'Enough! Stop this bloodthirsty ballad now!' They were hauled unceremoniously back to their seats by an irate Mother Mellus as Tarquin called upon the next performer.

'Sorry about that, chaps, bad form, y'know! Sister Sage, I don't suppose you'd like to warble us that absolutely splendid ditty about the robin an' the cuckoo?'

After a bit of persuasion the old Sister got up and began singing. Her voice was loud and clear for one of such great age.

The night wore on as performers came and went: singers, dancers and those who liked to recite poetry. Blaggut had eaten his fill and quaffed enough cordial to float a small boat. His head nodded fitfully, eyes closing as his chin dropped on to his chest. Slipp tweaked his nose, muttering, 'Wake yerself up, dozeyguts, we're going' t'get the treasure.'

They detached themselves stealthily from the gathering, creeping off into the night. Blaggut cast frightened glances about him as he clung to Slipp's tail.

'Couldn't we go back an' sit by the fire, Cap'n? I don't like it out 'ere in the dark night, the black shadder might get us both!'

Slipp whirled on his unfortunate companion. 'Bucketnose! I told yer never t'mention that agin, cummere!'

'Eeeyoowcheeyee!'

'Stop squealin', you limpet 'eaded oaf!'

'I can't 'elp it, Cap'n, yore bitin' me ear. Yeek!'

The mousebabe and Furrtil sat proudly with the cup between them. Saxtus looked enquiringly at Mellus. 'I thought you said that the mousebabe was a rogue and a scamp, the worst of all the Dibbuns?' he asked.

The old badger mother shrugged. 'That doesn't stop him and Furrtil being the best singers. Hahaha, that was the best laugh I've had in seasons, the Song of the Pirate Pond Dibbuns. They deserved to win, what do you think Simeon?'

The blind Herbalist seemed preoccupied, 'What? Er, oh yes, by far the most comical . . .'

Mellus could tell that Simeon's mind was elsewhere. 'What's wrong old friend, are you tired?' she said.

The blind one felt about until he found the badger's paw. 'Slipp and Blaggut have gone, and I didn't follow them.'

'But why should you follow them?'

'Because that one called Slipp is up to no good. Until now I have trailed them whenever they went off alone. Both of them think I am a black shadow that haunts them, and it keeps them out of mischief. But I was a bit slow tonight, I've let them get away.'

The badger stood up decisively. 'Right, leave it to me, I'll find 'em!'

'I have a pretty fair idea where they are,' said Simeon, standing up with her. 'Gone to dig up the Dibbuns' treasure at the southeast wall corner.'

The mousebabe and Furrtil picked up their trophy together. 'Hurr, us'n's show ee whurr that be at!' said Furrtil.

Tarquin was starting up another reel for all to join in as the four creatures went off after the searats.

Slipp was digging with the long kitchen knife he had stolen; Blaggut used a piece of stick. Together they dug and sweated until Blaggut felt his stick hit something hollow. 'Haharr, 'ere it is Cap'n – the secret 'idden treasure of the h'Abbey.'

Slipp ordered Blaggut out of the hole and began digging feverishly with the knife. In a short while he had unearthed a small rectangular box, of the type used in the Redwall kitchen to store salt or spices. It was oak, bound with brass strip, and had a broken lock. The searat Captain tugged it from the earth and, wiping it on his smock, he clambered from the hole grinning from ear to ear.

'You was right, mate. You ain't been right many times in yer life, but you was this time. We got the treasure!' Throwing open the box he turned the contents out upon the ground. They both stood speechless a moment, looking. It was typical Dibbuns' treasure: a pawful of mouldy acorns, some fragments of coloured glass, faded ribbons, two hawk feathers and a spinning top made from stone. Just the sort of things a Dibbun would consider precious.

Blaggut scratched his head with a soil-grimed paw. 'Boggle me braces, Cap'n, that ain't no treasure, 'tis only liddle beasts' playthings!'

Slipp picked up the box and hurled it at the wall, smashing it to pieces in his rage. 'Rubbish an' pups' trinkets! Secret 'idden treasure, eh, I'll secret 'idden treasure those two liddle scum when I get me claws on 'em!'

Walking slightly ahead of Mellus and Simeon, the two Dibbuns materialized out of the night. Mousebabe pointed accusingly at Slipp, his voice shrill with anger, 'Dirty ole searat, you breaked our treasure box t'bits!'

Slipp raised the long-bladed kitchen knife. 'Yew snoutfaced liddle spawn, I'll carve ye to slices!'

'No, Cap'n, don't 'arm the liddle uns!' shouted Blaggut, as he grabbed hold of Slipp.

The bosun reeled back in agony as Slipp slashed the paw holding him from getting at the mousebabe. Slipp rushed at the Dibbun brandishing the knife, and screaming, 'I'll bury ye in yer own treasure 'ole!'

He took a leap and was actually in mid-air when Mellus came bowling through like a furred thunderball. The two creatures collided with a roar and a scream, hitting the ground heavily. Simeon hurried forward, feeling the air about him as he called to the Dibbuns, 'Mousebabe, Furrtil, stay out of the way, come to me!'

Blaggut stood by helpless, his face a frozen mask of horror as Slipp rose from the ground. The great badger lay still, both paws clutching the knife handle as if trying to pull it free from her heart.

The screams of Mousebabe and Furrtil cut the night like shards of broken glass. Simeon's sightless eyes flickered this way and that as he pleaded, 'What is it, Mellus, are you all right?'

Blaggut fell on all fours beside the stricken form. 'Cap'n, you've slain the ole badger lady!'

The searat Captain stood trembling. 'The ole fool did it 'erself,' he snarled, 'jumpin' on me like that! Got wot she deserved, orderin' me round all the time!'

Tears rolled down Blaggut's face as he rocked back and forth. 'You killed 'er, Cap'n! Oh, what'll we do now, Cap'n?'

The Dibbuns were still screaming and clinging to Simeon. A brutal sneer lit Slipp's face as he moved into action. Grabbing the badger chalice, which the little ones had dropped in their fright, he kicked Blaggut upright. 'Well at least we ain't leavin' 'ere empty pawed. Come on, idiot, yore in this with me. Move yerself or stay 'ere an' get torn t'bits by the Redwallers. I'm savin' me own skin!'

He slunk off, letting himself out by the small east wallgate. Blaggut followed him into Mossflower, whimpering, 'O, wot've we done, Cap'n? That was an 'appy place, I would 'ave lived there an' been a searat no more. Now we got to run, we can't go back to the h'Abbey, ever . . .'

Slipp struck the weeping bosun a heavy blow in his face. 'Shut yer slobberin' an' git movin', they'll be comin' after us soon an' I ain't waitin' for yew!'

Blaggut nodded dumbly and followed his Captain into the night-time depths of the vast woodlands.

Father Abbot Saxtus sat on the ground, next to Mellus's body, numb with shock. Oak Tom and Tarquin kept the Redwallers back, whilst Brother Mallen and Sister Sage took the Dibbuns and the very old back to the Abbey dormitories.

Tarquin L. Woodsorrel sniffed back his tears and kept a stiff upper lip. 'Tom, as soon as it's clear here I'll get my lance and you get your bow. We'll track the murderers by night and have them slain by dawn!'

The big squirrel grabbed Tarquin's paw tight. 'No! First we must see Mother Mellus at rest, it's the right thing to do. Those two searats will be lost by now, they don't know their way around Mossflower. I do! When I'm ready I'll track them down. No need for you to go, I travel best alone. I'll leave their carcasses for the ant folk to pick over!'

30

Several hedgehogs stood atop a dune; shielding their eyes against the noonday sun they squinted at the curious procession coming their way. A sturdy female relaxed her grip on a warclub and turned to her mate, saying, 'They be not rats, Gawjun.'

The male hedgehog, a huge, primitive-looking fellow, shook his warclub in a businesslike manner. 'Mayhaps they be not rats, Deekeye, but who be a knowin', strangebeasts could be troublesome. One of they be's a hog, Gawjun will speak unto him. You there hog! Stand forward an' cease thy drums a bangin'!'

Bowly Pintips halted his recruiting party and silenced the four leverets, who were enthusiastically battering away at four small mole drums. He signalled Furpp, who was carrying a broom as a banner, to follow him. Both went forward, and Bowly called up to the hedgehog leader.

'My name don't be hog, I be Bowly Pintips the Warrior an' I would parley with you!'

Gawjun and Deekeye met with Bowly and Furpp at a spot halfway between their respective bands. Gawjun glared suspiciously at Bowly, and the young warrior stared back nonchalantly, tossing his hardened oat-cakes from paw to paw.

Gawjun nodded approvingly at the youngster's bold-ness. 'Be you with Foxwolf?' he asked.

'Nay, I be with Gael Squirrelking against Foxwolf. There be others like me. Our banner is a broom – we will sweep Nagru and his horde out of Southsward.'

'Big words for a little warrior. What be you doin' in these parts, Bowly Pintips?'

'Recruitin' an army to do battle with the Foxwolf.'

Deekeye began swinging her warclub. Bowly stood motionless as it whirled by his snout, trying hard not to show fear. The female hedgehog let out an unearthly roar:

'Spike'n'striiiike!'

The warclub struck the ground a hairsbreadth from Bowly's footpaw. Deekeye grinned ferociously. 'Recrui-tin' army to do battle with Foxwolf, eh! Not before time, say I. What say you, Gawjun?'

The big male bent his head, pressing his brow against that of Bowly until their spikes meshed in an antiquated hedgehog greeting. With his eyes practically touching Bowly's he gave a fleeting smile. 'The tribe of Gawjun an' Deekeye be with thee, Bowly!'

Untangling his spikes with great dignity, Bowly tossed an oatcake high, caught it flat on his footpaw and flicked it up into his grasp. 'Gather thy tribe an' follow this mole to his dwellin', 'tis our meeting place. Come armed!'

Bowly and his recruiting troop marched off, drums beating. The four leverets were all admiration for their companion.

'I say, well done, old lad!'

'Spoke their lingo too, good show!'

'Tough lookin' crew, but you out toughed 'em well!'

'Yes, very basic beasts, hedgehogs, don't y'think?'

Bowly glared at young Foghill. 'Aye, but not as chattery as hares! Now, where's those mice you told me about Runtwold?'

'Oh them, 'bout two hours march west of here, old lad.'

'Well, get those drums to bangin' good'n'loud, we're goin' to recruit 'em. An' I'm not ole lad, I'm Bowly Pintips, right!'

Mariel had her paws full in the gatehouse. It was a constant strain trying to hold back Muta and Rab from breaking out to attack the rats on the stairway; both the badger and the otter were growing more impatient by the hour. They did not seem to realize that it was vital the gatehouse be held. Snorting their impatience they lumbered around, banging the door hard with their paws.

Then the mousemaid had an idea. She had been peeking out of the window, watching the arrows and slingstones of her friends on the valley floor as they shot upward to the plateau at the horde in the open drawbridge space. A sideways glance and she could see the horde firing back in retaliation. The Foxwolf and Silvamord could be heard as they yelled commands at their troops:

'Front rank archers and slingers. Fire!'

'Over there, you fools! Fire higher!'

'There! There! Can't you see them?'

'Advance out on to the drawbridge, cut down the range!'

The mousemaid waited until forty or fifty archers and slingers were halfway out on to the open drawbridge, then she turned to her two silent companions.

'Take the drawbridge up. Quick!'

Glad to be doing something, the two beasts threw themselves upon the turning handles. The drawbridge went up like a rocket under their joint berserk strength.

Mariel watched in delight as screaming rats slid backward, though most tried clinging to the rough wood. She let her paw fall in a chopping motion. 'Down drawbridge!'

Leaping clear of the handles, Rab and Muta kicked the trip lever. There was an ear-splitting squeal and the handles spun in a blur, followed by a loud thud as the drawbridge crashed back down. Three rats were flung into the moat, the others lay stunned and groaning. Muta played with the winding handle like a toy, lifting and dropping the massive structure in small movements. It was a clear warning to the horde that they would not be allowed to use the drawbridge. Nagru was beside himself with fury.

'A mousemaid and two half-baked casualties controlling the only entrance or exit to my castle. Never! Grutch, take archers up to the south battlements, they should be able to send arrows through the gatehouse window from there!'

The Foxwolf looked around until his eyes rested on a hulking horderat, far taller and stronger built than most. 'Lumba, take fifty good fighters, use armour, spears and shields, and take the gatehouse. Smash the door and bring me the heads of those three beasts. Silvamord, take a third of our entire force up on to the battlements – it will be much easier to fire on the enemy from there.'

The vixen's tailed skirts swished as she turned. 'Where will you be while all this is going on?'

Nagru pointed downwards with the iron claws of his wolf pelt. 'Right here with the rest of my horde. We must defend this open gateway night and day until the gatehouse is recaptured.'

Silvamord signalled her approval.

'That's more like the Foxwolf of old. At last you're beginning to use that brain like a true commander.'

Dandin lay behind a rock with Meldrum and Iris,

watching the activity taking place within the open portal on the plateau. 'They're up to something and I have a feeling in my stomach it's not going to do us much good,' he said.

Meldrum the Magnificent squinted up at the figures beginning to appear on the battlements. 'That blighter's doin' what any sensible General should do. Gettin' them up high where they can sweep this valley floor with their arrows. We'll be pinned down an' slaughtered if we don't do somethin' soon.'

The three ducked behind the rock as a short cloud of arrows zipped down from the battlements. Somewhere close by there was a strangled cry as an otter fell to one of the shafts. Iris gnawed her lip anxiously, saying, 'We've got to stay here and face it out until help arrives. I've been thinking – Mariel can't be alone in that gatehouse. She couldn't raise and lower the drawbridge on her own.'

They kept their heads low as another salvo of arrows quivered into the ground around them. Iris pulled one out, fitted it to her bow and returned fire. She lay watching the path of her arrow's trajectory in disgust.

'We have to shoot upwards, they're out of our range. That arrow didn't get anywhere near 'em!'

Meldrum loosed a swift shaft in the direction of the drawbridge and was rewarded by a distant squeal. 'Good job we can still reach those villains in the gateway, isn't it? Fire away, chaps, keep y'heads down an' defend our position. Give as good as we get, that's what I always say, wot?'

An arrow hummed by Mariel's cheek, bounced off the wall and fell to the floor. She glanced at the window and threw herself flat against the side wall.

'Muta, Rab, over here – they're on the battlements firing in at us. Get against this wall, it's on their blind side.'

As the two warriors joined her more arrows zipped in. Then the door began shuddering under the impact of some heavy object. 'Look out, they're knocking at the door!' Mariel groaned.

Gael Squirrelking stood with his paws around Queen Serena and his son Truffen. The little squirrel felt his father's paw shake with emotion as he gazed around the crowded sward in front of Furpp's dwelling. Squirrels crowded everywhere carrying bows, slings and spears. A greying elder approached the King; bowing low, he placed his forehead against Gael's footpaw.

'Majesty, we thought you were dead, but you live and all of Southsward is glad of this.'

Gael raised the oldster up. 'Weldan, my old friend, how did you find me here?'

'Word is abroad of your escape. I have brought two hundred; they will not rest until you regain the royal house of Floret and the murderer Urgan Nagru lies slain, this I vow!'

Serena was about to reply when drumrolls and shouting broke out behind the squirrels.

'Make way an' stan' aside for the recruitin' party!' Bowly Pintips and his party marched up in grand style. Furpp gave an elaborate flourish of his broom, halting them in front of the royal family. Serena came forward and took the young hedgehog's paws fondly.

'Bowly, my young warrior,' she said, 'where have you been?'

He swept a nonchalant paw at the dunes around. 'Thither an' yon, Majesty, recruitin'. Watch this!'

To the north a dunetop suddenly bristled with hedgehogs brandishing warclubs. Another wave from Bowly's paw and a crowd of yelling mice carrying long pikes appeared on a dune to the south. Serena clapped her paws with joy, 'What wonderful recruiting!'

Bowly tossed an oatcake into the air and caught it neatly. 'Oh, that ain't all, watch this!' he cried.

He took the broom from Furpp and waved it at a hilltop next to the one the mice stood on. An instant roar went up as masses of moles appeared, each one armed with mace and chain. Furpp took one of the mole drums and banged out an irregular rat-tat. Between the hills marched another fourscore moles carrying oaken mallets.

Bowly and Furrp stood with the leveret squad as Gael and his family thanked them personally. The Squirrelking took the broom from Furpp and climbed the dune above the mole's dwelling. He held the broom aloft, its twig bristles pointing at the sky.

'Friends, good creatures all, I thank you for rallying to me, and this, your standard. It is only an ordinary broom, but it will be the symbol of our army. This will show those who try to conquer and enslave us that ordinary things can become very dangerous, like this broom. Where it is raised aloft you will follow and wait. When it falls with the broomhead down then we shall sweep! We shall sweep out the evil of Foxwolf and make Southsward clean to live in again!'

Gael let the broomhead fall and the hills shook to a mighty roar.

'Free Southswaaaaaard!'

The army took off like a hurricane, headed for Castle Floret with Bowly in the vanguard. Racing alongside the tribal leaders were hedgehogs, moles, mice, otters and squirrels. With the broom waving high in his paws, Bowly yelled his warcries to the four winds. He was a warrior!

31

Another heavy blow to the gatehouse door caused it to tremble and splinter. Mariel stood with her back against the wall, knowing she was not going to refuse the two dumb creatures who stood staring at her pleadingly. She nodded towards the door, saying, 'Somebeast ought to stop them smashing it in . . .'

Lumba backed up the stairs, heading the group that carried the battering ram. He was confident that the next charge would burst a way through into the gatehouse.

'Last time now, give it all you've got. One, two, charge!'

Ten rats were carrying the ram. They sped down the stairs with the other forty close on their heels.

Before they reached it the door swung open.

Unable to stop, they went pounding through the doorway. Muta and Rab met them head on – the two berserk warriors were like eagles among pigeons. Spears were swept aside broken, shields bent double and armour crushed like autumn leaves. The badger seized a rat in each paw and used them as flails upon the others. Rab Streambattle was among them like a flame, his swordblade flashing as he hacked through armour and hide alike.

Hooktail had carried on running as he entered the room. He dashed past Muta and was about to turn when a mighty smack from Mariel's Gullwhacker sent him sailing through the window where he met an arrow before falling to the moat. The mousemaid spun her weapon, punishing every head or face that appeared before her. With two rats clinging to her back Muta fought on, the bloodlust hot in her eyes; horderats bounced off the stone walls as she whirled her huge paws like a windmill.

Rab was out on to the stairs; dropping his sword in favour of a spear he went to it with butt and point, using the centrepole as a quarterstave until he made it to the top of the steps. Shaking off the two rats that clung to her like ticks Muta grabbed the fallen battering ram. A scream of pure terror came from the remaining horderats. Muscle and sinew stood out on the old badger's scarred hide as she swung the ram, flattening rats against both walls. The rest broke and ran up the stairs, only to find Rab armed with a spear on the top step barring their way. They turned, but Muta was coming through the door with the battering ram pointed at them.

Shutting her mind to the awful sounds, Mariel concentrated on unloading rats out of the window. One or two who had missed the wrath of Muta and Rab pushed past her and leapt howling into the moat. Mariel collected spears and began hurling them up at the archers on the battlements.

The battle won, Muta and Rab returned exhausted to the gatehouse. But there was still work to be done. The door had been torn off its hinges in the attack. Quickly they turned it on its side and, using the battering ram and the remaining spears, made a barricade.

Out beyond the plateau, Egbert the Scholar popped up

unexpectedly out of the ground beside Meldrum and smiled apologetically.

'You must excuse me,' he said. 'I could go no further because this large rock was in the way. My name is Egbert, how do you do?'

Meldrum was lost for words. He sat staring at the mole. Egbert shook his head despairingly and launched into mole speech.

'Bo urr zurr, oi'm Eggbutt ee mole, cumm to taken you uns out of this yurr place, burr aye!'

As Dandin and Iris turned to stare at him also, Meldrum regained his composure and spoke.

'Come to take us out o' here, wot?'

Egbert dusted earth from his paws impatiently. 'That is correct. Hmph! Amazing the things one must resort to when attempting to communicate. Listen, I've come to take you out of here before you are all slain.'

Dandin shook the mole's paw warmly. 'Well, I'll go along with that in any language. We're at your command friend, just lead on!'

Meldrum waggled his ears reflectively. 'Not so fast, laddie buck, some things are easier said than done. How can y'be so sure you can get us out o'here, eh, young molechap? Speak up, don't be shy.'

Egbert donned his spectacles and looked at Meldrum over the top of them. 'Hmm, shyness would be a virtue in some creatures, though I doubt it is widely practised among hares. How do I propose to get you out of here? Well, I could sit here discussing it at length with you. Duck!'

They crouched quickly as more arrows cut the air.

Egbert continued as if nothing had happened. 'Unfortunately I don't intend sitting about here and being shot at all day. Listen, I got Mariel into that gatehouse, trust me. I can get you out of here and into Castle Floret if you do as I say. Are you willing?'

Iris shouldered her bow. 'We're willing Egbert, always trust a mole, I say.'

Meldrum the Magnificent had recovered his aplomb. Jamming his hat tight over his ears he winked at Dandin. 'Trust a mole, that's what I always say too. Even if the blinkin' creature spouts like a library scroll, wot!'

Nagru joined Silvamord on the battlements to see how she was faring. The vixen explained the position to him.

'We're keeping that lot in the valley pinned down well, but your gatehouse scheme has failed. Lumba and his troop ended up in the moat and now that scurvy mousemaid has blocked the gateroom window, my archers can't get at them. Something has got to be done about the gatehouse. Come on, Foxwolf, where's your cunning?'

Nagru stared down at the boarded window hard and long, then his wicked eyes narrowed to slits. 'Keep your archers trained on that window. Mingol, get rags, wood, straw, lots of straw. Damp it all down well.'

A malicious smile lit up the vixen's face. 'You're going to smoke them out!' she crowed.

Sicant pointed down into the valley. 'My Lady, look! They're breaking and scattering!'

Silvamord's smile widened as she looked over the battlements. 'Well, well, what a pitiful little army. They've had a bellyful and now they're running off home. See them go! Archers, fire!'

Nagru swiftly countermanded her order. 'Cease, hold your arrows! I'm going to teach those upstarts a lesson they won't forget. You stay here and see that the gatehouse is taken. I'll leave Grutch and some others to hold the gateway in case of ambush.' He whirled and ran for the stairs.

'Where are you going?' Silvamord called after him.

The Foxwolf shouted back as he ran, 'I'm going to show 'em I'm not afraid to attack. I rule Southsward and they'll know about it before nightfall!'

Silvamord could taste victory. She threw back her

head and howled. 'Make an end of it, Nagru! Kill them, leave none alive! Sicant, go and tell Mingol to hurry himself – I'll smoke them out of there or choke them slowly to death!'

Benjy had scouted out a clear running stream, and Joseph and Finnbarr called a halt on its bank in the late afternoon. Log a Log's Guosim shrews came in from foraging the hills and woodland bringing lots of apples, pears and wild plums, even some cherries and a variety of roots and vegetables. The crew sat cooling their foot-paws at the water's edge, Joseph keeping an eye on Wincey and Figgs as they paddled in the shadows.

Finnbarr sunk his teeth into a large red apple. 'Ahoy, Bellmaker, great country 'ereabouts, plenty of eve-rythin' just agrowin' for the takin'.'

Joseph and Benjy were sharing cherries, seeing how far they could spit the cherrystones into the stream. Log a Log stretched out on the bank next to Foremole.

'Ah, this feels like home t'me, nothin' like bein' near a nice stream eatin' a pear. Though I wish we could've had a fire, my cooks would make a great soup from those roots and vegetables.'

'Hurr, oi loikes zoop zurr Log, tho' oi dearly loikes a purr too, burr aye!' said Foremole as he buried his face in a mellow pear with a squelch.

Rufe, Durry and Fatch had found an old willow further upstream. They swung on a springy limb as it bobbed them up and down into the water. Rosie munched her way through a heap of dark purple plums as she watched the young ones enjoying themselves.

'Y'know, we'll have to watch those young uns if we get caught up in a skirmish of any great size,' she said. 'I wouldn't like to think of my leverets havin' to fight battles.'

Wincey had wandered up on to the bank. Joseph cut up an apple for her, setting it out in slices. 'You're right,

Rosie,' he replied, 'I couldn't bear to think of these little uns being hurt in any way. Hi Figgs, don't go too far! Come back here this instant, d'you hear me, missie?'

Finnbarr tossed an apple playfully at Joseph. 'Yer a real ole mother 'en, Bellmaker. Stop fussin' o'er the liddle maid, she's an otter, ain't she? I'll wager Figgs can shift fer 'erself in water better'n you can.'

The Bellmaker, however, was not convinced. 'Figgs is far too little, Finn, she'll get lost if she goes much further downstream alone.'

Finnbarr grasped Joseph's paw, pulling him upright. 'Ho come on then, fussbudget, we'll go an' get 'er.'

Together they waded downstream, past willow and red-berried rowan mingled with balsam and reed mace, the trees closing in an arch over the streamwaters. Small clouds of midges flitted in and out of the sunpatterned shade, disturbed by the progress of the two wading creatures. Cupping paws about his mouth Joseph called aloud, 'Figgs! Where are you, Figgs?'

Finnbarr tugged the edge of the Bellmaker's jerkin urgently. 'Don't turn round too fast, matey, she's be'ind us.'

Joseph turned slowly. Figgs was there, seated on the brawny shoulders of an otter, who with about fifty others lined the stream holding javelins menacingly. Finnbarr glanced over his shoulder to see a similar number appear apparently from nowhere, merging between foliage, sunshine and shadow.

Figgs scrambled down from the otter's shoulders and swam to Joseph. The Bellmaker ignored the javelins hemming him in on both sides and clucked disapproval at the otter babe. 'Tch, tch, look at your smock and bonnet, they're saturated.'

This seemed to relax the otters. The big one spoke:

'I am Blerun Downriver, what names do you go by?'

'Joseph the Bellmaker. This is Finnbarr Galedeep, and there are more of us upstream.'

Blerun leaned on his lance and nodded. 'I know, we have watched you since you camped there. Do you serve Urgan Nagru the Foxwolf?'

Before an otter could lift javelin Finnbarr's twin swords had cleared their sheaths. He went into a fighting crouch, his single eye glittering hotly 'No, matey, we've come t'do battle with 'im, so if you're on the Foxwolf's side we'd best start the party right 'ere!'

Blerun left his javelin sticking in the streambed and extended a paw towards Joseph and Finnbarr. 'Your enemy is our enemy. We will fight him together, Finnbarr Galedeep.'

So it was that the *Pearl Queen*'s crew began the final stage of their march to Castle Floret.

32

Morning sunlight flooded a copse in the stillgreen depths of northeast Mossflower. Dewdrops hung heavy and bright on leaf and petal, plentiful as the tears shed by the former bosun of *Pearl Queen*, Blaggut. Exhausted after a night-time flight through dense woodland, Slipp had dozed a scarce hour when he was awakened by the sobs of his companion. Red eyed and irate, the searat Captain picked up the stolen badger chalice, and snarled, 'Yew keep snottin' an' slobberin' like that and y'll rot yer eyes. Now stow that wingein', d'ye hear?'

Blaggut did not even try, his whole body shook as more tears poured forth. 'Wot did yer kill the ole badger for, Cap'n, she never did us any real 'arm. You shouldn't 'ave slayed 'er!'

Slipp trampled the grass in a circle around Blaggut, speaking through clenched teeth. 'I killed 'er cos she was tryin' to kill me, can't you get that through yer thick 'ead! Any'ow, she needed killin', treatin' me like some kinda wet-eared galley slave. Look, wotcher goin' t'do, sit round 'ere cryin' until they catches up with us? Come on, stupid, we got travellin' t'do.'

Slipp punctuated his words with the usual kicks at Blaggut. He sat unmoved, head in paws, still heaving with grief. 'If I travelled for the rest o'me days it'll still be with me, Cap'n. That pore creature lyin' stabbed to the 'eart, the liddle uns screamin' an' ole Blind Simeon a wonderin' what was goin' on. You go without me, Cap'n, I'm no good to nobeast anymore!'

Slipp seized Blaggut roughly and pulling him upright he began shaking him furiously. 'Lissen, deadbrains, I'm still the Cap'n round 'ere, an' if I sez yore goin' then go yer will!'

No sooner had Slipp released him than Blaggut slumped down and continued weeping. The searat Captain's rage knew no bounds – he stormed about the copse, destroying flowers and tearing at the foliage as he gave vent to his anger.

Blaggut carried on as if unaware of it all. 'They're good an' decent creatures at the h'Abbey, I could 'ave been one too in time. Though a searat can't change 'is colours they say, and mebbe that's true. If we'd never stopped at Redwall everybeast'd still be livin' there peaceful an' 'appy, 'twas no place fer bad uns such as us.'

Slipp could stand no more. Snatching up a thick branch of dead wood, he laid into Blaggut. 'Up on yer paws, oaf. Leave the thinkin' t'me, I'm the Cap'n an' yore the fool! Come on, gerrup, you blitherin' empty 'eaded, no account, washed-up gobbet o' flotsam!'

Blaggut got up.

He came at Slipp with a strange light in his tear-stained eyes, paws outstretched and teeth bared, regardless of the blows that were being rained upon him. Slipp began backing away. The branch broke as he slashed and struck at Blaggut's head and body. Slipp tripped and fell and Blaggut was on him, his paws tight about the Captain's neck. The broken branch fell from Slipp's nerveless grasp as Blaggut's vicelike grip tightened. They lay face to face, the searat bosun's voice coming in gasps as he shook Slipp like a rag doll.

'Fool! Aye, yer right Cap'n, I was a fool, an oaf, an idiot, an' all those other names you called me. That's cos I took up with you Cap'n, yore bad right through, you'll never change, that's why I gotta do this. Sorry Cap'n!'

It was well into noontide. The mourners stood around the flower-strewn heap of earth at the southeast corner of Redwall Abbey's ramparts. Redwallers and Dibbuns alike gazed sadly at Mother Mellus's last resting place. Simeon leaned upon the paw of his Father Abbot, who had gathered strength as the day progressed. At the start of the day Saxtus had moved about like a creature in a trance, doing things automatically. Gradually the realization of his position as Abbot took over. Duty could not be ignored, so with a great effort Saxtus pulled himself together. He patted Simeon's paw comfortingly before turning to address the Abbey dwellers.

'My good friends, the poems have been recited, the prayers all said. Mother Mellus has moved on to sunnier pastures, quieter noontides and more peaceful woodlands, though she will always live in our hearts. But I can hear her speaking to me now, guiding me as ever she did from the time I was a Dibbun, right through until I was chosen as Abbot. I always heeded the wise words of Mellus, as I do now. She is telling me that Redwall life must continue.'

Saxtus paused to smile and tweak a leveret's ear.

'Mellus says that there is fruit to be picked in our orchard, boats to be sailed on the pond, work and play for all. As the summer fades to autumn we will have a great feast one day, to celebrate the memory of our dear friend. Go now, think about this as you work hard and rest well!'

There was a flash of sunlight and something glimmered through the air in a bright arc, falling to rest quietly on the fresh-dug earth of Mellus's grave, where it lay unharmed.

The mousebabe was quicker than anybeast. He scurried forward and picked up the object. 'Furrtil, lookit, our badger cup wot we winned!'

'Take it an' live long in peace!'

Every eye turned upward to the east walltop. Blaggut stood there looking unhappily down at where the badger lay buried. Oak Tom's paw flew to his dagger and he moved towards the wall. Saxtus called out to Tarquin, 'Stop him, I will not have that creature slain!'

Tarquin intercepted Oak Tom as he began climbing. 'Steady on old lad, I know how y'feel, but the Father Abbot must be obeyed, wot? Let's hear what he has to say.'

Blaggut walked around the ramparts and descended by the south wallsteps, stopping on the final stair. His voice was raw and husky with sorrowing.

'I killed me own Cap'n this morn. Yore badger was a good creature, 'e did wrong to slay 'er. I would've stopped 'im but it all 'appened so quick. Any'ow, I brought back the cup fer the liddle uns an' that's that, you kin kill me now.'

Saxtus took the dagger from Oak Tom and stowed it in his wide habit sleeve, then he turned to the mousebabe. 'You saw what happened. I leave it to you, does he deserve to die, or would you let him live?'

There was a moment's silence. Every Redwaller looked on anxiously as the mousebabe trundled over to the wallsteps and took Blaggut's paw in his.

'Mister Blackguts is good, norra killer, he makes boats.'

Furrtil joined him, latching herself on to the searat's other paw trustingly. 'Hurr, that be roight, ee'm a gennelbeast, oi loikes 'im.'

Saxtus spread his paws wide. 'There you have it friends, from the mouths of Dibbuns. A little un can sometimes see things in others that us older ones cannot because our judgement gets clouded.'

Simeon retrieved the dagger from Saxtus and gave it back to Oak Tom. 'Well, do you still wish to slay him, Tom?'

The big squirrel sheathed his blade. 'No, I acted in haste out of my grief for Mellus. This Blaggut is no killer, if he was he'd still be running. But he returned, after he slew the guilty one. I can see that he is still confused about it, aren't you, Blaggut?'

The searat sat down upon the steps, ruffling the Dibbuns' heads absent-mindedly. 'We lied when we told you we was travellers, we was searats, always 'ave been. Tho' I never 'eard tell of a searat who killed his Cap'n. I did, but I was drove to it. Cap'n Slipp was a bad un, he'd 'a killed more if he lived.'

Oak Tom sat on the steps next to him. 'You did right, Blaggut, it was only justice long overdue. Good will always defeat evil, and there is good in you.'

Tarquin L. Woodsorrel had been waiting to speak up. 'Hmm, you'll 'scuse me askin', old chap, but what'll you do now, I mean where'll you go?'

Furrtil looked pleadingly at the Abbot. 'Ho say ee'm can stay yurr zurr, oi'll mind 'im.'

Blaggut smiled for the first time since the previous night. 'Bless yer 'eart, liddle matey, but you'll 'ave enuff t'do mindin' yerself an' growin' up pretty. I'd like to stay at yore h'Abbey, but I don't think I can after wot 'appened. One thing's sure, I ain't a searat no more. There's a snug cove by the sea, close to where I come ashore. It was an 'andsome place as I recalls, fresh water, vittles a growin' out o' the floor, and the sea close by. That's where ole Blaggut's bound for, I could live there.'

Saxtus respected the searat's decision, though he felt bound to enquire, 'What will you do there?'

Blaggut stood up, lifting his chin proudly. 'I'll build boats, Father, I'm good at boatbuildin', tho' tis a skill I never knew I 'ad til I came 'ere. I'm a good boatbuilder, ain't I, messmates?'

The mousebabe and Furrtil chorused together, 'Black-guts makes the best boats!'

By late afternoon Blaggut was ready to set out, laden with provisions and tools donated by kind Redwallers. Saxtus had detailed a small party, headed by Oak Tom and Tarquin, to go with him. They would help him to build a dwelling at his chosen place. The searat stood by Mellus's grave and shuffled awkwardly.

'G'bye marm, sorry about yore trouble. I'll try to be as good an' 'elpful to others as you was, I promises.'

Furrtil and the mousebabe began weeping inconsolably at their friend's departure. Blaggut pressed a pawful of candied chestnuts on them, saying, 'Ho, stop blubberin', mates, you'll 'ave me at it again. You can come an' visit with me next summer if yer good an' stop that cryin'. Lissen now, there's the Joseph Bell, it's tea-time, 'urry along or y'll be late!'

He stood watching them until they disappeared into the Abbey. Wiping away a tear, the former bosun of *Pearl Queen* hitched up the pack on his back and set off.

'Come on, Mr Tarquin, I promise you I won't make no skilly an' duff fer supper. Me'n you will build the fire, an' may'ap Mr Tom'll do the cookin'.'

They set off up the path with Tarquin muttering darkly, 'Oak Tom as cook, hmph! I should say not, the blighter'd prob'ly have us eatin' treebark an' drinkin' water. Now Brother Mallen, there's a useful mouse, good cook too. Hi, Mallen old chum, c'mere, I want a word with you!'

The shadows lengthened as they left the dusty path and cut off into Mossflower Wood.

33

The Urgan Nagru buckled a belt over his wolfhide to hold both sword and dagger and strode purposefully to where two-thirds of his horde awaited him in an inner courtyard. Grey rats in serried ranks held aloft banners, spears, lances and pikes. They stood silent in the calm that comes before storm, every eye upon their Lord as he positioned himself at their head. Drawing his sword, Foxwolf gave a bloodcurdling yell and charged out of Castle Floret.

'Owoooooh!'

The drawbridge shook to the pounding paws of the grey tide; they thundered out down the plateau steps, their barbaric war cry ringing into Southsward.

'Urgan Nagruuuuuu! Kiiiiiillll!'

Mariel watched from the gatehouse window. As soon as the last horderat was clear of the castle she rapped out an order to her two silent helpers.

'Up drawbridge!'

Muta and Rab had the huge timbered structure slammed shut seconds after the mousemaid had given her order. Mariel stood watching through a slit in the wrecked table which shielded the window, smiling with grim satisfaction.

'Foxwolf is locked out of Floret!'

Muta moved anxiously from side to side, nostrils twitching, eyes wide. Mariel grabbed the big badger's paw, saying, 'Muta, what is it?'

Rab dived – throwing himself at them he knocked both to one side as a smoking mass of debris crashed through the barricade. It was swiftly followed by two barrels, both alight and packed with wet straw. Smoke billowed thickly around the confines of the room, as more bales of damp green branches bounced down the stairs into the gatehouse. Coughing and spluttering, Mariel made it to the window, and pushed aside the table that covered it. A hail of arrows whined in. The mousemaid threw herself flat upon the floor, her mind racing. The barrels would not go through the window, they were too large, and now the window was no longer shielded by the table. It was time to leave the gatehouse.

'Muta, Rab,' she shouted, 'We must get out of here, but first the handles of the winding drum have to be broken, so that the drawbridge stays up. Can you do it?'

Coughing and gasping for breath, their eyes red and watery, the three friends felt about in the dense smoky gloom. Muta gave a strangled grunt as her formidable paws fell upon the handles. With strength born of desperation the badger threw herself upon the mechanism. Mere wooden handles were no match for her fury – they cracked and splintered momentarily before snapping clean off. Now the drawbridge was shut and locked. Gasping for air, Muta rushed out on to the stairs, still holding the broken handles in her paws. Rab materialized out of the smoke to join her. Wiping their eyes, both creatures looked at one another.

Mariel had not made it out of the gatehouse!

Under Egbert's instructions none of the creatures on the valley floor stayed together. When Iris gave the word they scattered widespread, each one tacking and dodging as they made for the cover of the wooded hills surrounding the valley. Once they were under cover of trees and clear of arrow range, everybeast made for the gathering place, a thicket on the north side, behind the castle. Egbert met them there.

Meldrum was last to arrive. He plucked an arrowhead from his tunic epaulette, saying, 'Huh, if I'd been a hareslength backward in comin' forward that blighter would have ruined me tunic. Good job it's not the dress one. Right, Educated Egbert, where to now?'

The mole glanced severely over his spectacles at Meldrum. 'Let us strike a bargain. Do not refer to me as Educated Egbert and I will not call you Hollow-Headed Hare. Agreed?'

Field Marshal Meldrum Fallowthorn the Magnificent sniffed. 'As y'wish sah. Hmm, touchier than most moles this lad, wot?'

Egbert pushed aside the shrubbery of bush and plant to reveal the cave at the north side of the plateau base. Dandin whistled softly. 'A secret entrance to the castle, wonderful! Lead on friend.'

The mole removed his glasses and polished them busily. 'I'd rather not, thank you. I think it would be propitious if I stayed in this area, to show others the way in. You must realize that Floret is still full of rats under the vixen's command. As I do not profess to be a warrior there would be little use for me to accompany you. I am sure you understand.'

Meldrum raised his eyebrows at Iris. 'Propitious, wot? The fellers a walkin' wordsmith!'

'Righto, that's fine with me friend,' said Dandin, watching Egbert nervously polishing his glasses. 'But how do we get up into the castle, is there a secret way?'

Relieved to be out of the action, Egbert smiled. 'There are many secret ways. Follow any of the tunnels and you are bound to come out in some part of Castle Floret.'

Dandin unsheathed his long dagger. 'That's good enough for me, let's go!'

Heading a band of horderats, Silvamord waited in the corridor that led to the gatehouse stairs. She fanned smoke from her nostrils as Mingol lit another barrel of wet straw.

'Send it down to the gatehouse, Mingol. They must be well choked in there by now, but it's best to be certain.'

Mingol kicked the barrel and it rolled off down the corridor. Bouncing down three small steps, it hit the wall and vanished from view as it trundled off down the gatehouse steps. Silvamord ran her tongue delicately along the edge of a vicious looking curved sword.

'I hope at least one of them staggers out still alive!'

Muta was very much alive. She came thundering into the corridor carrying the burning barrel and hurled it straight at Silvamord and her rats. They leapt aside with cries of horror as the barrel smashed to staves and the mighty badger came at them, smoke pouring from her fur.

Rab had been into the gatehouse and rescued Mariel. Carrying her across his brawny shoulders, the otter made it to the portion of the corridor on the far side of the stairs. Depositing the gasping mousemaid gently on the floor beside a window, Rab left her there to recover. Then, sword in paw, he launched himself into the attack.

The corridor was a mêlée of smoke and noise. Silvamord had got over her initial shock, and now she urged her rats on in front of her, staying well distanced from the two creatures she feared most.

'Rush them!' she screamed. 'Hack them to bits, they're well outnumbered!'

Rab and Muta were separated – both had their backs to opposite walls. The otter fought with berserk fury, his blade flickering as it sought, thrust and parried. Muta had a winding handle and a barrel stave as weapons, and any rat who came in range was smashed flat by a swinging blow from either one. The badger fought with the strength of ten.

Through the smoke and chaos Silvamord could see that the pair would not last. She dropped to the back of the pack, striking out with the flat of her swordblade as she urged the horderats on. 'Keep at them, we've got them, press in on them!'

Mariel stuck her head out of the window and gulped down clean fresh air. She rested a moment, regaining her balance. A sound of running caused her to pull her head in and look down the corridor. Reinforcements under the command of Grutch were coming to help Silvamord from the opposite direction. Galvanized into action, the mousemaid unlooped the knotted rope from around her body.

Thwack! Whock!

The first two rats fell to her Gullwhacker as Mariel whirled it in the teeth of the oncoming foe.

'Redwaaaaallll!'

Faced with overwhelming odds, the mousemaid's warrior spirit rose; the hard, knotted rope end was everywhere like a blur. Foerats tripped over their fallen comrades as they tried to get at her. Teeth flew, heads cracked and limbs splintered as Mariel of Redwall made her stand.

The smoke was beginning to clear under the trampling paws of horderats. Silvamord could see that the hard-pressed trio had only moments to survive under the numbers that assailed them. Waving her sword she pressed forward, crying, 'Don't stop, get in there, kill them!'

Dandin emerged from behind a wall tapestry to find himself in a broad passage, broken at intervals by short flights of steps. Iris and Meldrum held the tapestry aside as the rest of the otters came out of the secret tunnel. Dandin suddenly held up a paw for silence. Echoing along the stone hallway came a faint cry.

'Redwaaaaalll!'

Breaking into a headlong dash he tore off, shouting, 'This way, it's Mariel! Redwaaaaaaalllll!'

Taking up the Abbey warcry the small force followed him at a flat-out run.

The rear followers of Grutch's command were hit hard and fast by the charge. Dandin came vaulting in on a spear, flattening a rat as he took up position alongside Mariel. Swinging the Gullwhacker full in a rat's face she yelled at Dandin over the noise of combat, 'Get help to Muta and Rab. Quickly!'

But there was little need for the mousemaid's plea. Iris tore past them, wreaking havoc with a broken javelin as she screamed with joy.

'Rab! Rab Streambattle! It's me, Iris!'

Suddenly, Rab's swordblade was revolving like a windmill in a gale as he fought his way towards her, the words ripping unbidden from his throat.

'Iris! Iris!'

Meldrum battered his way with a pike until he was at Muta's side. The old campaigner winked at her. 'Right, here we go, back to back now, bet I wipe out more vermin than you do, marm, wot?'

The big badger took up the challenge with a grunt. Placing her back flat against the hare's, she moved with him. They were unassailable, a complete fighting machine.

Silvamord saw the tide turning against her. She was puzzled as to how the intruders came to be inside Floret, but not unduly worried. There were still lots more horderats at her disposal. Slipping away from the rear of her contingent she hurried up to the battlements, where most of her force were stationed to sweep the valley floor with their bows.

'Sicant, Hooktail, get every rat here down to the gatehouse corridor. Follow me!'

Muta, Rab and Mariel were safe among the otters. They regrouped in the corridor. The horderats milled about on the other side further up, uncertain of what to do without somebeast to lead them. Rab Streambattle soon made up their minds for them. Exercising his new-found voice he led what remained of the small rescue force against the foebeast.

'Chaaaarge!'

The rats took one look at the howling warriors leaping over battle debris and fallen bodies, and panic set in. They broke and ran off in retreat.

Eyes blazing, weapons swinging, the avengers came after them, with Mariel, Dandin, Rab, Iris, Meldrum and Muta in the lead.

34

Urgan Nagru stood on the wooded hillside, sword and dagger drawn. His chest heaved with exertion as he gazed around at the silent trees. 'I'll find them, they've got to be here somewhere!'

A rat Captain named Bladetail slashed the undergrowth with his spear. 'The way they were running, Sire, I'd bet they're right out of Southsward heading north now.'

'They can run to the gates of dark ice, I'll still find them and put an end to it all.' Nagru began walking uphill resolutely. 'I never left an enemy alone in my life until victory was mine. Deadbeasts never come back to fight again, remember that, Bladetail!'

The rat Captain recalled Muta and Rab, but held his silence. Nagru was in a killing mood. All along the hillsides horderats began moving upward with their leader. Nagru pointed his dagger at one rat. 'Viglim, scout ahead, get up on top and see if you can pick up their trail. Look sharp!'

Viglim saluted and dashed off ahead. Two horderats toiling side by side climbed upward; they watched Viglim reach the top and then he was lost to sight.

One of the rats slowed to regain his breath. 'I think we're chasin' shadows, they're long gone.'

His companion pushed on, replying as he went, 'That'll suit me, anythin' fer an easy life, mate. Though we've got to wait until Nagru gets tired of the chase.'

Nagru was nearly at the top, when a scream caused him to look upward. This was followed by a noise like a thousand dull drums. Viglim came toppling back downhill, a small circular object rolling behind him. Letting the body of Viglim roll past him, the Foxwolf trapped the circular object with his footpaw. He picked it up, inspected it and passed it to Bladetail, saying, 'What do you make of this?'

'Sire, it looks like an old stale oatcake, though it's too hard for that. Maybe it's some kind of rock. What's that noise up above?'

Nagru quickened his pace. 'We'll soon find out, let's take a look.'

The Foxwolf was first to breast the hilltop. The drumming noise was the ground thrumming to legions of paws. Bearing down on him like a tornado came Bowly Pintips at the head of an army of otters, mice, moles, hedgehogs and squirrels. As they ran, a mighty cry arose from the battle host.

'Freeeee Southswaaaaaard!'

Nagru was a seasoned warrior, and he did not panic as most creatures would have done. Waving his sword, he shouted urgently to his horderats. 'Rally to me!'

Every rat hastened to obey. Nagru was not given to idle commands – they sensed the urgency in his voice. Scarce had they grouped when the Southsward army came pounding over the hilltop and the two forces clashed. The battle broke over Nagru with a vengeance.

Squirrels immediately raced up treetrunks and began hailing arrows downward into the horderats. The front ranks were mainly the tribe of Gawjun and Deekeye; wielding their warclubs, the hedgehogs waded in, only to be met by Nagru sending spears and pikes straight at them.

Bowly and his leverets cut to one side. Picking up a lance from a fallen otter, the young hedgehog and his troop fought their way into the horde's flank, only to find themselves surrounded. They gathered round Runtwold, who had taken a swordthrust in his foot-paw, and tried fighting their way out. Luckily a party of moles saw their predicament and came to their aid with maces swinging.

Nagru sought out Bladetail. 'Retreat, sound a retreat!' he shouted. 'We'll take them on the valley floor.'

Bladetail blew on a bone whistle; the response was immediate. Like a tide of grey, the horderats flooded down through the trees of the wooded slope to the open valley. Nagru had arrived before them. He positioned a line of archers to fire at the first wave of Southswarders emerging from the trees. Those carrying spears and lances were sent back to lay in a slight dip in the ground, while the rest grouped behind them. It was hastily done, but the Foxwolf was satisfied that his more disciplined horde would triumph against the wild rabble.

With a rousing yell, the Southswarders broke the tree cover and charged out on to the valley floor. Gael Squir-relking was at their head, holding high the broom banner. Gawjun saved them both by throwing himself on the King and bringing him down. The arrows zipped over their heads, felling the first rank of Southswarders. Bowly called from behind the old spread oak, where he was supporting the wounded Runtwold. 'Back to the trees, don't charge into the open!'

Keeping their heads down, Gawjun and Gael made it back to the trees. Now Nagru ordered his archers to drop back. They lay in the land dip with the spear and lance rats. Arrows and slingstones, like clouds of vicious hornets, rattled back and forth between the two armies.

Gawjun thumped his warclub against a tree and slumped down moodily. 'I thought 'twould be a straight battle against yonder vermin, now we be caught in a standoff!'

Bowly nodded knowledgeably. 'I been in one o' them standoffs. We bide 'ere until help arrives, that's what we do!'

'Where'd thy sense come from?' said Deekeye, curling her lip. '*We're* supposed to be the help that's arrivin' – who'll help us?'

Nagru had assessed the situation now that the field of combat had been established. The cunning that had made him Lord of the cold lands came to the fore as he laid plans.

'Bladetail, Coldclaw, take two squads and drop back. Retreat until you are out of range, then split up and go to opposite sides of the valley. Make your way through the trees and attack them from both sides. When you go at them, create lots of noise – that should provide enough distraction for my main force to mount a surprise charge from the front.'

Gael had all the squirrels up in the trees – it was a good position to fire arrows from. He was joined by Bowly and as many others with slings who could climb up into the high branches. They pelted the horderats hard, harassing them constantly every time a head or paw showed from the dip in the valley. Bowly saw the two squads retreating and chuckled, 'We're drivin' 'em back, see!'

Gael shook his head doubtfully. 'Foxwolf is no fool, he's up to something.'

Inside Castle Floret, Mariel and her friends found their fortunes reversed abruptly. They had pursued the remnants of their foes up a flight of stairs, only to be met by Silvamord's counter attack. Masses of horderats poured down the stairs from the battlements, and the friends were forced to turn and retreat. Back down in the corridor a tide of grey swept in from every available entrance. Whooping and screeching, they chased the small depleted army of Southswarders. Dandin, Rab and Muta fought a way through, protecting the rearguard as Mariel ushered her fighters along the corridor. It was no easy task. Meldrum had taken a spear thrust in his shoulder and he hobbled along, supported by Troutlad and Greenbeck, complaining loudly.

'The old tunic's ruined now, good'n'proper. Foul villains, chuckin' their spears about with no regard at all to a chap's good togs, wot? This place must be a flippin' rat paradise, never seen so many of the vermin in all me born days – there's no end t'the blighters!'

Iris saw two of her otters fall to arrows; she appealed to Muta as they passed a side chamber. 'What about that place, is the door locked?'

Locked doors did not stop the big badger. She hurled herself at the door. Hinges and lock gave way together and the door fell flat. Iris shook her head. 'It's just a room, we'd be trapped in there!' she said.

Mariel saw that the horderats had slowed now, distancing themselves, but still advancing under Silvamord's shouted commands. 'Stay your distance, don't clash with 'em. Archers, keep firing and following until they're all cut down!'

Two more Southswarders fell to the horderat arrows. Iris flung back a fallen spear at the rats, shouting, 'Muta, the door, can we use it for a shield?'

The badger grunted and strained, manoeuvring the fallen door until she was carrying it lengthways across her back. Meldrum dismissed Troutlad and Greenbeck. 'Go and help her, two big stout lads like y'selves shouldn't be totin' me about. I'll shift for meself, wot?'

They took the ends of the door, lightening Muta's load. The shield proved quite effective; the small group made its way down the corridor until Rab stopped them. 'Not that way, it's the banqueting chamber – it's too wide, they'd be able to surround us.'

Dandin ran ahead and took a look at the chamber. He came hurrying back with bad news. 'There's more rats coming through from that side!'

Mariel cut off down a passage. 'Come on, this is the only way left!' she called.

Rab Streambattle hesitated. 'But it doesn't go anywhere, there's only a small room down there, we'll be blocked in!'

'Better than bein' in the middle of a rat sandwich,' said Meldrum, prodding him forward. 'Hurry up, old lad, any port in a storm!'

Silvamord relaxed at the entrance to the passage and congratulated Sicant and Hooktail. 'Good work, well done! They're bottled up tight!'

She eyed the rats around her, settling on one who looked bolder than the rest. 'You there, what's your name?'

'They call me Ugrath, Lady.'

The vixen clapped Ugrath's back, her tailed skirt tinkling musically as she paced around him. 'I watched you Ugrath, you fought well. There's a little job you can do for me, do you think you're up to it?'

Ugrath pulled in his chin and stuck out his chest proudly. 'I am yours to command, Lady!'

'Good. I want you to take a message to those fools. Tell them if they throw down their arms, bind the badger and the otter tight, and come out here, I will spare their lives. But it must be done immediately, or I will strike at them and leave none alive. Go now!'

Ugrath's throat bobbed as he swallowed, then, grasping his pike tight, he set off down the passage. Sicant exchanged glances with the vixen. 'You'll let them live, Majesty?' she asked.

Silvamord drew her curved sword, testing its edge on

her paw. She raised one eyebrow at Sicant. 'Well, what do you think?'

There was silence from down the passage, followed by a sound of voices and an anguished yelp. Ugrath came staggering back, minus his pike and nursing his nose with both paws. He squinted at the vixen through a swollen eye. 'Mousemaid with a rope, she . . .'

Silvamord silenced him with a glare, and turned to the massed rats crowding everywhere. 'Pikes and long spears, archers behind, follow up with swords. Charge!'

35

Egbert the Scholar was not feeling very happy as he
stood with one paw in the valley and the other inside
the cave entrance. The mole knew that there was fighting and bloodshed inside Floret – he could hear the faint
sounds of conflict from the south side of the valley
where Nagru was battling with Gael Squirrelking's
army. Egbert gave a whimper of anguish – his former
relatively peaceful life was now shattered by war.
Timidly, he ventured beyond the bushy screen which
hid the secret entrance to Floret, intending to escape
from it all up the north slope, which faced the castle's
rear side.

Suddenly, a sound in the undergrowth startled him.
He turned to run back to the cave and was immediately
swept off his paws by a murderous-looking beast. Lying
flat on his back, the terrified mole covered both eyes, so
that he would not have to see the dreadful apparition. It
was a big, villainous-looking otter, covered in tattoos
and scars, with one eye and a musselshell, and carrying
twin curved swords. Egbert curled into a ball, hoping
his end would be swift and painless. A voice, firm but
friendly, sounded close by. 'Put up those swords, Finnbarr, you'll frighten the poor mole to death!'

Egbert uncovered his eyes and looked around. He was surrounded by a host of javelin-wielding otters and shrews armed with rapiers. The speaker, a strong-looking mouse, with twinkling eyes and a grey beard, helped him upright and shook his paw in friendly manner. 'Hello there, I'm Joseph the Bellmaker. Don't be afraid – you've nothing to fear from us. You don't look like one of the Foxwolf's creatures.'

The knowledge that he was out of danger restored the scholarly mole's voice. 'Creature of the Foxwolf, me, Egbert the Scholar?' he said, indignantly. 'Never! I, sir, am what is known as a casualty of war. It is no small thing having to leave Castle Floret because the place has been turned into a battleground, I can tell you!'

Foremole was astounded at Egbert's lack of mole accent. 'Burrhurr, ee talken wunnerful pretty, zurr Hegbutt!'

'Battleground?' Log a Log interrupted. 'You mean that there's fightin' goin' on inside that castle? Who's battlin' with who, matey?'

Egbert adjusted his nose spectacles prissily. 'I think the phrase is, with whom . . .' He caught an impatient glare from the sea otter and hastened to explain. 'Actually, it's the forces of Silvamord – she's the mate of Nagru. They're battling with a small mixed group led by my friend Mariel . . .'

Suddenly the mole's footpaws left the ground and he found himself hoisted up in front of Joseph's burning stare. 'Mariel! How do we get into that castle, tell me!'

The words flew in a babble from Egbert's mouth. 'Secret castle into the cave I mean secret cave into the castle, put me down, I'll show you!'

Driven by the Bellmaker's urgency, Egbert scurried willy-nilly through the passages and tunnels leading upward into Floret. Joseph and Finnbarr followed close on his heels, with Log a Log and Blerun the otter leading the large band that was strung out behind in the dark narrow passages. Finnbarr Galedeep ducked his head low, following the mole on all fours. 'I 'ope ye know where yer goin', messmate.'

Egbert had become lost in his haste, but he did not admit it. 'Aha! Wood panelling. This is it – halt and give me space!' He tugged aside a thin oak slat and squeezed through, looking about speculatively at the new entrance he had found. He was forced to jump aside with a startled squeak as three sections of the wainscot were slammed flat on the floor and armed creatures began pouring in. Joseph took the mole's paw in a gesture of friendship.

'Thank you, Egbert. There is one more favour I would ask of you. Back in the entrance cave you will find three small creatures, Wincey, Benjy and Figgs. Would you be so kind as to watch over them until this thing is finished?'

A smile of relief crossed the mole's face. 'Indeed I will, Joseph. If you will excuse me I'll go and attend to them straight away!'

Foremole stopped him climbing back into the tunnels. 'Noice place ee 'ave 'ere, zurr Hegbutt, hurr aye!'

The Scholar lapsed into mole dialect to reply. 'Bo urr, she'm noice awroight zurr. Oi be off naow to lukk arter ee liddle uns. Gu'bye moler!'

Finnbarr's teeth gleamed white in the gloom of the dim chamber they had emerged into. 'Must be summat wrong with that un, he's goin' to miss all the fightin'. Come on, buckoes, git yerselves through 'ere, we ain't got all summer!'

Finnbarr had been one of the first through the opening. He made a quick scouting trip, accompanied by Durry, Rufe and Fatch. Sliding silently back into the chamber, he found Joseph among the creatures crowding the ill-lit room. 'Bellmaker, I found where the fight's at. Along the passage outside an' down some stairs, you kin 'ear the 'ullabaloo from the top o' the stairwell!'

Joseph hefted a long ash stave that he favoured as a weapon, crying, 'Then that's where Mariel and Dandin will be. Are we ready?'

Finnbarr was already racing Blerun for the door. 'Las' one down there's a flat crab!'

Mariel saw the charge coming. She swung her Gull-whacker as Troutlad, Greenbeck and Muta picked up the door and headed the counter charge. Behind them, the small force swung slingstones into the horde's front rank as they dashed down the passage with only a battered door between them and the crowds of grey rats.

'Redwaaaaaalllll!'

They met with a crash, the door flattening several rats as the long spears and pikes sought out the Southswarders. Dandin led them under the spearpoints, ducking low as he dived in with his long dagger drawn. Arrows came hissing over at the slingers; those who were not struck returned slingstones fast and hard. Grunting and slashing, roaring and striking, the conflict went on in the narrow passage.

Silvamord stood on the backs of two rats who were bent double. They gasped as she leapt up and down excitedly, shrieking, 'Finish them off! Kill, kill, kill!' A mighty blow from Joseph's stave sent her spinning.

Suddenly the air was filled with wild warcries.

'Logalogalogalog!'

'Galedeeeeeep!'

'Southswaaaaaaard!'

'Redwaaaaaaaalllll!'

Then the crew of *Pearl Queen* and Blerun's otters were in the thick of it. The horderats fought viciously, knowing they were fighting for their lives. Mariel and her company gave a ragged cheer as the rats who were attacking them turned and retreated down the passage. The battle flowed outward; clashing steel echoed as Southswarders, aided by *Pearl Queen*'s crew and Blerun's otters, matched their courage against the savagery of Silvamord's horderats. Joseph beat his way through the mêlée until he was at the side of Mariel and Dandin. Laying a rat senseless with a sweep of his stave, he grinned and bowed his grizzled head to them both.

'Daughter!'

'Father!'

'Dandin!'

'Sir!'

The Bellmaker flinched as Mariel's Gullwhacker whipped by his ear, taking out a rat who was sneaking up on him. 'I see you still favour the old knotted rope,' he said.

Gullwhacker hummed as Mariel swung it in a blurring pattern. 'Aye, it's as good as any weapon when there's fighting to be done. Come on, let's give 'em blood'n'vinegar!' With a hearty roar the three warriors threw themselves into the fray.

Log a Log and the Guosim shrews had fought their way across the banqueting chamber. Several shrews fell to horderats' spears until the Guosim got the measure of their enemies, then they fought in close, their deadly shrew-rapiers laying the foebeasts low as they ducked in under the spearshafts. Blerun and his otters put bows and javelins to good use as they battled along the corridor and up flights of spiral stairs. Sometimes they would fight paw to paw, javelin against spear and pike, at other intervals they found themselves crouching in doorways as they exchanged arrows with the rats.

Durry, Rufe and Fatch were fighting as a team. Slinging hard pebbles they would pop up in strategic places, hurl off a volley and drop down again, only to appear in another place. Rufe spotted Silvamord slinking along the side of a corridor – the vixen was looking for an avenue of escape. Threading her way between the horderats that were backed to the wall, she weaved sinuously towards one of the staircases, staying well away from the area where Muta and Rab were beset by a crowd of grey foebeasts. Setting a good-sized stone in his sling, Rufe swung it hard and accurate. It struck the vixen somewhere between neck and shoulder, and she went down. Yelling triumphantly, the young squirrel threaded his way through the chaos to where Silvamord lay. Durry saw him go and followed him, calling out, 'Rufe, come back here, stay with me'n Fatch!'

Fatch had not realized Rufe was elsewhere until he heard Durry's shout. Seeing the danger his friend was in, the shrew overtook Durry, crying out a warning. 'Rufe, stay away from her!'

The young squirrel had reached Silvamord. He turned his back on her, shouting to his friends, 'I've captured their leader!'

Silvamord sprang up and slashed at his back with her sword. Fatch saw Rufe go down. He hurtled forward and threw himself upon the vixen; swinging his stone-loaded sling, he caught her in the face as she brought the sword up to finish Rufe off. Silvamord thrust backward at the shrew clinging doggedly to her back – she felt him go limp and slide off. A slingstone caught her paw and Durry rushed in howling as he readied another stone to his sling. With a snarl the vixen raced off up the stairs.

Freeing himself of a rat, Rab Streambattle glimpsed Silvamord disappearing up the steps and pointed in her direction. Flinging aside a stunned rat, Muta grunted and took off in pursuit. Rab went in an entirely different direction, as fast as his paws would carry him. He knew Floret and he was certain of the exact point on the battlements where the vixen would emerge.

Rufe staggered upright helped by Durry. The hedgehog saw the rent in his friend's tunic and the blood seeping from his back. 'Rufe, she got you, are you all right?'

Rufe crouched beside Fatch, cradling the shrew's

head in his paws as he replied, 'I'm wounded, but I'll live. What's wrong with Fatch?'

Durry saw the rips on both sides of the shrew's tunic and the spreading dark stains. Silvamord's sword had gone right through. Fatch's head lolled to one side as he smiled weakly into Rufe's face. 'Told you I'd look after you, didn't I, mate?'

The eyes of Fatch the loyal Guosim shrew clouded over and closed for the last time. Durry Quill turned and guarded both his friends. Rufe had both paws around the body of his protector, weeping softly as he rocked him back and forth.

Silvamord panted hard as she pushed herself upward on the stones of the spiral stairs. Behind her she could hear the relentless pad of Muta's paws getting nearer. Not daring to look back, the vixen pressed onward and upward, fear clutching her heart in its icy claws. Fumbling hastily, she unlatched the roof door, slamming it behind her as she dashed out on to the battlements with a sob of relief.

Rab Streambattle stepped out from behind a turret, sword at the ready. Silvamord heard the door behind her burst into matchwood as the badger came cannoning out on to the battlemented roof. Whirling like lightning, she struck at Muta. The badger dodged aside, catching the blade in one paw as it hit the stonework. Though the edge cut into Muta's paw, she hardly felt it – the hated vixen standing before her was all that she could see. Dragging the sword from Silvamord's nerveless grasp, the big badger snapped the blade between her paws like a twig. With a scream of terror the vixen took a running leap over the battlements.

Muta and Rab dashed to the edge and watched Silvamord falling, down, down, down, to land with a dull splash in the moat.

Rab smiled into Muta's angry, frustrated eyes. 'She's mine, friend. Nothing escapes from an otter in water!'

Dropping his sword, Rab sailed in a graceful arc as he dived from the battlements of Floret. He struck the water cleanly with hardly a splash. Muta watched the still moat from her high vantage point for a long time, but nothing disturbed the water save ripples. Then she saw Rab slip from the water and sit watching on the bank. Moments later a still-bloated form bobbed to the surface. Rab had spoken truly, nothing did escape an otter in the water. Silvamord, the mate of Urgan Nagru, was no more threat to any living creature than the weeds she floated amongst. A great calm fell over the badger as she waved to her friend below.

The horderats were broken and defeated inside Castle Floret. *Pearl Queen*'s crew and Blerun's otters had helped Mariel and her friends to carry the day. Parties of the victors scoured passage and chamber, combing out any final pockets of resistance. Mariel and Dandin watched a wall curtain moving slightly.

'Looks like a couple hiding behind that curtain, let's give them a Redwall greeting!' the mousemaid whispered as she readied her Gullwhacker.

A lump stuck out of the curtain fabric and Mariel gave it a sharp tap with the knotted rope.

'Ouchooch! I say, go easy there, you rotters!'

Dandin ripped the curtain aside to reveal the Hon Rosie Woodsorrel, rubbing her rear end ruefully. 'Hah, so there you are at last, where've you been?' she cried.

Mariel thoughtfully hid the Gullwhacker behind her back. 'Hello, Rosie. I think we should be asking you where you've been?'

The garrulous harewife shifted a fallen rat and sat down wearily on the floor. 'Well may you ask, young uns, well may you ask! I've been doin' a passable impression of a bloomin' mole. Lost underground in all those bally tunnels an' turns, trekkin' this way an' that until I was dizzy. Don't snigger you two, s'not funny y'know. Moles have my undyin' sympathy if they have to tramp around tunnels all their lives, no wonder they speak funny. I say, have I missed the jolly old battle? Not a scrap left for Rosie, eh, well there's a fine thing, come all this way through shipwrecks an' sharks t'be disappointed. Tchah!'

Finnbarr Galedeep stood in the banqueting chamber watching groups of defeated horderats being marched off to the dungeons by Blerun's otters. Their weapons were stacked in heaps on the floor. He turned to Joseph, who was anxiously scanning the valley from a window, and said, 'Ahoy, what's goin' on out there, Bellmaker?'

Joseph continued to peer at the far side of the valley floor as he spoke. 'More fighting! It looks like some creatures need our help down there, Finn – take a look at this.'

Finnbarr and Joseph were joined at the window by Meldrum. The old hare assessed the situation right away. 'Hmm, that must be the Foxwolf an' his force in the dip – those chaps in the trees have got to be Southswarders. Hullo, looks like old Foxwolf's layin' some sort of trap for those lads in the trees. Look at those two squads droppin' back towards here – I'll be bound they're out to ambush from both sides, sneak around through the trees at the Southswarders in the old pincer movement, wot?'

Joseph took up his stave. 'You're right! Come on Finn, let's rally our crew and get down their fast. Meldrum, keep a small squad here to watch those prisoners. Where's Mariel and Dandin? There's not a moment to lose!'

36

The two horde Captains, Bladetail and Coldclaw, had the tables turned on them so fast it made their heads spin. One moment they were about to split their forces and go separate ways, next instant they were engulfed by two silent waves of hard-eyed warriors rounding both sides of the plateau. The ambushers found themselves ambushed. The rats who were not immediately cut down dropped their weapons and lay on the ground in token of surrender. Coldclaw was laid low by a single blow from the Bellmaker's stave. Bladetail dodged Dandin's dagger and made a run for it, back to Nagru and the main force.

The Foxwolf was busy directing his rats to keep up constant barrages of arrows, javelins and slingstones at the Southswarders in the trees. He had the advantage of numbers and it was beginning to tell.

'Archers, take aim at those rowans to the left, about midway up the trunks. Shoot!' A hail of shafts zipped viciously into the swaying rowans.

The Urgan Nagru laughed savagely – he was in his element. 'Southswarders, hah! They don't know what a real battle is. I am the Foxwolf, I was Lord of all the lands of ice and snow beyond the great seas! These fools will weep blood before I am done with them!'

He was revelling in the screams of the squirrels who had fallen from the rowans pierced by arrows, when Bladetail tumbled breathlessly into the dip and collided with him, shouting, 'Lord, they're coming!'

Gael Squirrelking pointed out into the valley at the silent masses sweeping to the aid of the beleaguered Southswarders.

'Bowly, Gawjun, look!'

Weldan, the older squirrel leader, came to the King's side. 'When they get close enough, Majesty, then we'll charge. That way Foxwolf's forces will be hit from both sides at once.'

Finnbarr Galedeep drew his swords as he ran alongside Mariel and Dandin. 'Haharr, they've spotted us mateys, there's no goin' back now!'

They were close enough to see the eyes of the horde when yelling warriors broke from the tree cover. 'Free Southswaaaaard!'

Hon Rosie Woodsorrel passed Finnbarr at a bound, javelin at the ready, as she yelled, 'Whoohahahooh! Here we go chaps!'

A roar arose from the charging creatures around her. 'Redwaaaaaaaaalllllll!'

The valley floor shook to the pounding of paws as both sides closed in on the dip like a gigantic double tidal wave, clashing with the horde of Nagru as they joined battle. Gael Squirrelking was brought down by a loaded sling – Bowly Pintips snatched up the broom standard as he leapt over the senseless squirrel. A ring of pikes pointing outward protected the Foxwolf as he shouted above the din.

'Circle and fight outward!'

Mariel found her Gullwhacker caught as it wrapped around the crosstree of a rat's pike. She tugged furiously, as three more rats ran at her with drawn swords. Joseph was in at her side, laying two low with blows from his stave. The third fell to a blow from Deek-eye's warclub. Hon Rosie and Log a Log were fighting side by side, javelin and rapier points flickering in deadly patterns. Rosie spotted the four leverets and Bowly; beset by rats on all sides they struggled valiantly to retaliate. Hacking a path through to them, Rosie took them under her wing. 'Stick with Auntie Rosie, young uns, and watch your backs!'

Bowly took a crack over his head from a spearbutt and fell on all fours, still trying to uphold the standard. In the heat of battle Foremole had formed an alliance with the Southsward mole tribe. Heading a band that swung maces expertly, he fought his way to Bowly and took up the broom, waving it high as he threw himself into the fray. 'Yurr, follow oi moles, rally to ee standard!'

Suddenly, Gael was hauled upright. Rubbing a size-able lump between his ears, he stared into his rescuer's face joyously. 'Muta!'

The big badger peered at him, recognition dawning upon her. Planting the King firmly at her side she began fighting off all comers with mighty blows of her paws.

Joseph had fought his way to the edge of the conflict. He rested a brief moment, noting happily that the battle was going in their favour – Redwallers and Southswar-ders were beginning to overcome Nagru's force. Finnbarr appeared at his side breathing heavily.

'We're doin' well, Bellmaker,' said the big sea otter, as he wiped both his sword blades on the grass. 'But that Foxwolf is still goin' strong. Look, the rogue's got a group o' spearbeasts about him, fightin' their way over to the trees!'

Joseph gripped his stave as he set off towards the action. 'Nagru must be stopped – if he reaches the trees he'll escape!'

Escape was indeed the uppermost thing in the cun-ning brain of Urgan Nagru. He knew that the

Southswarders were fighting for a cause, the freedom of their homeland. His horderats had only the fear of him to keep them fighting, and that was not enough. Small groups were beginning to lay down their arms and make their way beyond the edges of the mêlée to sit in surrender on the ground, heads in their paws.

The wolfskull clacked against Nagru's head as he turned to see Finnbarr Galedeep coming after him. The Foxwolf had seen the big sea otter do battle with his twin blades, and he did not relish the prospect of having to face him. Muttering to his ring of spear rats, Nagru urged them towards the wooded hillslope.

'It's fight or die, now, my warriors – you get me to the trees and I'll get you away safe. We'll get to the cove where our ships are hidden; they won't follow us into the sea. Keep going, it's not far now!'

Joseph and Finnbarr were joined by Mariel and a small force, who circled around the outer edges of the fray until they were in the trees. It was the last thing Nagru or his spearguard were expecting. Joseph's heavy stave, aided by Finnbarr's twin blades and Mariel's Gullwhacker, broke through the surprised rats. Joseph was tripped by a spearbutt in the confusion and Mariel rushed to his side, defending her father hard with the knotted rope until he was able to stand upright. A thud and a roar came from within the broken ring of spears. Finnbarr Galedeep had found the Fox-wolf.

Creatures from both camps leapt aside as the fox and the sea otter locked together in a death struggle. Finnbarr could not use his swords in such close quarters – hurling them aside, he grabbed Nagru bodily and flung him to the ground. Nagru raked viciously at his foe's face with the metal wolfclaws, his teeth seeking the sea otter's throat as he called to his guards, 'Help me, kill him!'

Bladetail drove his spear into Finnbarr. The handle

snapped as the two creatures on the ground rolled over and over in a shower of dust and torn grass. Bladetail reached for another spear, but before he could grab it, Dandin's long dagger ran him through.

The dust crimsoned as Foxwolf and Finnbarr fought like madbeasts around the small clearing, fangs snapping, claws raking, limbs kicking furiously. Then Finnbarr was standing upright; grabbing the fox by his neck and tail, the sea otter ran his enemy across the open space. Nagru's paws flailed helplessly as he was propelled head down, and the last thing he heard was Finnbarr's warcry.

'Galedeeeeeeep!'

Crack!

With a sickening thud, the mighty sea otter ran his opponent's head on into the unyielding trunk of an oak tree. The Urgan Nagru died by his own symbol of power. The wolf fangs of the skull that rested on his head were driven deep into his evil brain by the force with which Finnbarr charged him against the treetrunk. So perished the Urgan Nagru and his dreams of conquest.

Joseph dashed to Finnbarr's side. 'You old battledog, you did it! You slew the Foxwolf!'

The sea otter sat upon the ground and smiled at his friend. 'You would've done it if you'd reached him first, Bellmaker.'

Joseph took Finnbarr's scarred and tattooed paw. 'The battle is won, come and we'll find someplace to rest while I bind those wounds of yours.'

But the sea otter stayed upon the ground. 'Let go of my paw, matey,' he said. 'This is where I rest!'

Joseph knelt by his friend's side. 'Finnbarr, are you all right?'

Finnbarr winced as he shook his head. 'There's 'alf a spear inside o' me, Bellmaker. I ain't gettin' up from 'ere. Pass me swords, will yer, messmate?'

Joseph took the fallen swords from Mariel and Dandin, and pressed them into Finnbarr's paws. The Bellmaker realized then what had happened. Bladetail's spear had done its work; his companion was dying. Joseph's brown eyes radiated sorrow as he put a paw about Finnbarr's shoulders and whispered to him, 'Is there anything else you need, mate?'

Finnbarr squinted through his one good eye. 'Turn me t'face the west, that's the direction the sea lays in, ain't it?'

The Bellmaker nodded silently, turning his friend gently, so that he faced west.

'Thankee shipmate,' Finnbarr grunted. 'Now stop 'ere with me awhile until I leave yer t'go on me last good voyage.'

Joseph the Bellmaker stayed. He held on to Finnbarr Galedeep the sea otter until his eyes clouded over and finally closed. Finnbarr smiled as the sounds of land faded. Calm as a millpond and blue as aquamarine, the sea stretched away to meet the sky on a far horizon. He stood alone at the tiller of his beloved *Pearl Queen* as the sails billowed silently and it took him away.

37

Pennants and gaily coloured streamers fluttered on high from every tower of Castle Floret. Below the plateau every creature in Southsward sat feasting on the valley floor. The plateau steps were garlanded with flowers and green boughs; squirrel choirs sang, young ones danced and played, older ones dozed peacefully in the warm noontide.

Muta danced too, and perched upon her shoulders the little squirrelprince Truffen laughed and clapped his paws. Queen Serena watched them as she sat upon the steps with her friends Rab Streambattle and Iris.

'Muta has had my Truffen on her shoulders since first light, do you think she'll ever let him down again?'

Iris laughed as she watched the antics of the two. 'D'you think he'll ever let her, the rascal? There's nothin' he likes better than bein' carried about all day by her, eh, Rab?'

Her mate sprawled lazily across the steps. 'Muta's happy, she's no longer a fugitive, or a berserk slayer. They both deserve their happiness.'

Log a Log and Blerun marched up with both their tribes in tow. Sitting themselves between Foremole and Weldan, they accepted beakers of blackberry cordial.

The shrew Chieftain unbuckled his rapier and put it to one side. 'Ah well, that's the horderat prisoners gone. We shoved 'em aboard one o' their ships an' pointed them off to the open sea. They come back under pain of death, I told 'em.'

Egbert the Scholar sat a few steps above them, surrounded by Furrp and his tribe and Foremole. They inspected the huge medal he wore about his neck.

'Burr, et be a vurry noice thing, zurr Hegbutt,' said Furrp. 'Urr, wot be et furr?'

Egbert felt very important as he explained to the rustic moles. 'This is my symbol of office. By Royal appointment I am now Castle Librarian and Archivist of Floret, Official Recorder for Southsward Country and Dynastic Concordance Coordinator to the House of Gael.'

Furrp scratched his snout with a heavy digging paw. 'Gudd luck to ee, zurr. Oi wuddent sleep wi' a gurt 'eavy medal an' a name long as a wurrm's tail loik that, hurr no!' Egbert sat with a look of injured dignity as the moles all fell about chuckling.

The four leverets and Bowly Pintips were demolishing a weighty plumcake, listening to their uncle Meldrum and Hon Rosie as they discovered ancestral connections.

'Hmm, Woodsorrel y'say marm, not one of the Long Patrol Westshore Woodsorrels by any chance?'

'Whoohahahooh! The very fellows, that's my Tarquin's branch of the family, d'you know them, Meldrum?'

'Know 'em? Listen m'dear, my great uncle Bracken was the head of the bunch, marvellous old cove. They called him Bracken the Brave y'know.'

'Did they indeed? That's not what my Tarquin told me. He said the story goes that Bracken told so many fibs about his exploits, that the Long Patrol nicknamed him Old Bracken the Blowbag. Whoohahahooh, good name, wot?'

Amidst the laughter that followed young Foghill piped up, 'I say, uncle Mel, your ears have gone all red!'

Meldrum the Magnificent addressed his nephew sternly. 'Never mind my ears, you young pup. What've I told you about callin' me uncle Mel? Confined t'barracks for two days, sah, for incorrectly referrin' to a senior officer!'

Joseph lay full stretch in the soft grass of the valley floor, shaded by a rowan. He was watching Durry Quill and some young shrews, who had borrowed Mariel's Gullwhacker and made a swing from the branches of a sycamore. Rufe Brush sat by Joseph, his eyes red from weeping. The Bellmaker nudged the young squirrel gently. 'Come on, Rufey, how about a smile for an old greybeard?'

Rufe stared at the daisies which brightened the grassy shade. 'I can't get Fatch out of my mind, I'll never forget him.'

Joseph saw a teardrop spill from Rufe's cheek to the grass. 'I should hope you never will forget Fatch,' he said. 'He was a brave shrew to give his life for you. I'll bet wherever he is now he must be in a fine old temper.'

Rufe rubbed a paw across his eyes and sniffed. 'Why would Fatch be in a temper, Joseph?'

The Bellmaker plucked a dockleaf and gave it to his young friend. 'Here, wipe your face, I'll tell you why. Fatch gave his life so that you could live on and enjoy yours. If I were Fatch I'd be in a real temper now, knowing that you were not enjoying the life I'd given you, sitting weeping amid the joys of freedom on a summer day.'

Durry Quill had been listening from a distance. Now he trundled up and stood looking down at the Bellmaker. 'You're right sir, an 'ole Finnbarr would be in an even worser mood lookin' at your face, 'tis more miserable than a frog who's swallered a bumblebee. Come on, you two, let's play on the swing!'

'Look out, Durry!'

A young shrew had swung the wrong way. He came spinning in on the rope, knocking Durry ears over tip into Joseph and Rufe, and now all three lay in a heap.

Joseph sat up glaring at the swinging shrew, then he began to chuckle. Rufe tried to sit up and fell back on to Durry; the hedgehog pushed him off. 'Gerroff me y'great Rufey lump!'

Rufe could not resist the smile spreading across his face. 'Fat wettysnout pricklybottom cakeface!'

All three stood up laughing heartily. Joseph dashed off towards the rope, shouting, 'Me first, you two are so fat you'd burst the swing!'

They raced after him giggling.

'You great big Dibbun!'

'Wait'll we tell Mariel you was playin' swings!'

Afternoon drifted on in a warm summery haze. Gael Squirrelking supervised the lowering of the drawbridge that Deekeye and Weldan had repaired. Gael looked anything but a king as he sat on the edge of the bridge with his newly adopted young ones, Wincey, Benjy and Figgs, competing to see who could skim flat pebbles the furthest along the moat.

Dusk fell like a velvet mantle, and by the light of myriad lanterns twinkling across the valley Mariel paced out an area by the dip, where the final battle had been fought.

'Here, this is where the monument shall stand!' she announced.

Joseph, Gawjun the hedgehog and Blerun the otter stood forward from the crowd who had gathered to watch. Gawjun pointed out a hill. 'Yonder stands a great boulder on the hilltop. Blerun, thy tribe can roll it down here. Together we will set it straight and hew it with chisels. Egbert shall write the words to be carved upon it.'

Joseph stared up at the boulder perched on the hill. 'And I shall stay and make a bell to crown it. Each dawn it will ring out to honour the courage of those creatures who gave their lives to free Southsward from the Foxwolf and his horde. Their memory will live on into legend!'

38

Autumn leaves turned gold, drifting down to carpet the path outside Redwall Abbey in the soft misty mornings. Fruits that had ripened on bough and vine were harvested in to larder and storecupboard. It was time for the fine October Ale to be brewed, chestnuts to be candied and berries to be preserved in honey. Abbot Saxtus stood over the threshold on the gatehouse wall with Blind Simeon.

Saxtus folded his paws into wide habit sleeves, saying, 'Well my friend, we are a fine pair, standing up here admiring the season. By rights we should be down in the kitchens, helping to make jams, jellies and preserves.'

Simeon stared sightlessly out as a breeze rustled the dry leaves of Mossflower. There was a twitter and flurry of wings overhead. 'The birds fly off to follow the sun where fresh harvests are ripening. Let us earthbound creatures stop here awhile and talk, Father Abbot. It would spoil the Dibbuns' fun if you appeared in the kitchens, they'd have to behave with an Abbot hanging around. This feast you once talked of, to celebrate the memory of Mother Mellus. When is it to be?'

Saxtus ran a paw over the worn red stones of a battlement. 'Soon now, I hope.'

'When our friends return from their quest?'

'I didn't say that, Simeon.'

'I know you didn't, Saxtus, but that is what is in your mind.'

The Father Abbot clasped the blind one's paw warmly. 'There are no secrets from you, old friend.'

Simeon's whiskers twitched, and he leaned forward, listening. 'Here comes another of your secrets, Father. A carrier of information, if I'm not mistaken.'

Saxtus peered into the grey autumn distance. 'I can't see anything,' he said.

Simeon pointed to where Mossflower Wood bordered the path. 'There, it's Blaggut, scurrying along at the woodland's edge.'

There was no mistaking the bulky shape of the former searat as he waddled into view. Saxtus shook his head in amazement. 'How did you know it was him?'

The blind mouse held on to his Abbot's paw as they made their way down the wallsteps to the main gate. 'That one is a stranger to bathwater, I always smell him before others can see him. But don't tell him that, one can forgive a little ripeness from a creature with a good heart.'

Blaggut sat in the gatehouse, drinking old cider from a beaker and bolting warm damson scones as he related his information.

'Twas last eve I saw 'er, Father h'Abbot, just afore twilight, a ship I once knowed, the *Pearl Queen*. She was out t'sea, comin' up from the south. So I stowed meself be'ind some rocks an' watched 'er. When the crew sighted land they started shoutin' the name Redwall. I figgered they must be yore friends who went a questin'. Well, t'cut a long story short I came straight 'ere to tell yer the news. Y'll fergive me, but I never let 'em see me, 'cos not knowin' who I am, they might've mistook me fer a searat an' slayed me.'

Saxtus refilled Blaggut's beaker. 'You did well, friend. Thank you for travelling all night to bring me the good word. If you go to the kitchens you can visit your friends, mousebabe and Furrtil. I will tell Brother Mallen to fill a sack with food for you, knowing how you like our Redwall fare.'

Blaggut bobbed his head respectfully at Saxtus. 'There ain't no tastier vittles in all the world, sir, thankee. Haharr – I bet those Dibbuns are growin' big an' plump now, bless 'em.'

Early noon brought breeze, sunshine and scudding clouds. Simeon and Saxtus stood with Furrtil and the mousebabe on the path outside Redwall, waving goodbye to Blaggut as he shuffled off, sack on shoulder, into the treeshade of Mossflower.

'Fare ee well zurr, doan't eat ee vittles too farst!'

'Gu'bye, mister Blackguts, thanks for fixin' me boat!'

Blaggut turned and winked roguishly. ''Appy sailin', mateys, see yer agin soon, I 'opes!'

He disappeared into the woodlands. Simeon addressed Saxtus. 'Well?'

'Well what, friend Simeon?'

'Well, what about the feast, friend Saxtus?'

The Father Abbot kept a straight face as he replied, 'You can stand there all day saying "well", or get yourself off to the kitchens and tell the cooks to get started on it!'

Simeon felt both his paws grabbed by the two Dibbuns, and he was whisked off at a run, with Furrtil and the mousebabe roaring, 'Party! Party! There's goin' t'be a partyfeast!'

The great Joseph Bell tolled three hours before midnight. Furtively cloaked in a dark coloured curtain, Tarquin L. Woodsorrel poked his head around the main gateway, which had been left open. One glance confirmed what he was looking for. Ears streaming out behind him, the long-legged hare sprinted for the Abbey. He arrived with a bound through the doors of Great Hall. 'What ho, they're comin' along the path, chaps!' he yelled.

Saxtus gazed around at the laden tables of the festive board. 'Is everything ready, Sister Sage?'

'Ready as ever, Father Abbot, as soon as the Harvest Vegetable soup arrives. Ah! Here it is now.'

Brother Fingle, assisted by several helpers, wheeled in a trolley weighted down by a huge, steaming cauldron. Halting it in front of the main table, he bowed proudly.

'One large pot of Harvest Vegetable soup, simmered since mid-morning, Father. The best of celery, carrots, cabbage, mushrooms, leeks and white turnips, cooked to perfection!'

Tarquin threw off his cloak and gave a smart salute. 'Cellar supplies all up an' waitin'. First barrel of last October's Ale tapped, strawberry cordial, mint tea, dandelion an' burdock fizz, oh, and a small firkin of blackcurrant wine, to keep out the chill. All correct!'

Saxtus walked around the tables twice, taking note of everything that had been laid out to welcome back his companions. The centrepiece was a massive moist fruitcake, decorated with sugared maple leaves, and surrounded by trifles of various colours – bright redcurrant, green gooseberry, pale pink rose and delicate woodland violet. Loaves with shining fresh crusts – seeded, patterned, farls, cobs and batons – ranged between cheeses of white and yellow. Pies and tarts, apple, bilberry, plum and pear, latticed or open, twinkled as their fillings caught the candle and lantern lights. The last of the fresh summer salads were laid in flat wooden bowls, chopped and dressed with herbs from the woodlands.

Saxtus's paw strayed near a confection of meadow-cream and whipped honey piled high and fluffy in a basin. The mousebabe clucked disapprovingly. 'Tch tch, Sister Sage smacka paw, naughty!'

Despite the warning, Saxtus took a quick dip. Sucking his paw, he winked at the mousebabe. 'She can't smack my paw, I'm the Father Abbot – good job, isn't it? Mmmm, delicious!'

A knock sounded loud on the door of Great Hall. Saxtus scurried to his Abbot's chair and held a paw to his lips for complete silence. All round the tables Redwallers sat, decked out in their best habits, shining-eyed with anticipation, waiting quietly.

The knock sounded again, louder this time. Still the creatures at the festive tables sat in silence. Dibbuns clapped paws tight across their mouths, shaking with glee at the joke their elders were playing.

Boom! Boom! Boom! Boom!

Four loud knocks that sounded suspiciously like the knotted end of a Gullwhacker hitting the door, followed by the unmistakable voice of Dandin.

'Ahoy there, anybeast home?'

Mousebabe wriggled uncontrollably, stuffing the tablecloth edge into his mouth to keep from laughing aloud. The great, heavy, curled-iron handle turned. All eyes were riveted on the door as it opened slightly.

Hon Rosie Woodsorrel poked her head into Great Hall.

'Whoohahahooyaaaaah!'

She banged the doors open wide, they thudded against the walls either side and the homecoming adventurers flooded in. Redwallers dashed from their seats at table to meet them.

'Rosie, Rosie, dear old thing, you're home!'

'Tarquin! My babes, come here! Mmmmmch!'

'I say, Mater, steady on with the kissin'. Yukk!'

'Dandin, you rogue, you haven't changed a bit!'

'Haha, you have though, Saxtus, you look more like an old Father Abbot than ever! Dearie me, what a tummy!'

Blind Simeon felt the contours of the face before him. 'Mariel, the Warriormaid of Redwall, welcome home!'

Mariel hugged the ancient herbalist. 'Simeon, the sight of you is worth a thousand quests!'

'Aha! Is that my old friend Foremole?'

'Burr aye, zurr Mallen, tis oi, 'appy as a buzzybee. See yurr, Bowly Pintipers, an' all ee shrews, well fam ishered an' willin' to eat, hurr, hurr!'

'Logalogalog, we be shrews an' sail in boats onna pond!'

The Guosim Chieftain chuckled as he was bowled over by a gang of Dibbuns. 'Hohoho! Lookit you, y'great fat mousebabe, I'm goin' to tickle you thin!'

'Yeeheeheehee! Stoppit! No, more! Yeeheeheehee!'

It took quite a while to get the greetings over and every-beast seated at the festive board. The Abbot was about to ring his bell when Sister Sage broke down weeping piteously. They gathered round to find the cause of her distress. The old Sister shook her head despairingly.

'The rhyme, the rhyme, don't you remember?'

Oak Tom's wife Treerose repeated the first lines:

'Five will ride the Roaringburn,
But only four will e'er return . . .'

In the silence that followed, Oak Tom could be heard calling off the names of the questors.

'There's Rufe Brush, Durry Quill, Rosie Woodsorrel and Foremole. Four came back!'

Sister Sage left her seat and threw herself sobbing upon the mousemaid. 'Oh Mariel, your poor Father, what a good brave creature our Bellmaker was . . .'

Saxtus looked stricken. 'No, not Joseph?'

Simeon provided the voice of reason amid the upset. 'Silence please, the rhyme said that only four would re-turn. It never said anything about death. Mariel, tell us what happened to your Father!'

Mariel looked gratefully at Simeon. 'Thank you, friend. Now if I can get a word in edgeways let me explain. Joseph the Bellmaker is far from dead; here is a letter he told me to deliver to Abbot Saxtus.'

Unrolling the small scroll, Saxtus read aloud:

'To my good friend the Father Abbot and all Redwallers. The needs of Southsward are great, and I have decided to stay here to help rebuild their home. I am fashioning a beautiful bell to ring out over this land to honour those who died in the great Battle of Southsward and to remind me of my friends at Redwall.

I wager you are in the midst of a feast. I wish I were there with you. But as I am not, do not let me detain old friends from their enjoyment. Mariel, Dandin and the crew of *Pearl Queen* will have plenty of time to relate the story, around a good fire on cold winter nights. Be happy, grow strong, take care of each other and your beautiful Abbey of Redwall. No doubt we will all meet again some day.

Each of you has a special place in my heart.
Joseph the Bellmaker.'

Mariel smiled fondly as she added, 'He has been honoured with the titles of King's Advisor, Honorary Commander to the Army of Southsward, and Lord Warden of Floret. But you know my dad, he wishes to be known only as Joseph the Bellmaker. Lift your beakers, friends, I give you a toast to my father, Joseph.'

The very rafters rang as every Redwaller shouted aloud, 'To the Bellmaker!'

As they drank, Saxtus finally got to ring his bell. 'All talk and tales, both sad and happy, must wait until tomorrow. The hour grows late and we have a feast before us. Let full justice be done – but only after I have said the grace.

'Autumn comes, the summer's flown,
Travellers' journey ends.
Harvest is in, the table laid,
Sit you down 'midst friends!'

And so they did, until dawn's light flooded through the ancient stained glass windows. Nobeast crept away to bed, not even Dibbuns. Good food, songs and poems, close comradeship and a few tears, all combined to welcome the return of the questors and honour the memory of Mother Mellus.

Father Abbot Saxtus blinked against the morning sunlight reflecting off his bell, mentally composing what he would write in his Abbey Record book. 'One of Redwall's great feasts, to be remembered for long seasons to come.'

The mousebabe sat in Rufe Brush's lap, half awake as he nibbled a redcurrant tart. Mariel was about to doze off in her chair when she noticed mousebabe watching her. 'What are you looking at, cheekywhiskers?' she asked.

'I wanna be a warrior like you.'

The mousemaid winked at him as she took a sip of mint tea. 'Then you'll have to grow up honest and true to your friends – a warrior needs good companions to learn from. One day you may become a warrior, as great as the squirrel who is taking care of you right now. Isn't that right, Rufe?'

Rufe Brush smiled down at the Dibbun. 'Aye, it's right enough, but first you'll have to get Durry Quill to teach you to roar like this.'

Rufe threw back his head and roared.

'Grooooarrarrarrrrgh!'

Mousebabe leapt with fright, and Rufe stroked his tiny ears until he began to doze. The young squirrel talked to him in a low, gentle voice. 'But that's only part of it. I had to learn many things, but I was lucky, I had the right teachers to guide me. The fighting spirit of Finnbarr Galedeep, the friendship of Durry Quill and a brave Guosim shrew named Fatch. Wisdom and strength are needed by a warrior, and I got them from Mariel's Father, Joseph the Bellmaker.'

Mousebabe repeated the final word before sleep overtook him.

'Bellmaker!'

Epilogue

The Bellmaker's tale took three days in the telling, three days in which the storm never once abated. Food and blankets were sent in to the gatehouse, and each night the two old friends and the Dibbuns slept there. On the fourth day they woke to find the sun beaming through the windows from a gentle blue sky. But the Dibbuns would not move until certain questions had been answered.

'Did our Abbey get another badger, sir?'

The ancient squirrel smiled and shook his head. 'Ah, that's a story for another day.'

The little mouse Jerril climbed down from the arm of the chair. 'What 'appened to Mariel an' Dandin?' he asked.

The old hedgehog answered from the depths of his armchair. 'They stopped at Redwall for a season, then one mornin' Dandin, Mariel an' Bowly Pintips took the *Pearl Queen* an' sailed out, to see what was over the horizon they said. I was goin' to go with 'em, but in the end I stayed home with my old matey 'ere.'

The bass-voiced molebabe wiped a tear from his eye. 'Ee sea h'otter, Finnenbarr Galeydeep, 'twere sad ee was slayed, oi would've loiked to 'ave met 'im.'

The squirrel exchanged glances with the hedgehog. Rising slowly they went over to a cupboard. The squirrel talked as he rummaged among objects that he treasured. 'Finnbarr Galedeep was a mighty warrior, maybe you'd like to see his swords.'

He drew the pair of matched curving blades from the cupboard, passing one to the hedgehog. A gasp of wonder arose from the Dibbuns as they stared open-mouthed at the two shining weapons. The molebabe clambered into the armchair vacated by the hedgehog. 'Whurr did ee get em frumm, zurr?'

The ancient squirrel straightened his back proudly. 'Joseph the Bellmaker presented them to us when we left Southsward, a token of our bravery as warriors in the battle, he said they were. Right, Durry?'

Durry Quill whirled the blade he was holding above his head and it glittered in the morning sunlight. 'Aye, right Rufe, I'll never forget that day. I named this sword Finnbarr!'

Rufe Brush blinked back a tear as he stared at the name engraved upon the blade of his sword. 'And I named mine Fatch!'

The Dibbuns poured out yelling into the spring morning. They roared and shouted as they fought again the Battle of Southsward. Rufe and Durry stood in the gatehouse doorway watching. The young mouse Jerril ran back to them for a final word.

'Did any of them ever come back to our Abbey?'

Durry leaned on the doorframe and nodded. 'Aye, quite a few times as I recall. Log a Log, Blaggut, even Joseph the Bellmaker and his three friends one summer. Though Wincey, Benjy an' Figgs was so big I scarce recognized 'em. But y'know what we always say?'

The molebabe came trundling past, stick in paw, serving as his sword as he fought off two small squirrels. 'No, wot do ee allus say zurr?'

335

Rufe answered for Durry. 'We always say that Redwall is here to welcome any with a good heart. Call in, our door is open to all friends.'

The molebabe thought about this for a moment before replying, 'Hurr, vurry good zurrs, but ee know wot I allus say?'

Rufe smiled at him. 'No, tell me what you always say.'

The bass-voiced molebabe waved his stick in the air and charged off shouting.

'Redwaaaaaaaaaallllll!'

Other great reads ⤳ *from* **Red Fox**

Further Red Fox titles that you might enjoy reading are listed on the following pages. They are available in bookshops or they can be ordered directly from us.

If you would like to order books, please send this form and the money due to:

ARROW BOOKS, BOOKSERVICE BY POST, PO BOX 29, DOUGLAS, ISLE OF MAN, BRITISH ISLES. Please enclose a cheque or postal order made out to Arrow Books Ltd for the amount due, plus 75p per book for postage and packing to a maximum of £7.50, both for orders within the UK. For customers outside the UK, please allow £1.00 per book.

NAME_____

ADDRESS_____

_____

Please print clearly.

Whilst every effort is made to keep prices low, it is sometimes necessary to increase cover prices at short notice. If you are ordering books by post, to save delay it is advisable to phone to confirm the correct price. The number to ring is THE SALES DEPARTMENT 071 (if outside London) 973 9700.

Humour and Adventure in the Redwall Series

A bestselling series based around Redwall Abbey – the home of a community of mice and the adventures they find themselves in.

REDWALL

As the mice of Redwall Abbey prepare for a feast, unknown to them, Cluny, the evil one-eyed rat, is preparing for almighty battle . . .

ISBN 0 09 951200 9   £4.50

MOSSFLOWER

The gripping tale of how Redwall Abbey was established through the bravery of the legendary mouse, Martin.

ISBN 0 09 955400 3   £4.50

MATTIMEO

Slagar the Fox is intent on bringing destruction to Redwall Abbey and the fearless mouse warrior, Matthias. He'll stop at nothing – including Mattimeo, Matthias's son.

ISBN 0 09 967540 0   £4.50

MARIEL OF REDWALL

A young mousemaid is washed ashore on the fringes of Mossflower country. Battered and bruised, she makes her way to Redwall Abbey, where the story of her horrific ordeal unfolds.

ISBN 0 09 992960 0   £4.50

SALAMANDASTRON

Why did the sword fall from the Abbey roof? Who is the white badger? And can the good creatures triumph over Ferahgo the Assassin?

ISBN 0 09 91461 5   £4.50

MARTIN THE WARRIOR

Bedrang the Tyrant stoat holds many creatures prisoner in his fortress on the coast. But a young mouse, Martin, refuses to obey the Evil Lord, and plans a daring escape.

ISBN 0 09 928171 6   £4.50

Other great reads ⌒ *from* **Red Fox**

Teenage thrillers from Red Fox

GOING TO EGYPT   Helen Dunmore

When Dad announces they're going on holiday to
Weston, Colette is disappointed – she'd much rather
be going to Egypt. But when she meets the boys who
ride their horses in the sea at dawn, she realizes that
it isn't where you go that counts, it's who you meet
while you're there . . .
ISBN 0 09 910901 8   £3.50

BLOOD   Alan Durant

Life turns frighteningly upside down when Robert hears
his parents have been shot dead in the family home. The
police, the psychiatrists, the questions . . . Robert
decides to carry out his own investigations, and pushes
his sanity to the brink.
ISBN 0 09 992330 0   £3.50

DEL-DEL   Victor Kelleher

Des, Hannah and their children are a close-knit family
– or so it seems. But suddenly, a year after the death
of their daughter Laura, Sam the youngest son starts
to act very strangely – having been possessed by a
terrifyingly evil presence called Del-Del.
ISBN 0 09 918271 8   £3.50

THE GRANITE BEAST   Ann Coburn

After her father's death, Ruth is uprooted from town-
life to a close-knit Cornish village and feels lost and
alone. But the strange and terrifying dreams she has
every night are surely from something more than just
unhappiness? Only Ben, another outsider, seems to
understand the omen of major disaster . . .
ISBN 0 09 985970 X   £2.99

Other great reads ❧ *from* **Red Fox**

Chocks Away with Biggles!

Red Fox are proud to reissue a collection of some of Captain W. E. Johns' most exciting and fast-paced stories about the flying Ace, in brand-new editions, guaranteed to entertain young and old readers alike.

BIGGLES LEARNS TO FLY
ISBN 0 09 999740 1 £3.50

BIGGLES IN FRANCE
ISBN 0 09 928311 5 £3.50

BIGGLES IN THE CAMELS ARE COMING
ISBN 0 09 928321 2 £3.50

BIGGLES AND THE RESCUE FLIGHT
ISBN 0 09 993860 X £3.50

BIGGLES OF THE FIGHTER SQUADRON
ISBN 0 09 993870 7 £3.50

BIGGLES FLIES EAST
ISBN 0 09 993780 8 £3.50

BIGGLES & CO.
ISBN 0 09 993800 6 £3.50

BIGGLES IN SPAIN
ISBN 0 09 913441 1 £3.50

BIGGLES DEFIES THE SWASTIKA
ISBN 0 09 993790 5 £3.50

BIGGLES IN THE ORIENT
ISBN 0 09 913461 6 £3.50

BIGGLES DEFENDS THE DESERT
ISBN 0 09 993840 5 £3.50

BIGGLES FAILS TO RETURN
ISBN 0 09 993850 2 £3.50

BIGGLES: SPITFIRE PARADE – a Biggles graphic novel
ISBN 0 09 930105 9 £3.99

Other great reads ❮ *from* **Red Fox**

Gripping Red Fox Fiction for Older Readers

BETWEEN THE MOON AND THE ROCK
Judy Allen

Shy Lisa feels that she has finally found a voice when she joins the
Christian fundamental group that have recently moved in next door –
but her best friend Flora feels that there is something frighteningly
evil behind their mesmerising services.

ISBN 0 09 918651 9   £2.99

TINA COME HOME
Paul Geraghty

New to England, Murray is fascinated by Tina, the most unusual, in-
teresting girl he's ever met. Not daring to approach her, he starts secretly trailing her home from school . . . which is when he stumbles
upon her secret.

ISBN 0 09 971710 7   £3.50

PAUL LOVES AMY LOVES CHRISTO
Josephine Poole

Paul and his sister Amy have always been the greatest friends, and he
takes it for granted that he is the most important person in her life.
When she falls in love, his whole world is suddenly shattered, and he
has to face the violence of his emotions.

ISBN 0 09 974040 0   £3.50

YOU'LL NEVER GUESS THE END
Barbara Wersba

Joel's black sheep brother has hit the bestseller lists with a novel Joel
knows is rubbish. Life's not fair, and it's beginning to get him down –
until a bizarre chain of events lead Joel into the spotlight . . .

ISBN 0 09 911381 3   £3.50